Syndicate Rules Books 1 & 2

Copyright © 2024 by Lucy Monroe

All rights reserved.

No part of this publication may be reproduced, distributed, or transmitted in any form or by any means, including photocopying, recording, or other electronic or mechanical methods, without the prior written permission of the publisher, except as permitted by U.S. copyright law. For permission requests, contact [include publisher/author contact info].

The story, all names, characters, and incidents portrayed in this production are fictitious. No identification with actual persons (living or deceased), places, buildings, and products is intended or should be inferred.

ISBN 978-1-961214-18-7

SYNDICATE RULES BOOKS 1&2

Arranged Marriage Mafia Romance

Convenient Mafia Wife

Urgent Vows

Lucy Monroe

Lucy Monroe LLC

CONTENTS

DE LUCA FAMILY TREE

Enzo (d) 💍 Aria   Ilaria 💍 Big Sal

Severu 💍 Catalina   Bianca 💍 Salvatore

Miceli 💍 Róis   Nerissa

Giulia 💍 Raffaele

Neri

New York Cosa Nostra

Italian Mafia Hierarchy

New York: Five Families

Bonanno, Colombo, Gambino, Genovese, and Lucchese: each founding mafia is led by a don who could be from any of the families loyal to them.

New York Genovese family

Don/Boss:

Severu De Luca

(Titles: Don, Boss & The Genovese)

Underboss:

Miceli De Luca

(Severu's brother)

Consigliere:

Francesco Jilani

Capos:

Domenico Bianchi, Big Sal De Luca, Tomasso Marino, Niccolo Costa, Lorenzo Ricci, Stefano Bianchi

Head Enforcer:

Angelo Caruso

(Called *Angel of Death*)

Soldiers:

Luigi, Carlo, Aldo (Severu's men)

Fausto, Marco (Francesco's men)

Las Vegas

Don/Boss:

Patrizio Mancini

Underboss:

Raffaele Mancini

Detroit

(Don: Pietro Russo)

* All names and positions are fictional or used in a fictional capacity, a product of the author's imagination, loosely based on La Cosa Nostra structure in America.

CONVENIENT MAFIA WIFE

SYNDICATE RULES PREQUEL

LUCY MONROE

LUCY MONROE LLC

A NOTE FROM LUCY

Dear Reader,

This story takes place before Urgent Vows. We get to see the lead up to that story, but we also get to know Giulia and her husband, the underboss of Las Vegas. Their marriage of convenience is about to explode in ways neither expects.

While it ends on a cliffhanger for one couple, there is an HEA for the other.

Happy reading!
Lucy

A NOTE FROM SEVERU DE LUCA

Severu De Luca
Don of the Genovese

I am don of the strongest of the New York Cosa Nostra Five Families because my grandfather was smart enough to avoid the roundup of made men in the 1980s. And none of his men ever turned traitor, so the power of the Genovese grew while others waned.

When La Cosa Nostra was founded, all Five Families in New York had pretty even territories and power. Nothing stays the same though. Fortunes and influence rose and fell over the decades.

When the government passed the Racketeer Influenced and Corrupt Organizations Act, the law cracked down on all the Families. Made men turned rats. Dons and underbosses ended up in prison by the bucketload. One of the dons who didn't, retired (and I don't mean that the usual way – he went to fucking Florida) and wrote a damned memoir, if you can believe it.

The only way through that mess was down and then back up again.

The Families convinced the FEDs and the public that the Cosa Nostra was all but extinct. That the lion had been detoothed. When in fact our crime syndicate went back to our roots of secrecy and subterfuge. We have more members, more money, and more influence than ever, but we pull the strings of power from behind the curtain.

Mafia dons are the ultimate puppet masters. We are the billionaire CEOs that don't get caught with our pants down by the press or hanging our asses out on social media. No one questions our armored cars or security details that could lock down a small city because who wouldn't protect this kind of wealth?

I rule my city without mercy or remorse.

I expect total loyalty from my mafia and every single one of their family members. They belong to me, and I am their king.

Don't break my rules and I won't break your fingers. Betray me and you'll beg for death.

CHAPTER 1

Las Vegas, Nevada
Mancini Mafia
GUILIA

Busy finalizing the guest list for the next celebrity *charity* poker tournament, I'm not paying attention when the car stops.

All proceeds will go to funding research for heart disease in women. By *all*, I mean what is left after the mafia takes its cut.

As the wife to the Las Vegas Cosa Nostra underboss, it is my responsibility to organize four events like this every year. Not only does the mafia take its cut, but the events launder less legitimate income from the Mancini mafia businesses.

My father, who was a don in New York, would never have allowed my mother to materially participate in mafia business. My father-in-law has different expectations. While I am not allowed to know anything else about the business, I am given a dollar amount for each event I am supposed to *wash*.

My husband shows his appreciation for me organizing each event. Sometimes with a piece of jewelry. Sometimes with a short trip abroad. Which I go on alone. Naturally.

Raffaele Mancini is too busy with his position in his family's mafia empire to accompany me. It's not as if we love each other. Well, not as if he loves me.

I stupidly fell for Raff soon after our engagement was announced when I was sixteen. All right, at first, it was probably just a crush on the gorgeous, charismatic man I had been promised to since I was twelve.

However, those feelings matured as the years went on. First, because he treated me with respect every time we were together. Then because he fought his father so that I could attend university before the wedding. It helped that my own father insisted on it as well.

But the Mancinis could have pushed for the marriage to take place as soon as I turned 18, and for me to attend university online. However, Raff understood how important it was to me to have the full college experience. Or so I thought.

I also didn't want to be a teenage bride, and looking back, I realize he had no more interest in having a teenager for a wife.

When I got married, I thought it was a fairytale. I was a mafia princess, and he was my prince.

Unlike other arranged marriages in the mafia, we were going to be happy. We were going to love each other.

Like my parents.

My bubble burst on the second day of our honeymoon when he left me with bodyguards in Paris to return to Las Vegas to deal with something that to this day remains a mystery to me. I soon learned that no matter what, mafia business took precedence over our marriage.

Over me.

I figured out that Raff hadn't supported me attending university because he *understood* me. He was happy to put off the wedding because work always came first and not having a wife was even more convenient than having one. Even one that cemented the alliance between the strongest of the Five Families in New York and the Mancini mafia in Las Vegas.

Lara opens my door and waits for me to step out of the car.

Six feet tall with a musculature many men would envy and the beauty of a cover model, Lara could have gone to college on a basketball schol-arship. Instead, she joined the Marines, but delisted after making it into MARSOC. One of less than a hundred women in the Marines' elite special forces, she was stuck in support job because she is a woman.

Returning to Vegas, she requested the opportunity to follow in her father's footsteps as a Cosa Nostra soldier in the Mancini mafia. Though her mother is a schoolteacher from Nigeria, her father is the descendant of one of the original Sicilian Cosa Nostra families.

My father-in-law has many faults, but an inability to recognize talent for the life because of gender isn't one of them.

He has a higher percentage of female soldiers working in his ranks than MARSOC and he doesn't keep them in support positions.

My head bodyguard, Lara is in charge of my security team.

I unclip my seatbelt, slip my tablet into my Balenciaga hourglass tote and climb out of the back of the luxury sedan. It's black, just like all the other luxury sedans in Las Vegas.

I could be the head of a casino, a celebrity, a high roller, or what I am...a mafia wife.

Looking up, I see that we are at a medical facility. Unsurprising. My husband put this appointment on my calendar. I assume I'm here to meet with one of the doctors involved in the heart disease research associated with the event I'm working on.

Raff isn't always great at communicating, but I was raised in the life, and I'm quick on the uptake. My mother trained me well for my role as wife to the future don.

The driver stays with the car while Lara accompanies me into the building.

"Hello, Mrs. Mancini. If you will just follow me?" A woman around my age indicates a hallway off the main reception area.

I hadn't even had to tell them why I was here. Which is a good thing, since I'm not absolutely sure what that is. However, I'm used to this treatment.

Keeping a Mancini waiting in Vegas is like expecting a member of the President's family to check in with reception in Washington D.C. – it's not going to happen.

I'm a little startled when I am led into an exam room rather than one of the doctor's offices. Lara waits outside the door.

"Let's get you into a gown and then we'll check your weight and vitals." The woman hands me a folded garment.

Not wanting to reveal my confusion, I take it.

"I'll give you a minute to change." She leaves.

I drop the gown on the exam table and whip my phone out of my purse to check my calendar again. Maybe I missed something. I've already had my yearly physical. So, what is going on?

The note in my calendar reads:

Dr. Hewitt

11:15 a.m.

The Smithson Building

I do a quick search on Dr. Hewitt and find several in Las Vegas. One is a psychiatrist. Doubtful. Two are general practitioners. Possible. Another is a podiatrist. Unlikely. Another is a fertility specialist. Yeah, no. There is a physical therapist as well and even a naturopath by that name.

None of them list the Smithson Building as their location, but that doesn't mean much since not all of them have locations listed, and those that do give physical addresses.

So, I search on the Smithson Building and find a physical address to compare. Is it ridiculous that I have no actual idea where I am in Las Vegas? Mamma would chastise me. I should always be aware of my surroundings and location.

I've grown lax, trusting Lara and my driver to get me where I need to be when I need to be there.

Usually, my personal assistant is with us as well, but not always. I hadn't questioned when Janine wasn't in the car. I'd assigned her several tasks for today and had assumed she was working on them.

I wish she were here now because I'm certain she knows why I am here.

Before I can cross-reference the physical address for the building with the Dr. Hewitts I found in my search, the door opens.

"Oh, you aren't changed." The woman isn't smiling now. In fact, she looks annoyed. "Dr. Hewitt made time in his schedule for you despite being fully booked. Patients have to wait months to get in to see him, but Mr. Mancini insisted."

Okaaay. "For what exactly?" I ask.

The woman's mouth twists in a frown. "For an exam." She says it like I'm not very bright.

Her attitude irritates me, but one thing a mafia wife learns to deal with is people, especially made men, thinking she's not as smart as they are.

I'm no ornament, but this woman clearly doesn't know that.

"I'll change. Give me another minute."

"I hope you mean that literally," the woman says and then leaves in a huff.

Regardless of her clear annoyance, I don't rush removing my dark pink Chanel sheath dress and cream colored short cardigan. While February in Las Vegas is nowhere near as cold as New York City, it stays under seventy degrees most days, making a light jacket or sweater necessary.

I lay my clothes neatly over the back of a chair before donning the examination gown. I don't take off my jewelry or shoes since I wasn't asked to. Besides, there are no socks or booties provided.

I keep my purse nearby. Though I'm positive Lara wouldn't allow me to be in a dangerous situation, I feel better having easy access to my gun.

The woman returns in just over the minute allotted and gives my shoes a dirty look but doesn't tell me to take them off. "Good. Let's get your weight and vitals, shall we."

Her tone is less friendly and more officious.

I step onto the scale with a grimace. Although it has been three years since my son's birth, I never lost all the weight I gained when I was pregnant with Neri.

The nurse, as I'm sure that is what she is now, tuts and then instructs me to sit on the exam table. She takes my blood pressure and I wonder, not for the first time, why it has to hurt so much when the cuff tightens.

Maybe I'm just sensitive.

The nurse checks my heart rate and oxygen levels before saying, "The doctor will be with you soon."

Despite how put out she obviously is, I'm sure I won't be kept waiting. I am a Mancini. And this is Vegas.

As expected, a light knock sounds a couple of minutes later.

I roll my eyes. The nurse hadn't knocked once. "Come in."

A tall, thin, grey-haired man wearing a white lab coat and stethoscope enters the room. He looks like a doctor, but I'm shocked that he is a man.

I haven't had a male doctor or nurse treat me since my marriage. Per my husband's requirement. Now, I'm not sure what to think because Raff arranged this exam.

"I am Dr. Hewitt." He puts his hand out to shake. "It's a pleasure to meet you Mrs. Mancini."

I shake hands with him. His palm is dry and cool.

"Why am I here?" I ask bluntly.

"We're just going to run some tests and do a basic physical exam. Nothing to be afraid of."

"I am not afraid." But I am still confused. "What kind of tests?"

"Mr. Mancini wants us to determine if there is a physical and/or treatable reason for your infertility."

"Infertility?" I gasp, stunned. "I have a son."

"Whom you gave birth to over three years ago."

"Yes." I do not say: *Thank you for stating the obvious.* Sarcasm is not considered an attractive trait in an underboss's wife.

But neither do I smile.

"Coupled with the two years it took you to get pregnant initially, Mr. Mancini is understandably concerned about the lack of a second pregnancy since your son's birth."

Is he kidding me? Embers of rage come to life deep inside me. "He made an appointment for me with a fertility specialist because he wants to know why I haven't gotten pregnant?"

I keep my tone even. Just. When what I really want to do is yell so loud it bursts this condescending asshole's eardrums.

"I understand how difficult and embarrassing this might be for you, but you need to understand that whatever the cause of the infertility, it does not make you less of a woman."

This man counsels couples on their inability to have children? *This man* does? Those poor couples. Especially the women.

Embarrassing. Infertility. Neither are words that reflect any level of sensitivity.

What a jerk.

"The ability to have children has absolutely nothing to do with being a woman," I grit out as calmly as possible.

His, "Hmm," could be taken for either agreement or disagreement. "If left untreated, it could impact your marriage."

Again, insensitive much?

"If what is left untreated?" Why does he assume the problem lies with me? If there is a problem. Which there isn't.

What there is, is highly effective birth control.

"Your inability to conceive."

"Have you had even an hour's worth of sensitivity training?" I wonder out loud.

"I assure you. I am the best in my field. My success rate is higher than any other fertility specialist in the Western United States."

I just bet he hates having to qualify that claim with a geographical designation. This guy just oozes condescending arrogance.

"And I assure you, this is unnecessary." I put my hand up when he opens his mouth to say something else. "I have an IUD. I had it inserted the day after my son's birth."

It was either that or wait eight weeks. And the one area in which Raff does not and has never disappointed me is our sex life. I knew we'd be having intercourse as soon as I got the go ahead after my six-week check-up.

Dr. Hewitt's eyes widen. "Mr. Mancini will be relieved to hear that, I am sure." Judgement for me not telling Raff about the birth control laces his already supercilious voice.

I manage to hold back my angry retort. Dr. Hewitt is annoying, but he's not the person I'm most furious with. That would be my husband.

If Raff wanted to know why I hadn't gotten pregnant, why didn't he talk to me about it? Instead, he'd made an appointment for me with a fertility specialist without consulting me.

I'm used to my husband being high handed. He's a mafia underboss after all. But this is beyond ridiculous. This is insulting and hurtful.

My mind goes to the gun in a specially designed, concealed outer pocket of my handbag. All of my purses have them, regardless of designer. It makes it easy for me to access my gun quickly and discreetly without opening my purse.

If my husband was here right now, I'd shoot him with it. In the arm, or something. I'd want it to hurt him, but not leave him permanently incapacitated.

I bet my father-in-law has something to do with this, too. Now, him? I would like to kneecap. He's always banging on about us having more children, but I'm not having another baby until I'm ready.

Ironically, I have an appointment with the OB/GYN who inserted the IUD to remove it when I visit my family in New York next month. I'm seriously tempted to cancel that appointment.

The doctor washes his hands and then puts on a pair of sterile gloves. "I need you to remove your shoes and lay back on the table."

"Why?" I already explained I don't need an examination.

"To remove the IUD." He frowns. "I was not expecting this additional procedure."

The nurse comes back into the room carrying a tray with some sealed hypodermics and empty vials for blood sample collection. She sets it down on a portable table near me.

"I need forceps," the doctor tells her. "After I remove the IUD, I will still do the exam Mr. Mancini requested to make sure there are no complications."

What is this guy's damage? I am the patient. Not my husband, and sure as hell not the nurse.

"She's on birth control?" The nurse glares at me reprovingly.

I don't wait for him to answer her. "You are not touching me," I tell them both firmly.

The nurse ignores me and reaches for my shoes. I was raised by my mother to be a lady, but my dad taught me to defend myself.

So, I kick my leg out just missing her because she jumps backward. She's surprisingly fast.

"Get away from me. I am leaving." I jump down from the exam table. "You both need to get out of here so I can get dressed."

Dr. Hewitt opens the door and calls out for someone. Neither he, nor the now scowling nurse leave the room like I told them to do.

A couple of seconds later a man wearing scrubs comes in.

"Mrs. Mancini needs some help calming down. Prepare a sedative," Dr. Hewitt says to the woman. "Dolph, help her back onto the exam table."

Oh, heck, no.

Dolph reaches for me and it's my turn to jump back. I grab my handbag and quickly pull out my Glock 19, training it on the big man. "Step back."

"Put that away," the doctor barks, not sounding worried at all.

Does he think I won't shoot?

The female nurse approaches me with the hypodermic.

I let my gun's barrel shift slightly so it's pointing at her and I snarl. "Stay away from me."

She retreats and Dr. Hewitt turns his condescending arrogance on her. "She's not going to shoot you, Lynne."

"Don't bet on it," I say.

I should call for Lara, but I'm angry with her. She brought me here. And though I'm sure she knew why too, Lara didn't say a word to me about it.

Dolph leaps toward me and I quickly aim and fire. Lynne screams. Dr. Hewitt shouts and Dolph crashes backward, red blooming on the right side of his scrub top. I wasn't aiming for a kill shot, but to stop him.

Lara bursts into the room, her gun drawn. As soon as she sees where I have mine aimed, the woman with the sedative, she trains hers on the doctor.

"Get this woman out of my clinic. When Mr. Mancini arranges another appointment, she needs to be sedated and cannot be armed."

Lynne gasps. "You are going to let her come back? Why aren't we calling the police?"

The doctor ignores her.

So does Lara. "Giulia?"

Almost everyone in the Vegas mafia calls me by my first name. They do things differently here than in New York. There is a lot about Las Vegas that is different from where I grew up.

The weather, for one thing. I like the sunshine, but the extreme heat in the summers is why I plan my longest trip each year to visit my family in August.

"Guilia?" Lara prompts me again.

Oops. My mind is wandering. I've never shot anyone before. It's disconcerting. "Dolph needs assistance before he bleeds out."

Neither Dr. Hewitt nor Lynne move to help their colleague, who is sitting on the floor, bleeding against a cabinet.

"Why did you shoot him?" Lara asks me.

"He was going to force me onto the exam table where he..." I indicate the still fuming doctor. "Planned to shove his fingers up my vagina without my consent." I point to Lynne. "She was going to sedate me."

Lara narrows her eyes at the doctor. "Explain."

With that one word, Lara puts herself firmly in the same doghouse as my husband. Instead of threatening the doctor, she requests an explanation. As if there is *anything* that could justify the man's actions.

Apparently, like Raff and Dr. Hewitt, Lara doesn't believe my body belongs to *me*.

It's not about being a woman. It's because I'm the wife of the underboss and any children I have are heirs to the don.

"She has an IUD. Mr. Mancini wants her to get pregnant and she won't as long as it's in her uterus. I was going to remove it, per his instructions to treat her infertility."

Furious, I say, "I am the patient. You don't do anything to me without my permission. And also, the use of the word infertility could be triggering, as I'm sure you are aware."

This man needs more than a weekend seminar on sensitivity. He needs to have his brain rewired.

"Mr. Mancini knows that in order to do the exam, I would have to touch Mrs. Mancini's vaginal area. Even if she did not have an IUD he is unaware of," Dr. Hewitt further explains to Lara, completely disregarding my words.

He thinks Raff will approve of his actions. He may be right.

But I am livid. "I should have shot *you*."

"Perhaps psychiatric treatment is in order," Dr. Hewitt says, still speaking to Lara. "Tell Mr. Mancini I can refer him to someone discreet."

I shift my gun and pull the trigger. The bullet whizzes past the doctor's head and hits the wall behind him. Dr. Hewitt scream is just as high pitched as Lynne's. He's not so sanguine when the gun is pointed at him.

"Shut up," I demand with a fierce glare. "Or the next bullet goes right through your mouth."

Dr. Hewitt blanches and shuts his mouth tight. Good. A puddle of urine pools around Lynne's feet. That shouldn't make me as happy as it does.

Lara sighs. "I knew the boss should have talked to you about this before making the appointment."

"You think?" I put my gun down at the end of the exam table closest to me and rip the exam gown off.

"What are you doing?" Lara demands, showing her first sign of shock.

"Getting dressed."

"You shouldn't be doing that with everyone in the room."

"Really?" I roll my eyes. "My husband was going to let that man feel up my coochie. I don't think him, or his staff, seeing me in my bra and underwear is a problem."

I pull my dress on and do the zip with an angry jerk, and then put on my sweater. After smoothing my hair as best I can with my fingers, I grab my purse and my gun. "Let's go."

Not waiting for Lara, I sail out of the exam room. The lack of an audience outside is testament to the quality of sound proofing in the exam rooms. Which is not a comforting thought, honestly.

Now that I'm no longer in a room with people intent on sedating me, I tuck my gun back into my handbag.

Fertility clinic, my backside.

This place should be shut down. Trying to treat a patient without consent.

Thinking they can sedate me.

Assholes, every one of them. But the biggest one is my husband, the underboss.

Lara is right behind me by the time we get outside. "Our people will take care of this. The doctor and nurses know not to talk."

I get into the back of the car without a word to my bodyguard.

Lara isn't doing me any favors.

Dr. Hewitt and his medical staff are not going to talk because if they report my actions to the police, they will need to answer hard questions about why I felt threatened. Why they aren't HIPAA compliant.

Doing so and revealing such an egregious breach of my privacy could lose him his license and shut the clinic down.

There's no point in me filing a complaint though. Because, at the very least, my father-in-law will have it suppressed. That doesn't mean I'm okay with letting things stand.

But right now, Dr. Hewitt and his nurses aren't the ones I'm focused on. That would be my husband. The rat.

"Take me to the casino," I instruct the driver.

Although he has an oversight manager for the casino, Raff and his top lieutenants have their offices there.

"The boss is in a meeting right now. I will let him know you want to talk to him," Lara says.

I don't reply. As soon as we are back in Vegas proper, I wait for a red light. When the car slides to a stop, I get out. We're near the back side of the Luxor. I head to their taxi stand.

"Guilia!" Lara is right behind me. "Stop."

I listen to her just like everyone in that clinic listened to me today. Which is not at all.

Walking right to the front of the line of guests waiting for a taxi, I say, "I am Giulia Mancini. I need a taxi to..." I name the Mancini owned casino.

The concierge whistles up a taxi and opens the door for me. Lara runs around to the other side when it becomes clear to her that I'm not sliding over to make room.

I tell the taxi driver where I want to go.

"Guilia, you know he can't see you right now."

I know that Raff won't prioritize seeing me right now. It is not the same thing. He *can* see me, and he *will*.

CHAPTER 2

Fucking Irish.

I kick the body on the floor.

Even his own mother wouldn't recognize him now. It's not the missing fingers, or the broken legs. His face is a mass of cuts and bruises, eyes swollen shut. He's missing teeth. His hair is so matted with his own blood, it looks black.

My Head enforcer, Angelo, and I do damn fine work together.

My consigliere disapproves of me taking a personal role in interrogation. He wants me to leave it to the enforcers. Fuck that. If Pietro Russo had taken a more active role in his mafia business, the Irish and Russians could have never moved in on him in Detroit.

"Open it," I bark.

Miceli, my brother and my underboss, places his palm over the biometric reader on the wall. The steel plate in the center of the floor drops eight inches and slides to one side, creating a man size hole.

I shove the body with my foot until it tumbles through the opening. A soft splash sounds. The scent of chemicals mix with the metallic scent of blood in the chilled room.

We don't fucking dump bodies with cement shoes in the Hudson River like our grandfathers. We dispose of them without a trace.

Our chemist created a solution that dissolves all organic tissue in a matter of hours. No stray bits of fiber. No bones to be found for forensic analysis. No fingerprints for identification and no goddamned DNA. Not his. Not ours.

Any metal in the body, including bullets, gets strained out and put in the smelter. No medical device serial numbers. No ballistics.

"Fucking Irish," I say out loud this time. "They aren't moving in on my territory like they did Russo's."

That was a bloodbath and five years later, the mob and their bratva allies still control Russo's clubs and warehouses in Detroit. The supply routes through all of Wayne County are under their jurisdiction now too.

I am Don of the Genovese, the strongest of the Five Families in the New York Cosa Nostra.

My grandfather and father fought like hell to rebuild the Genovese family, to make us what we are today. I'm not giving up so much as a goddamned laundromat to the Irish or anyone else. Much less a whole fucking county's supply routes.

We operate under an uneasy truce, not an alliance, with the New York Irish mob and the other organized crime factions in the city. We have our boroughs and businesses we control; they have theirs.

Someone's always trying to push against the boundaries we've been protecting for the last hundred years and rebuilt over the past decades. When they do, we push back. Hard. And they learn to mind their manners.

What the Irish did in Detroit? That was fucked. And it's not happening in my territory.

"Someone's feeding them information," Miceli says, brown eyes just like mine filled with fury. "Too many shipments compromised. One of our safe houses burned."

Cold rage surges through me making my teeth grind and my muscles clench. "If it is *famiglia*, they will die slowly and in more pain than they have ever known."

"It could be an outsider." Angelo finishes cleaning and putting away his tools.

He keeps them in a titanium lined briefcase, which goes with the dark suits he wears. He wouldn't look out of place on Wall Street but he's a bigger predator than any of those jackholes ever could be.

He snaps the briefcase shut. "Too many people working for us that aren't family."

It's an old complaint.

And I'm not in the mood for it today. "You got a problem with how I run things?" I ask, stepping toward my head enforcer.

"No, boss." Angelo's tone is even, his expression stoic like it always is.

He's loyal. He wouldn't be in this room otherwise. I'm still not taking any shit from him.

Miceli, who is both my brother and my underboss, says, "We have too many businesses to keep them staffed at the lower levels with made men."

Success has its downside.

Like any of us needs that reminder. But he knows how close I am to snapping and this is his way of keeping the peace.

"You think an outsider knows our business that well, even one who works for us?" I ask Angelo.

The Irish scum we'd just interrogated had been told what warehouse to hit and where to place the incendiary devices in order to make the fire look like a combination of faulty wiring and unlucky product placement.

Too bad for him, whoever gave him that information hadn't known about the security measures we added to all our facilities after a shipment got stolen from another location.

Measures only the men in this room and my chief of security are aware of.

"Fuck if I know," Angelo says. Which means he still thinks it's possible.

No matter how pissed off the idea makes me, I have to consider it. Just like I can't rule out one of my own as the informant.

"Either his instructions were a hell of a coincidence, or—"

"Someone arranged the merchandise to be arranged the way it was," I interrupt Miceli.

Warehouse logistics are handled by either the warehouse manager or the inventory coordinator. The managers are usually higher ranking and older made men, but the inventory coordinator could be a foot soldier. The forklift drivers, on the other hand, might not be Cosa Nostra at all.

They don't know the true contents of the boxes and crates though.

"It could be a compromised location," Miceli says with a frown.

"You think somebody bugged us?" We have better anti surveillance equipment and protocols than the military.

Miceli shrugs. "Unlikely, but not impossible."

"New surveillance shit is getting developed all the time," Angelo adds.

Miceli closes the floor again, so it looks like the steel sheets are welded together.

"Fucking Irish." This time it's Miceli who says it.

He presses the button that will send powerful jets of chemically treated water across the floor, the metal chair and table we use for detainees, and over the walls. Leave no trace. We have thirty seconds to exit before it starts.

Angelo and Miceli go first, to clear the room on the other side before I follow.

~ ~ ~

The next morning, I call a meeting with my consigliere, Francesco Jilani, Angelo, and my brother. They come to my office on the 35th floor of the high-rise that belongs to *la famiglia's* legit business front, Oscuro Enterprises.

I sit behind my desk, answering the never-ending stream of emails I get as CEO, while my assistant ushers the three men in. Miceli and Francesco sit in the two chairs facing my desk. Angelo remains standing. He could pull another chair over, but I know he won't. Miceli lounges, but his casual demeanor is an act. He's relaxed like I am. Never. Aware of everything around him.

It's how our father trained us, and the security team outside my office door doesn't diminish that awareness one iota.

Francesco, on the other hand, sits straight up, his manner respectful, but about as alert as a sleeping spaniel. The consigliere I inherited from my father when I took over as don five years ago, he's twenty years my senior and damn complacent for a made man. He trusts his bodyguards and our security team to protect him.

Though we have bodyguards, Miceli and I see them as backup, not the front line. Angelo is the same, if not more paranoid than us. He only sits down when social strictures absolutely require it. Even then, I've yet to see him stay in his chair throughout an entire meal.

I shut down my email and close my laptop. "We aren't waiting for those whiskey-soaked assholes to move in on me like they did Russo. We take the fucking war to them."

Last night, I updated Francesco on the results of the interrogation.

Miceli nods. "I'll call a meeting."

"I don't like that he didn't name his boss," Angelo says.

His words drop into the room like bomb. We all stare at him.

"He said he got his instructions from the mob," Miceli says.

"But when we asked which boss, he never used Brogan Shaughnessy's name."

The poor bastard had been nearly dead at that point, and he'd just kept muttering, "My boss. It was my boss."

We all know who the biggest mob boss in New York City is, but Angelo's right, the Irishman didn't name him. "You think he was from a different crew?"

Angelo shrugs. He's not prone to speculation.

"There are several organizations that would benefit from a war between us and the Irish," Francesco says. "Waiting to strike back might be prudent as it's possible that is exactly whoever is behind these recent attacks wants us to do."

I don't like waiting. It pisses me off, but that's why the man is my consigliere. He's supposed to give me smart counsel and I have to admit he could be right.

"We need to do some digging. Find out if Shaughnessy is looking to expand his territory."

"Domenico told me the I.D. we found on the Irishman is fake," I tell them.

It's not uncommon to carry fake I.D. when on a job. It can obfuscate even better than having no identification at all. But its presence *could* mean that Francesco's theory has merit. Angelo thinks something is shady and I trust his gut.

I look at my brother. "Get Domenico to run facial recognition on the Irishman."

Domenico is my capo in charge of online money laundering, but he has tech geniuses on his crew that do a lot of other stuff for the organization too.

"Talk to your contacts in the mob," I say to Francesco. Besides respect for my father, I keep him as consigliere because he has built a lot of connections in his decades as a made man. "Maybe they know if their boss is targeting us."

Francesco's mouth tightens, but he nods. He doesn't like taking orders from me. Too bad. I'm don.

I look at Miceli. "Order a full sweep for surveillance equipment. Offices, meeting rooms, bars, restaurants. Anywhere our plans could be overheard."

"Consider it done."

I nod. Then I look around the room, meeting each man's eyes before I say, "It's not the Irish stirring up shit with my capos."

There has been grumbling about lost revenue from the hit shipments, about stability in *la famiglia*. Like I fucked up. Like I'm weak.

Francesco crosses his legs, trying to look more relaxed, so I know whatever coming out of his mouth isn't going to be something I like.

"What?" I growl.

A Don has to have patience, not just power. But mine is on a knife edge ready to gut someone.

"You need to get married."

It's not the fact that Francesco says it that pisses me off so much. It's that Miceli nods his agreement. Angelo's expression doesn't change.

Again with this shit? "Now is not the time."

"You're the youngest don in the last four generations," Francesco says.

Like I don't know. "I am aware."

"Even so, you are thirty-five."

"So?"

"You are don. You were born when your father was 30 and still an underboss."

"I've got time." We're facing war with Irish mob and he wants me to worry about finding a wife?

"Like Papà had time?" Miceli asks.

Fuck.

"He was only sixty and if he'd waited to have you until he was in his forties," Miceli says, "You would not have become boss after him."

"You sure about that?" I demand, but I don't let the rage I feel at being questioned like this, even by my brother, show on my face.

A don does not show emotion, even anger, unless it is strategic to do so. I learned that before I learned to read.

"No, but it would have taken a lot more bloodshed. We would have lost strong capos."

He was right. Even at 30, some of the capos had not wanted to follow me as their Don. I hadn't been forced to kill anyone we were better off keeping, though.

Hell. Francesco is right. So is my brother. I don't want a wife, but I am The Genovese and I owe *la famiglia* security. "After I settle this shit with the Irish, I'll find a wife."

"I don't think you should wait."

"Noted," I say to Francesco, ice in my tone.

Angelo's raspy voice sounds from his place against the wall. "I agree."

My gaze snaps to him. "Why?"

"Timing." Even for Angelo, that's a short answer.

"He's right," Miceli says. "This Irish thing might be more complicated than we thought. Who the hell knows when we'll get it sorted. And when we do, it might lead to war."

"A wedding for their don will give *la famiglia* something to celebrate, especially if we start losing soldiers." Francesco clears his throat. "It's about doing what's best for the *la famiglia*. Being a don your capos can trust, not just to kill for them, but to provide security and continuity into the future."

Every word out of my consigliere*'s* mouth increases my fury, but I rein it in. Because damned if he doesn't have a point. I don't want a wife, but it's not about what I want.

"Fucking hell."

The other men in my office can take that for the concession it is.

CHAPTER 3

Las Vegas, Nevada
Mancini Mafia
GUILIA

When I arrive at the casino, I head straight to the private elevator that services the office floors. I bring up the access key on my phone and place it in front of the reader before pressing the button for Raff's floor.

"I texted the boss and he's making time in his schedule for you in thirty minutes," Lara says to me as we ascend to the 32nd floor.

"Hmm."

The elevator doors open onto the impressive lobby with a man and a woman seated behind a large half oval shaped reception desk. Everything is modern elegance in here, including my husband's corner office.

Even though the only access to this floor is with an electronic key, like the one on my phone, there are still armed guards stationed in strategic locations.

"I'm here to see my husband." I yank off my cardigan, dropping it and my purse on the reception desk.

"He is in a mee—"

I don't wait for the receptionist to finish, but storm past their desk and head for Raff's office.

The door is locked. Of course.

I don't let that deter me and pound on it. "Raffaele Mancini, you had better open this door right the fuck now."

My mother would be appalled, but that fiasco at the fertility clinic? That is so beyond okay, I don't have words. So, I pound again.

"Giulia..." Lara tugs at my upper arm. "Come on."

I put her on her back before and take only a second to enjoy the look of shock on her face before turning back to pound on the door again. We spar three times a week. Did she think all those martial arts lessons were for nothing?

Lara jumps to her feet just as the door opens.

His face a study in shock and fury, Raff stands on the other side. "What are you doing, Giulia?"

I sweep past him, crossing the large expanse of his office and scramble up onto his desk. I whip my dress off and have my bra unclasped before Raff can reach me. I yank the lingerie off just as he grabs me around the waist.

I throw it. "This is what you want isn't it? To take away my privacy and expose me to whoever!"

I don't even look at the people he is meeting with. My ire and attention are directed entirely on the son-of-a-bobcat I am married to.

"Get out!" he barks.

I hear people moving.

"Funny how that didn't work when I told Dr. Hewitt and his minions to leave me alone." I'm so angry, my throat aches with the need to scream.

Tears are burning at the back of my eyes, but I blink them back. I will not cry. Not right now.

Raff's suit jacket comes around my shoulders as his office door closes with a bang.

He holds me near him with a grip on the lapels of his jacket. "Is there a reason you want me to have to gouge out the eyes of three of my top capos?"

"They're your father's capos."

He growls.

I usually find that sexy. Right now, I just want to punch him. So, I do. Right in his rock-hard abs, which is what I can reach the way he's got me trapped close to his big body.

Without much oomph behind it, he doesn't even grunt from the impact. But my hand stings.

"What the hell is wrong with you?" he demands.

Raff is a full foot taller than my five-feet-three-inches. With his Italian good looks, chiseled features, and that sexy divot in his square chin, he's easily the most gorgeous man I have ever seen. Dark hair. Grey eyes that go molten when we are naked together. Sculpted muscles, including drool worthy eight-pack abs and a backside I could look at for days.

All of it makes for a devastating package.

Right now, his grey eyes burn into me like molten steel.

I force myself to ignore my body's usual response to his closeness and that intensity in his gaze. Unfortunately, anger seems to heighten my reaction to him, not dim it.

But my ovaries are not the boss of me.

"What is wrong with me?" I yell. "You made an appointment with a fertility doctor without talking to me."

"Apparently you had an IUD inserted without talking to me."

So, Lara can tell him that, but not tell me that I'm on my way to a visit with a fertility specialist? My absolute belief that I am safe with my husband's people, but especially my personal security detail is shaken.

And that hurts. It also makes me angrier.

I shove against Raff's chest, but it's like trying to move a brick wall. "Step back."

"No." He maneuvers me around his desk and sits down in his executive chair.

Sleek black leather and imposing in size, the three-thousand-dollar chair is the equivalent of a modern throne. There's no doubt that the man who sits in this chair commands the room.

Pulling me into his lap, he slides his hand inside his suit jacket and presses an arm around my naked waist. "Talk to me, *cara*."

"Why? When you won't listen." For six years, I've convinced myself that the physical closeness is enough. That his need to touch me and the way I feel when he does makes our marriage strong.

I've been fooling myself.

"This. This is what is wrong." I wave between the two of us. "You sit here acting like you don't know why I'm mad when I just told you..." I shake my head. "Let me up. I don't want you to touch me right now."

Eyes narrowed in anger, now widen and reflect pure shock.

We've been married more than a minute. Of course, we've argued. Though I keep it under wraps most of the time, I *do* have an Italian temper. However, I have never before told him I don't want to be near him.

In fact, sex is usually how we resolve most of our conflict.

That is so far off the table right now, it might as well be in another country. No matter what my body wants. My mind and my heart are screaming in accord.

I need distance. I shove off of his lap and he lets me go.

"I did not think you would be upset about the appointment."

"You were wrong."

"I see that. I didn't like you seeing a man, but he's the best." Raff says this like I'm supposed to give him points for allowing a male doctor examine me for the sake of supposed superior care.

Yeah, not happening.

"So he told me." I search the room and see where my bra landed after I tossed it.

All I want to do is to get out of here, to get away from him and the knowledge I am not, and have never been, anything more than a body to slake his lust and a womb to carry his children.

"Newsflash, a doctor who would treat a patient without her consent, who would try to sedate me to do so? That's not *the best*. That's a creep."

CHAPTER 4

My beautiful wife walks to where the bra she tossed is in a puddle of pink lace on the floor, her large breasts swaying with each angry step. Damn, she turns me on when she's like this.

"He threatened to sedate you?" Lara didn't say anything about that in her text.

While a lack of chattiness can be an asset, sometimes the Marine trained bodyguard can be too taciturn.

"Why the heck do you think I shot Dolf?" my wife demands.

She shot someone? What the fuck went down in that clinic? "Who is Dolf?" And why did my gentle and proper wife feel the need to shoot him?

"I thought Lara texted you."

"Her text said your appointment didn't go well and that you wanted to talk to me. I thought you were upset by bad news."

Her bra dangling from her hand, Giulia's brows furrow. "Then how did you know about the IUD?"

"Dr. Hewitt emailed me." Along with a summary of the visit, that does not include shots fired, the email has a recommendation for a psychiatrist I do not mention.

I assume the birth control somehow damaged my wife's ability to conceive. Dr. Hewitt believes she needs someone to help her work through that. Setting aside my personal disappointment at not having any more children with her, I am determined to be that person.

Not some damn shrink.

I had my admin reschedule everything on my calendar for the rest of the day, after my meeting with the capos. I hadn't expected Giulia in avenging Fury mode to come pounding on my office door.

She slides her arms through the straps of her bra and pulls it up, covering her luscious tits and reaches behind to do the clasp.

"Don't get dressed on my account." I let my eyes roam over her lust inducing curves.

I cannot get enough of her fuller figure since giving birth to Neri. Her pillowy softness is as much of a turn-on for me as her tight, wet pussy.

She ignores me and fastens her bra, hiding her mouth-watering tits from my gaze. Standing in my office in nothing but her black bra and panties and vibrating with temper, my wife is fulfilling one of my favorite sexual fantasies.

"We might as well take advantage of the free time in our schedules." And this unexpected opportunity to live out that sexual fantasy. But as soon as I say the words, I realize they are the wrong ones.

Giulia's body goes stiff and eyes that are shooting daggers at me once again glisten with moisture. Her temper is sexual kryptonite, but I hate seeing the hurt in those pretty brown depths.

Okay. Talk first. Sex after.

"Tell me about this morning."

Giulia doesn't start talking. That would be too easy. She goes hunting for her dress and then puts it on.

"Why did you strip in front of my capos?" I ask her. I get she was angry. Still is angry, apparently.

But to reveal her body to my men?

And they are *my* men as much as they are my father's. To be loyal to the don is to be loyal to me, his oldest son and underboss.

But some capos are more loyal to me than others. Those men were three of them.

My threat to gouge out their eyes wasn't hyperbole, however. But my men are smart. The second she climbed up on my desk, giving them a view up her skirt, they averted their eyes.

She faces me defiantly. "You didn't care about stripping me bare in front of that doctor." Her tone is scathing when she says the word *doctor*.

"I did not strip you." I knew I should have gone with a female specialist, but my father had been adamant that Dr. Hewitt was the best.

The more the men look to me for leadership, the more my father seeks to assert his authority in *my* life, not just *la famiglia's*. I thought going with his suggestion for the specialist was an easy give.

Clearly, I was wrong because my beautiful wife is upset.

"Didn't you?" she taunts.

Giulia is not being literal. Damn it. There's no winning when her words mean something different than what she says.

I try anyway. "You believe me sending you to a specialist took something from you?"

"Ding. Ding. Ding. Give that man a prize." Her small hands are curled into fists at her sides and there's not one relaxed muscle in her body. "You should never have *sent* me to him. You are my husband, not my parent. And regardless, I am no longer a child."

Telling her that *my* father insisted she seek fertility treatment is more likely to fan the flames of my wife's anger than douse them. Even if he is her don.

We both know that I could have refused. I didn't. Assuming she was probably as concerned as I was by the fact she hadn't gotten pregnant again since Neri's birth, I went along with my father's suggestion.

A miscalculation on my part.

Giulia believes my father is overbearing and too involved in our marriage. I'll do no favors reminding her he is only as involved as I allow him to be.

Her father was a don in the Five Families and a very different man than mine. His death five years ago has nearly canonized Enzo De Luca in my wife's mind.

"I went first," I tell her.

She stares at me. "What do you mean?"

"I saw Dr. Hewitt first." If the problem had been with me, then my wife would not have had to undergo any tests.

"To talk about me?"

"To discuss potential reasons for the lack of a pregnancy since Neri when I *thought* we weren't using birth control."

Not looking even a little guilty by that reminder, she just narrows her rich chocolate gaze.

"He tested my sperm count."

"You gave him a sample of your semen?" she asks. "How?"

"I jacked off into a cup. Does it matter?"

"No. I suppose not. Only, I find that really hard to picture."

"Maybe we should rectify that." Not that I will use a cup, but the idea of having her eyes hot and needy on me while I jack myself has my already hard cock twitching.

Her temper trips my switch every damn time.

"Sex doesn't solve everything." Her ire deflates, leaving behind a sadness I do not understand. "You can get back to your meeting. I won't interrupt you again."

Why do I hear *ever...for anything* echoing around us?

"Neither does barging into my office and stripping in front of my men. We both have our ways of coping."

"Fuck you, Raffaele." Just that fast, she's pissed again. She skirts around me and grabs the door, but it doesn't open. "Let me out."

"No."

She makes an adorably frustrated sound and spins to face me again. "Stop with the games, Raffaele. You have work to do and so do I."

"I cleared my schedule for the rest of the afternoon."

"Well, I didn't."

I just look at her. Does she really think I didn't have the foresight to text Janine on her behalf?

Giulia makes a sound like steam coming from a tea kettle. "After everything else, you had the audacity to cancel my afternoon appointments?"

"I am efficient that way."

"Damn it, Raff!"

At least she's calling me Raff and not Raffaele.

"Come and sit down with me."

She storms over to one of the couches in the seating area that almost never gets used. I prefer to meet people from behind my desk.

Our made men are not my colleagues. I am the underboss. The only man with more power than me in Las Vegas is my father, the don. The only time

I use the couches by the window is on the rare occasions my father or his consiglieres come to my office.

Even Giulia's brother, Miceli, sits in a chair facing my desk when he comes to Vegas to discuss business. And like me, he is underboss. Their older brother, Severu, has been don since Enzo's death.

As much as I would prefer to sit beside her, I don't. She didn't react well to me putting her on my lap earlier. Though I did so because I thought she needed comfort. Her telling me she didn't want me touching her makes it very clear that if she wants comfort, it is not from me.

I don't like it. However, for now, I will respect her wishes.

Her impromptu striptease still confuses me, but I now get it was motivated entirely by rage. At me.

We sit in silence for a tense minute before she says, "You're the one that won't let me leave until we talk. So, talk." She waves her hand at me in a come-on gesture.

"You knew we expected you to have more children."

"We," she derides. "Is that we, you and your father? Or we, you and your parents?" She shakes her head. "Only I have a hard time believing your mother cares one way or the other whether we have another child. She sees Neri less than my mom does."

I cannot deny the truth. Aria lives in New York, but she visits several times a year and my wife goes back to New York at least once a quarter.

"My mother has yet to reconcile herself to being a grandmother."

"Neri is three years old. Do you think that is ever going to happen?"

"No." Why sugarcoat it? Viola isn't maternal. Becoming a grandparent did not change that.

My son calls her Bea just like me and my brother.

Aria De Luca is Neri's only real *nonna*.

"So, the Mancini family expects me to pop out babies like a brood mare."

"Don't pretend you didn't know that having children in the plural was part of the bargain." Hell, our fathers had negotiated the point when Giulia and I were promised. I had been seventeen, but Giulia had still been a child of twelve. "Even your sainted father agreed that you would bear a minimum of two children."

"He's not sainted."

"I was certain you thought he was." She has compared our fathers too many times to count during our marriage.

Mine never wins in the comparison. Of course, he is alive and able to interfere in our lives...in her life. De facto, Patrizio Mancini will never be able to compete with the dead don who by all accounts was both a good don *and* father.

Patrizio is a good don.

However, my uncle and nannies can take the credit for any real parenting my brother and I received growing up.

"You're being sacrilegious."

"And you are avoiding the point."

"Yes, I have always been aware that you and Patrizio expected me to carry more than one child."

"So?"

"I have an appointment to have the IUD removed next month when Neri and I go to visit my mother."

"Why did you go on birth control?" And why not tell me about it?

She looks at me like she can't believe I asked that. "Do you even remember how hard my pregnancy with Neri was on my body?"

I remember how sexually hungry she was.

After the first few months of debilitating morning sickness. That had been rough on her, but I hadn't been around much because we'd been dealing with a bratva infestation in Reno.

I'm a hell of an exterminator. The Mancini family controls organized crime in Nevada, not just Vegas.

Giulia had told my father that either someone else had to plan the money-laundering charity events during her pregnancy or they had to be cancelled. She'd also taken a lot of naps her last trimester.

"You didn't have your usual energy. I thought that was normal."

"Based on?"

I shrug. I am an expert on running our mafia. I am not an expert on pregnancy. "If it wasn't, why didn't you tell me?"

"My being unable to work for almost my entire pregnancy didn't clue you in?"

"Viola doesn't work at all."

My aunt had run the charity events before Giulia took over, and she still helps bring in big name celebrities.

"I am not your mother."

"No." That became even more obvious after our son's birth.

While still running the galas with the precision of a general, my wife is nurturing and present in Neri's life.

"My OB said I should wait at least a year before getting pregnant again after Neri's birth," Giulia says, like she has to force every word out.

"She said nothing to me."

"Wow, shocking," my wife mocks. "Only you are not her patient."

I grit my teeth at her sarcasm, but right now I need information and the only way to get it is patience. I know my wife that well at least. Though clearly there are things about her that I am in the dark about.

"You didn't say anything either."

"We don't talk about stuff like that."

"Things like your health?" Okay, so my own sarcasm slips past my grip on my patience.

She crosses her arms, lifting her gorgeous breasts into prominence. "Yes, things like my health."

"I asked how you were doing every day when you were pregnant." She'd been carrying my child. "And you told me you were fine."

"I was fine."

"No, you were not."

She sighs. "I didn't think you wanted a blow-by-blow of my fatigue, lower back pain and swollen ankles."

"You were wrong."

"Fine. I'll make sure and tell you every time I have to throw up and how often I have to pee and all the rest of it with the next pregnancy."

Does she think that bothers me? "Good."

"We'll see how good you think it is when it's happening."

"Bring it."

"You can be ridiculously competitive."

"It is not competitive to want to be made aware when my wife is finding the side effects from pregnancy difficult to navigate."

"I never said they were hard to deal with, just hard on my body."

"Noted."

"I don't want something like this morning happening again, Raff." And we are back to what caused her to come pounding on my office door.

"Tell me about the appointment."

"Let's see, I arrived at the clinic believing I was going to see a doctor involved with heart research, but I was shown into an exam room and told to change into a gown. Do you have any idea how humiliating it was to realize you'd made an appointment with a doctor for me without talking to me about it?"

"It is my job to take care of you."

"Your idea of taking care of me is telling one of your men to do it."

"What the hell are you talking about?"

"You abandoned me on our honeymoon and left guards to watch over me."

I barely knew my wife when we married. I assumed it would make little difference to her enjoyment of Paris, if I was there, or not. "You know I had to leave."

"When I am sick, you move into a guest room and the staff takes care of me," she says as if I have not spoken.

"I check in on you nightly." But I keep my distance and do it from the doorway because I cannot get sick.

No weakness is tolerated in an underboss. Not even the flu. The few times I have been ill in my life, I have hidden it and soldiered on.

Just as my father expected me to.

"What about your detached version of taking care of me would make me believe you want the nitty gritty details of my life?"

"Going on birth control is hardly a tiny detail. You should have discussed it with me." Damn it. I boxed myself into a corner with that one.

"You mean like *you* should have talked to *me* about visiting a fertility clinic?" she asks with sugary sweetness.

"In future, I will discuss it with you before making doctor's appointments for you."

"How about you discuss any medical concerns you may have in regard to *my* body with me and *I* will make whatever medical appointments *I* deem necessary."

"Agreed."

"Just think, if you'd brought up your concerns to me, you could have avoided masturbating into a cup."

CHAPTER 5

Las Vegas, Nevada
Mancini Mafia
GIULIA

The twist of my husband's lips lets me know just how distasteful he found coming into a sample collector cup.

Poor, beleaguered underboss. Not.

At least no one tried to knock him out and take the sample against his will.

"My father has been bringing up your lack of pregnancy at least weekly since Neri turned one," Raff points out.

"I am aware."

"You—"

"Do not pretend that if I'd told him about the IUD, that would have shut him up. Patrizio would have insisted I have it removed."

Raff inclines his head, making no attempt to deny it. "He is your don."

"That doesn't give him the right to dictate when I get pregnant. This isn't the 1950s, not even in the mafia."

"I am your husband."

"Yes. And if *you* had brought it up to me, I would have told you about the birth control."

"Don't you think that as your husband, I should have been involved in the decision to use it in the first place?"

"No. Again, not the 1950s. But I would have told you about it, if I knew you were worried." No one had been worried about me though, just whether or not I could not conceive again.

"So, you are saying this is all my fault?"

"Has there been a single word out of my mouth since my arrival that would imply I think anything else?"

His face goes blank. I'm facing the *underboss* and not my husband now. He's about to say something about duty and the mafia and it will lacerate my already sore heart.

"Don't," I say, trying to fight the hopeless pain leaking in at the edge of my fury.

"Do not what?"

"Don't go *underboss* on me, right now, Raff."

"I am the underboss."

"You are also my husband."

"I have never denied it."

"If you are mad at me, just say so. But don't start yammering on about duty to *la famiglia*. Don't shut me out." Though that last is more his default setting than not.

"I *am* pissed you are on birth control and didn't tell me." For just a second, the blank mask slips and I know that by pissed he means raging. "But according to you, that's my fault."

I shrug. If he's hoping I'll argue with him on that point, he'll be disappointed.

Maybe I *could* have told him about the IUD, but no, I don't feel like I *should* have. I hadn't had a tubal ligation. I hadn't taken away the chance to have more children, just put it off.

For the sake of both my physical and mental health.

"Aria would not have hidden something like that from Enzo. And he would have been furious if she had."

He's right, but that's still a low blow. Also, not relevant to our marriage. "My parents loved and trusted each other implicitly."

"Are you saying you don't trust me?" His deep tone is infused with outrage and disbelief.

Of course, he ignores my reference to *love*, an emotion my controlled husband has no use for.

Instead of firing back an automatic response to his question about trust, I take a moment to really think about it.

An arrow of insight pierces me to the core.

"I thought I didn't tell you because you didn't need to know," I explain. "I wasn't putting off having more children indefinitely, just until I knew I could handle another pregnancy and what came after."

I had believed I didn't feel the need to tell Raff about the IUD because of the emotional distance in our marriage. Which, yes, is something he fosters.

When we first got married, I'd been more than willing to build the kind of relationship my parents had. I craved closeness with the man I'd foolishly fallen in love with. Raff has made it clear he is not interested in me as anything but a convenient mafia wife, easy access bed partner and baby maker.

"You thought?" he prompts.

"Yes, but you're right. I don't trust you."

"How the hell can you say that? I am your husband."

"But you are the mafia's underboss *first*. And your father's son *second*. Your role as my husband comes in a distant *third*, if that."

"You cannot tell me that Enzo put your mother ahead of his responsibilities as the don." He doesn't mention the fact his role as son comes ahead of being my husband.

Raff probably sees it one and the same with being underboss and keeping his vow as a made man.

"If my father knew that pregnancy would risk Mamma's health after Severu was born, he would have suggested the birth control himself. And he would not have allowed her to go off of it unless he was absolutely sure the pregnancy would not put her at risk."

Even if that meant potential instability for *la famiglia*.

"The key phrase there being *if he knew*, which I didn't because neither you, nor your OB told me you should wait a year after Nero."

"Even if my pregnancy hadn't been so exhausting, waiting at least a year to get pregnant again is not exactly rocket science." All he had to do was show the slightest interest in me as a person, and not a baby making machine.

"My degree from Stanford is in business, not medicine, or engineering."

The sarcasm is thick between us. So is the anger and once again my lady parts start sending all sorts of messages about how to resolve this argument.

Doing my best to ignore them and remain rational, I say, "You don't need a medical degree to Google *why is my wife so tired during pregnancy*. But first you have to actually care about said wife's welfare."

"I am not a mind reader. You should have said something to me."

"If one of your men was suddenly unable to do their job, wouldn't you ask why?"

"I thought I knew why. You were pregnant."

"Lots of pregnant women can work. I avoided having to go on bedrest because I didn't."

"How the hell are you holding me accountable for not knowing what you did not tell me?" Raff sounds beyond exasperated.

"As long as I popped out a healthy baby, I didn't think it mattered to you."

"You believe I would have pressured you to get pregnant before you wanted to, before it was safe?"

"Yes."

"That is bullshit."

I laugh, though the sound is hollow. "This morning proves the opposite."

"In what way does my concern about your health prove that I would willingly put it at risk?"

"Because you weren't concerned about *my* health, only the viability of my reproductive system."

"They are one in the same."

"No, they are not." The longer we talk, the more my fury dissipates and is replaced by sorrow. "There is no scenario in which you sending me to a fertility specialist without consulting me is an expression of concern for *my* wellbeing."

"Lara said the appointment did not go well. Since I now know that did not mean you got bad news, what does it mean?"

Good strategy. When you don't have argument to make, change the subject.

Done with talking about what cannot be changed, I go with it. "It was a disaster but my reasons for thinking so are probably not the same as Lara's."

"Tell me about yours."

We've already covered the ground about me not knowing why I was at the clinic and how humiliating that was.

So, now, I tell him the rest. "Lynne, that's the nurse who first showed me into the exam room, was rude. Dr. Hewitt was worse though. If I was a woman with fertility issues, he is the last doctor I would want to consult about it."

"He's supposed to be the best in his field."

"Oh, he told me. Dealing with him is an awfully high price for the chance to have a baby."

"What do you mean?"

"His was arrogant, condescending and borderline psychotic. When I told him I was on birth control, he decided he would remove the IUD without my consent. When I argued, he told Lynne to sedate me and when I balked, he called in Dolph to hold me down."

With every word I speak, the aura of menace around my husband grows. "This Dolph laid hands on you?" My husband's tone is chilling. "Where the hell was Lara?"

"My bodyguard was waiting outside the door, like the good little Mancini lapdog she is."

"You are angry with Lara?"

He has to ask? Men! "What was your first clue?"

"You don't insult your security detail. Or anyone else." He pauses. "Except my father."

"I don't insult Patrizio."

Raff's right brow raises, calling me a liar.

I sigh. "I don't *mean* to disparage my father-in-law."

Unable to meet Raff's eyes after telling that whopper right after the first one, I look away.

Sometimes I *do* mean to insult Patrizio. He's worse than autocratic. He's selfish and arrogant and unfeeling. I've never seen him say one positive thing to either of his sons and he treats our son, Neri, like a not very interesting chess piece on the board of *his* life.

My biggest fear since getting married is that my husband, for all his faults, will become more like his father. Raff can be an arrogant jerk. Case in point: this morning. However, he is a loving father, and he has never treated me like I'm a brainless ornament, like his dad treats his mom sometimes.

Patrizio may respect women as soldiers and treat then the same as his other made men, but mafia wives and mistresses are another category to him.

When Raff doesn't say anything else, I continue. "Anyway, I shot Dolph before he could touch me. Then I shot at Dr. Hewitt but missed him on purpose."

I wait for my husband to tear into me about putting *la famiglia* at risk with my actions.

He asks, "What happened after that?"

"I got dressed and left." Remembering a detail, I add, "Oh, and Lara came crashing in after the first shot."

Now Raff's eyes narrow and his jaw looks hewn from granite. "You removed your clothes with all of them still in the room?"

"The exam gown. I put my clothes back on."

"The doctor and his nurses saw you naked?"

"I never removed my bra and panties," I correct.

"Lara will lose a finger for this."

"You would punish her for your mistake?" That's something his father would do, but not Raff. At least I didn't think so. "Lara didn't send me to that psycho doctor, you did."

"I did not tell Hewitt to touch you without your consent," Raff grinds out.

"He thinks you did."

"A mistake he will regret."

My husband's righteous wrath gives me pause.

"Was it you, or your dad, who made the appointment for me with Dr. Hewitt?" They never referred to my husband, just Mr. Mancini.

For once, I have no trouble reading Raff's expression. *To lie, or not?*

"If you're going to lie to me, don't bother answering." I jump up and head for the office door. I'm done.

What is the point of continuing this conversation? He doesn't think he did anything wrong. He's definitely not going to admit his father, the don, is out of bounds.

His voice stops me halfway to the door. "My father made the appointment, but I insisted on being seen first."

"How chivalrous of you."

"I thought so." He's right behind me. "Come back and sit down, *cara*. We are not done talking."

"I am."

His hand comes around my waist, turning me to face him. "Please."

Has he ever said *please* to me before? If he has, I don't remember it.

I nod, but step away from his touch. It's too distracting. Something filters through his gaze, but I'm not sure what.

I retrace my steps, but don't return to the couch. The view outside the floor to ceiling windows draws me to them. Vegas is in a constant state of flux with old casinos and other buildings being torn down to make room for the city planner's vision.

Influenced in no small part by Patrizio Mancini.

It's so different from New York and yet, there's an undeniable beauty in the Las Vegas skyline.

I put my hand on the window, heat radiating through even the insulated, bullet proof glass. "If your father made the appointment, he probably *did* tell Dr. Hewitt to do whatever was necessary to get me pregnant, up to and including artificial insemination or IVF using that sperm sample you so helpfully provided."

"I will talk to my father."

"Do that. Because if I am ever put in a situation like that by him again, the nurse won't be the only person I shoot and I will be aiming to kill, not wound."

"You're fucking sexy when you go all Annie Oakley."

Expecting censure for daring to threaten the don, Raff's words shock me.

"More Ma Barker surely." At least she was a figure in organized crime.

"If you say so." His big hands land on my shoulders, providing more comfort than such a simple, not overtly personal, touch should.

As angry as I am, I need that comfort. Even though I wouldn't admit it to him under torture right now. But I don't move.

"Were you on birth control before Neri?" he asks.

Ah, he's remembering the two years it took me to get pregnant after our wedding. Dr. Hewitt said that contributed to Mr. Mancini's (i.e. Raff's father) certainty something is wrong with my lady parts.

"Yes."

"An IUD?"

"No. I used the implant, but I didn't like the headaches or the lack of libido." I didn't even realize the effect it had on my sex drive until I had it removed a month after my father's death.

I hoped bringing new life into my family would help all of us with our grief. It worked.

The other benefits, besides getting pregnant, of having the implant removed are that I no longer have daily headaches and I cannot get enough of physical intimacy with my husband. The sex is so much more intense than our first year of marriage.

The IUD has none of the negative side effects for me that I experienced with the implant. My OB told me that other women experience the opposite. Every woman's body is different.

"I thought you got pregnant because we were having more sex."

Cause, meet effect. "I'm sure that helped."

He turns me to face him and puts one hand under my chin to lift my head, so our eyes meet.

His gaze searches mine. "Why did you get the implant? You knew everyone expected us to try immediately for a child."

"Not everyone. My mom didn't." In fact, Mamma had been the one to suggest I go on birth control before the wedding.

"Aria knew?"

I nod, my chin sliding against his finger. "Mamma was nineteen when she had Severu. She knew how hard it would be for me to find my footing among strangers in a new city while pregnant."

Because that was exactly what she'd had to go through.

"You wanted a chance to settle into Vegas before pregnancy hormones hit."

Isn't that what I just said? I manage not to roll my eyes when I nod my agreement again. "Besides, I wasn't ready to become a single mom at twenty-two."

"You are not a single parent."

"No, I'm not. You're a lot more hands on with Neri than I expected." Raff has always been more committed to his role of dad than husband, but there is no way I could know he would be that way. "I didn't know what to expect and what I did know about your dad didn't give me a lot of hope."

"I am not my father."

"Keep it that way."

"He is a strong don."

"One day, you will be too, but that doesn't mean you have to stop being a decent father."

His thumbs brush up the column of my neck sending shivers of arousal down my arms. "You have an appointment to remove the IUD when you go to New York next month?"

"Yes." I try to ignore the way my body is reacting to his nearness.

You'd think with all the experience I have doing that, I'd be better at it. Six years married to a man who turns my crank just by being in the same room makes for a lot of practice not showing my sexual excitement in the company of others.

"Thank you."

My brows furrow. "For what?"

"For being willing to give me another child."

"Like you said, it's part of the agreement."

"You are too good of a mother to see our children as a means to an end."

"Which is why the timing of my pregnancies matter. I needed to know I could handle parenting Neri with my other responsibilities before adding to them."

"You don't have to run the galas."

"That's not what our don said."

"As you have pointed out, he is not your husband."

Now he wants to take the stand that Patrizio's word isn't law in our marriage? When it's something I actually don't want?

"I like using my education," I point out. "Even though we're using the benefits to launder money, the mafia's take from them is no more than most charitable organizations' overhead costs. And each gala finances important endeavors. It makes me feel good to be part of that."

Sliding out from under his hands, I say, "I think we've hit our quota of talking for the month."

Not one word of it has assuaged the pain in my chest at the knowledge that I'm just a walking, breathing *womb* to the Mancinis.

Needing some time to myself to process and put my game face back on, I go back over to the door. "Can you unlock this for me? And I'll let you get back to work."

"Not just yet." He's closer now. I can hear it in the nearness of his voice.

But he moves like a darn shadow and it startles me when his hand covers mine on the doorknob.

He tugs me around to face him. Molten grey eyes devour me. "You stripped in front of medical staff, your bodyguard and my capos."

I frown. "I was angry."

"Yes."

"With good reason."

"Perhaps."

"So, unlock the door."

"We have one more item on the agenda."

What agenda? "This wasn't a planned meeting."

"You are not leaving without an undeniable reminder of who this delectable body belongs to."

CHAPTER 6

Las Vegas, Nevada
Mancini Mafia
RAFFAELE

I'm a damned Neanderthal when it comes to my wife.

She knows it. I know it. It's not changing.

When she stripped in front of my capos, she knew there would be consequences.

Lara will take care of the incident at the clinic, but I will take care of Giulia. Specifically, reminding her who she belongs to.

I never should have listened to my father about sending her to Dr. Hewitt. But that is another problem I will handle later. Personally.

"I belong to myself, Raff." She looks up at me, defiance burning in her chocolate brown eyes.

There is only one response for that bit of provocation. And I give it to her. Yanking her body into mine, I slam my lips down over her saucy mouth.

Her lips remain impassive under mine for nearly five full seconds, but as I run my tongue along the seam of them, she opens and kisses me back with angry passion. She bites my bottom lip, drawing blood.

The copper tang coats our kiss as her tongue fights with mine for dominance.

I grab her ass and lift, her legs coming around my torso instantly, forcing her dress up and exposing her silk clad pussy.

Images of taking her against the door tempt me, but this is about more than getting off.

I carry her to my desk, shoving everything off the surface with a wide arc of my arm. This is where she bared herself for my men. This is where I remind her that *I* am her husband.

It only takes a second to unzip her dress and then I work it up her body, breaking the kiss only long enough to yank it over her head. She slams her mouth back to mine as I toss the dress to the side.

Her bra is next, and we don't have to stop mauling each other's mouths to get it off of her. As soon as her generous tits are naked, I squeeze them in both of my hands.

They are so fucking soft and perfect. I play for long seconds as our kiss turns more carnal.

She buries her fingers in my hair, yanking my hair to hold my head close. I revel in the small bite of pain.

Then I pinch both of her nipples at once and she cries out into my mouth. Ever since her pregnancy with Neri, Giulia's nipples have been more sensitive. With enough patience, I can make her come from breast play alone.

But I have something else in mind for right now.

I pull out the knife I keep in a sheath on my hip and cut both sides of her silk panties before yanking them from her body. Cupping her pussy, I slide my middle finger between her folds, finding slick wetness.

No surprise there. Anger makes my wife horny.

We're even. I'm hard enough to drill through stone.

I push my finger inside her silky tightness while brushing her swollen little clit with my thumb.

Giulia moans and cants her hips. She wants to come, but I'm not letting her do it on my fingers.

Lowering her back onto the desk, I slide my mouth from hers and begin to lick and bite my way down to her pillowy mounds. She writhes on my fingers as I suck up a mark on the top swell of one breast.

Her body is tensing in preparation to climax, and I pull my hand away.

"No! Don't stop. Damn it, Raff, I'm so close."

Lifting my head, I stare down at her flushed face. Sweat dews her forehead and her chest rises and falls with her rapid breaths.

"You are so beautiful like this wife."

"On the verge of killing you?"

I smile and dip my head to take one of her nipples into my mouth. Without any lead up, I suck hard and she screams, her body bowing again. I let go with a pop and then lave the turgid nub, soothing it.

"You bastard. You are doing this on purpose."

"What was your first clue?" I don't wait for her to answer but move to her other tit and give it the same treatment, stopping the stimulation she needs just before she comes.

She tries to shove her hand between us so she can touch herself, but I grab it. "Uh uh uh."

"Damn it, Raff!"

"Who do you belong to, wife?" I demand.

She glares and I kiss her red and swollen nipple. Softly.

"You! I belong to you!"

"Good answer."

I don't go back to her breasts but shift back so I'm kneeling in front of the desk. Grabbing her ass, I pull her forward until her pussy is right in front of my face.

"Oh, Raff, please..."

I don't make her ask again. I feast on her, licking her cream and eating at her pussy until she's writhing against my mouth. I shove two fingers into her vagina at the same time I suck her clit between my lips and press against it with the hardened end of my tongue.

She screams and her pussy clamps around my fingers as her body tries to bow off the desk in ecstasy.

I take her through aftershocks until she's begging me to stop. "It's too much," she gasps. "Too sensitive."

I smile. I've just gotten started.

Undoing my slacks, I pull my hard cock out and shove it into her tight channel.

She groans, her hands scrabbling at the desk edge, like she's trying to find something to hold onto.

I grab them both and slam them onto the desk by her head, my palms pressed against hers. Then I start to move, thrusting in and out of my wife's beautiful body over and over again.

This time when she comes, she sobs out her pleasure.

Her inner muscles milk my cock and I go over with her, filling her with my seed and not caring that it cannot take root. I want her marked with my scent and my essence.

My dick does not soften, and I pick my wife up, keeping our bodies connected as I carry her to the sofa I was sitting on earlier. I sit down with her straddling me and let my big hands roam over her small, silky body.

When my finger dips between her ass cheeks, her head falls forward against my chest. "Raff?"

It's not the first time I've touched her little pink bud, but every time she has to settle into it. Knowing every part of her body is mine to explore makes me feel like a king. Her king.

And she is my queen.

"Let me, *dolcezza*."

"Yes."

I reach down further and spread our combined cum over her silky soft flesh until her asshole is soaked with it, then I press my finger inside. Her sphincter tightens around it, and I wait until she relaxes before I start moving in and out up to my second knuckle.

Eventually she begins to move against me, fucking herself on my cock in her pussy and my finger in her ass.

I cup her tit with my other hand and play with her nipple and her body moves jerkily, up and down and side to side as she seeks maximum stimulation.

Thrusting up, I take control of the rhythm and drive her to a climax that goes on and on, her body contracting around mine for long seconds until I finally cannot hold back any longer and I come inside her again.

She goes boneless against me, my cock and finger still buried deep inside her.

"You are mine, *dolcezza*. Always."

"Yours," she slurs and kisses my chest before laying her head against it.

Usually, she claims I am hers, just as possessive as I am. That she doesn't this time bothers me.

So, I do it for her. "As I am yours."

"Yes."
It's enough.

CHAPTER 7

Las Vegas, Nevada
Mancini Mafia
GIULIA

I'm dozing in my husband's now (and finally) naked lap when his phone rings. I'm not surprised when he answers it, but his tone makes me sit up in shock when I realize the person on the other end is his dad.

"None of your fucking business."

His dad barks something.

"Leave it," Raff slams back.

His body tenses under me at whatever his dad says next.

"This is a family matter. As don you do not interfere between a husband and his wife."

Oooh, no way does Patrizio like hearing that.

I go to lift off of my husband, but his hand clamps down on my hip and holds me in place. "Interfere between Giulia and me again, in any way, and you'd better start training Fabrizio to take over as underboss."

My lungs seize and I can't draw in a single breath of air. I can't believe what I'm hearing.

"I don't have to leave the Cosa Nostra to leave you."

Jerking upward, I stare in shock at my husband's harsh features. No matter how angry Patrizio is, it has got nothing on Raff's fury right now. He's a volcano ready to blow.

"He was going to fucking drug her and touch her!" Raff's shout makes my ears ring.

But my heart soars. He is really pissed on my behalf. He screwed up not talking to me about the appointment, but he would never have made it if he thought the doctor would not treat me with deference and respect.

Dr. Hewitt's hubris and belief he could get away with sedating me is all on my father-in-law. I'm sure of it.

"When we have children is between me and Giulia. Stay the fuck out of it."

Patrizio says something.

"No, I will not insist she has the IUD removed."

I can't believe what I'm hearing. Why doesn't he just tell his dad that I have an to remove the birth control device?

Or is Raff leveraging this situation on purpose for more independence from his father, the don? My husband can afford to lay down the law with Patrizio when he already knows I'm getting my IUD taken out in a couple of weeks. He'll get what he wants while maintaining a position of strength with his father.

He and Fabrizio have such a different relationship with their father than my brothers had with my dad.

"Get someone else to do it," Raff says forcefully. "I'm taking the day off to spend with my wife."

If I have a heart attack from shock right now, who will finish raising Neri? Because that is the first time in six years Raff has put spending time with me ahead of business.

Raff hangs up and tosses his phone on the low table near the sofa. "Put your dress back on."

"I thought you weren't leaving." I knew it was too good to be true.

Not that I can blame my husband. He cannot refuse a direct order from his don without serious consequences. Even I'm careful how I subvert my father-in-law's directives. Mostly, I avoid direct communication when at all possible with my don.

"We are leaving. I'm not near done with you, but my ass is sticking to this leather. I'll arrange for a suite for us."

We're going to a suite? To make love some more?

We don't just spend the rest of the afternoon exhausting each other's bodies, but the evening and the entire night. Raff answers his phone a couple of times, but he never leaves to take care of business.

We don't do a lot of talking, but I'm not complaining when my vocal chords get a work out screaming from multiple orgasms.

~ ~ ~

A week after the doctor appointment debacle and subsequent sexfest with Raff, I am packing for my upcoming trip to New York with Neri. We both need warmer clothes than we wear in Las Vegas.

My phone dings and I check the text. It's from Raff.

He sent me a link that leads to an article about the tragic death of a well-known local fertility specialist. Apparently, Dr. Hewitt died of an unexpected heart attack.

Chills run up the back of my legs. I should have expected this. I'm not sure why I didn't.

Raff isn't just protective, he is over the top possessive too.

Ever since I stormed into his office and we spent the rest of the day and night together naked, Raff has been even more insatiable than usual. He claims my body over and over again, both physically and verbally. It's hot and sometimes a little overwhelming, but still, yeah...really hot.

He's always a little extra attentive in the bedroom before and after one of my trips to NY, but this past week he's been downright insatiable.

I didn't connect it to what happened with Dr. Hewitt though. Or realize Raff's response would be so permanent.

After how he told his dad off like I never in a million years thought he would, I should have known Dr. Hewitt's days were numbered.

I'm not sure how I feel about his death. I can't help thinking I'm not the only female patient Dr. Hewitt treated like a walking womb, but did he deserve to die for it?

Clearly my husband thinks he did.

In Raff's world, justice is dispensed by the mafia, not the authorities and usually with some level of violence.

I call my husband.

He picks up on the first ring.

"Was it you?"

"What do you think?"

I think Raff has a very medieval outlook sometimes. "I purposefully didn't hit a vital organ when I shot Dolf," I say.

Our phones are encrypted, but even so, I probably shouldn't be talking about shooting people.

"You have very good aim," my husband acknowledges.

"That's not the point."

"No?"

"He and Lynne don't deserve to die."

"Are you sure about that? Because I am not."

I knew it. "Please, Raff, don't do anything rash."

"I am not a reckless man."

"Not usually."

"Not ever."

"You took an entire day off from work and told your don to find someone else to do whatever it was he wanted you to do."

"I had more important things to do."

Sex. He never considered it a top priority before.

"Are you packed for your trip?" he asks when I don't say anything more.

"Working on it."

"How long will you be gone?"

He already knows the answer to that question, but I tell him anyway. "Two weeks."

"Your trips to New York are growing longer."

"No, they aren't."

"You used to be gone for only a week."

I roll my eyes, though he can't see it. "This visit is lasting two weeks so I can get to know my brother's intended bride and help with the wedding preparations."

My oldest brother has decided to get married and in typical Severu fashion, has given my mother and the bride three months to plan a wedding with hundreds of guests. I'm not sure the bride even realizes she's getting married yet.

Mamma said the dinner we are attending is the first time she'll officially be meeting Carlotta Jilani.

"I would prefer you kept it to a week."

"And I would prefer that Dolf and Lynne did not die in the near future, or ever at your hand."

"If I agree, will you return home next weekend?"

He's negotiating. With the lives of two sort-of innocent people.

"That is not fair. You know my family needs me."

"I am your family."

My brow furrows. "Is something wrong, Raff?"

"No."

"Are you sure?"

"I don't like how frequently you travel to New York."

It's the first time he's complained about it. Well, not really. He always says he thinks I'm going to be gone too long. He gets downright grumpy before the annual month long visit I make in August.

With the exception of the last trimester of my pregnancy with Neri, I've been making four trips a year to see them since we got married. And he's never before told me I go to see my mom and brothers too often.

"I know going without sex for two weeks is a challenge for you..." I let my voice trail off teasingly as my heart squeezes.

I assume my husband remains celibate while I am out of town, but fidelity in a mafia marriage is not a given.

"I don't just miss sex, *amate*. I miss you."

My heart skips a beat. He calls me *cara*, darling. Not *amate*, beloved. It's a typical Italian endearment and doesn't necessarily mean he has feelings that he's never given voice to. Like love.

But it feels significant.

My knees wobble and I sit down on the bed with a thump.

"Don't you miss me when you are gone?" he asks sounding almost like a petulant child.

"You know I do."

"Do I?"

"What is this about, Raff?"

"If you missed me, you wouldn't leave Las Vegas so often and take our son with you."

Oh. This is about me taking Neri away.

"He enjoys his time with his *nonna* and uncles."

"I know he does."

"I'm sorry you miss our son, but if I left him here, he would spend more time with the nanny than you." Raff is a good father and way more present in Neri's life than I expected from his parents' example, but he is still a mafia underboss and busy CEO.

His hours away from our home exceed his hours here by many.

"I think it would be hard on Neri to be away from me for that long," I add.

"Of course, it would. He's a young boy. It is hard on me having you gone for a week and I am an adult."

"Now, you are just being dramatic. Hard on you?" I scoff.

"You find that difficult to believe?" he asks, his tone almost angry. "Maybe because it is *not* hard on you."

"Seriously, Raff, what is this about?"

"Do you remember who that tight pussy belongs to when you are in New York?"

"My body belongs to me," I assure him. Though we both know that's only part of the truth.

I *do* belong to him. I only wish I was as confident that he truly belonged to me.

"What you are really asking is if I let another man touch me and that is insulting." If deep down, I am also just a little bit thrilled by his jealousy, I'm not admitting it out loud.

That's for sure.

"I apologize. I know you have too much honor to desecrate your wedding vows."

"Desecrate. That's a serious word. Can I assume you also have too much honor to *desecrate your* wedding vows?"

"I am no cheater." His voice is just bursting with affront.

"Neither am I."

"I know. I should not have asked that."

"Are you admitting to a mistake? Only it's the first time I've ever known you to do that."

"Don't be so gleeful. I can admit when I am wrong."

"When have you ever?"

"I do not recall, but if I had been wrong, I would have admitted it."

I want to tease him and say that is a lie, but the arrogant man would just say he is never wrong. Except, he just admitted he'd made a mistake asking what he had.

Which touches me way more deeply than it should, and I find myself saying, "The only man I want is you, Raff."

"I crave you like a drowning man craves air."

I gasp, hating that this conversation is happening over the phone and not in person. I want to touch my husband so badly right now, it physically hurts that I can't.

And I won't see him again for two full weeks.

Neri and I will be flying out on the Mancini jet before Raff gets home from work. I prefer to travel in the evenings with my son, eating our dinner on the plane.

My rambunctious boy is not quite so energetic then as during the day. He will fall asleep about an hour before we arrive and won't wake on the transfer to my family's home in the top three stories of an Art Deco building in Manhattan. Since it is three hours later in New York, letting Neri sleep through until morning helps him to adjust to the time change more quickly.

"Text me when you arrive in New York and call me before you go to bed."

"Alright."

"Be safe."

"You too." I think my admonishment is more needed.

My husband's life is saturated with violence. In comparison, a flight on a well-maintained private jet represents no risk at all.

CHAPTER 8

CATALINA

Papà is beside himself. The don is coming for dinner.

I don't understand why my father is so happy. As Severu De Luca's consigliere, he has dined with the don many times. Don De Luca has been to our home as well, though this is the first time he is coming to dine with us.

All of us. Papà, my Zia Lora, Zio Giovi, Carlotta and me.

Zia is my father's widowed sister and she's lived with us since mamma died. She and Zio Giovi came for the funeral and never left. I like Zio Giovi. He is kind. He's much older than Zia though, his hair more silver and his face more lined than papà's.

Zia's full name is Madonna Candelora, like mine is Madonna Catalina and my sister is Madonna Carlotta.

It's Jilani family tradition to name the girls Madonna and use our middle names when speaking.

Zia shortens her name to Lora and mine to Lina. Zio calls me *tesorina*, even though I am twenty-five. Carlotta calls me *soru*, sister. Papà doesn't use my name. He prefers other epitaphs.

I check the table again, to make sure everything is right. Using the hem of my t-shirt, I rub at a small smudge, so nothing mars the sheen of the dark wood table. The runner down the middle and the placemats are from my mother's wedding trunk. They are all hand tatted Sicilian lace, sent to her by family in the Old Country.

In the center of the table is a large bouquet of flowers arranged in Zia Lora's favorite crystal vase with matching crystal candelabras on either side. They catch the light from the chandelier and sparkle.

I make sure all the flatware gleams, without any spots of tarnish on the silver. The nearly hundred-year-old hand painted ceramic dishes are from my father's side of the family. His great grandmother brought the original set over from Sicily.

Everything is set for a formal dinner and even though Zia is cooking, when the time comes, maids will serve the food.

Zia Lora, tall and slim like most of the Jilanis, comes bustling in, her face creased in a smile. "This looks lovely, Lina, but it is time you got yourself ready."

"Are you sure you don't need me to do anything else?" I ask.

"No, no, you do not have time. Your sister went up to dress an hour ago."

My sister is considered the most beautiful mafia princess on the East Coast, maybe in the whole country. Papà has been receiving offers for her hand since she was twelve years old. In the Cosa Nostra, mafia princesses can be promised from any age, though the formal engagement is never announced before they are sixteen.

With the same build and dark brown hair as Zia Lora, Carlotta also has amber eyes and perfectly symmetrical features. Wherever she goes, she turns heads. First it was always, "What a beautiful child," then "What a beautiful girl," and now they say, "What a beautiful woman."

At nineteen and six years younger than me, I know my sister is a woman, but I still think of her as a girl.

Papà has refused to arrange a marriage for her; he is holding out for someone powerful.

Like the don? Is that why *he* is coming for dinner? Is he going to make an offer for my sister?

As papà likes to point out, though I was born into the mafia, I am no princess. I will probably never marry, though when I say that to Zia Lora, she gets upset. But papà has no desire to arrange a marriage for me.

Because I know the truth.

If he gives my hand to someone with integrity, I might tell my husband my father's shameful secret and papà would be removed as *consiglieri*. If he gives me to someone like himself, I might tell that man too, but then my husband would have leverage over my father.

One day, my father might kill me, like he did my mother, but he won't risk giving my hand in marriage so I can tell others what I know.

I walk upstairs, keeping a steady pace. If I don't try to rush, I won't limp. Sometimes, no matter how slowly I walk, I cannot hide that I am defective, as Papà calls me, though.

Is defective the right word? My right leg is shorter than my left because of the fall I took down the stairs, the same day as Mamma. Isn't that wounded, not defective?

Papà thought we were both dead that day. I'm sure of it. But he was wrong. I lived. And I remember.

Carlotta comes rushing up as I reach the hall outside my bedroom. "You aren't dressed yet. *soru*, you must change now. There's barely time to do your hair and makeup."

"Brushing my hair will only take seconds and I don't wear makeup," I remind my glowing sister.

Carlotta is wearing a soft pink dress by one of her favorite designers. Her luxurious dark brown curls are brushed to a sheen that falls like silk down her back. Her nude heels add four inches to her already above average height, making her tower over my own five-feet-three-inches.

She might be only nineteen, but she looks as regal as a queen.

"You look wonderful," I tell her as we walk to my bedroom.

Carlotta's pretty lips twist in a moue of discontent. "I don't like all these pastel colors. I would look so much better in red."

With her darker coloring, she's absolutely right. But red is not a color for an unmarried mafia princess still in her teens.

"Once you're married, I'm sure your husband will buy you dozens of red dresses." Who wouldn't want to spoil my sister?

She is not only beautiful, but she is sweet natured, if a tad selfish, but that is not her fault. She isn't just a mafia princess, she is the princess of our family. Everyone loves her. Even our father.

"I don't want to have to get married to wear colors like red and...and black." Carlotta's tone is filled with discontent.

It worries me. "Black is the color of mourning."

"Not in the real world, it's not."

Carlotta talks like everything outside *la famiglia* is the real world. She thinks the traditions and the culture of the mafia are antiquated and un-realistic.

In some respects, I agree with her. The prospect of living the rest of my life under Papà's roof, simply because I am unmarried, fills me with dread. It's supposedly for my safety, but I am in more danger here than if I lived on my own. I'd much rather get a job and support myself, but he'll never allow that.

Running away would be considered betrayal. Betrayal to *la famiglia* can be punished by death. I'm not ready to die, so I don't run away. Not yet anyway.

I have plans, plans I can't even tell Carlotta because once I implement them, I'll never see her, my aunt or my uncle again. Most importantly, I'll never have to see my father again and I will be able to stop wondering if today is the day he is going to kill *me*.

When I run, I'll have what I need to make sure I will never be found.

"Please do not mention the *real world* as you call it at dinner," I implore my sister.

"Of course, I won't. I never tell Papà what I really think of mafia life. It would hurt him."

Hurt him? I'm not sure. But it certainly would make him angry. And when he gets angry, it is never my sweet, sunny sister who he takes his ire out on.

It is me. Whether it is because I look like Mamma and not a Jilani, or because I know his secret, my father despises me.

At five foot three, with more padding on my curves than Carlotta will ever have, I am the spitting image of our mother. At least before the plastic surgery, the incessant diets and the blonde highlights my father insisted on.

Papà even made her wear contacts that turned her hazel eyes green. Trying to make her into the image of the woman he'd wanted to marry when he'd been forced to settle for my mom.

I push away the unhappy memories of the past. "What do you think I should wear?" I ask my sister.

She grins and eagerly opens the door to my wardrobe. There is no closet in my bedroom because it is part of the original house, built over 150 years ago. It's a small bedroom too, but I don't mind. It has its advantages. Like a fireplace and being far away from my father's suite.

After perusing my dresses, yanking hangers this way and that, Carlotta's grin turns into a frown. "Don't you have a single decent dress?"

I'm not the clothes horse that my sister is. I don't care about designer labels or wearing the latest fashions. Most of my dresses are at least two years old. Not because papà doesn't give me a clothing allowance. His pride would not allow that.

It is because I've been buying designer clothes and returning them for the past three years, putting the money I get back in my runaway fund kept hidden in my room.

Papà doesn't notice my lack of fashion. Carlotta does.

"Where's that dress we bought when we were out shopping last week? It looked amazing on you."

I wave my hand dismissively. "I didn't like it and took it back."

"You'd never know you were so picky looking at the state of your wardrobe," she says repressively. She grabs the navy chiffon skirt I wore to my cousin's wedding a couple of years ago and hands it to me. "Hold this. I've got a top that's perfect for it."

"None of your blouses will fit me," I warn her.

Carlotta gives me a mischievous smile. "Well, it won't fit the same, that's for sure. It'll show off your girls."

I instinctively cross my arms over my generous breasts. "I don't want my boobs on display, thank you."

"Do you really think I have anything that would put them on actual display? I'm not allowed plunging necklines. I'm too young." Her tone makes it clear what she thinks of that.

Carlotta is gone only a few minutes before she comes back with a white silk blouse and I breathe a sigh of relief. Until I have it on. It's sleeveless, which I don't mind so much. Papà isn't stingy with the heating.

The soft cowl neckline is not at all provocative, but the silk must have some spandex in it because it's stretchy, clinging to my curves. Once I have the skirt on, my waist looks tiny, but my chest and hips look even bigger than normal.

When I complain, Carlotta assures me that I look great. Knowing no one's attention is going to be on me at the dinner, I decide it's not worth the argument with my sister to change into something else. I put on a pair of navy blue ballet flats.

I don't wear heels. Walking in them makes my hip ache like really, really.

Carlotta insists on putting my mousy brown hair up in a messy bun leaving tendrils to curl around my heart shaped face, but I put my foot down when she wants to put makeup on me.

I don't have to imagine what Papà would say. The last time I wore make up, he shook his head and asked of no one in particular, "What's the point of gilding a turnip? It still looks round and like it was grown in the dirt."

I knew he was talking about me. I didn't let it make me cry though. I don't let him see me cry at all anymore.

We run into Zia Lora coming out of her room and she stops to look at us. "Don't you both look lovely?" She cocks her head to one side looking at me. "Wait, I think I have a pair of earrings for you."

She rushes back to her room and is back only moments later with a pair of teardrop pearl earrings in her hand. "Put these on."

So, I go down to dinner wearing my aunt's earrings and my sister's blouse.

"At least my underwear are my own," I grumble.

My aunt and sister laugh.

Zio Giovi comes down the hall. "I see I have three gorgeous women to escort to dinner," he says gallantly, putting his arm out for Zia to take.

Carlotta and I take each other's hand and follow them. My sister's palm is sweaty and I realize she's perfectly aware of what this dinner might mean. She's nervous and I don't blame her. It's not every day a don comes looking for a wife.

We reach the foyer and Papà points to his side. "Come here, Madonna Carlotta. You will stand with me to greet the don."

"Both of your daughters should stand with you," Zia Lora says, her voice filled with censure. "What will Don De Luca think of you otherwise? That you are ashamed of one of your daughters?"

While it might be true, my father's pride would never allow him to reveal that truth to someone outside the family, particularly his boss.

He glowers, but nods. "You stand beside your sister. It will give Severu a comparison that will highlight what a diamond my princess is."

Carlotta frowns, but soon her expression clears. I do not show any reaction to Papà's stinging comment. Starve a bully of his attention and he will grow tired of tormenting you. That's the idea, anyway.

Zia Lora clicks her tongue. "You have two lovely daughters, Francesco."

"The Don will be spoiled for choice," Zio Giovi says with a warm smile directed at both myself and Carlotta.

Papà just harrumphs.

"We will wait for you in the drawing room," Zia Lora says before she and Zio turn to go.

After a couple minutes of silence, Carlotta asks, "Is the don really coming because he's thinking of marrying me?"

"Do not be so forward *stellina*," Papà chides. "That is not a question you should ask."

"I shouldn't?" My sister sounds naïve, but I can hear the undertone of frustration in her words. "Isn't it my life?"

Our father takes her hand and pats it. "It is not something for you to worry about. I will see to your future."

Carlotta's features tighten for just a moment and then they smooth into placid sweetness again. My sister is not as accepting of our father's pronouncements as he believes.

The doorbell rings. A maid answers and leads not only the don, but his mother, brother, and sister toward us. The don's bodyguards take up unobtrusive positions in the hall. One remains by the front door. All are alert and serious.

I've had glimpses of the don before, from a distance when he was let into our house and when he was leaving. I have never actually spoken to him though. Unlike Carlotta, my father has never taken me to a social gathering where I might meet Severu De Luca in person. Not as his father's underboss, nor as the don he has been for the past five years.

This close, he takes my breath away. Don De Luca stands more than a head taller than my father's five-feet-ten-inches. The don has a muscular, broad chest that makes his upper body look like a V. The slacks of his bespoke suit hint at long, muscled legs. It isn't merely his size that fills the space around him though; it is his unmistakable aura of power.

His gaze traps mine and I cannot look away even though I know I should.

He's 35, but there are no smile lines around his eyes or mouth. His brown eyes eerily reflect no emotion at all. Not eagerness to spend time with his potential bride, not pleasure in his consigliere's company. Nothing. His masculine lips do not crease in a smile of greeting. Dangerous and intimidating, it feels like he's on alert for any source of danger despite being in the home of a trusted associate.

My father, who has always been the greatest threat in my existence, appears diminished in the dominant presence of his don.

Unbelievably, my vagina, which has been silent for twenty-five years, decides to wake up. It looks at the terrifying head of the Genovese Family and says, "Yes, I want that."

I feel a sensation between my legs I have never experienced before. A feeling of emptiness that needs to be filled. Heat suffuses my body, making the drafty foyer feel suffocatingly warm.

In that moment, I realize that I have figured out the timing for my exodus from my precarious life. I'm running away the day after my sister's wedding. I'll leave my father's house right after Carlotta does.

My reaction to the don isn't just shocking. It's embarrassing. If I don't get it under control before they are engaged, it will be a betrayal of my sister too. I cannot lust after her fiancé, much less her husband. That is just wrong.

I may not be a made man, but I am Cosa Nostra. I have a sense of honor and I won't compromise it.

Not even if my ovaries are sending up fireworks and cymbals are crashing in my vagina for the first time in my life.

I am not a sexual person. I'm not ignorant. I considered the possibility I preferred women, but my body reacts to no one. I am simply sexually inert.

Until this moment.

I break my gaze from the don, the man who is one thousand percent off limits and force myself to take in his brother. They look alike. Dark brown eyes, black hair, huge and muscular. But my vagina just yawns and goes back to sleep when my eyes land on Miceli De Luca.

Carlotta doesn't seem to be under the don's spell like I am. She gives a barely there smile and greets him and his family demurely, but she doesn't offer her hand.

Papà frowns but covers it up with forced bonhomie. "Severu, you remember my daughter, Carlotta."

"And this must be your oldest daughter," Signora De Luca says with a warm smile after my father neglects to introduce me. "Madonna Catalina, isn't it? We have not met."

She's beautiful. Though I know Aria De Luca is in her fifties, with her golden blonde hair and unlined face, she looks like she could be the don's older sister, rather than his mother. As well as their dark hair, her children must have gotten their brown eyes from their father. Hers are green.

"Please, call me Catalina."

"And you may call me Aria." She offers her hand and I shake it as the fragrance of rose, jasmine, vanilla and just a hint of citrus wafts around us.

I know it well. It was my mother's perfume and I keep a bottle to spray on my pillow when I need the comfort to fall asleep.

Choking back unexpected emotion, I say, "Welcome to our home." I can't make myself use her name and still think of her as Signora De Luca in my head. I am almost as awed by this elegant woman as I am intimidated by her powerful son.

The don's brother shakes my hand as well. "Miceli," he says by way of introduction.

"It is a pleasure to meet you," I reply. Though that isn't strictly true.

Where I find the don's forceful presence inexplicably exciting, this man just scares me. The cold look in his dark eyes doesn't help.

My gaze skitters away from him only to land once again on his brother and I have to stifle a gasp. This is so unfair. My first taste of sexual desire and it's for a man who is completely off limits and so out of my league, we might as well be on different planets.

Miceli gives my hand a squeeze. My gaze snaps back to his face. Miceli releases my hand with a frown. I try to give him an innocuous smile in return, but am sure it looks more pained than banal.

Miceli steps away and his sister takes his place. "I am Giulia Mancini. It's nice to meet you, Catalina."

It doesn't escape me that all of these people have met my sister before. Because she is not kept like a prisoner in our home.

Then Severu De Luca is standing in front of me and my feelings of resentment are overshadowed by the reaction of my ladybits to his presence. His masculine scent overpowers the comforting fragrance of his mother's perfume, eliciting an entirely different reaction in me.

Don De Luca takes my hand. More heat rushes up my neck and into my face. Moisture pools between my legs, soaking my panties. My ovaries practically explode and my vaginal walls contract with need. Oh. My. Gosh. All of this from his hand touching mine?

Can I fake a sudden illness and go hide in my room? I certainly feel fevered.

The don says in his deep voice, "Catalina, thank you for having us in your home." Like I am my father's hostess.

Papà has never afforded me that distinction, but his boss assumes it and my father doesn't have the courage to deny it as I'm sure he wants to.

I manage a quick handshake before jerking my hand away and tucking it behind my back, so I don't accidentally touch him again. For the love of Mike. "Uh, Don De Luca. Thank you for coming."

He doesn't offer the use of his first name, and I would never presume to use it otherwise.

I can't read his expression, so I have no idea if he notices my improper reaction to him. Though why should he? It's not like he can just guess my panties are now damp. Can he? I have zero experience with men and sexual attraction.

His dark eyes look like they can see right into my soul. He turns away, showing no more reaction than if he'd shaken the hand of a mannequin. Relief and dis war inside me, but my brain reminds my body that relief should win.

Carlotta slides her hand into mine and holds tight. Her body is tense, and her fingers are cold to my touch. She's nervous and no matter how difficult I know this dinner is going to be for me with my newly awakened sexuality, no way am I abandoning her.

I tell my vagina to go back to sleep. It shouldn't be hard. Awake is not its natural state. And I walk with my sister into the drawing room.

CHAPTER 9

New York City, New York
Five Families
SEVERU

Dinner is excellent and Francesco's family are good hosts, but my mind is occupied with the problem of who is passing mafia information on to the Irish.

Although she never made a lasting impression on me when we have met in the past, my intended is as beautiful as her reputation claims. Demure, with good manners, she does not put herself forward in the conversation. I hope this bodes well for the future.

I have no time for a spoiled wife who will expect to have my constant attention. Despite her beauty, she is not inspiring, but I don't expect her to be the love of my life. I almost smile at the ridiculousness of the thought.

I care for my family and would die to protect them. Though I would rather kill. But love? That is for other people. Not the don. While my future wife can expect the same protection as my family, I have no intention of giving her anything else.

A don cannot afford weakness.

Miceli and the older sister seem to be arguing about something. I tune into their conversation and am surprised. Miceli favors bitcoin for money laundering. He's calling it investments, naturally. We don't talk real business with women present. Catalina thinks the market is too volatile.

The way they bicker back and forth amuses me. I notice, Francesco doesn't look entertained however.

He glares at his daughter. "That is quite enough. Discussing topics beyond your comprehension, much less arguing a point of view you cannot possibly understand is not how I expect a daughter of mine to behave."

It's a harsh reprimand, but Catalina doesn't look cowed. Her face shows no expression at all, but her hazel eyes darken so they appear green.

She sits with her back straight, her head held high and gives her father a steady look. "As you say, Papà."

The words are right. Even the brief dropping of her gaze is exactly what is expected and yet there is something in her tone, the set of her shoulders, something that denies victory to her father.

Miceli frowns at Francesco and then admits grudgingly, "Catalina makes the same argument Domenico does."

Which is why we don't use bitcoin to launder our money. Miceli is underboss, but Domenico is capo with responsibility for all our online money laundering operations. We don't override our capo's decisions without strong motivation. And if it's strong enough to counter their orders, the capo is in serious trouble.

"Is he the investment director for Oscuro Enterprises?" Catalina asks.

"Madonna Catalina!" her father barks. "Our business is none of your concern."

"As you say, Papà." This time Catalina's tone is perfectly neutral, with no subtle undertones, but her shoulders do not slouch. Her head does not bow. "Is there a topic you prefer I discuss?"

"I would *prefer* you keep your mouth shut."

I know Francesco is a chauvinist. Hell, the world of the mafia is filled with chauvinism, or so my sister informs me. But I do not like the way he is speaking to his oldest daughter. Neither does my brother, if his clenched jaw is any indication.

And Giulia is glaring daggers at my consigliere.

"Come now, Francesco, I am sure you don't mean that," my mother says, surprising me. We do not interfere in the family affairs of others. "I am enjoying visiting with both of your daughters."

"You are too kindhearted," Francesco replies.

My mother's mouth tightens but I doubt my consigliere notices the tiny sign of Mamma's displeasure. Sensing I may have missed something about the dynamic of my consigliere's family, I scan the other guests at the table.

Candilora shoots a look of clear gratitude toward my mother. Her husband is eating, but the grip on his fork is tight. Carlotta looks oblivious to the tension at the table, her lovely features showing no concern. My brother gives me a look and I know what it means.

He has never liked that I kept Francesco as my consigliere after our father's death. He considers the man too hidebound. However, it would be a disservice to my father's memory to replace the man. The idea of appointing a second, or even a third consigliere has merit though. Some dons have a counsel of three.

"Come, Lina, you can help me put the finishing touches on desert." Candilora stands and puts her hand out to her niece.

Catalina nods and stands, her expression stoic. She does not take her aunt's hand, but she does follow the older woman from the room.

"Carlotta will play the piano for us after dinner," Francesco says, his voice warm with approval. "She is quite an accomplished musician."

"Not as accomplished as *soru*," Carlotta says sweetly, smiling innocently at her father.

Francesco ignores his daughter's claim and asks Miceli what he thinks of the Yankees this season. I do not understand my brother's fascination with baseball. It is a hella boring sport. At least football has a chance for some bloodshed.

"Perhaps your sister will accompany you tonight," my mother says to Carlotta.

"Papà doesn't usually ask her to play."

"You will both play," I say. It is not a question. I don't ask. I tell.

My mother gives me a startled look, but nods. "I think that would be lovely."

"You are in for a treat." Giovi has been mostly silent throughout dinner. "My nieces are both very talented." He smiles benevolently at Carlotta.

She returns his smile sweetly, her undeniably beautiful features made even more so by the expression. I do not know why my mind insists on remembering the stoic expression her sister has worn throughout most of the evening.

And why it is thoughts of the older woman that make my dick hard.

CATALINA

Don De Luca has decreed that both Carlotta and I will play the piano after dinner. Papà is furious, but he's doing his best to hide it. He wants to show off the daughter he loves. His little beauty.

Playing the piano is consuming and personal for me. I prefer to do it without an audience. I do not dare demur though. For one thing, even I know you do not tell the don no. And for another, the only thing that will make my father angrier right now is for me to embarrass him by refusing to play at the don's command.

I think Carlotta must have instigated this, but I do not know if it is because she doesn't want to play alone, or because she wants to highlight my worth. It is something she has done since we were little. She's very subtle about it and I'm not sure anyone else in the family notices, but I do.

It is one of the reasons I adore my younger sister so much. She has always seen my value, no matter what kind of cutting remarks our father makes about me. He cannot diminish me in her eyes. Zio and Zia are the same, though they usually reserve their approving comments for when papà is not around.

Carlotta and I take our places side by side on the piano bench. She starts playing *Clair de Lune* and after the second note, I join her. We have been playing this way since she first learned the instrument. We play three songs like that, finishing with *Bella Ciao*, the lively notes garnering both vocal praise and applause from our listeners.

We turn to face our dinner companions and I notice that even the don's lips are tilted up infinitesimally on one side of his mouth. It's not a smile like Zio Giovi's, but it does funny things to my heart. And my traitorous vagina.

Carlotta smiles shyly and blushes. I duck my head, uncomfortable with being the center of attention even though I share the spotlight with her.

"Now, you play a song for us by yourself, *stellina*." My father's tone is jovial, but there is no doubt in my mind he expects to be obeyed.

I stand from the piano bench and join my aunt and uncle on one of the sofas placed in the music room for just this purpose. There are three arranged in a c shape, the opening toward the piano. The don, his mother and his sister sit on the one facing the piano. My father and Miceli sit on the sofa across from where I am.

I keep my attention on my sister, having no desire to meet my father's gaze or that of the don, or his family, for that matter. I desperately want to retreat to my room, my emotional reserves used up. I am not used to being around people besides my family and have gotten adept at avoiding my father. Spending so many hours in his company is draining.

Continuing with the theme of Italian folk songs, Carlotta plays a cheerful rendition of *Tarantella Napoletana*. When she is finished, there is more applause and smiles.

"Your turn," my uncle says to me.

I stiffen. I don't want to play alone in front of the audience.

"I'm sure Catalina is too tired to indulge you, Giovi," my father says repressively. "The don and his family are here to get to know Carlotta."

It's as blatant of a claim to what this visit is for as my father could make. No one denies it, least of all the don himself. He is looking at Carlotta with approval.

My heart falls. A tiny part of me was still hoping that all this talk of marriage and engagements was just that. Talk. That Don De Luca was not interested in my nineteen-year-old sister. It was a ridiculous hope.

He is the most powerful mafia don in the country, who else would he choose for his bride than the most beautiful mafia princess? The don isn't going to settle for just any woman. He will take for a wife only a woman that will make others envious. Just as his father did before him.

At least Carlotta is not already promised to another like Signora De Luca had been all those years ago. Aria De Luca was supposed to become Aria Jilani. It was considered a good match. My father was the oldest son of a capo. Everyone expected him to become capo one day, but instead he was promoted to the role of consigliere at a very young age.

I wonder if Severu De Luca is aware my father's appointment to such a prestigious position was part of the bride swapping bargain between his father and my own?

My father gave up his claim to Aria and accepted my mother as his substitute bride. Mamma came with an impeccable pedigree and advantageous connections, but she was not the elegant and charming beauty that Aria was. Mamma was short, curvy and worst of all, according to my father, painfully shy.

Despite his pretense to the contrary, my father never got over losing the woman he'd been promised, and he'd made my mother pay for it every day of their marriage.

A touch on my arm makes me jump. It is my aunt, and her expression is filled with concern. "Is your father right, are you too tired to play?"

I look around me and realize everyone's attention is on me.

"Of course, she is," my father states with authority. "You know Catalina lacks stamina."

"Oh, if you are not up to it, that is quite all right," Signora De Luca says.

And I realize two things. One, I missed part of the conversation while I was lost in memories and two, apparently the don's mother has added her request to my uncle's for me to play a solo.

The look of smug triumph in my father's eyes spurs me on as nothing else could and I stand. "I am happy to play for you." I speak directly to the don's mother.

Then I turn and go back to the piano while Carlotta takes my place on the sofa with our aunt and uncle.

I hear a quickly indrawn breath when I start playing and am sure it is my father. He knows this song choice for the act of rebellion it is. *La Campanella* had been my mother's favorite piece and was one of the last songs she taught me to play before her death.

Losing myself in the music, I forget about getting back at my father. I forget my audience. I simply play and feel the peace I knew as a little girl sitting on this very piano bench beside my mother.

As my fingers still on the piano keys, I want nothing more than to slump into myself. I am more than drained, I am hollowed out. But I keep my spine straight and my shoulders back. I will not let my father win. I show him no weakness.

The applause barely registers as I stand. "I will have coffee brought into the living room," I say, prepared to make a quick exit to the kitchen.

The don stands. His mother and siblings follow suit.

"No coffee for us." Don De Luca catches my father's gaze with his hard eyes. "I will call you tomorrow to discuss the particulars of the engagement."

Does anyone else see the way my sister's eyes narrow?

She deserves so much better than this. She deserves a proper proposal, even if this is a mafia arranged marriage.

Signora De Luca shakes her head. "That's my son, ever practical."

I would have said abysmally insensitive, but nobody asked me.

"We'll meet for lunch tomorrow to start planning the wedding," she says to my sister. "I would like you both to join us."

This time she meets Zia Lora's eyes and then my own. We both nod, but I notice my sister says nothing. Everyone takes her acquiescence for granted and that worries me.

Carlotta is used to getting her own way. She's never run right up against the wall of our father's intransigence. Rock, meet hard place.

One of them is going to shatter and I don't think it's going to be the consigliere, no matter how indulgent he usually is toward my sister.

CHAPTER 10

After our return to the De Luca building, I check on Neri. The nightlight reveals both the nanny and Neri sleeping peacefully, in their respective beds.

With his dark curls and square jaw, Neri looks so much like his father, I sometimes wonder what there is of me in him. Raff says he sees it in Neri's enthusiasm for life and affectionate nature.

An affectionate nature I know will be trained out of him by the time he becomes a made man. Raff has agreed to allow our son to finish high school before being inducted into the mafia. And like my husband and brothers, Neri will get a business degree before taking any official role.

It's as normal of a life as I can negotiate for my son.

Raff has already started training our son for life in the mafia. Thankfully, he's implementing my father's methods of using play to teach Neri, rather than the much stricter, formalized training Raff started when he was a mere toddler.

As part of the marriage alliance bargain, Raff spent the four years that I attended university in New York, learning under my father. His choice to follow my father's counsel regarding our son, rather than Patrizio's, is one of the reasons I can't help but love the infuriating man.

There is one area of Neri's training I insist on following neither father on. I refuse to teach my son to bury his emotions at such a young age. Neri is allowed to show his anger, his sadness, his hurt and his happiness...around family. Raff insists Neri cannot cry, or even laugh too loudly, in public.

It's a compromise I can live with.

Because that freedom to show any emotion was not afforded to either of my brothers. By the time I was born, neither Severu nor Miceli ever cried, and they almost never laughed.

I grew up knowing my father and brothers would both die and kill to keep me and my mom safe. However, I craved the hugs I saw school friends receive from their fathers. I was jealous of the joking camaraderie they had with their siblings.

Life as the daughter of a don prepared me in many ways for my life as the wife of an underboss who will one day rule over Las Vegas. But deep inside, I'm still starving for the affection I will never receive from the people I need it most.

I lean down and kiss my son, silently promising him that as much as I can make it, his world will be a different place than mine.

Returning to the guest room I have used since my marriage, I prepare for bed. My phone rings as I'm drying off from my shower.

It's Raff requesting a video call. I yank the shower cap I'd worn to keep my hair dry off my head and wrap the large, fluffy towel around my torso, tucking it above my breasts to hold it in place.

Swiping my finger across the screen, I answer the call and then prop the phone up on the counter. "Hello, Raff."

It's only eight o'clock there, but his handsome face is drawn in lines of weariness. "*Amate.* How was the dinner with your brother's fiancée?"

I pause in smoothing lotion down my leg. There is that word again. Beloved.

"Honestly? Strange."

"In what way?" The familiar hunger in his gaze tells me that he's watching my post shower routine closely.

Do I let the towel edges part to show more of my naked thigh? Why yes. Yes, I do.

"Francesco Jilani has two daughters and one of them is in her mid-twenties," I say as if I'm not doing my best to tease my husband with my body. "But I've never seen her at any of the social functions."

Raff's eyes narrow, but he replies in kind. "I didn't realize he had an older daughter. Is she married?"

"No and she'd be a better fit for Severu. You should have heard her arguing the merits of bitcoin with Miceli." I lift my other foot onto the stool and administer lotion down the length of my leg.

"Your brother doesn't seem to get that bitcoin is as big a gamble as the games in our casinos."

Really? He can still talk about ways to launder money? I need to up my game.

Giving a not-so-accidental peek at my feminine center, I lower my foot to the floor. "I think she convinced him."

"I'm impressed."

"I was too. And I could tell Severu enjoyed the way she schooled our brother, but he's marrying her younger sister." Carlotta is only nineteen. My brother is 35.

It's a significant age gap. Almost an entire generation. Catalina is closer to my age, and Severu's. There's only a decade between them, which is still a gap, but she's more mature than her sister. It's not just about years, but attitude.

"I wasn't talking about Catalina."

"Oh?" I ask, smoothing lotion onto my arms.

"Drop the towel, wife."

I play with the top of my towel but don't part it. "You want a peep show, husband?"

"I want to see my wife." His eyes are so hot, they are melting my feminine core.

I let the white terrycloth drop to the floor.

"Beautiful," he growls.

"You want to see beautiful? You should have been at dinner. Carlotta is as stunning as everyone claims."

"No one is as gorgeous as my wife." His phone shakes, making his image wobble and then it rights itself.

"Did you put your phone on a stand?" I ask.

So he could touch himself? With all the trips I've taken during our marriage, this is the first time we've done this. If we're doing what I think we are.

"Cup your tits, Giulia."

Okay, we are definitely doing it.

I curve my hands under the bottom of both of my breasts, squeezing just the way I like. My nipples are already hard, but I don't touch them. I'm teasing us both.

The growl that comes out of his throat is pure masculine arousal.

"What are you doing with your hands?" I tease him.

"Do you want to see?"

"Yes."

He shifts the phone stand so I have a view of him sitting in his office chair, his trousers open, his erection dark and engorged with blood sticking straight up. One of his big hands has it grasped at the base, the other is gripping the arm of his chair with white-knuckle intensity.

He is so into this.

Wetness gushes from my center, sliding down my inner thighs.

"Squeeze your tits together, like you do when you let me fuck them."

My knees want to buckle, and I drag the vanity stool to where I am so I can sit on it and still give him a view of my naked body. I sit down with my legs spread, letting him see my glistening folds.

"Fuck." He rubs up and down his shaft, his hand almost a blur.

I press my boobs together, my nipples sticking out like big, round erasers. I love when he uses my breasts to get off. The feel of his velvet covered hardness between my pillowy softness is so darn sensual. And he plays with my nipples until I'm begging to come by the time he paints my chest and neck with his cum.

"This fucking phone screen is too small. Put your camera up to your pussy. I want to see how flushed and wet you are."

"What? No." The blush he's so sure is in my lady bits travels up my body and makes my face hot.

"Do it, *amate*." His dark, commanding tone sends arousal zinging along every one of my nerve endings.

I lean forward and grab the phone, and then lower it so he can see my wet slit. "I can't believe I'm doing this."

In the little rectangular inset that shows my camera's feed, I can see what Raff is seeing. An up close and personal image of my coochie. Why does that turn me on so freakin' much?

His expression is harsh and intent. On me. I can feel the impact across 2500 miles.

"Touch yourself. Slide your fingers into those pretty pink folds and spread your honey up to your clit. Get it good and wet."

"I hope your office door is shut," I huff. But my hand goes exactly where he wants it.

I'm so wet, I'm going to need another shower after this. Sliding my forefinger and middle finger between my labia, I scissor them and send jolts of pleasure from my clitoris outward.

I moan.

"Giulia." Raff's voice is laden with sexual need.

"I wish you were touching me," I tell him.

"Whose pussy are you touching?" he asks gutturally, his hand spreading his own precum over his turgid penis.

"Yours," I moan, unable to give him my usual sass on this.

I miss him. I ache for him. I need him in ways he'll never understand.

"And whose cock is this?" he demands, like he's angry.

"Mine." He might not love me, but my husband belongs to me.

"Put your fingers inside. Come on, *cara*, fuck yourself for me."

Pushing both fingers into my slick heat, I shudder at the sensation. Both full and nearly full enough.

"I'm going to have to buy a dildo for these trips," I joke, my voice breathless as I slide my fingers in and out of myself.

I'm holding my phone so he can see what I'm doing with my other hand, but my clitoris needs stimulation. I'm so close to coming, my body is shaking with the need to orgasm.

"No dildo!" Raff looks and sound feral. "No cock in your pussy but mine."

"Alright, caveman." I'm not about to order a dildo online and have it delivered to my family's home.

Going into a sex toy store is out of the question too.

"I mean it, *amate*. Your fingers and nothing else until you are with me again."

"You're so bossy sometimes," I complain, though the words come out in broken gasps.

I'm so close and for whatever reason this conversation is only increasing my excitement.

"Come for me, wife. Come. Now."

Bossy.

I press my heel into the bundle of nerves at the top of my labia as I shove my fingers as deep as I can into my swollen vagina. Ecstasy detonates inside me with the power of crashing comet. My whole body seizes with the pleasure and I yell Raff's name.

I hear him shouting, "Giulia," but my eyes are closed and I can't even watch his ejaculate shoot out of his shaft. I imagine it in my mind's eye though and it sends another wave of pleasure through me.

Thump.

My side hits the bathroom floor with a painful jar. This time when I cry out, it's not in bliss.

Oh, man, that hurt. I sit up and look around for my phone. It landed a couple of feet away, against the wall.

"Giulia!" Raff is yelling. "Are you alright?"

I crawl to the phone and grab it, holding it so he can see me. My hair is a mess and I'm sweaty and red in the face. I'm definitely going to have to step back into the shower before going to bed.

"Next time, I think I need to be on a bed for that. Softer landing."

"Damn it, Giulia, this is no joking matter. Are you bruised?"

I look down at the side I landed on. My hip is a little red, but there's nothing that's going to turn into a bruise tomorrow. "I'm fine."

"Show me."

"Are you kidding? I told you I'm fine."

"I want to see."

Knowing it will be easier, and faster, to just show him than to argue over it, I scan my phone's camera over my left side.

When I'm done, I bring it back up to my face. "Satisfied?"

"Yes," he says grudgingly.

He doesn't look satisfied. He looks like he wants to come through the phone and do a personal inspection himself.

As the adrenaline fades from the ignominious fall off the stool, I yawn.

"You are tired. You need to go to bed."

"I have to shower."

"You just got out of the shower."

"You got me all messy," I tease him with a tired blink.

"No shower. Get some sleep."

"You're getting bossier the older you get. I'm going to have to start reining you in," I tease. But honestly? Bed sounds really good right now.

My body is replete and I may be able to fall asleep without tossing and turning from missing my husband. I never sleep as well when he's not in the bed with me.

"Good luck with that."

"Was that a joke, Raff?"

"Go to sleep, Giulia."

"Goodnight, husband."

Something intense flares in his eyes, and he says, "Goodnight, wife. Dream of me."

I don't tell him that's all too likely.

As I'm drifting into sleep, I remember the expression on Severu's face when Catalina played the piano. He'd been mesmerized, like the rest of us, but there had been something more there. The same look Raff had tonight on our video call.

Pity for Carlotta makes my heart hurt. Severu will never love the girl, but she'll never inspire the kind of passion in him that has made my own marriage bearable either.

Because it's not her my brother looks at like a steak dinner to a starving man.

It's Catalina.

CHAPTER 11

New York City, New York
Five Families
CATALINA

Our lunch with Aria De Luca, Giulia Mancini and Zia Lora is more like a war council.

Apparently Don De Luca expects a full Sicilian wedding in three months. Three!

His mother informs us that she will be his voice in the wedding plans. As her maid of honor, Carlotta insists on me being present for everything. So, I'm glad the don isn't going to be underfoot.

If I could go without seeing him again until the day of the wedding, that would be great. My vagina disagrees, but she's a lazy twit who has spent two and half decades dormant. She doesn't get a vote now.

However, between my sister's unenthusiastic response to her engagement and the groom's lack of interest in the wedding, I can't help worrying their marriage is a disaster in the making.

~ ~ ~

I chew on my bottom lip and watch my sister as the car eats up the miles between Long Island and Manhattan.

The last week and a half have been a whirlwind of activity.

Yesterday, Carlotta picked out her wedding gown. As much as my sister loves fashion, she reacted to picking out the dress she's going to be married in like she was choosing a flavor of ice cream. But with less excitement.

Right now, we are on our way into the city for a consultation with the catering company. We'll be meeting Aria De Luca and her daughter again. Not the don.

Zia Lora won't be able to make all the trips into the city because it's all so rushed, but she's convinced Papa to give us a car and a driver. Even with a second soldier acting as bodyguard, it is freedom unlike anything either of us have ever known.

"I'm so excited to try this tasting menu," Carlotta says with her first spark of real enthusiasm. "The head chef said I could tour the kitchens and watch different preparations."

"Does it matter how they make the food, so long as you like how it tastes?" I ask.

My sister's lovely face is flushed, her eyes fever bright. "Oh yes. I can't wait to see how they make the chilled dessert. The chef does it in individual portions with liquid nitrogen."

"That sounds dangerous." Not to mention challenging for the number of guests expected to attend.

Even with the short notice, there are nearly two-thousand people on the guest list. At least a thousand of them, or their representatives, will definitely be there.

It is not every day a don gets married. Guests are coming from all over the country and even Italy. There will be dons, or their underbosses, from all Five Families in New York and the other Cosa Nostra territories, as well as the Camorra we count as allies.

Carlotta shrugs. "It's molecular gastronomy," she says with reverence.

"I could barely get you to give an opinion about the flowers." She'd agreed that having mom's favorite white camelias included in the arrangements would be nice, though Carlotta hadn't actually shown a preference for anything herself.

"Flowers are boring."

"And the dress?"

"Aria has impeccable taste. The dress she picked out is fine."

"I don't think your future mother-in-law should pick out your wedding dress," I admonish.

"Why not? She's got experience being a don's wife. She knows what's expected. I don't. You know what Zio Giovi says..."

"Go with the experts and you won't go wrong," we say together and then burst out laughing.

"She may be an expert on being a don's wife, but she is not an expert on you, Carlotta. And this is your wedding."

"That's why you're here, to be the expert on me," Carlotta says.

It's disturbing that Signora De Luca and even her daughter have had more input on the wedding plans than the bride-to-be, but I don't say anything. I can tell my little sister is overwhelmed by the prospect of becoming the don's wife.

She doesn't find him even remotely sexy. She told me so and I had to bite my tongue to keep back my astonishment. "He's nearly twice my age and you've seen how cold his eyes are."

I don't tell her how a simple look from those dark eyes warms up my insides faster than a shot of whiskey.

"Well, I'm glad you're excited about the food," I say now.

Only I realize later that it's not choosing the food for the wedding menu that excites my sister.

She's happy to leave the final choices for each course up to the rest of us, but Carlotta peppers the caterer with questions about *how* each dish is prepared and she's transfixed when we are taken on a tour of the kitchens.

I see cooking as a means to an end, a way to avoid my father. He wouldn't step foot in the kitchen. However, Carlotta *enjoys* our time learning how to prepare our family's signature dishes from Zia Lora. I mean, I don't dislike cooking, but given a choice between doing it and listening to a lecture on ancient history, I'll go for the lecture every time.

Carlotta is busy trying to guess the ingredients of a soup she's been invited to taste by one of the sous chefs when Signora De Luca touches my arm.

I turn to face her.

"Carlotta is very lucky to have you as her older sister. I worried she would struggle with the wedding plans without a mother to help, but you stepped in and are doing a wonderful job."

I feel my face heat at the compliment. "Zia Lora would be doing more if the plans were not so rushed."

"When Severu makes up his mind about something, there's no changing it," his sister, Giulia, says, with a look toward Carlotta that could be construed as worried.

She has the most adorable three-year-old son, Neri. She's brought him with her when she could, but right now he's at the De Luca's taking a nap.

"Carlotta is young." There is something in the don's mother's voice and she's looking at my sister with an identical expression to her daughter's. "Beautiful, but young."

"She is smart and she's good with people. She'll learn what she needs to," I say loyally, though in my heart I agree with Signora De Luca. I hate that my sister is being pressured into marrying at such a young age.

"Let us hope that she does not lose herself in the process."

Surprised by the older woman's sentiments, I admit, "If it were my choice, she wouldn't have been pushed into marriage at nineteen."

"I was eighteen when I married Enzo."

I cannot tell from Aria De Luca's tone if she thinks that was a good, or a bad, thing.

"Do you wish you had been older?" As soon as I ask the question, I wish I could take it back. "I'm sorry. I shouldn't have asked that. It's much too personal."

"We are becoming friends, are we not, Catalina?"

Are we? We've known each other less than two weeks, but I like Aria De Luca very much. And her daughter, Giulia. They are both very easy to be around and neither lords their position over others.

Huh. The don's mother and I *are* becoming friends. I smile.

Aria returns my smile. "In answer to your question. I had many good years with Enzo. We were never in love, but we grew to love each other. We respected each other. He was good to me."

"That's not actually an answer to my question." Which is another thing I probably shouldn't say, but it is something I *would* say to a friend.

"No, it isn't, is it? I'm so used to being circumspect. Yes." She expels a breath like a sigh. "I wish I had been older. I spent the first few years of my marriage feeling like a fraud, terrified of doing or saying the wrong thing. I believe I would have been more confident and less afraid if I had been older when I got married."

Giulia doesn't look like this is news to her. Maybe that's why she was allowed to attend university before marrying the underboss in Las Vegas.

"I'm glad you will be there to help Carlotta navigate her life as a don's wife," I say to Aria.

Aria gives a smile tinged with something else. Sadness? Concern? I'm not sure.

She says, "I will do my best, but I'm sure she will continue to rely on you."

Only I am not going to be there. Even if I didn't have these totally inappropriate cravings for my sister's future husband, I must get away from our father.

My plans are set. I will be leaving New York after the wedding.

CHAPTER 12

New York City, New York
Five Families
CATALINA

We are on our way home and I relax on the leather backseat of the family Mercedes S-Class sedan. It's luxurious and comfortable, but not armored like my father's personal SUV with a 3rd row of seating for additional guards.

Carlotta is still talking about everything she learned from the chef and sous chefs.

"You should ask Don De Luca for cooking classes. I am sure he won't object."

Carlotta's eyes fill with hope and then they dim. "Even if he wouldn't, I don't think I could ask him for anything. He scares me."

"He's going to be your husband. You do not need to fear him."

"You don't think so?" Carlotta shivers. "He's ruthless. I bet he tortures men for breakfast."

"Don't be dramatic."

"I'm still a teenager," she sasses. "I'm allowed."

"You'll soon be married. Teenager, or not."

Carlotta frowns, but then her expression lightens. "You could bring cooking school up to Aria. She'll suggest it to her son if you tell her you think it's a good idea for me."

Not sure how we went from cooking classes to cooking school, I say, "Aria is going to be your mother-in-law, not mine."

"But you two get along so well."

"She wants to help you, Carlotta. Let her."

My sister's mouth twists in a grimace. "I suppose."

"To tell you the truth, I'm a little jealous," I admit.

"You are?" Carlotta asks, like there could not possibly be anything in her current situation to be jealous of.

"Most women would be jealous of you marrying the don."

"You're not though. I know you."

She doesn't know how I react to Don De Luca. No, I'm not jealous of her being a don's wife, but being *his* wife? I'm ashamed to admit, even to myself, that I am.

I say what doesn't shame me though. "I miss having a mom so much and now you are going to have a really kind and caring mother-in-law."

"I've never needed a mom," Carlotta says dismissively. "I had Zia Lora and I had you. I don't want a mother-in-law."

Carlotta was only four when Mamma died. She doesn't remember our mom's gentleness, her loving nature, her sweetness despite being married to a man who never accepted her for herself. Mamma had never let it make her bitter.

"I'm sorry you don't want a mother-in-law." I don't tell her she needs to get over it. There are enough people in Carlotta's life ignoring her feelings right now. I'm not going to be another one of them. "I know this is hard for you. I wish I could make it easier."

"You are."

I wish that were true. "Your light has dimmed since the engagement was announced."

"Can you blame me?" Carlotta's eyes fill with tears. "All anyone sees or talks about is how beautiful I am, like I'm nothing more than my face and body. Like I'm some kind of prize. But I am a woman with thoughts and feelings. I'm not just a broodmare who will make pretty children. Oh, God, *soru*, I'm terrified of my wedding night. I can't stand the thought of him touching me."

I pull my sister into my arms and hug her tight, my own eyes burning. I can't stop this wedding, and neither can she. I can't make my sister be attracted to the don any more than I can rid myself of my own inexplicable desire for him. If I could give it to her, I would. For so many reasons.

The window behind us explodes, glass shattering over our heads. Carlotta screams, but she quickly undoes her seatbelt and drops to the floor of the car, curling up into a ball. I do the same.

We've been trained since we could walk in how to respond in situations like this. Not that either of us has ever been in one before.

"What's happening?" Carlotta screams the question.

"Stay down," one of the bodyguard orders.

My sister's terror suppresses my own. I have to take care of her. I have to protect her. I know where the extra guns are kept in the cars.

Zio Giovi showed me. He also taught me how to shoot. My father would be furious if he knew, but both Zio and I are good at keeping secrets.

I press the lever that allows me access to the hidden compartment under the backseat and pull out a gun. It's a Glock. Good. I've used one of these before. I check that it is loaded. It is.

A loud thump sounds and then the car swerves, a kathunk, kathunk telling me that whoever is after us has shot out one of the tires. The car fishtails wildly but it keeps moving forward. Toward the safety of our home.

Suddenly the kathunk gives way to the sound of metal scraping on asphalt. I don't know how long the driver can keep the car going, driving on the rim.

Seconds later, I learn the answer to my question as the driver brings the car to a stop.

"Stay in the car with the doors locked," he says before he and the other bodyguard jump out, slamming doors behind them.

Why don't they use the doors as shields? The car is already compromised with the missing back window. It's not armored, so if our pursuers get past the bodyguards, all they have to do is shoot through the windows.

Unless they don't want to kill us. Kidnapping is a bigger worry for my sister and me. Regardless, this car is no refuge.

"It's going to be okay, *stellina*," I say, using my dad's endearment for my sister. "We're going to be alright."

Shaking with fear, Carlotta doesn't answer.

Gunshots sound from behind the car, but I don't raise my head to see what's happening. I wait. There is a cacophony of shots and the thump of a body falling. Was it one of the pursuers, or one of the bodyguards?

I'm scared, but I have to know.

I lift my head just high enough to peek through the missing back window. Our bodyguards have taken a stance behind trees to the side of the road, drawing the fire of our pursuers away from the car.

There is a masked man lying in a pool of blood on the road. There are three additional masked men still standing. They are using their SUV as a shield. One starts running toward our car while his associates lay down covering fire toward my father's men.

Regardless of the bullets hitting the trees all around them, our driver comes out enough to shoot the man headed toward us. He falls and remains unmoving. Then our driver takes a shot in the shoulder. My throat tightens with dread as I see the blood and the way his body is thrown backward.

He gets up again almost immediately though, keeping up a steady barrage of gunfire toward the remaining pursuers. Seconds later, he's shot again and this time, he doesn't get up.

The second bodyguard manages to hit another one of the masked men and that one falls to the side of the SUV. He tries to get back up, but can only pull himself into a sitting position against the SUV. The last masked man standing runs toward the back of their SUV and pops around it out of sight.

I want to scream a warning to our bodyguard, but we are trained not to do anything that could compromise the focus of the men trying to protect us. The bodyguard is scanning the area to both the front and the back of the SUV, like he knows the masked man could come at him from either direction.

Just as I decide the warning is worth it and shout, "At the back!" as loud as I can, more gunfire erupts.

The bodyguard is shooting in the right direction, but the other man's aim must be better because he goes down.

It feels like an hour has passed, but it's probably less than five minutes. Both of our bodyguards are either dead or incapacitated. If we try to make a run for it, we're as likely to get shot as not. I don't think it's worth it.

There's only one of them left. I see that he's moving toward the car, his stride confident. He thinks we're sitting ducks in an unarmored vehicle. He doesn't know about me though, that I have a gun and I know how to use it.

I've never shot at a person before, but I will do whatever I have to in order to protect my little sister.

"Do not move," I tell her in a harsh whisper. "No matter what. Stay still."

She doesn't reply, but I have to trust Carlotta will do as I say and not bump me at an inopportune moment. I take the Glock in both hands, like Zio Giovi taught me. I'll need to raise my head and shoulders above the backseat to take aim through the glassless window.

I have only seconds before the gunman reaches us and I know I will only get one chance. If I miss, the man will have a chance to shoot me and then there will be no one left to protect either of us.

Hoping my mom is watching over us, I rise up and take aim as I breathe in and fire the gun as I expel that breath. Not once, but over and over until I see the man fall backward with a shocked expression on his face.

I watch, but he doesn't move. Nobody moves outside the car. Even the man propped up against the SUV appears passed out. Or dead.

I'm sure the bodyguards would have sent an emergency call to my father, but I still say, "Carlotta, call Papà."

She doesn't move or reply.

"Carlotta," I say with more forcefulness, never taking my eyes of the men lying on the street.

It's like my fingers are frozen on the gun, my gaze locked irrevocably on the scene of carnage outside.

"What?" she finally asks in a shaky voice.

"Call Papà. I think I got the last one, but there might be more coming." They'd made their move on a stretch of road with trees on both sides and no houses.

That doesn't mean no one heard the gunshots. The cops might have been called. That's not my problem. Keeping my sister safe is. And there's no way of knowing if the masked men have reinforcements on the way.

"You shot one of them?" Carlotta asks, sounding dazed.

"Yes. Are you dialing Papà?"

"I am."

Then I hear the ring and realize my sister has her phone on speaker.

"We're on our way." My father says rather than answering. "Don't worry, *stellina*, we'll keep you safe."

"Catalina already did," Carlotta says.

"Catalina?" That's not my father's voice. It's Don De Luca.

My father must have his phone on speaker as well.

I don't know if the don is asking what Carlotta meant or for me to speak.

"I think all of the gunmen are dead, but they might just be passed out," I say, deciding to answer. My voice sounds weird to my own ears. "The bodyguards are down, but I don't know if they're dead."

Carlotta starts to cry. "*Soru* shot one of them."

"She shot one of our bodyguards?" my father demands, his tone filled with anger.

"No," my sister wails. "She shot one of the bad guys. She kept me safe. Why don't I know how to shoot a gun?"

Carlotta is sobbing now and it's hard to understand her, but my father's reply proves that he does. "Because ladies don't handle guns," he says with stark judgment toward me.

It's such bullpuckey. There are women all over the world that compete in shooting tournaments, even actual ladies of the nobility. I know because I watch the competitions online. They're fascinating. No one dies when those guns are fired. There is no blood.

I wish I could join them. I'm a very good shot.

I look at the man lying in the road that proves that and my heart skips a beat. What if I killed him?

"It is a good thing one of your daughters knows how to handle a gun," Don De Luca says. "Or they both might be dead right now."

My father doesn't answer. I hear a vehicle speeding towards us from the direction of our home. I don't want to turn away from the men in the street, but have to make sure it's our father coming toward us. Only I can't move.

"We see you," my father says, for once diminishing my stress, rather than adding to it. "We are almost there."

The sound of the approaching vehicle grows louder. Then the call drops and I hear not one, but multiple cars come to a stop, one after the other, their engines still running.

I hear doors open and soon after, men swarm past the car, checking on the fallen shooters. "This one's alive," a man shouts after checking the pulse on the man leaning against the SUV.

"Take him to the box," Don De Luca barks, the low gravel of his voice inciting a feeling of safety I do not examine.

Someone knocks gently on the window nearest Carlotta. "*Stellina*, open the door," my father calls coaxingly.

Still sobbing, Carlotta shakes her head. "What if there are more?"

"I will take you home where you will be safe."

"I'll never be safe," Carlotta says.

"Madonna Carlotta, open this door," my father says in a voice he never uses with my sister.

The door opens. "Papà," Carlotta cries.

"Come here, princess, Papà has you." Our father pulls Carlotta out of the car. I don't see it, but I feel the movement behind me. "Catalina put that damn gun down before you shoot someone."

I can't let go of the gun. I can't move at all.

Because I already shot someone, didn't I? I don't know if he's dead. I'm waiting for someone to check his pulse. No one does.

"For God's sake. Bring her back to the house," my father orders someone.

"Yes, sir," Marco, one of my father's men, says. "Miss Jilani, come with me." After a couple of seconds, he adds. "Please."

I hear a car pull away, tires rumbling over the gravel on the side of the road.

I don't move.

"Miss Jilani," Marco says, his tone strange.

"You have to check," I say.

"Check what?" Marco asks.

"His pulse. You have to see if he's dead."

"Who?" Marco asks. "Your father's men? They are both headed toward the hospital."

He doesn't mean a regular hospital. That's not how it works. The mafia has a private clinic here on Long Island and a fully functional hospital in the city. I wonder which one he means, but I don't ask.

"Him," I say, jerking the gun like a pointer toward the man I shot.

"Move," I hear. Then the sound of shuffling.

"You did well, Catalina." That's not Papà's voice. It is a voice that should not affect me, but it does.

Tension bleeds from my body and suddenly I'm able to turn my head.

Don De Luca crouches beside the open door, his expression unreadable. "You can let go of the gun now. You and your sister are safe."

"Is he dead?" I ask.

He knows who I mean. I can see it in the don's expression. Don De Luca's lips thin, like he doesn't want to answer, but he says, "Yes."

"I didn't mean to kill him," I admit. "I had to stop him though."

Will the don think I am weak? His men would not have hesitated to kill the masked man. But I am not a made man.

"You did well," he says again.

"I did?"

"You did."

My fingers, curled so tightly around the gun, relax.

"That's good, Catalina."

The approval in his tone allows me to release my frozen hold on the gun. It falls, thunking against a large piece of glass that rests on the carpeted area behind the headrests.

A big warm hand curls around my upper arm. "Come here, Catalina."

That touch breaks through the last of my paralysis and I turn to surge toward the don. He guides me out of the car. "Are you alright?" he asks.

I stare up at him, unable to make my dry mouth form words, but I nod.

"You have glass in your hair, can I brush it out?"

I nod again.

He does it with gentle movements. "We have to go. We don't want to be here when the cops arrive."

I force a word out, "Carlotta?"

"Your father is taking care of her." There's a strange quality to the don's tone. I don't know what it means.

"We can't leave, can we? I shot someone. The police will want my statement."

"There will be no statements."

I look around and realize that the bodies are either gone or being carried toward the SUVs that arrived with my father and the don. The mafia Soldiers are efficient and fast. I realize that if the cops do come, there will be nothing for them to find.

I follow the don toward a black Porsche Cayenne with tinted windows. I know the make because my father was angry when the don bought it because it cost more than his Mercedes Maybach. It's armored and has bullet proof tires. Papà insisted on getting them on his own SUV as soon as he learned the don had gotten them on his Cayenne.

My father is both competitive and vain. I notice his SUV is nowhere to be seen. He and Carlotta are already gone. He left me. It's not unexpected, but it sucks. Even when my life has been threatened, my father can't find a modicum of concern for his oldest daughter. Well, I guess he did tell Marcus to bring me back to the house.

I find myself sitting next to the don in the back of his SUV, his driver and a guard are in the front.

"Where's Marcus?"

"In the SUV in front of us."

I recognize it. It's one of my father's. Another SUV pulls out behind us.

It's weird, the way the don is taking care of me. Does he feel responsible for me because I am his fiancée's sister or because I'm his consigliere's daughter? I know it's not personal. It can't be. I'm nothing to him.

"Don't you have to stay, to take care of all that?" I wave my hand toward the back, not turning to look at the receding scene behind us.

"Aldo will handle it," he says.

"Who's Aldo?" I ask.

"One of my men."

"Oh. You must trust him."

"I do."

"That's good."

"Who taught you to shoot?" he asks when I don't say anything else.

"My zio."

"He's a smart man."

I nod.

"But he didn't teach your sister to use a gun?"

"He and Papà don't always see eye to eye." Is that an explanation? I don't know, but it is the truth.

"I am glad in this instance that your uncle did not listen to my consigliere."

Because Carlotta is okay. That makes sense. The approval in the don's tone warms my insides, dissipating the chill of shock.

"Will you teach your daughters to shoot?" I ask, curious.

"*Sì*. I will also make sure they always travel in an armored car as you and your sister will do going forward."

I'm sure my father will not be happy about that. The only armored vehicle he has in his fleet is his personal SUV.

"I will provide the car and bodyguards," Don De Luca says, like he knows what I'm thinking. "It is my prerogative as your sister's fiancé."

That isn't going to make it any easier for my father to swallow. I don't look forward to navigating his temper for the next couple of months.

CHAPTER 13

New York City, New York
Mancini Mafia
GUILIA

I can hear my son's excited voice coming from the living room as the elevator doors open onto Severu's level of the penthouse.

"Look, Miss Connie!" Neri puts his Deadpool figure in the center of the train track and holds it there.

When the train engine comes around, it hits the figure and derails, falling on its side, its wheels still spinning.

My son dances around in glee. "Didja see? Didja see?"

"Yes, he won again," the blonde woman replies with an indulgent smile.

A fully trained bodyguard, Connie Dane has been Neri's nanny since birth. My son adores her.

And the feeling is mutual.

"Look, Neri, your mamma and *nonna* are back." Connie rises gracefully from her spot on the floor near the train track.

She dusts off the seat of her slacks, though I doubt very much there is a speck of dirt on Severu's floor.

My son jumps up and runs over to throw himself against my legs in an exuberant hug. "I missed you Mamma."

"I missed you too, *ometto*." My little man. I bend to lift Neri up to hug him back just as tight. "You were still napping when I left, or I would have taken you with me."

"I don't need a nap," Neri says forcefully.

It's a familiar argument and one my little man is not going to win anytime soon. Overtired, Neri can rival any made man's temper.

"Your zios Severu and Miceli took naps until they turned five," my mother says.

"They did?" Neri asks suspiciously.

His *nonna* smiles and kisses both his cheeks before saying, "Yes. And Miceli was like you. He tried to get out of his naps, but Severu never did."

That has my son's active brain whirling, I can tell. My oldest brother is only second to his father in Neri's hierarchy of heroes. He adores Miceli too, but Neri is in awe of Severu.

I mouth, "Thank you," silently to my mother over Neri's shoulder.

She gives her familiar Mona Lisa smile and nods. "I need to get ready. I am meeting some capos' wives for tea."

Aria De Luca's social calendar is daunting. I enjoy the whirlwind of activity with her when I am in New York but can't attend everything. I'd never see my son otherwise.

Besides, I'm not sure anyone could keep up with my mother and her social engagements.

Neri squirms in my arms and I let him down.

Throwing a greeting to Lara over his shoulder, he rushes back to the center of the large living room. His toys are spread out on a thick art deco carpet and the coffee table that is usually there has been moved under the window.

My bodyguard returns the greeting and takes up a position near the entrance of the room.

Things have been cool between us since the appointment with Dr. Hewitt. Lara apologized for not telling me what the appointment was for, as did my assistant, who I left in Vegas for this trip.

I would have left Lara too, but Raff would not hear of it.

I'm sure neither will make the same mistake again, but I'm not one of those people whose temper burns hot and bright and then dissipates. It takes me time to get over genuine anger.

Miceli says I can hold a grudge better than he can hold a gun. Considering how deadly my brother is, the implication isn't lost on me.

I kick off my heels and settle on the floor near where Neri is playing. My narrow skirt forces me to sit with my knees bent and my legs off to one side. Not nearly as comfortable as Connie is in her dark pantsuit designed for ease of movement while looking professional.

But I'm used to it. This way, I can get up and back into my heels in seconds if anyone outside the family arrives.

Neri enacts a fight sequence between his superhero figurine and the remaining train cars. "Deadpool is the bestest!"

The antihero superhero is Neri's favorite of all of them and he never goes anywhere without the action figure. Considering all of the men he most looks up are themselves more Deadpool than Captain America, it makes sense he's so enamored with the mask wearing superhero.

Neri zooms across the living room and stops in front of my bodyguard. "Look, Lara. He's the bestest and the strongest. Just like Papà."

Lara nods. "I see that, *piccolo.*"

My son shoves one of the other action figures out toward me. "You be him, Mamma."

Soon, my figure is in a mortal battle with Neri's. My son's wins, of course and he crows in victory.

Looking like the perfectly put together mother to the don that she is, Mamma comes into the living room, her heels tapping with each rapid step. "Connie, I believe the chef has some chocolate chip cookies fresh from the oven she wants Neri's opinion on."

Realizing immediately that my mother wants to talk to me without my son present, Connie jumps up and says, "What about it, Neri? Are you up for taste testing some cookies?"

"Yes!" Neri starts running toward the kitchen.

"No running," my mother mildly rebukes.

While I say, "Keep it to a walk, *ometto.*"

Neri slows down. Barely. And is soon out of sight.

"What is it?" I ask my mother in a quiet voice. Just because I can't see my son, doesn't mean our voices can't carry.

"Carlotta and her sister were attacked on their way back to Long Island."

I jump to my feet. "Are they okay?"

"What happened?" Lara asks, coming to stand less than a foot away.

"They are fine physically." Mamma shakes her head. "Their attackers shot out a tire on their car and forced them off of the road. Both bodyguards were wounded, but they managed to take out three of the four assailants."

"What about the last one?"

"Catalina shot him." My mother's tone is laced with shock.

I'm not surprised though. Catalina has a depth to her that is lacking in her younger sister. Whether it is the six years difference in their ages, or simply a matter of temperament, I don't know.

"But they are both alright?" I ask.

Mamma nods. "Nevertheless, we should send a care basket to them."

"Good idea. I'll arrange it while you are at your tea."

"Severu insisted I cancel my engagements for this afternoon and evening. He doesn't want either of us leaving until he's determined the motive behind the attack."

"I have my appointment with the OB tomorrow," I say. "I cannot miss it, but I'll take extra security with me."

"I'll arrange details with Matteo," Lara says, mentioning Severu's head of security. "We have a team of four with us and will need four additional men from the don."

I don't argue over the size of detail she wants to take. It wouldn't do any good if I did, but in this instance, I agree that more is better.

I don't want any of my guards ending up wounded, or worse, because we aren't ready for an attack.

Las Vegas, Nevada
Mancini Mafia
RAFFAELE

I read the text from Lara with disbelief. My brother-in-law's fiancée and her sister's car was forced off the road. Both women are fine, but Severu has yet to determine who is behind the attack and what their motivation is.

A quick look through my notifications confirms that my wife has not called or texted in the hour since Lara sent her message. In a meeting with one of my capos, I did not see the text until now because Lara didn't use urgency protocols sending it.

I will discuss that oversight with her later.

There is also a voicemail from Miceli and I listen to it. He gives a few more details than Lara's text and tells me that Severu has the house on lockdown.

However, there is no text from my wife. I know better than to expect a missed call from her.

The first couple of years we were married, Giulia used to call me whenever she had a question, or wanted to tell me something. When she went to New York, she would call me each night.

I didn't always answer. When her message didn't require any response on my part, I didn't return the call either. I thought I was being efficient.

One day, she called me repeatedly but left no message. I finally picked up on her fifth attempt to reach me. Having just finished interrogating a man who had been skimming at one of our casinos, I wasn't in a great mood.

She didn't ask what was wrong, like she usually would do. Not that I could tell her ninety percent of the time, but the question soothed me all the same.

This time, she asked why I had not picked up before.

Like a fool, I told her I had more important things to do than answer personal phone calls throughout the day.

She apologized for bothering me and said it wouldn't happen again.

It took me until later that evening to wonder why she had called me to begin with, much less so many times. But I didn't get a chance to ask her because it was three weeks before I saw my wife anywhere but in our bed at night.

And when we are in bed, talking is not what I want to be doing.

Four Years Before

I am disappointed to see Giulia dressed to go out when I come to the breakfast table. The last three weeks have been hell.

It all started with that miscreant, Paolo. He was the manager of one of our small, out of town, casinos and he stole over three-hundred-thousand dollars before our redundancy accounting caught him.

My father was so infuriated, he demanded an immediate in-person audit of all of our businesses, not just the casinos. I was busy from morning to late into the night, but it's finally done.

We found three more casino employees that had to be dealt with and cremated afterward. Two dealers and one croupier were on the take.

"Do you have plans this morning?" I ask my wife.

"I'm meeting with the director for the shelter benefitting from the upcoming casino night."

It was Giulia's idea to make it a 1920s themed evening with famous mobster impersonators hired to mingle among the guests. She's laundering more money for us than ever before with these charity events and manages to make a large donation to the benefitting charity too.

When my aunt ran the events, most of the time the charity was just a shell organization for the Mancini mafia. Giulia agreed to take over the events only if she could donate 75% of the legitimate proceeds to actual charities.

Since legitimate business is always a better cover for mob business, even my father agreed.

"Do you have time for lunch later?" I ask her.

I've missed my wife, which is not something I ever expected to feel when we got married two years ago.

We're not in love. We married to cement ties between the Mancini mafia with one of the Five Families in New York. They have port access on the east coast that we need, and we control necessary shipping routes through Nevada.

She looks surprised by the question, but her expression tells me her answer before she shakes her head. "I'm sorry, but I don't."

I don't ask about dinner. We're scheduled to eat with a group of our top lieutenants and their wives to celebrate the promotion of our newest capo. He's replacing the man who should have been aware of the crooked casino employees.

The former capo isn't dead, but he probably wishes he was.

Giulia shuffles her silverware around her plate and then looks up. "I have something to tell you."

"What?" I ask, but my attention is on the way her fitted dress shows off her delectable breasts.

Is this shelter director a man, or a woman?

"I'm pregnant."

She says it so calmly, that it takes a few seconds for her words to register. I jump up and grab her from her chair, kissing her until she's breathless and smiling.

"When are you due?"

"In the fall. I'll be pregnant over the summer." She pretends to pout, but the twinkle in her beautiful brown eyes belies the complaint.

"My father is going to be over the moon. You should call your mother. It will give her something good to think about."

Don Enzo, my wife's father, died of a heart attack a year ago. Giulia spent more time than usual in New York, comforting her mother.

I can still feel the hollowness of his loss. When I spent four years training under Don Enzo in New York, we connected in a way I don't with my own father. Losing him was a blow to all of us.

This baby will bring healing and hope to both of our families.

"I already told her," Giulia says.

Waiting for my father to answer his phone, I nod. My wife's words surprise me, though. Do women tell their mothers before their husbands that they are pregnant?

My father is thrilled by the news. "We'll announce it at the dinner tonight and have a drink to celebrate."

I agree and hang up.

Giulia is looking at me intently. "What did your father say?"

"He wants to announce it at the dinner tonight."

She frowns. "So soon?"

"Why not?"

"I wanted to hold onto it for a little while longer. To keep it just our news before it became all about the next Mancini mafia heir."

"But that is what he, or she, will be." My father has backwards views on women, especially wives, or maybe it's just my mother.

But if I'd had a sister, she would have been trained to help run the business.

Giulia lays her hand on my arm. "Yes, but our baby will be *our* child before he, or she, belongs to the family."

It's a sweet sentiment, but not a true one. "You know the mafia comes first."

"Here, more than anywhere else, I think." Her lovely features are cast in sadness.

Is she thinking about her father again?

It's only later, after my wife leaves for her meeting, that I wonder if this was what she wanted to tell me that day she blew up my phone but refused to leave any messages.

CHAPTER 14

Las Vegas, Nevada
Mancini Mafia
RAFFAELE

"Call Giulia," I tell my phone.

She picks up on the second ring.

"Why the hell didn't you text me?" I harshly demand.

Silence greets me. And then, "Hello, to you too, Raff."

My teeth grind. "Don't, Giulia."

"Don't what? Be polite?"

"You should have texted me as soon as you heard about what happened." Hell, she should have called me, but we both know that isn't going to happen.

"Why?"

Did she really just ask me that? "Two women connected to your family were attacked. Why the hell do you think?"

"Didn't Lara text you? I thought she would."

Thought as in, Giulia wasn't sure? "Did she tell you she would?"

"No, but I assumed."

Which means my wife did not know for certain that *anyone* would contact me and tell me what was happening in New York. And she apparently didn't think it was important enough for me to know to ensure that I did.

Fury explodes inside me, but I force myself to keep my voice calm. "Is this about the appointment with Dr. Hewitt?"

"How would the Jilani women being attacked have anything to do with a dead doctor?"

She's pretending ignorance, but I'm not fooled.

When she's riled, my wife can hold a grudge with every fiber of her stubborn being. It has been four years since the day I foolishly told her I had more important things to do than talk to her on the phone.

She has not called me once in all that time.

If I don't call her when she's in New York, then we don't talk.

She texts me, though not often. It is not the same. I miss the calls I used to consider superfluous. I've told her I like to hear her voice. I've even said it would be nice if she called me occasionally.

She smiles and nods and does not call.

This is different though. This is her damn safety.

"What time will you arrive tonight? I'll have extra security meet you at the airport." I will be there too.

"We aren't flying back until Sunday night."

"No. You *weren't* coming home until Sunday. Now, you are getting your beautiful ass on a plane with our son and flying home to Vegas."

"No."

"Giulia," I growl.

"Because of this whirlwind wedding planning, I had to reschedule the appointment with my OB to tomorrow."

"I don't care. You need to come home."

"I'm not having my IUD removed by a stranger."

My stubborn wife. Her obstetrician is based in New York, though she made trips to Las Vegas to oversee my wife's pregnancy with Neri. The OB flew in once a month until Giulia was eight months pregnant. Then the doctor came to stay until Neri's birth.

We provided her a penthouse to live in and king's ransom to focus solely on my wife's wellbeing.

"Your OB can come out to Vegas."

"No."

"Then wait to get it taken out until your next trip to New York." We would all be there for Severu's wedding. My wife could have it done then.

"I'm sure your father would not approve of waiting an extra three months."

"I don't fucking care. You are my wife and I want you safe." My father may be don, but I am the ultimate authority over my wife. And she damn well knows it.

This *is* about the Dr. Hewitt debacle. Killing him wasn't enough. Giulia still wants her pound of flesh. From me.

"I'm safe here," she says, like that should sway me. "Severu will send extra guards with our security detail when I go to the doctor's tomorrow."

"Tomorrow? Has he learned the reason behind the attack then?"

"No."

"Cancel the appointment."

"That's not happening." She huffs out a sigh. "We can't come back tonight anyway. Have you forgotten? The jet returned to Las Vegas so your father could use it last week."

"Use Severu's jet."

"You're being ridiculous. Both Neri and I are perfectly safe here."

I'm done arguing. I know when my wife is being intransigent and when she's willing to listen to reason. The only way she's getting on a plane is against her will. And the only person who will carry my resisting wife onto an airplane is me.

I text our pilot and tell him I want to be wheels up within the hour. We use a private airstrip, so we don't have to wait for a takeoff slot. However, the ground and flight crews have to hustle.

"I will see you in a few hours, Giulia. Do not leave your brother's house *for any reason* in the meantime."

"What? You can't fly to New York on a whim, Raff."

"The safety of my wife and child is not a whim, *amate*."

"You can't think I would ever put Neri's safety in jeopardy." There is no mistaking the hurt in her tone.

"No, but yourself is a different matter and somehow you don't understand how important *you* are to both me and our son."

"I'm well aware of how important my incubation abilities are to you."

"You are a hell of a lot more to me than a uterus."

She makes a *pfft* sound and it infuriates me even more than her not contacting me about the attack. It is time my wife realizes that she is fucking vital to me.

"Do me a favor and be there, Giulia. That is unless you want to give me a stress related heart attack."

"Don't say things like that! I already told you I'm not leaving until the OB appointment tomorrow. I just don't know why you think you need to fly out here."

"You don't?"

"No."

"Think about it, wife." I read the text telling me that the plane will be ready to go in twenty-five minutes. *"Ti amo."*

It's the first time I've said the words, but not the first time I've felt them. It would take a stronger man than me not to fall in love with my stubborn, temperamental, soft-hearted wife.

I thought I didn't need to say it, that she knew. Like I know that she loves me.

She gasps, her shock showing how wrong I am in that assumption. "You did not just say that."

"Take a nap, *amate*, because when I get there, I'm going to exhaust you showing it. Again."

Does she think that men who have no feelings for their wives crave them like I crave her? I know I haven't said the words, but damn it if I haven't shown her with my actions.

How has my highly intelligent wife missed it?

CHAPTER 15

"We were supposed to kidnap her." The Albanian screams as Angelo tightens the clamp around his balls.

Blood is already pooled on the steel floor beneath where he sits tied to a metal chair.

"Her, not them?" I ask.

The would-be kidnapper looks at me, fear registering. Considering his predicament, it is odd that he's more afraid to answer me than deal with Angelo's methods of extracting information.

Then it hits me. "You were supposed to kidnap my fiancée." The man doesn't answer, but I don't need him too. He already has. "What about her sister, what were you supposed to do with her?"

He tries to shrug but his broken clavicle makes the move disjointed and causes his face to twist in a rictus of pain. "We were supposed to leave her, I guess."

"Why don't I believe you?" I ask, inexplicable fury roiling in my gut.

I don't let it show. I am not ruled by my emotions.

Angelo takes one of the man's fingers and slides it into the tool he uses to remove them. If he presses the handles together a strong, sharp blade will slide up and cut right through the flesh and bone.

"Don't. Please," the man begs. He's already lost two. "I am not lying. Our instructions were to let her go and only take the sister."

"And was that your plan?" Miceli asks from where he is leaning against the wall, looking bored.

The expression that crosses the Albanian's face is all the answer I need. His crew had no intention of letting Catalina go. They planned to take her too, probably to sell her.

New York Cosa Nostra stays out of human trafficking, but there are plenty of gangs and cartels that operate in and around the city who don't observe those limits. Including the Albanians – who don't just work with the Irish, but are in bed with fucking Russian bratva.

"What were you going to do with her before you sold her?" I ask in a deadly quiet voice.

"Nothing."

The sound of his finger being severed is followed by another scream and more blood spilling onto the floor. Angelo cauterizes the wound so the Albanian doesn't bleed out before we're ready for him to die.

The smell of burning flesh assaults my nostrils, but I don't react. That would be weak and a don never shows weakness.

"I don't believe you," I tell the now crying man and wait to see if he answers.

"We were going to take turns with her," he admits. "You got to break them before they're any use in a brothel."

Fuck that shit. The idea of the surprisingly fierce woman being touched by this piece of garbage and his buddies makes my vision go red with rage. I punch him in the face so hard, his head snaps back and we have to use smelling salts to wake him up again.

"Who hired you?" Angelo demands as soon as he wakes.

"I don't know," the man says. Again. His accent has gotten thicker the longer he is tortured. "It was anonymous through the web."

I know his crew makes money as hired muscle, usually for organizations that don't want a direct connection whatever is going down. Like kidnapping a don's fiancée.

We continue the interrogation but get nothing else of use out of him. The closer he gets to death, the more he slips into Albanian. Not one of the six languages I speak, but Miceli is familiar enough with it to shake his head, indicating nothing said is useful.

When we are done, I walk behind him, grab his head and twist until the bones of his neck crack, the break killing him.

We drop him into the pit under the floor and leave the box.

Back in my office, thirty-two floors above the box, Miceli asks me, "Is it true that Catalina killed one of the kidnappers?"

I nod. "Her uncle taught her how to shoot a gun."

"That's pretty badass. Maybe you should have picked the older sister," Miceli jokes.

I don't smile. I've thought the same thing, but ultimately, it's better this way. I want a wife who will not interfere with my life. Catalina calls to something inside me that feels too much like a heart.

She is dangerous. Carlotta is not. The younger sister is demur with no hidden depths like her sister, nothing to spark a passion I do not want to feel.

I am don. I do not indulge in emotions better left to others.

CATALINA

Carlotta is inconsolable tonight and insists I sleep with her. I don't mind really. We have less than three months together before her marriage. Before I leave New York for good.

I've been researching places to live. According to my sources, Mississippi has the lowest cost of living, so my nest egg would last the longest. However, Colorado and Massachusetts have the strongest job market.

I wouldn't even know to look into these things if it weren't for the online seminar I watched on setting goals and making plans to achieve them. It seemed like an infomercial for the woman's book at first, but she gave some pretty good tips.

I even read her book. On my ereader, of course. I don't need anyone in the family seeing a book like that lying around in my room.

I've read everything I can about living economically because that is not something even Zio Giovi is going to teach me. No one in my family ever has to worry about money.

Although Washington state is down the list for both affordable cost of living and job opportunities, it is still in the top ten and has the added benefit of being on the other side of the country.

My chances of disappearing are better if I go to a large city with which we have no familial or business ties. Like Seattle. There's mafia in Seattle, but they are Camorra and there's no chance I'll be recognized by someone I know there.

"Are you asleep?" Carlotta asks in the semi-dark. She insists on having a night light on tonight.

I would prefer the peace of complete darkness, but it's her room.

Turning to face her, I say. "No."

"Will my life always be like today?" she asks, her eyes growing shiny with tears.

Having just got her calmed down less than hour ago, I nearly groan, but I hold it in and force a smile. "No. Today was an anomaly."

"An anomaly we've trained for since we were children."

I can't deny that. "It's the life in the mafia."

"I don't want this life."

"You mean life in the mafia?" I've thought about taking Carlotta with me when I leave.

Only, as much as I love my sister, I don't think she is capable of living economically. She's too used to having what she wants when she wants it. The don can give her that.

"Not exactly. I love my family and friends," she says. "It's restricting being a mafia princess though. I don't want to be the don's wife."

"Are you sure about that? As his wife, you'll be the queen bee in the family. You'll be able to set fashion trends and live in a home even bigger than this one. You'll be able to go to plays and nightclubs."

"You think he's going to take me to nightclubs?" Carlotta demands, ignoring the rest because she knows it's true and the indecision on her face says she wants those things.

"Maybe not, but he'll let you make friends and as long as you don't do anything you shouldn't, I bet he'll let you go to clubs with them."

"I already have friends in the city," she says petulantly.

I smile encouragingly. "There you go then."

"I like the idea of being queen bee and all the rest," she admits and then bites her lip. "But I don't want to have to marry Severu to get it."

Part of me wants to be patient and understanding. This is my little sister and she's understandably nervous about the future. But part of me simply can't comprehend how blind she is to what a sexy and dynamic man it is she's marrying.

"You don't get one without the other," I say as consolingly as I can.

"But today, we could have died. That never happened before I was engaged to him."

"I've never heard of it happening to his mom, or his sister, either."

"Just because we've never heard of it, doesn't mean it hasn't happened. I'm sure no one except immediate family will ever hear of what happened to us today either." Carlotta flops onto her back and glares at the ceiling.

"But they've never actually been kidnapped or harmed, right?"

"How do you know that?"

"Because they are both living peacefully in their homes," I point out.

Carlotta harrumphs, clearly unconvinced.

"Would you run away if you could?" I ask reluctantly.

I don't want to take her with me. She'll make everything harder, and our father will never stop searching for her, which will put my own freedom at risk. If we are caught, I have no doubt my father will kill me after torturing me.

But if she says yes, I can't leave my sister behind to pay the price that makes my own escape from Papà's house possible.

Carlotta laughs a little hysterically. "Right? Like I know how to function in the real world. Papà has made sure we are totally unequipped to take care of ourselves."

I know she's younger than me, but Carlotta has been out of school for a year. She could have spent time learning about how to navigate life outside the mafia if she'd wanted to. Like I have. No, I haven't left yet, but I didn't want to leave my sister until I had to. Or my aunt and uncle. They love me, even if my father doesn't.

"I will talk to Aria about convincing Don De Luca to get you cooking classes," I offer, hoping that will assuage my sister.

She turns back to me, her face glowing with excitement. "You will? There's a bunch of amazing culinary institutes in the city. I don't care which one I go to. I mean I have my favorite of course, but attending any of them would be a dream come true."

"What's your favorite?" I ask, wanting to keep this positive attitude going.

"Oh, you wouldn't know it," she says vaguely. "It doesn't matter anyway. Like I said, I'd go to any of them. When I graduate, maybe I'll be able to create new dishes for some of the mafia owned restaurants."

That sounds like a teenager's dream, not set in any kind of reality, but I smile anyway. She'll learn more than cooking techniques if she gets to attend culinary school. She'll learn the hierarchy in the kitchen.

I watch a lot of cooking shows with my sister. From what I've seen, I'm pretty sure Carlotta would have to work her way up to creating dishes. It's not surprising that she hasn't drawn the same conclusion.

In Carlotta's world, she can have and do what she wants. Except pick her own husband.

"I don't think it will be safe for a don's wife to work in a kitchen, even in one our restaurants."

"Oh, I don't want to work. Not like full-time, or anything. I want to experiment with food and preparation techniques."

She'll be able to do that in her own home. The don can refurbish his kitchen to restaurant standards and I'm sure he won't mind doing so. I get the feeling that he wants to do whatever he needs to in order to keep my sister occupied and happy.

And out of his hair.

Even though I don't like thinking of her in that kind of passionless marriage, my worry for her future dissipates a little.

"If only I knew him better. I don't think the prospect of marrying him would be so scary." Carlotta sighs. "Though nothing is going to change that he's old enough to be my father."

"Only if he was a precocious teen." The don is sixteen years older than her, not twenty. Stifling the little voice in my head that says the age difference between the don and myself is less daunting, I say, "You'll get to know him before the wedding. Isn't that what the weekly dinners in his home are for?"

Carlotta has been to one dinner with the De Lucas and was supposed to go with our father again tomorrow. Will that still happen?

Carlotta snorts. "He and Papà spent the whole time last week talking business and it will be the same at the next one."

I want to grind my teeth in frustration. These dinners are for Carlotta to get to know her future husband, and Papà is commandeering them with his usual self-serving attitude, oblivious to anyone else's needs. Even those of his favorite daughter.

I'll be talking to Aria about more than Carlotta going to culinary school.

CHAPTER 16

New York City, New York
Mancini Mafia
GIULIA

Knowing Raff will be arriving tonight, I don't even try to sleep. I didn't take a nap like he suggested either.

Infuriating man.

I don't understand why he's dropping everything to come to New York. Neri and I will be back in Las Vegas Sunday night.

Raff must know that Severu will never allow anything to happen to his sister or nephew.

I didn't tell our son that his papà was coming to New York. If I had, we would have never gotten Neri to sleep tonight. He'll see Raff in the morning and be thrilled at the surprise.

Waiting in the living area on the floor for extended family in my family's building, I answer emails and messages related to the upcoming charity gala. Raff texted forty-five minutes ago to say the jet had landed and he was on his way. He should be here any minute.

I'm nervous. I don't know why.

Something just feels different between us. I wish I knew what.

The elevator dings and my heart speeds up.

Dropping my phone on the occasional table near the sofa, I surge to my feet.

The doors open and my husband is there. Wearing his usual tailored suit, but no tie, he exudes power. He already carries himself like the don he will one day be.

His dark hair and handsome face are so familiar and *necessary*, I feel an ache of both longing and recognition in my chest.

The moment his grey eyes alight on me, they go molten. He crosses the space between us in two long strides and pulls me into his arms, his mouth coming down on mine in a ferocious, claiming kiss.

Melting into his body, I kiss him back for all I am worth.

The sound of his bodyguards walking past to drop off his luggage in our room, barely registers. Except to make me aware that other people are seeing us kiss like sex starved teenagers.

Or a married couple deprived of each other's company for ten long days.

Only, Raff is not usually big on PDA.

Cupping my bottom, he lifts me against him, and I let my shoes drop to the floor before latching my legs around his torso. We start moving but I don't take my mouth away from his.

The door to our room slamming behind us breaks into my sensual haze and I finally separate my lips from his.

Gone is the controlled, urbane man I married. In his place is a ravenous beast whose gaze sears me.

"Raff." His name comes out on a puff of air as want courses through me.

He lets me slide down his body but keeps me close. "*Amate.*"

Beloved. There is that word again.

He unzips my dress and tugs it down my shoulders. The floral crepe de chine slips from my body and pools around my feet on the carpet.

I shove his jacket off of him and start working on the buttons of his shirt with fervent fingers. Raff unclasps my bra and manages to remove it with minimal interruption to my efforts.

Big, warm hands cup my breasts and squeeze. Pressing forward for more, I shudder with desire. A feral sound comes from deep in my husband's chest sending wetness gushing from my core.

Reaching down he rubs my folds through the silk of my panties. "So wet, wife."

"You make me that way."

"Only me. No one else," he growls.

I don't know where this caveman moment is coming from, but I lean forward and kiss his naked chest, biting just hard enough to leave a red mark. "Only you, Raff."

His trousers are in the way. He helps me get them off, our hands working in urgent tandem until he stands there gloriously naked. His big, muscled body gives off pheromones that have my vagina clenching and my heart racing.

Clasping his big shaft, he runs his hand up and down the length. "You make me so damn hard."

Precum weeps from the tip and I want to taste it. I drop to my knees and do just that, reveling in the familiar flavor. The essence of my husband.

Knocking his hand away, I curve my fingers around his velvet covered hardness. This is mine. I've got my own primitive responses going on inside me.

My fingertips do not touch. They never do, unless he's soft. And he almost never is when we are naked together.

Our gazes lock and I open my mouth to take more of his sex in. I lave my tongue back and forth on the underside of his penis and suck until my cheeks hollow out.

"Fuck, I've missed you," he growls.

I pull my head back and my mouth comes off of him with a pop. "Me, or this?" I tease. And then take him back into my salivating mouth.

His taste is addictive.

"It is all one package, *amate*. I'm fucking addicted to your body, but when you are gone, I miss everything about you."

The words settle into my heart like seeds that instantly bloom into something more.

I grab his butt and pull him toward me, taking him to the back of my throat and swallowing. It took me a long time to be able to do this without gagging, but we both love it.

He pulls back, allowing me to breathe before surging forward until his pelvis presses against my lips and his balls brush my chin.

"You are so perfect, *amate*."

I need to breathe, but I don't shift away from him.

He draws his hips back though, allowing me to suck in air through my nose. "I miss your spitfire personality."

I would smile, but my mouth is stretched too wide.

"I miss the sound of your voice." He surges forward again, dominating my throat.

Humming with approval, I draw another deep groan from my husband.

"I miss the sound of you breathing in the bed next to me." His voice is hoarse, heavy with passion.

I swallow over and over, bringing him to the brink.

But he jerks back again, allowing me to take another breath.

"Look at me, wife."

I shift my eyes up, his molten gaze, filled with emotion I don't dare name, trapping them. "I miss the way you smile and how it lights up your gorgeous eyes."

This time when he thrusts into my mouth, he shouts and hot, salty liquid shoots down my throat. I suck and lick him as he draws back, cleaning his still hard sex.

He lifts me up and carries me to the bed. "Your turn."

My panties, the only piece of clothing I still have on, fly over his shoulder after he tears them from my body.

I expect him to push my legs apart and assuage the growing ache in my lady bits, but he brings his body over mine, holding himself up on his arms. His lips find mine, but the kiss is tender. Passionate.

"I miss your laugh when Neri does something to amuse you." He kisses down my neck, suckling up a love bite that will be a bruise tomorrow.

I shiver in reaction.

Raff moves down my body, kissing, licking, sucking, and nipping at my heated, sensitized skin. He suckles each nipple until I'm begging for more and then he bites down gently with his teeth.

I scream and my body convulses with a mini orgasm, but Raff is not done with me.

He keeps traveling down my torso, tormenting me with his mouth. And the words he's saying.

They are too much.

"I miss holding you at night and waking with you wrapped around my body in the morning." Finally, he presses my legs apart and pushes my legs up so my knees are bent.

I know what is coming next and I don't know what I want more. His mouth on my clit or the words he's using to seduce my heart along with my body.

"I miss this pink little pussy." He inhales. "Your scent." He licks me from my bottom to my clit, slurping my juices from my folds. "Your taste."

He doesn't speak again for long minutes while his mouth and fingers drive me to first one and then another climax. I try to shift away as he continues to nibble and suck on my overused clitoris.

Strong fingers lock down my thighs like manacles and Raff continues to pleasure me until my body explodes again in a cataclysm of pleasure. I am wracked with sobs of ecstasy and an overload of emotion.

In a single powerful move, Raff comes up my body and he settles on top of me, his penis pressing against my opening.

He cups my face. "You are alright, *cara.*"

Tears still streaking down my cheeks, I nod. I am beyond alright. I feel reborn in pleasure and love and it terrifies me.

He claims my body with a single, commanding thrust, forcing swollen tissues to give until his pelvic bone presses against my clit.

I moan, my tears drying up. In this moment we are connected body-to-body, soul-to-soul and heart-to-heart.

His expression is so fierce it could be either love, or hate. "I miss your stubborn determination and your cranky reaction to be woken up too early."

I reach up and cup his face. "Raff."

His name *is* love to me.

He turns to kiss first one of my palms and then the other. "I miss every single fucking thing about you when you are gone. You take it all away when you leave."

"Then maybe you should come with me," I practically yell.

He starts pounding into me. "Maybe I should and maybe you shouldn't spend so much time in New York." He's not yelling, but his tone is just as forceful.

I cry out as he hits my cervix and I feel near painful pleasure coiling tight in my belly again.

"I..." There is no more room for words between us.

Arching up, I meet Raff, thrust for thrust until every muscle in my body clamps down in otherworldly ecstasy and I scream his name. He shoves deep inside and goes rigid. His shout is so loud it makes my ears ring.

We stay like that for long seconds, the warm wetness of our combined spend leaking out from my core around him.

I reach up to kiss him and he meets me halfway, driving my head back into the mattress as he owns my mouth and lets me claim his.

Eventually, the fierce kisses turn gentle and our hands roam over each other in soft caresses. When our breathing has returned to something like normal, my husband pulls out of me and scoops me up from the bed.

"No," I say.

"No what?"

"No shower. I like smelling like us together. I'll shower in the morning."

He is already moving so he can pull the duvet back on the bed. "I know."

CHAPTER 17

New York City, New York
Mancini Mafia
GIULIA

Once we are situated under the covers, facing each other, his hand on my hip and mine on his chest, he says, "So, I will come with you to New York twice a year and you will not spend an entire month here in August."

"Las Vegas is so hot in August," I complain, but my heart is pounding with what all of this means.

"New York isn't exactly an icebox."

"Okay."

"Okay?" He looks at me like he's trying to figure out the catch.

"Yes. I don't like being away from you either, Raff. If you are willing to carve time in your schedule to come with me and Neri twice a year, I am willing to give up my month in August."

"And the other week?" he asks, referring to the fourth trip I usually take.

"I won't plan for a fourth week, but there may be times I have to come to New York without you."

"May be?" He presses.

"Not every year. Just sometimes. Like once Severu's wife has their first baby. I'll want to come out to visit and if it doesn't coincide with one of our joint trips, I'll still want to come."

My husband gives a grudging grunt of what I assume is agreement.

This moment feels profound, but I'm afraid to analyze too closely why that is.

"We should sleep." But the looks in his eyes makes it impossible for me to close my own.

They reflect a raw emotion I never thought I would see in my husband's gaze. Only...it isn't new, I realize. I've just never let myself see it before. I always dismiss this emotional intimacy as lust.

He doesn't say anything, but his gaze stays locked on mine, as if he is willing me to acknowledge that emotion.

"You don't love me," I blurt. But for the first time I doubt. Does he?

"Of course, I fucking love you, Giulia."

"You never said."

"Neither have you."

Is he saying he knows I love him? Maybe he's pretending to feel the same, so I'm not hurt. He's so protective, he would do something like that.

He sits up and pulls me with him until I'm sitting on his lap, my legs sideways over his thighs. "Whatever you are thinking, stop it."

"You can't tell me what to think," I assure him.

His smile is devasting. "There is the feisty woman I am married to."

"We got married to cement an alliance between our families." There's no love in that.

"Only a fool would refuse to see you as anything more than the guarantor of an alliance," he informs me. "All evidence to the contrary, I am not fool."

"I never said you were."

"And yet, I have somehow convinced you that your only value to me is your ability to carry my child."

"If that's not true, then why send me to Dr. Hewitt?" That trauma inducing visit is certainly not evidence against Raff seeing me as a walking womb.

"I thought you were worried too but hadn't said anything." His hand runs up my side in a distracting caress.

"How can you say you love me when you don't *talk* to me?"

"I do talk to you, but I didn't about this and that was a mistake."

Wow. He's admitted making a mistake for the second time in our marriage. Is this some kind of new precedent?

Sighing, I admit, "I should have told you about the IUD." I've had a lot of time to think in my lonely bed at night since coming to New York. "If I had told you what my OB said about waiting, you would never have pressured me."

When it comes down to it, Raff has *never* been willing to compromise my safety, much less my health.

"No, I wouldn't have." He kisses me quickly and softly, like he just can't help himself. "You can trust me. I will always protect you."

A lump forms in my throat. "It doesn't always feel like it."

"Because of my father." It's not a question.

I nod anyway.

Guilt flashes across Raff's eyes. "I made more than one wrong assumption."

"Okay, this whole admitting to being wrong is weirding me out. But also, what do you mean?"

He smiles. "I expected you to know how important you are to me. I thought you would see my father's meddling in our lives as harmless, like I did."

"You're not a tolerant man." Which is one of the reasons I believed I wasn't important enough to Raff to push back against his father. "Why let him meddle at all?"

"It's complicated."

"I'm sure I can keep up."

He kisses me. Again. "No doubt. When I returned to Las Vegas after training with your father for four years, my own was ready to hand over the reins, or so he thought."

"Patrizio is too controlling for that."

"He assumed that I would continue business in his image."

"But you didn't."

"No. While he was out golfing with his buddies and romancing his latest mistress, I instigated a major shift in how we operated both our legitimate and mafia businesses."

"Those changes made things better." Capos talk. So do their wives.

Profits have steadily increased in the past few years and many of the wives have said they feel their families are safer with the new direction the mafia business is taking. Not a single made man in the Mancini mafia has gone to jail, much less prison, since I moved to Vegas.

The Cosa Nostra in Nevada isn't as big as the Five Families in New York, but there are enough made men to make that an impressive statistic.

"They did." Raff's shaft is hard again...did it ever go soft? And it's pressing against my hip.

The man is one big distraction.

Taking a deep breath, I attempt to focus on our conversation. It is important. "That's a good thing, isn't it?"

"Yes. However, by the time Neri came along, loyalties had shifted. With the exception of a couple of capos and their crews, the organization looked to me for leadership."

"But your father hadn't retired."

"Not in his mind, but the minds of his men? He had. He wasn't there for the day-to-day."

"He's still their don." The vows taken by made men (even if they are women) are more binding than the promises made during a wedding.

A man will be forgiven for cheating on his wife, but will die for cheating on his don.

"I am his son, his acknowledged heir and the underboss. *He* left me in charge of daily operations. Showing loyalty to me and our family, is not a betrayal of the don. He told his capos and the rest that I speak for him. Even his consigliere comes to me first."

"I didn't know that."

"Because I didn't tell you. I should have." He squeezes my waist in comfort? Acknowledgement?

Or just because he likes touching me?

This is not working.

I shift around to straddle his thighs but keep my sex away from his. "We should have talked about a lot of things."

"So, we will talk about them now." He presses against my bottom, drawing me inexorably forward.

"Is it...uh..." His hardon presses against my still slick and swollen nether lips.

"Is it what?" he asks, his voice rumbly with passion.

Is what...um...what? Then I remember what I was trying to ask. "Is it that easy?"

"Yes."

How is he talking so easily? "You're so certain about everything." And inhumanly resistant to the effects of his arousal.

"I learn from my mistakes."

And apparently, he doesn't have any trouble admitting them. To me. Right?

Just to confirm, I ask, "Do you ever admit being wrong to anyone else?"

"No."

As I thought. Warmth radiates out from my heart and suffuses my body. "What now?"

"Now you tell me why you insisted on staying in New York when I told you to bring our son home to Vegas." All tolerant compromise has disappeared from his set masculine features.

"You're not my boss." It's my kneejerk reaction but I was expecting him to talk about something else.

Maybe even tell me he loves me again. Not take me to task for refusing to fly home today.

"When it comes to your safety, I am."

"If you think that, why didn't you arrange for the use of my brother's jet and have me and Neri taken there by our security?" I might sound a little testy.

"Would you have gone without physical coercion?"

"No."

"There is your answer."

"So, you came to New York instead?"

"Don't misunderstand, wife. I am here to bring you home. But the only one that will carry your resistant body onto that airplane is me."

"You can't do that."

"Can't I?"

We both know he can. And more importantly, that he would.

I cross my arms over my bare breasts, hiding them from his gaze as much as I am showing my annoyance with body language. "I'm perfectly safe here with my family."

"I am your family."

"So are they."

"Neri and I are your *primary* family," Raff says, no give in his deep tones.

"And am I *your* primary family?"

Raff kisses me. Hard. "Yes."

"Then you should never have let your dad make that appointment with the fertility clinic."

"You are right."

I am? I mean, I know I am. But he does too?

"The shift in the power dynamic in our syndicate has been hard on my father and I chose to let him meddle in our lives rather than business." Raff sounds almost ashamed.

"That's a crappy thing to do." How am I supposed to believe he loves me?

Raff's smile isn't a happy one. "Yes. But remember, I was operating on the false belief it would not hurt you."

"What did you think was going to happen?"

"I damn well didn't think you would see allowing my father to insert himself into our lives as proof that I don't care about you."

"How was I supposed to take it? It sure as heck wasn't a compliment, or proof that my opinions mattered to you."

"When did I ever dismiss your opinions?" He shifts my body against his, rubbing my nether lips up and down his shaft.

My clit is so sensitive that I jerk every time he brushes against it.

"Stop that."

He stops moving me, but doesn't let me shift back on his thighs.

I roll my eyes. "Do you really have to ask that?"

"Yes, I do. Even the appointment with Dr. Hewitt was made under the assumption you *wanted* to get pregnant. You'd never told me otherwise."

I think back to all the times my father-in-law stuck his oar into my marriage. He insisted on me and Raff moving into the mansion Raff and his brother had been raised in. I'd wanted to buy our own home and build our own memories.

But I'd never told Raff that.

All the heavy hints about getting pregnant were annoying and I mentioned that to my husband, but how was Raff supposed to know that they hurt me as well? First, I didn't tell him and second, he had no idea I didn't *want* to get pregnant.

Patrizio had inserted himself into the search for both Neri's preschool and then elementary school. However, my husband refused to simply go with his father's suggestions for either school. We made the decisions together, and neither brought up his father's stated opinions when doing so.

My whole marriage, I've taken Patrizio's interference as proof that Raff valued his opinion over my feelings, but looking back, I can't help seeing that my husband isn't the only one who should have done a better job of communicating.

"I've been operating under some mistaken assumptions myself," I admit.

The hand not holding me pressed against him like a safety bar on an amusement park ride, brushes my hair back from my face with tender softness. "That right there is only one of the many reasons I love you."

He said it again. Why don't I say it back? What is holding the words inside me.

"What reason?" I ask instead.

"You are fair."

"Oh."

"You are also stubborn and hold onto a grudge like Super Glue."

He is not wrong. "Thank you."

He chuckles and shakes his head. "Both can be a strength," he agrees.

"But they can also hurt me and the people around me."

Raff doesn't reply, but I see in his stormy grey eyes that he's one of the people who has been hurt.

"I love you too, Raff. I always have."

The lovemaking that comes after my confession is no surprise, but the way he holds me after, listing all the things that made him fall in love with me? It's a lot. And one of the most amazing moments in our marriage. I will treasure his words forever.

It is only *fair* for me to tell him what made me fall in love with him too.

"You loved me before we got married?" He sounds stunned.

"Yes." He'd lived in New York the four years I went to university.

We'd spent time together when I came home for visits and every summer, he was there. We didn't date. My father wouldn't have allowed us to spend time alone. My college was an all women campus.

But I got to know Raff and what I knew I learned to love. Only now, I realize I didn't know him as well as I thought I did.

And the love I feel for him is deeper and stronger than what I experienced before our marriage, despite the challenges that marriage has been to my emotional equilibrium.

"You should have flown home, Giulia."
"I told you, my OB appointment is tomorrow."

CHAPTER 18

I call the don's mother the next day and after the initial pleasantries, I put the idea to her about Carlotta enrolling in culinary school.

"I'm not sure how Severu would feel about that. It's not what young ladies in our family usually do."

"Neither is getting a bachelor's degree, but Guilia did before she married," I point out.

"You are right. But why doesn't Carlotta bring this up to Severu herself?"

I almost laugh, but I realize Aria is serious. Either she's blind to how my sister sees her son, or she's blind to how intimidating her son can be.

"Because he makes her extremely nervous," I say with honesty. Pretending otherwise serves no one. "That's something else I wanted to discuss with you."

"What do you mean?" Aria asks warily.

Hmm...I wonder what she thinks I'm going to say. "Carlotta told me that when she came to your home for dinner, the don and my father spent most of the time discussing business."

"Nothing that shouldn't be discussed in front of a young woman, I assure you."

"That's not what I'm concerned about. How is Carlotta supposed to get to know her fiancé when he spends all their time together talking to my father?"

"She'll have a whole lifetime to get to know him," Aria says patiently, like she thinks I should know this.

But this isn't the last century, and my sister deserves to be wooed, if only for her very short engagement.

"I don't want my sister walking down the aisle terrified of what is to come," I say bluntly.

Aria sighs. "Unfortunately, my son has the habit of discussing business whenever his men join us for dinner."

"Then maybe he should take Carlotta out to dinner alone."

"Like a date?" Aria asks, sounding amused. "I'm not sure he would take such a suggestion from me seriously."

Well, he definitely won't if Aria herself finds the idea laughable. I ask, "But you will talk to him about culinary school?"

"Cooking classes at the very least," she assures me.

I thank her and ring off. Someone has to talk to Severu about acting like a fiancé and not just a don. If his mother won't do it, I know my father won't. Heck, he's part of the problem.

I consider asking Zio Giovi to do it, but that feels cowardly. I am not a coward, no matter what my father wants to believe. I will call the don myself. I do ask my uncle if he has the don's cellphone number.

"No. I may be married to your aunt, but I'm not one of his men," he says to me. He doesn't sound bitter exactly, but for once he's not smiling when he's talking to me either. "Why do you want it?"

"Oh, I just need to ask him something about the wedding." Since I'm helping to plan the wedding, that sounds believable.

And technically, I'm not lying. Having a good wedding requires a happy bride, at least by my estimation.

"I'm sorry I can't help you."

"That's all right. Thank you, anyway, Zio." I give him a quick peck on the cheek and turn to go, but he grabs my arm.

I stop and look at him inquiringly.

"I haven't told you how proud I am of you for how you handled yourself yesterday. If you hadn't been there, your sister would have been taken."

Or we both would have been killed. I shiver, but smile my thanks. "You're the one that taught me to shoot."

"Your father isn't happy about that," Zio says with a grimace.

"I know, but if I only did things that made Papà happy, I would spend all day, every day, holed up in my room."

Zio doesn't deny it. In fact, he laughs. "You've got spunk, *tesorina*, despite how your father has tried to beat it out of you."

It's the first time anyone has acknowledged to me aloud what my father does. Zia always pretends to think I'm clumsy. Though it has been a long time since she's had to patch me up. I've gotten very adept at avoiding Papà. Carlotta is either completely unaware, or she too chooses to tell herself my injuries are somehow self-inflicted.

But Zio has said the painful truth and my heart nearly bursts with all the feeling that acknowledgement provokes. I give him a spontaneous hug, squeezing him really tight. "Thank you, Zio."

"You know I would stop it if I could."

"I know." Like he said. He may live here, but he's not part of the New York mafia. Not really.

And my father is the don's consigliere. Even if my uncle went to the don, Zio's word wouldn't be taken over my father's. And if it was, the only thing that would happen would be for the don to remove my father from his position. That would devastate my father, but it would not protect me, or my uncle, from his wrath.

"He hardly hits me anymore," I reassure my uncle.

"You intimidate him because you don't cower."

I think it's more because I'm good at staying out of my father's orbit, but I don't mind my uncle believing I am stronger and more influential than I am. It feels good to have someone believe in me.

~ ~ ~

I remind myself of that belief in my strength after I sneak into my father's room while he is showering before dinner. I use Carlotta's birthday to unlock his phone and quickly memorize the don's number before dropping the phone and leaving the room as silently as I entered it.

It's the next day before I can call the don to talk to him about Carlotta.

"Yes?" he barks in an unfriendly tone when he answers.

I don't let that deter me. He wouldn't recognize my number. "Hello, Don De Luca, it is Catalina Jilani."

"Catalina." He sounds shocked. "If you are looking for your father, he is not with me."

"No, I called to talk to you."

"About?" He sounds wary.

"My sister. She's nervous about the wedding."

"This sounds like something for my mother to handle."

Is he kidding? No wonder Carlotta is finding it so difficult to get to know him.

"She's not marrying your mother," I say, trying to keep my voice even, but unable to keep my annoyance out of it completely.

"I am aware of that," he says in an even tone.

The lack of anger in his voice gives me the courage to continue. "She needs to get to know you better. She still sees you primarily as her don and not as her fiancé."

"I do not see the problem with that."

"You don't?" I ask, having difficulty keeping my voice respectful as I know I should. "She'll be your wife soon."

"Is there a point to this phone call, Catalina?"

The way he says my name sends shivers through me and they are not from fear. It's a good thing I'm running after the wedding. If his voice can do this to me, I have no business remaining anywhere in his and my sister's orbit.

"You need to take Carlotta on some dates."

"You want me to court her?" Incredulity infuses his tone.

"Is that so shocking?" I demand. "You are her fiancé."

"Exactly. We are already engaged. There is no point in a courtship."

"Not for you, maybe. But you are not a 19-year-old, afraid of marriage and the man she's supposed to spend the rest of her life with. Is it so much to ask that you take her out and let her get to know you? Let her see the softer side of your nature."

"I have no softer side to my nature," he informs me in a hard voice.

"I don't believe that." He was careful with me after the men attacked us. He was the reason I was able to let go of the gun and get out of the car.

"What you believe is irrelevant."

The words hurt. Though there is no reason they should. After all, that is exactly what my father believes. My opinions are as irrelevant to him as I am.

"That may be so." I cannot keep the hurt entirely out of my voice, no matter how hard I try. "However, Carlotta is not."

"I did not say you are irrelevant." He sounds offended. "Merely that your belief about my character does not matter to the truth of who I am."

Oh. It's weird having the don explain himself to me, but it sends a curl of warmth through my heart. Only my heart isn't the one he needs to penetrate.

"Please, think of Carlotta. Do you really want her terrified as she walks up the aisle?" I never plead with my father. I know it's useless. I can't help hoping Don De Luca will be different.

"Do you have a suggestion for these dates?"

Oh, my gosh, he's listening to me. He's willing to try.

"Maybe dinner at a trendy restaurant with a tour of the kitchen after?" I suggest.

"We have weekly dinners scheduled with my family." He sounds impatient now.

I don't let that deter me. "Yes, where apparently you spend the entire time discussing business with my father."

"What else should I discuss?"

"Anything that you can talk about with Carlotta, not your consigliere."

"I am a don. Carlotta must become accustomed to not being the center of my attention."

"No doubt," I say, too frustrated to hold back my disdain. "However, that should not mean that you ignore her entirely. I am sure your father did not treat your mother with such disregard."

Aria would not be the confident, self-contained woman that she is if that were true.

"My father and mother were practically strangers when they wed."

"And I'm sure if she could have had it differently, she would have."

"Fine, I will take Carlotta to dinner. Are you satisfied?"

"With a tour of the kitchen?" I press.

"I will arrange a tour of the kitchen if you believe that will please her."

"I do."

"Are we done here?"

The *I have more important things to attend to* remains silent, but I hear it all the same. I don't care. He agreed to take Carlotta to dinner and do something that will make her happy. That's all that matters.

"Yes. Thank you for giving me some of your precious time." Okay, maybe gratitude isn't the only thing I'm feeling, but I managed to say the words without a bit of the sarcasm I feel.

I'm taking that as a win.

He hangs up without saying goodbye. I don't know why that makes me smile, but it does. I have never seen the don be anything but meticulously polite when talking to women. My aunt. His mother. My sister. Myself.

Hanging up without saying goodbye is definitely rude. It might be something he does with his men, but I doubt he has ever hung up on his mother without a proper word of parting.

It should not make me feel so pleased to have gotten under his skin. But it does.

CHAPTER 19

After the strange, but exhilarating conversation with Catalina, I get another unexpected phone call.

I slide my finger over the phone's screen to take the call from the New York Irish mob boss Brogan Shaughnessy.

"I hear that someone attacked your bride-to-be," he says without a greeting.

Rage brings everything in my office into laser focus. "Brogan, you bastard. You think your family is safe after that?"

"It wasn't my mob."

"Convince me."

"A team hit one of my betting establishments."

"I care why?"

"Because although they wore masks, they were speaking Italian."

"None of my guys would be that sloppy. When I hit you, my men won't be hiding their faces and the only speaking done will be the bullets from our guns."

"I know."

"The fuck you do. You just accused me of hitting your betting shop."

"No, I said it was hit by a team who spoke Italian. Badly, as it happens."

I stay silent, my mind whirling, because blaming the Irish for what has been happening is too easy.

"We've held a truce between our families for more than a decade," Shaughnessy says. "Someone is trying to get us to go to war."

"To what end?"

"I don't know, but we have a better chance of figuring it out if we cooperate."

"What do you want?"

"We work together to figure out who the bastards behind this shit are. They've got someone in my outfit feeding them information."

That's a big thing to admit. I don't take the bait and say I believe the same about my own syndicate. "You've got a relationship with one of *my* people, or you wouldn't know about the attack against Catalina and Carlotta."

"I spy on you; you spy on me. It's the way it's always been done."

I can't deny that. It's why I'm unconvinced the would-be arsonist is part of Shaughnessy's mob. My information says otherwise.

"But ask yourself this: if I've been spying on your syndicate since I signed that truce agreement in blood with your father, why aren't my hits more successful?" the mob Boss asks. "If I'd gone after your fiancée, I'd have her."

His style is to hit and hit hard, just like my father's was. Like mine is. Shaughnessy would have sent two teams after the women, and they would have been taken, regardless of Catalina's abilities with a gun.

If he had wanted to burn down one of my warehouses, he would have done it, and his man would not have gotten caught because he wouldn't have been sent in with faulty intel.

Is it possible the would-be arsonist hadn't been given the intel about our security upgrades, not because the informant didn't know about them, but because whoever hired him *wanted* an independent contractor, who happened to be Irish, caught?

"If you went after the women, I would burn your boroughs to the ground in retaliation."

"That you haven't says you've already considered the probability that my mob isn't behind these attempts."

He's right. Damn it.

"The bratva want my docks." I'm not telling him anything he doesn't already know.

He replies, "And they want my brothels for their sex slaves. The fekkers."

Neither the Irish mob nor my mafia engage in human trafficking, much less keep slaves to work in any of our businesses. We are not good men, but we have our codes and we've been living by them for generations.

"It could be the bratva," I concede. "But it was Albanians that attacked my fiancée and her sister. The surviving kidnapper claimed to be hired by an anonymous source."

"I'm sure your interrogation techniques got the truth out of him, but his own people could have set them up to believe his team was hired by an outside source."

"Yes."

"I'll have my people do some digging."

I don't bother saying I'll do the same. Shaughnessy knows I will. Whether either of us shares what we find is still up for question.

CHAPTER 20

New York City, New York
Five Families
RAFAELLE

After texting Lara to tell her she is in charge of Neri's morning routine, I wake my wife with kisses.

To her soft, delectable pussy.

"No, Raff. I'm sore," she complains.

But she's the one enthusiastically riding me fifteen minutes later. I tell her I love her just before her pussy walls tighten around my cock like a vice.

Giulia's shout, "I love you, Raff," as she comes, sends me over the edge right along with her.

My beautiful wife soaks in a hot bath while I shower and is still floating, her gorgeous tits peeking through the bubbles when I'm finished dressing.

"Are you ever going to get out?" I tease.

"Not anytime soon. My appointment with the OB isn't until after lunch."

No doubt she made it to coincide with our son's nap. Giulia is a doting and present mother, so different from my own. My wife spends as much time with our son as her schedule allows.

We both do, but he definitely sees more of his mother.

"I talked to your brother last night on the flight over from Vegas. He said the target was his fiancée and not even her sister. That doesn't mean his enemies won't go after other women in his family, but he's downgraded security from red to yellow."

"Oh, joy. That means I get to take eight guards with me to the doctor's office."

"I didn't say I agreed with Severu's assessment," I remind her.

Giulia has been my wife for six years. It is time she stopped seeing her brother as an authority in her life.

"Do you?" She crosses her arms over her chest.

She does that when she's mad because she knows how much I enjoy seeing her naked tits. My wife is a firecracker and I love her.

"I do."

Giulia rolls her eyes. "Does that mean you *aren't* going to cart me back to Las Vegas as soon as I'm dressed?"

"We can stay until Sunday, like you planned."

"Good. I didn't want to reschedule my appointment."

"About that. Are you sure you are ready to try for another baby?" I'm not taking anything for granted with my wife again.

Her hands sliding away from her breasts, she sits up in the water. "Aren't you?"

"My willingness to be a father again is not in question."

"I want more children, Raff. I just didn't want them too close together."

I kneel beside the tub and cup her face because I can't *not* touch her. "I know. What I'm asking is if it's still too close? You don't have to take the IUD out yet. They're safe for five years, aren't they?"

"Actually, the copper one I have can remain in the uterus for up to ten years."

Neri is only three. "Which means that the only thing that matters is if you *want* to remove it."

"I decided to have it removed before my trip, remember?"

"But did you make that decision because you want another baby right now, or because you felt obligated to fulfill our father's agreement?"

She doesn't answer immediately, which lets me know she's thinking about it. I don't assume either way. I'm done making assumptions with my wife. Which is why I'm asking.

"I want another baby. I'd like our children to be close enough to share their childhood."

A feeling very much like joy surges through me. "Okay, then. I will accompany you to your doctor." As well as a full compliment of my men.

"Lara said she would talk to Matteo about using some of Severu's people for the detail."

"I brought enough guards to keep you and our son safe." Giulia has a four-person security team with her, including Lara. I brought an additional eight.

I'm taking no chances with my wife and son's safety.

Neri is overjoyed to see me when Giulia and I finally leave the room. We play with our son until lunch time, though I have to take a few calls and answer some emails. It's not as bad as it would have been a year ago, when I started training both a junior CEO for our legitimate businesses and promoted one of my men to consigliere, giving us a council of three.

My man acts more as my second in command. Eventually, my father is going to have to hand the reins over officially. But until he does, I will make the necessary work arounds.

He and I don't see eye-to-eye on how to run the business, but he is still my father and the don. I made my vow to him the same as every other made man.

GIULIA

I knew having Raff with me to get my IUD removed wasn't the best idea, but there was no leaving him behind. I tried, suggesting he take the time to get some work done.

I swear sometimes *no* is my husband's favorite word. That must be where our son gets it from.

"You are not going into the exam room with me."

"I went to your appointments when you were pregnant."

"That was different."

"How?"

I'm stumped. Then it comes to me. "Because at those appointments, you got to hear the baby's heartbeat and see the ultrasounds."

Which he insisted on having at every single appointment.

"Yes, I did, but that is not the only reason I accompanied you."

Here we go. "Why else then?"

"Because no one is looking at your pussy without me present. Man, or woman."

"You make Cro-Magnon man look advanced sometimes, *cuore mio*."

The expression that comes over Raff's face when I call him my heart would be frightening. If I didn't know all that intensity is out of love for me.

But the man looks like he wants to eat me.

Right here.

"Not happening," I tell him.

He looks like he's considering convincing me otherwise, but finally he nods. Phew!

However, I don't try to convince him to stay in the waiting room when the nurse leads me back to the exam room.

"Remember, there might be some mild cramping after the removal, but it's nothing to worry about."

I nod, but Raff frowns. "Should you give her something for the pain?"

"No," I say before my OB has a chance to answer. "I'll be fine, Raff."

"That is what you said when you were in labor. You were not fine."

"Getting my birth control removed is nothing like giving birth, trust me."

He frowns, but inclines his head in acquiescence.

It only takes a few minutes for the doctor to remove the device. And she's right. I cramp. It's not so mild and because I'm no wilting flower, I tell her so.

Neither of us is prepared for Raff's reaction.

"Get her some pain meds," he barks, his hand going to his gun.

Oh, crap.

I grab his arm and pull him toward me. "I would rather have you hold me."

He slips both arms around me like I wanted him to and cradles me gently to him, but whatever expression is on his face has my usually unperturbable doctor ordering her nurse to get six hundred milligrams of ibuprofen in a tone I've never heard the OB use.

I'm glad to see they are in gel caps. The pain meds will take effect faster.

My cramps are already lessening by the time we reach the armored car Raff insisted on buying for my first trip to New York. It remains in storage in parking garage between trips, although my husband has told my brother to use it if necessary.

Why did I ever think Raff does not love me? The man is obsessively protective.

"You will not go through that again," Raff pronounces as we pull into traffic. "After you have our next child, I will get a vasectomy."

"Don't you think that's a little over the top?"

He looks at me like I'm the one being unreasonable. "No. That I am allowing you to give birth a second time is enough. There will be no other pain for you."

"Life doesn't work like that."

"It will for you."

Yanking his head toward me with both of my hands, I kiss my husband silly. He takes over, but refuses to raise the privacy partition so we can take things further. "Your safety and comfort are more important than an orgasm," he informs me.

"I love you, *cuore mio*."

"There needs to be a stronger word than love. You own my soul, *amate*."

"Whatever that word is, I feel it too," I tell him.

And he kisses me again.

But he still won't raise the privacy partition.

Bossy, wonderful, protective man!

CHAPTER 21

T he dinner with my fiancée is awkward and mostly silent. Carlotta shows no enthusiasm for my company, but her sister's *suggestion* that I arrange a tour of the kitchens elicits a huge smile and gushing thanks.

Suggestion? More like order. Catalina seems so quiet and shy, but she is actually strong-willed and courageous. I doubt even her father would have had the guts to call me and take me to task for not showing his daughter enough attention before the wedding.

I'm glad that Carlotta is happy. However, I have to acknowledge to myself, if no one else, that I'm more concerned about pleasing her sister than the woman I am engaged to. I tell myself *again* that it is a good thing I am engaged to the younger sister. There is no room in my life for preoccupation with a woman.

A week later, when I ask my mother to help me choose a jewelry ensemble for Carlotta to wear on our wedding day, I ignore the little voice in my head that says Catalina will approve of the gesture.

~ ~ ~

The rehearsal dinner is the night before the wedding. Neither I, nor my soon to be bride, are particularly interested in the rehearsal. Our wedding will be like every other mafia wedding I have attended, though with more guests and fewer attendants.

Because I am don, choosing groomsmen and bridesmaids would have been rife with potential pitfalls. Which is why we are both only having a single attendant. Our siblings. No one can take offence at being left out. No one can use being chosen as leverage for more prestige within the family.

I will wait at the front with my brother standing beside me. The flower girl is one of Carlotta's second cousins, and thankfully the one child related that closely to her that is the appropriate age and sex.

The ring bearer is my nephew, Neri. They will go first.

My sister is not part of the wedding party and Giulia has made it clear she does not mind. Catalina will walk down the aisle before everyone stands for her sister's entrance.

The rehearsal follows the plan without incident, which is exactly as I expect.

We adjourn to a rooftop restaurant that Carlotta has shown interest in for the family dinner afterward. The outside seating area is surrounded by bulletproof plexiglass walls and is a popular spot for politicians, celebrities and mafia.

As the don, I sit at the head of the table. Carlotta sits to my right and her father beside her. My brother sits to my left with my mother beside him. As the second most high ranking member of the Cosa Nostra, my brother-in-law sits at the other end of the table, my sister to his right.

I notice that Catalina has taken a seat as far away from me as possible, on his left. I don't like that, though it shouldn't bother me. I'm not sure why I even notice.

"Your fiancée looks beautiful," my mother says to me.

I nod my head in agreement without looking at Carlotta. As the most beautiful mafia princess of her generation, she would naturally look nothing less than that tonight.

Instead of being happy with my quick acquiescence, my mother frowns before her facial features smooth into a placid expression. What is that about?

"I think Mamma expected you to compliment your fiancée," my brother whispers in my ear, his amusement palpable.

I do not shrug. However, I am unmoved and I do not rush to give the expected compliment.

Carlotta doesn't like when I remark on her beauty. Her mouth tightens and her eyes narrow. It happens when others comment on it as well. I am surprised my mother has not noticed.

I'm sure Catalina is aware of how her sister responds to comments about her looks. She seems even more adept at reading people than my mother.

"You did well choosing this restaurant for the dinner," I tell my fiancée.

As I expect, this causes a genuine smile to appear on her perfectly made-up face. "I'm looking forward to trying one of their signature dishes."

Though traditionally my mother would have chosen the restaurant, as the rehearsal dinner is the responsibility of the groom's family, she was happy to go with Carlotta's suggestion. She made the comment that she'd had more influence on the wedding arrangements than she had expected to have.

"I will let you order for me." I do not care what I eat as I suspect there are no unpalatable entrees on the menu.

"Really?" Carlotta's smile grows. "Will you allow me to sample a bite of your dinner too?"

I shrug. "If you like."

This seems to please her, and I check to see if Catalina notices. She does and gives me an approving look.

"How romantic," my sister calls when she sees me offering Carlotta the promised bite of food after all the entrees have been brought to the table.

Carlotta stiffens, but her expression remains bland. Is she that unconcerned, or has she become that good at hiding her inner feelings? If it is the latter, that will be a benefit to her as my wife.

The don's wife cannot always show her true feelings. In fact, never showing them without careful consideration would be best.

Though I do not see a reason for it, Carlotta grows increasingly tense as the night progresses. She talks less and less, answering questions put to her with as few words as possible. A couple of times, she's so lost in her own thoughts, I have to prompt her to reply to someone's comment.

Catalina throws her sister a look of concern after each occurrence, showing that despite being at the other end of the table, she is paying close attention to us. Or at least to her sister.

Though I have caught her looking at me with an odd expression, almost like grief, more than once. When I meet her gaze, she turns her head away.

Is she that worried about how I will treat her sister? I may not be the most attentive husband, but I will not hurt Carlotta.

She will never see the harsh cruelty that comes out in my role as don to a crime syndicate. Just as my mother never witnessed that side of my father. To her, he was never less than a gentleman.

I will offer no less to my own wife.

CHAPTER 22

CATALINA

The morning of my sister's wedding, we are taken early to the church so we can get ready there. Carlotta expects it to take hours. I prepare myself for the tedium of having my hair and makeup done.

When we arrive in the room set aside for us, Carlotta seems agitated. We are both planning on keeping our casual clothes on until just before the ceremony so we do not crease our gowns.

I notice Carlotta's dress is not hanging up with mine. "Where is your dress?"

I know it was in the SUV, our extra bodyguards rode in. I put it there myself.

"I had it put in the other room."

"What? Why?" I ask.

She gives me a sad smile. "I want to get ready alone, *soru*. I need to get used to not having you to rely on as my security blanket."

"But—"

"You know that saying. Start as you mean to go on. This is the first day of this chapter of my life."

"I was looking forward to this morning." It will be my last time alone with her. The rest of the day, we will be surrounded by others and tomorrow, I will leave New York.

"You are such a good sister." Carlotta smiles at me. "But I need this time. Please will you give it to me?"

"Of course." No matter how hard it is to give up these final hours with her, I cannot refuse my sister if this is what she needs to ready herself for a marriage we both know she doesn't want.

If I could think of a way to protect her from it, I would. But there is no changing our father's mind once it is made up.

"I don't want to be pestered by anyone. Will you make sure that Aria and Zia Lora do not interrupt my time alone? It's going to be enough just having the makeup artist and hair stylist in there with me."

"If that is what you want, I'll make sure it happens."

Carlotta smiles. "I knew you would. Thank you, Catalina, you are the best."

I don't remember the last time she called me Catalina instead of *soru*. It feels momentous, like our relationship is changing. And it is. My sister is going to be a don's wife.

And I am going to be gone.

Two hours later, when Aria arrives already wearing a gorgeous light green designer gown that brings out the color of her eyes and her makeup done flawlessly, I explain that Carlotta does not want to be disturbed before my father's arrival at the church.

Severu's mother frowns, like this worries her, but says, "I will see to the guests then. You look absolutely stunning. I would have liked to have seen you wearing the wedding dress."

She leaves before I can reply to her astonishing comment.

She must have said *a* wedding dress, not *the* wedding dress and I simply misheard her. Yes, that must be it. I'm still reeling from Aria's words when Zia Lora arrives.

She is not happy when I tell her about Carlotta's request to be left alone. "But I have not given her the talk yet," my aunt says a little hysterically.

I stare at her and then cannot help the laugh that bubbles up out of my throat. "Do not worry. Girls talk. Even in proper boarding schools like the one Carlotta and I attended."

"You are sure? I would not have her ignorant of what to expect on her wedding night."

I'm fairly certain Carlotta knows exactly what to expect and that is half the reason she's so nervous about getting married. I finally convince Zia Lora to join the wedding guests.

And then I am alone for the first time that morning. The makeup artist and stylist are both gone. Papà will be here any minute, but for this moment in time, I am utterly alone and I am grateful.

Because in less than thirty minutes I have to watch my sister walk down the aisle toward the man I crave.

~ ~ ~

Papà arrives a few minutes late, but that is to be expected. I'm sure he got sidetracked talking to people he deems important.

People that are not me. I do not think he would even deign to speak to me, except that Carlotta is not here in the room where he expects her to be.

"Where is your sister?"

"She wanted to get ready alone. She is in the room through that door." I point to the door that connects to another room.

Without replying, Papà crosses to the door and opens it without knocking. I hear him call for my sister. She should be right there. Unless she had to use the restroom one last time before putting on her wedding dress.

My father curses and then goes silent. A minute later, he comes storming back.

His face purple with rage, he waves a piece of paper around. "Where is she? What have you done with her?" he whisper shouts the demand.

That in and of itself is concerning. When my father is angry, he does not whisper. He yells.

"I haven't done anything with her. Maybe she's in the bathroom," I say.

Papà backhands me and I stagger backward, both from the blow and the shock of it.

"This does not say she went to the bathroom." He shoves the paper toward me.

I look down, but it is hard to focus on the words. My eyes sting with tears of pain making the writing blurry. When I can finally read it, my heart climbs into my throat.

Dear Papà,

I am too young to get married. I do not ever want to marry a man so much older than me either. I want to go to culinary school. I want to have a life, not be an ornament on some man's arm.

I know you love me, so you will understand.

I'll call or write when I can.

Your Loving but Desperate Daughter,

Madonna Carlotta

What has she done? There is no coming back from this. Not with Papà and not with the don.

"Get in there and put the damn dress on, Catalina."

I stare at my father in confusion. Why does he want me to put my sister's wedding dress on?

"We need to find her." But even as I say the words, I realize what this morning's solitude was really about.

If Carlotta left right after closing herself into the room, she had had more than two hours to disappear. In a city the size of New York, with both a train station and two airports accessible, she could be anywhere. Or on her way to anywhere.

I never saw her makeup artist or hair stylist arrive, but assumed she let them in through the door to the hall in the other room. Doom settles over me.

Carlotta ran and she's not coming back. Not to marry the don.

CHAPTER 23

CATALINA

Pain explodes in my cheek, and I go flying. This blow is much harder than the last one and I land on my butt, my head knocking painfully against the wall behind me. My father stands over me, his face contorted with fury, his eyes burning with rage. His fist is raised, but it's not his fist I feel next. It's a kick to my thigh.

"Get up and get the dress on you useless piece of shit."

The words aren't anything new. I've heard them, and worse before. But I still don't understand. Why would I put on my sister's wedding gown?

"We have to tell Aria what has happened." She will know what to do.

Only I'm afraid even Don De Luca's mother will be stumped for how to salvage the mess my sister has wrought. She ran away. I almost laugh because I was so sure it was something she would never do despite planning to do it myself.

"I will not be made a laughingstock among *la famiglia*." He kicks me again. This time catching my ribs.

I gasp in pain but I do not cower. I push myself up against the wall and meet my father's enraged gaze, knowing I can't stop whatever is coming next. When my father is in a rage, there is no reasoning with him. However, I do not have to give him the satisfaction of showing fear in the face of it.

I have felt pain before. Either I will survive it, or I won't, but I will not cower.

No more blows come. "Get up. Get that dress on. It's the only way out of this mess you've made. Even someone as stupid as you should understand that."

I'm not stupid. If I were, I would not have lasted as long as I have in my father's home. I know how to avoid him, how to protect myself. Usually. I realize now that he would punch or kick me again, but his plan is for me to walk down the aisle, pretending to be my sister.

I can't do that if I cannot walk at all.

I climb gingerly to my feet, breathing shallowly, not sure if my ribs are just bruised. Or broken. Again.

"We can postpone the wedding." Unfortunately, I'm confident that between my father and the don's men, my sister will be found quickly.

"The dumb bitch ran away," my father growls. "There is no postponing. You will wear her dress. You will walk down the aisle. You will marry the don. Once he's spoken his vows, he cannot back out. He won't be happy though."

"Think about this," I urge my father. "The Don will be furious. He will punish you."

"The only one who is going to be punished is your sister and you for helping her." The malevolence in his eyes is terrifying.

"I didn't help Carlotta run away," I say, but I know it's no use.

My father glowers at me. "Of course, you did. She would never have thought of this on her own. Did you do it to get back at me?" He takes my arms in a bruising grip and shakes me. "Did you?"

I don't reply. He has already made up his mind to believe I'm the mastermind behind Carlotta's disappearance. Never mind the fact that I didn't run with her.

"I thought she was *my* daughter, but just like you, she belongs to your pathetic mother." He says that like it's the worst insult imaginable, but I know it's not.

I'd much rather be my mother's daughter than my father's.

"What are you going to do to Carlotta?" I ask, fear for my sister making my skin clammy with sweat.

"You have to ask me that?" my father sneers. "I'll deal with her like the traitorous bitch she is."

Cold chills run down my spine. I know what papà means when he says *deal with*. Carlotta ran away. That's considered a betrayal of him, her promise to the don and the Cosa Nostra. Our father won't just beat my sister. He'll kill her. And no one will stop him.

I cannot believe she's done something so reckless.

Yes, I was planning to run away, but I have a plan. I have money. She has none of that. And I know my father would be just as happy to see me gone.

Carlotta is engaged to the don though. She is Papà's *stellina*. He will never forgive her for this. And he will never stop looking for her so he can punish her for the blow she's dealt his pride.

Carlotta thinks she can do anything because Papà has always indulged her. Her note to our father proves that. She thinks he'll understand. Why?

I know Papà doesn't hit her like he does me, but even if she doesn't want to, she knows. She's seen me when I couldn't get out of bed to come down to dinner after one of his rages.

My thoughts are racing. I have to save my sister, but I don't know how.

Only one man can save Carlotta now. Her fiancé, Don De Luca. I have to talk to him before my father gets a chance to poison his mind against Carlotta.

I'm not just worried about what Papà will do to her either. Anything could happen to Carlotta right now. She's too trusting. Too vulnerable. She needs to be found and found quickly.

Facts click, click, click in my brain and I see my one chance. The only way to talk to Don De Luca before my father can is to walk down the aisle of the church.

"*Sì*, Papà, *sì*. I will put on the dress," I say, trying to make my voice soothing and to hide my terror driven determination.

He steps back and I go into the room that I thought my sister was in all morning long. Her wedding dress still hangs in its garment bag.

Papà has followed me into the room. "Get it on."

I just stare at him. He finally realizes that I'm not going to change with him standing there.

"I'm not leaving you alone for a fucking minute. Get that dress on now, or I'll dress you myself." He turns around but remains between me and both doors out of he room.

I limp as quickly as I can across the room to the wedding dress, while keeping a wary eye on my father. I should have gone up the aisle already in preparation for my sister's entrance.

Reaching around to unzip the dress I am wearing, I feel a piercing pain, but I do not pause. If I'm going to save Carlotta's life, I need to get that dress on. Now.

I let the blue chiffon slip to the floor, making no effort to pick it up as I step away from the pile of fabric.

I pull Carlotta's dress out of the garment bag and wonder how I am supposed to make this work. Where my sister is tall and slim, I am short and rounded. The gown was altered to her exact measurements. It does not matter, I'm going to have to make it work.

I step into the dress, the white silk cool against my skin. I'm so grateful the zipper is on the side. I do not want to ask my father for help. I have to expel all the air from my lungs and suck my stomach in to get the zipper closed.

When it's done, my breasts are encased tightly in the sweetheart bodice, creating more cleavage than I've ever shown in my life. I can barely breathe. The pain in my ribs is a steadily throbbing ache, but it's not stabbing. So probably not broken.

My mother's wedding tiara, something my sister insisted on me wearing, nestles perfectly in the updo Carlotta instructed the hair stylist to create with my long mousy brown hair. For a moment, I look in the mirror and see someone else staring back at me. An elegant woman with sensual curves.

Then I meet my own eyes in that same mirror and see the barely banked terror.

I know the don won't hurt my sister physically himself and I'm hoping he will protect her from my father, but there is no guarantee he will. She betrayed him too by running. And even if I can convince him to show Carlotta mercy, no one is going to be there to help me when I return to our family home with my father after this fiasco of a wedding gets cancelled.

"Miss Jilani? Are you and your sister ready?" The voice of the wedding planner comes from the other room.

I freeze, but my father replies to her calmly. "We'll be out in a minute. Send the flower girl and ring bearer out."

"Of course, Mr. Jilani." The woman sounds so perky. She has no idea the drama unfolding in this room.

There's a bruise blossoming on my cheek that the foundation the make-up artist put on me cannot hide. I pull the veil forward and it settles over my face and floats to rest lower than it would have on my taller sister, covering the deep cleavage of my decolletage.

I turn away from the mirror to face my father. "I'm ready."

He turns, eyeing me critically. Then nods. "Your face is hard to see through the veil. You will keep it on throughout the ceremony."

I say nothing and my father takes my silence as agreement.

"Well, come on then," he says.

I step forward and he scowls. "You forgot the shoes."

Toeing off my ballet flats, I consider my sister's shoes. Just as the dress is at least a size too small, they are a size too big. I quickly shove some crumpled tissue into the toe box of the modest pumps.

Thank goodness Aria had suggested the shorter heel for my sister's comfort. I don't wear heels at all and would probably fall right off the three-inch stilettos Carlotta usually has a fondness for

I put the heels back on and gripping with my toes, I move forward, only to nearly trip over the hem of the dress. My father curses. I gather the dress up with shaking hands, careful to keep the hem brushing the floor, but not so long it will tuck under itself and trip me again.

The wedding planner's eyes grow round when she sees us. "Where is the other Miss Jilani? She is supposed to go next."

"We have had a change in plans," my father says dismissively. "Start the wedding march."

We stand in the vestibule waiting for the doors to be opened and Papà puts his arm out for me to take.

I shake my head. "I can't. If I let the dress go, I will trip."

He glares at me but drops his arm. "You stay right beside me."

Like I'm going to run. Even if I had somewhere to run to, I have to speak to the don before my father goes after my sister. And the only way to do that is to take this opportunity.

I'm risking both men's anger, but it's worth it if there is even the smallest chance of saving Carlotta's life.

The End...For Now

Read Severu and Catalina's story in Urgent Vows.
If you enjoyed Convenient Mafia Wife, please consider leaving a review.
Thank you!

URGENT VOWS

Lucy Monroe

Lucy Monroe LLC

For the authors who made me fall in love with a new subgenre:Cate C.
Wells, Cora Reilly, Neva Altaj,
A. Zavarelli, J.T. Geissinger, & Michelle Heard.

I have read many other authors in the mafia romance genre since discover-
ing your books, but it was your stories that made me go looking for those
other books. You sparked my creative inspiration and desire to write my
own mafia romance series. Thank you all for the many hours of pleasure I
experienced spending time with your characters!

CHAPTER 1

SEVERU

The wedding march begins its sonorous tones from the organ, but the doors at the back of the cathedral remain closed.

The flower girl is standing alone on the other side of the altar, looking nervous. The maid of honor is supposed to be with her, but Catalina Jilani, my bride's older sister, did not walk down the aisle as she was supposed to do.

"What is going on?" My brother and best man, Miceli, asks me. "Where is the maid of honor?"

"I don't know."

Then the doors open and my bride steps in beside her father. She's not carrying her bouquet, nor is she holding onto his arm.

This is not what we decided on at the rehearsal either.

She takes one slow, halting, wedding march step and then two. Are my eyes playing tricks on me? Wishing cannot make it true, but the woman walking toward me does not move like Carlotta.

Even if she's wearing shoes with no heel at all, she's too short. Her veil hides her bustline, but I know those curves. They've been turning me on and featuring in my dreams for three months. They don't belong to the woman who promised to marry me.

It is not Carlotta walking toward me, but the missing maid of honor, Catalina. Miceli's harshly indrawn breath says he realizes it too.

My first reaction is relief.

I am not going to be forced by my honor to marry a woman I do not want while craving her sister. Quickly on the heels of that relief comes fury. Francesco is trying to perpetuate a bait and switch on me. Me? His don?

Why? And how the hell does he think he's going to get away with such an insult?

My consigliere often thinks he's smarter than anyone else, but there is no way he believes I will not notice I married the wrong woman. Is he relying on me staying silent because I don't want to look like an ass? Clearly, he assumes I won't notice it is Catalina until after the vows are spoken. My consigliere thinks I'm a fucking idiot.

More importantly, why in the hell is Catalina going along with this? The thought that she would try to dupe me pisses me off even more than her father's treachery.

I wait in silence, letting my consigliere and his oldest daughter dig the hole they are going to fall in deeper and deeper with each deceitful step. This wasn't supposed to be a red wedding, but I'm going to kill one of my top men today.

Francesco affirms that he is giving Madonna Jilani to me in wedded matrimony when the priest asks. He then shuffles away to take a seat in the front pew.

That was almost clever. Following the tradition in his family, both of his daughters have the first name of Madonna, but my bride's middle name and the one she goes by is Carlotta.

Her sister is Catalina.

The deceitful bitch standing at the bottom step of the altar.

I'm supposed to go to her and hold my hand out to guide her up the steps. I don't.

Seemingly unaffected by the slight, she takes each stair one at a time. She does not stop in front of the priest but continues until she is standing directly in front of me.

There, she stops and lifts her veil.

Hazel eyes turned green with strong emotion meet mine. "I need to speak to you."

My first thought is that she's not trying to trick me. My second one spawns from the hand size red mark on her cheek. I am going to kill that son of a bitch. He fucking hit her. Rage like I've never felt before turns my vision red.

I signal for six of my men to join us at the altar and to create a wall between us and the wedding guests, who have started whispering amongst themselves. Every single one of them has witnessed my consigliere's attempt to trick me into marrying his oldest daughter.

"Let me up there. I need to talk to the don. Take your hands off me." Francesco is making a nuisance of himself. I signal to Luigi to keep him back. If he gets within striking distance, I will kill him in front of too damn many witnesses.

Catalina is biting her lip and looking everywhere but at me now. Her gaze lands on the ring bearer, my three-year-old nephew, Neri, and then goes to the flower girl across from us. Both are fidgeting.

"Can we let the children go to their parents?" she asks, her soft voice strained.

I incline my head and my brother takes care of it.

"You said you need to talk to me," I prompt her.

She nods then looks directly into my eyes again and I'm struck by this small woman's courage. Whatever her father's plans and the violence he used to get her to agree, she is forging her own path.

"You need to save Carlotta."

That is not what I expect her to say.

My muscles tense. "Was she kidnapped?" I ask. "How long ago?"

"No." Catalina's eyes shut, like she wishes she didn't have to say what is about to come out of her mouth. "She ran away this morning while I thought she was in the other room getting ready."

"How do you expect me to save her?"

"First, someone needs to find her. She's too innocent to be out there alone."

"I'm sure your father has that in hand."

Catalina shakes her head. "He hasn't sent men after her yet." She sounds thankful for that fact.

Which makes no sense in light of her asking me to find my runaway bride.

"He was too busy getting you dressed up to take her place," Miceli says, revealing his return and showing he has heard at least part of the conversation.

Catalina shrugs and then winces, holding her body perfectly still. Is she hurt somewhere besides her face?

"Will you look for her?" she asks me.

A plan forming in my mind. "Maybe."

"Oh." My lack of commitment seems to deflate her.

"You said, first."

"Yes..." she lets her voice trail off, like she's hesitant to continue.

I'm not a patient man so my next words come out harsh. "What else?"

"Can you order my father not to beat or kill her?" Catalina looks at me with appeal shining in her eyes, that poor bottom lip taking further abuse from her teeth.

"Under certain circumstances, I can, yes." I reach out and tug her lip away from her teeth. "Whether I will, or not, depends on you."

Confusion fills her pretty eyes. "Me?"

"Yes, you. I expected to get married today. Fifteen hundred guests expect to see me get married. I do not know if you have noticed, Catalina, but I am missing a bride."

"Of course, I noticed. I'm stuffed into a wedding dress that's three inches too long and a size too small because my sister has gone missing." She sounds cranky.

"Ran away," I correct.

She frowns, but concedes with a nod. "Ran away."

"From me and her commitment to marry me." I spell it out for Catalina so there can be no doubt how I see Carlotta's actions.

Biting her lip again, Catalina studies me, but finally she nods her agreement. Not that I need her to agree. We both know the truth.

I remove her lip from her teeth again, this time brushing my thumb over it. "Stop that. You'll do yourself damage."

Her mouth parts on a slight gasp. I cannot help myself, I brush over her lip again. Her pupils dilate and I know my touch excites her, even under the current strained circumstances.

The attraction between us is too damn strong, which is the main reason I didn't demand Francesco give her to me as my bride. I am not looking for a wife to disrupt my life.

However, it looks like that is exactly what I am about to get.

"It would be against our traditions for me to order your father not to beat your sister." Catalina knows this, just as she is no doubt aware of my family's stance against domestic violence.

My father refused to have men under him in positions of authority who could not control their anger within their own home. He believed that if his capos, underboss, consigliere and head enforcer kept the violence we dealt with on a daily basis away from their families, it would set a good example for the men under them.

I have followed the same practice. But that is as far as our traditions allow the don's interference to go.

"As don, it is not my place to involve myself in family matters."

"But she's your fiancée. Doesn't that make her family?"

I disabuse her of the belief that her sister is mine in any way. "No, Catalina, the minute she ran away, Carlotta broke the agreement between our families. She is no longer my fiancée."

"So, you won't help?" Her eyes are awash with disillusionment.

She believed I would save her sister and I will. For a price.

"There is a circumstance in which I can fully protect Carlotta, but it requires something from you."

"Finally," Miceli says under his breath.

I ignore him.

"What?" She looks genuinely puzzled. Even after my hints.

"I need a bride and you're already wearing the dress, which fits you just right, by the way." I let my gaze slide over her beautiful breasts displayed so perfectly by the tight bodice.

She won't be wearing anything that shows so much cleavage in the future, but right now I'm enjoying the view. Her succulent hips are hidden by the full skirt of the gown, but that appeals to me too, that her sexy body is not on display for others to see.

"Right. If I try to walk without holding up the skirt, I'll trip and fall flat on my face." Choosing to take issue with my first statement, she ignores my comment about needing a bride entirely.

"If you are my wife, your family business becomes my family business." I watch as comprehension dawns.

Too many emotions chase across her expressive features for me to know which way she is leaning. She goes from relieved to reluctant, with several others in between.

"I can't marry you," she says, but her voice lacks conviction.

"On the contrary. You can and you will. Your family owes me a bride and you will be mine." Fucking *mine*. I like the sound of that too damn much.

"But it won't be legal."

I smile and whatever she sees in my expression makes her eyes widen. "The marriage license is for Severu E. De Luca and Madonna C. Jilani. So long as the priest uses your name and not your sister's for the vows, it is all good."

Not that the religious ceremony is necessary for the marriage to be legal and binding. All that is required is for both of us to sign the marriage contract along with witnesses and for the marriage record to be filed with the City Clerk's Office.

"But you don't want to marry me." She says it kind of desperately.

I smile again, like the wolf that I am. "Don't I?"

"Because you don't want to be embarrassed in front of all of these people," she says, like she's worked it out.

"If the marriage doesn't happen today, the only person that will be humiliated is your father. The person who will pay the highest price is your sister."

CHAPTER 2

CATALINA

I don't believe him about the humiliation.

Being stood up at the altar will make him look weak and a don cannot tolerate appearing anything but fully in control. Especially the most powerful don in New York, the head of the Five Families.

I believe him implicitly about my sister paying the highest price, however.

My father *will* kill her, especially now that his plan to foist me off as Don De Luca's unknowing surrogate bride has failed.

If I marry the don, my plans to run away will be ruined. But marriage to him will get me out of my father's house and away from his abuse, with no risk of being caught and dragged back into my own personal hell.

As the don's wife, I will be untouchable by anyone but him.

Unlike Carlotta, who has fantasies about living a *normal* life, away from *la famiglia*, I only ever wanted to be safe.

I never wanted to leave her, or our aunt and uncle, behind. Only our father. Marriage to the don will make it possible for me to keep my family in my life while putting me off limits to my father's fists.

I would also be marrying the only man who has ever starred in the kind of dreams that have me waking with my lady parts pulsing. Once his engagement to my sister was made official, my need to run away became even more imperative.

How could I stay, knowing I wanted the man she would call husband?

"Promise me you will never raise your hand to me. Not in anger, not as cold, calculated punishment. Never." I know what the rumors say, but if they were true, then my father would not be Severu De Luca's consigliere.

And he wouldn't have kept his position as the former don's consigliere all those years either.

The don's expression turns dark and forbidding. "The De Luca's do not beat their wives."

"I'm not concerned about your whole family. I want your personal vow."

"You have it," he grits out, obviously offended I need the assurance.

Too bad. This is the only thing I will ask for myself. Because I will not jump from the frying pan directly into the fire, not even for Carlotta's sake.

"Any other conditions?" he asks, his tone implying there had better not be.

I shake my head.

He frowns. "Are you sure?"

I am shocked he asks and even more so that he seems to want me to think about it before answering.

"Nothing else."

"Then you agree to become my wife." It's not a question.

I nod anyway.

"Say it."

"Yes, I will marry you." My ovaries sing the Hallelujah Chorus while my nerves jangle to an acid techno beat.

No matter how stressed I am, my ovaries are winning. I can only hope I'll get a chance to change my panties before we consummate the marriage. If he discovers how soaked they have become just from being this close to him and talking about getting married, I'll die of shame.

"I will find your sister and stop your father from punishing her," he promises in return, reminding me and my unruly body why I'm supposed to have agreed to this in the first place.

"Thank you."

"Where are the necklace and earrings I sent for Carlotta to wear? Did she take them with her?"

"No. I think she realizes pawning them would make her too easy to track." Or that stealing them would be one step too far for the don. Anyway, I'm not sure my sister would even know how to pawn something. "They're still in the dressing room."

"Get them," he says to his brother.

We stand in silence, waiting for Miceli to return. When he does, he hands the necklace to his brother. Don De Luca reaches out and puts it on me, his fingers brushing the back of my neck as he does the clasp. I shiver from the sensation. His lips quirk in response, like he knows what his touch does to me.

The necklace is cool against my throat and chest. Heavy with diamonds and emeralds in a chandelier setting of white gold, it feels like something a queen might wear. Although it was meant for my sister, I can't help the sense of rightness that I am wearing it now. Because he put it on me.

The don removes the modest blue amethyst earrings I'm wearing that were meant to go with my maid of honor gown. Then he puts a drop earring that matches the necklace in my right ear. I make no move to try to do it myself.

It feels like he's marking me as his and a primitive part of me wants that.

After he has affixed the second earring, he trails his finger over the outside of my left ear. "Beautiful."

A shudder of desire cascades through my body. He's talking about the earrings and not me, but I can't help my reaction. And that look in his eyes?

It isn't about pretty jewelry. It's pure, hot sexual desire. I only know because it calls to a matching well of need inside me.

My knees nearly buckle. He wants me.

"My bride," he says, his voice dark with possession.

I lick my lips, my heart beating a mile a minute. And I can no more stop the word that wants to come out than I can stop the earth from turning. "Yours."

Satisfaction covers his brutally handsome features.

With a flick of his wrist, his wall of made men disperse, allowing the crowd of guests to once again gawk at us. He takes my hand in his big one and turns us to face them all. My skirt swishes against the floor but moves with me easily enough.

I notice my father is seated again, with one of Don De Luca's men on either side of him. He's shooting me a death glare, but I do not care. The deal I just struck puts me out of his reach and Carlotta too. Even if he doesn't know it yet.

I look away from him to the other side of the church and my gaze lands on Don De Luca's mother. Aria is smiling, like she's really happy about something. Her daughter is sitting beside her and she seems equally pleased.

They both must realize that it is me standing here, and not my sister, so I don't understand their apparent happiness. But I hope it means the don's family will not resent the change in his bride too much.

I'd gotten to know them during my sister's engagement while I helped with the wedding plans, and I really like the De Lucas.

"May I call you Severu?" I ask in a whisper to the man beside me, sick of referring to him as don, even in my head. He is going to be my husband.

"Yes, Catalina. I do not want my wife calling me don, though sir might be fun. In the bedroom." His voice is low, like mine.

But my cheeks still go hot as fire at his teasing. I try to ignore the fact that the rest of my body reacts with a *yes, please and how soon can we get to the bedroom?* My grip on his hand tightens convulsively.

He squeezes back. "You like the sound of that."

"Shh..." I hush him, so embarrassed I could combust with it.

He chuckles and then raises his hand to silence the loud whispers coming from the guests. "There has been a change in plans. Madonna Catalina Jilani has agreed to be my wife."

With that he turns us back to the priest. That's all he is going to say?

"You may proceed," he adds to the priest.

"Madonna *Catalina*?" the older man asks, sounding dumbfounded.

"That is right." Severu's tone doesn't leave any room for discussion.

The priest nods. "Did you still want me to say the mass?"

"Of course." Severu laces his fingers through mine.

The priest asks for quiet so he can begin. The renewed whispers and rustling movements stop.

He starts the ceremony and after the opening prayer, Severu leads me over to the wedding bench on the left side of the altar. We sit in the pew designed for two people, while his brother joins their mother in the front pew on the groom's side.

During the homily the priest talks about the sanctity of marriage and what it means to submit one to the other. It's an interesting choice for a mafia wedding. I don't think Severu has ever considered the idea of submitting in any way to his wife, but I'm sure he's got lots of ideas on how the reverse should be handled.

Sir, indeed.

I'm not sure how submissive I am after the last fifteen years dealing with my father. I've been practicing quiet subversion of his authority and dictates whenever I can since my mother's body landed on top of mine at the bottom of the stairs because he struck her.

We return to the altar and stand before the priest for the Celebration of Matrimony. Severu speaks his vows in a confident, deep voice, that I'm sure even the guests at the very back of the church can hear clearly. Awed by the moment, my heart in my throat, I speak mine in a much quieter voice, but with no less commitment.

When it is time for the exchange of rings, I quietly panic. But I don't need to. The circle of diamonds meant for my sister to wear with her engagement ring is the one item that fits perfectly. We both have our mother's long, slender fingers, ideal for playing the piano. Severu brushes over the ring with his fingertip, seemingly happy to see it on my finger.

I choke up with unexpected emotion when it's my turn to put his on and my voice shakes as I speak my vow. "With this ring, I thee wed."

Whatever the priest says after is muffled in my head until it is time for communion. Then I watch with strange fascination as Severu drinks from the cup first, before offering it to me. He does the same with the wafer. It feels incredibly intimate. The priest seems flustered by Severu's actions, but he doesn't protest them.

After the nuptial blessing, he pronounces us man and wife and gives Severu permission to kiss the bride.

Severu turns me to face him and then cups the back of my head with one hand, while sliding the other around my waist, above my full skirt and pulls my body flush with his. I gasp at the near full body contact that I've never before experienced with a man, and his mouth slams down on mine, his tongue sweeping past my lips parted in shock.

It is no chaste kiss meant for a wedding. His mouth claims mine and my body goes up in a blaze of sensation.

I grab the lapels of his tuxedo jacket, holding myself up and pulling him closer at the same time. I have never kissed a man, but my lips instinctively mirror the movements of his and I am lost to a world he has created where only we exist.

He ends the kiss and steps back. I do not let go of his jacket. He smiles. "Later, *cara*."

I nod, though I don't know what I'm agreeing to. I'm still lost in the fog of desire created by his lips on mine.

When he begins to gently remove my fingers from his tuxedo, I come back to myself. Mortified, I let go immediately, not wanting to look out over our wedding guests and see the humor that is no doubt on several faces. I step back, but trip on the overlong skirt of my gown.

He doesn't let me fall but sweeps me up into his arms and begins to walk down the aisle toward the back of the church.

"You can put me down," I say with embarrassment. "I can walk."

"I like carrying you."

I'm not sure how to respond to that and my hip is already hurting from all the standing in heels during the wedding. My mom's life wasn't the only thing shattered by that fall down the stairs so long ago.

My hip was too, and it has never been the same.

So, I wrap my arms around Severu's neck and let myself enjoy being carried like a princess.

CHAPTER 3

SEVERU

Two bodyguards walking in front of us and two behind, I carry my new wife out to the waiting armored car. Carlotta had wanted a limousine, but it was the one thing I vetoed.

Safety is more important than living out a girlish fantasy. Does Catalina care that we are riding to our reception in my Mercedes SUV instead of a limo?

She is silent, staring out the tinted windows and I can't tell what she's thinking from the look on her face.

"How are you feeling?" I do not forget the way Catalina winced when she tried to shrug. Throughout the wedding, she showed brief moments of pain, quickly masking her reactions.

Her head turns and her hazel gaze locks on mine. "About the wedding?" she asks, confusion lacing her voice.

"From what your father did to you beforehand."

"Oh, that." She seems surprised I remember.

I don't point out that the red mark on her cheek is already darkening to a bruise. I am not likely to forget. "Yes, that."

"My ribs hurt, but they're bruised, not broken."

Her ribs? Fuck. How badly did he hurt her?

"And you know this how?" I keep my rage at her father, my now *former* consigliere, banked.

She does not need it right now and we have a wedding reception to get through.

"Because I've had both before and I can tell the difference."

"This is not the first time he hurt you?" The lying piece of shit, pretending to adhere to the requirements set by me and my father, while being a fucking child abuser.

"Not even close."

No wonder Francesco made such a big deal of keeping his family out of the limelight. He'd always said it was for their protection, to keep them from becoming targets because of his role in the mafia.

If my consigliere can hide this shit from me, we need to take a closer look into how my married capos treat their families.

"A doctor will be there to give you a thorough examination once we reach the hotel."

"That's not necessary." She seems to be under the mistaken impression that it is her decision.

"I do not agree."

"I don't want to take my dress off and have to get back into it for the receiving line," she says like she's ashamed of the admission. "Right now, the bodice is acting like a compression bandage for my ribs."

"Wrapping your ribs is not the best thing for them," I inform her. It can lead to complications like a collapsed lung or pneumonia.

"In the long term, you're right. But to get me through the rest of today, I'm willing to risk it. I'll do some deep breathing exercises once it's over and I can take my dress off for good."

Though I'm tempted to take her straight home, I can't. There was enough scandal at the wedding with the change in brides, a well-orchestrated reception is more necessary than ever. This isn't just about me and my pride, but the strength and stability of the Genovese family.

The New York Cosa Nostra is only as strong as its leaders. And I am at the top of that food chain.

"The list of guests that will be allowed through the reception line is limited." Though no doubt long enough to make it difficult for her. "Is there anything we can do to make it easier for you?"

"Yes," she says, surprising me. "If I could have something to stand on, so I can take off my shoes, that will help. My sister and I don't wear the same size. No one will be able to see under my dress, so I won't embarrass you."

"I am not easily embarrassed."

"That's good to know." There's humor in her voice.

I like this proof of her spirit.

"You'll have to wear your shoes for the rest of the reception," I warn her.

"That's what you think. I'll have my shoes off while we're sitting at the head table, and no one will be the wiser."

I am amused, rather than irritated, by her sass and smile. "So long as you remember to put them back on before we leave the dais for our first dance."

I'm surprised that wearing heels makes her bruised ribs hurt more.

"I like it when you smile." Her lips curve in response to mine.

I don't reply. Smiling isn't something I do a lot of.

CATALINA

By the time we finish with the obligatory receiving line, despite the pain relievers Severu made me take, my hip is on fire and my ribs feel like my bodice is lined with rocks, not silk.

I am exhausted and there is still the whole reception to get through. Thankfully, it will start with the meal being served and that will be followed by the toasts. I can stay seated for both.

I hope the makeup job done by his sister when we arrived at the venue holds. Severu said the mark on my face is covered completely, but if I sweat off the makeup, it's going to show through. I'm careful not to touch my face regardless.

"Are you going to allow my father to make a toast?" I ask Severu after he once again carries me to my seat.

The guests are going to believe the bride switch was all his idea because he wanted me and not my sister with how attentive he's behaving. Maybe that's his plan. If it is, it's a good one to armor his pride and standing as Don against the rampant gossip.

That explains the kiss. He was creating a narrative. One that left him looking ruthless and even selfish, but *not* abandoned by a runaway bride.

Marrying me had nothing to do with wanting me as his wife. Severu made the best of a bad situation, turning my walking down the aisle in my sister's wedding gown to his advantage. It is no less than I can expect but being a pawn in his game hurts all the same.

Will the guests forget that moment when I took off my veil and my father shouted? Maybe they will think he was as shocked by it being me as they were. What story will we tell to explain my sister's absence?

My thoughts are whirling with so many questions, I almost miss Severu's answer to my inquiry.

"Yes." The word comes out clipped and harsh.

He's no happier about it than I am, but in the mafia, appearances are everything.

I eat very little of the meal, though the food is delicious. My dress is tight and I'm fighting nausea, though I'm doing my best to hide it. The painkillers Severu gave me must have been some sort of opiate.

In addition to the nausea, they are making me loopy, which makes the happy bride façade easier to maintain, but also makes it harder to hide my nerves.

I'm worried to death about Carlotta. Has my father already sent men looking for her? What will happen if they find her? Severu promised to protect her, but what if he doesn't have the chance?

What if she gets herself in trouble before either man can find her? Let's face it, she's been raised as a mafia princess, the one daughter spoiled by our father. Carlotta is not equipped to navigate the real world.

Thoughts of the night to come only increase my inner turmoil.

Will Severu expect to consummate the marriage?

My ovaries may be swooning at the idea, but the rest of my body isn't. As the hours pass, my pain levels will only increase. I've been here before.

What happens if my husband expects to exercise his marital rights?

I've never been touched in any intimate way. The kiss at the wedding was the first one I've ever received. I have spent my entire life as a prisoner in my father's house or attending an all girls boarding school.

I've never seen a naked man in person, much less touched one with the intent of satisfying him sexually. How will I know what to do when the time comes? I don't want to disappoint Severu.

I'm no beauty like my sister. She could probably just lay there, and he would get turned on simply looking at her.

What if he doesn't want me? What if the look of desire I thought I saw at the church was something else?

"You are not eating," Severu remarks in an undertone to me. "We do not need to give our guests even more to speculate on."

"I'm trying."

"Try harder."

If we were alone, I would give him a look to let him know what I think of his order, but he's right about one thing. We *don't* need to give the people around us any more grist for the gossip mill. So, I give him a sweet smile instead. If it doesn't reach my eyes, that can't be helped.

I take a bite and chew, forcing myself to swallow the perfectly prepared pan seared salmon. Severu opted for the meat entrée of course. His change of bride doesn't seem to be impacting his appetite.

He didn't get smacked and kicked around just before the wedding like I did, though. If he had, I doubt he'd let anyone see his weakness. And I can't let the guests see mine either. I take another bite.

When my plate is finally taken away, I am relieved. By sheer determination, I managed to eat about half of it. But I cannot swallow another morsel without vomiting.

I can only pretend to take a sip of my champagne when Miceli offers the first toast. He is both funny and surprisingly warm in his welcome of me to their family. He even makes a joke about how his brother always gets what he wants in the end.

Further feeding that narrative that makes Severu look like the conscienceless don rather than the duped one. Though how anyone could believe he wants me over my beautiful sister is mystifying.

My father is next. His smile is smug, at least it looks that way to me. He believes he got away with what he did this morning. And I guess he's right, but Severu is angry with him. I'm sure he'll be having words with my father later, no matter how chummy they appear right now.

Appearances.

"You could have knocked me over with a feather when Severu decided to marry my oldest daughter instead of my youngest," he starts.

And I realize he's aware of the impression Severu has been at pains to present and he's doing his best to perpetrate it, probably to try to gain his don's favor after that pathetic attempt at tricking him.

"I am sure it came as a shock to all of you as well," he continues.

The guests laugh, finding my father charming. I choose to look at Severu, rather than my father, during the toast. At least then I can force a semblance of a smile. If I look like a lovesick calf, that is the price I will pay. I will not play into my father's theatrics.

And I notice how he has taken two digs at me already, though I'm sure no one else has.

Severu doesn't smile, but that's not unexpected. He's not a smiling kind of guy, which is why his smile in the SUV on the way here had such an impact on me.

Not because everything he does makes my body and emotions go haywire.

Note to self: if you are going to try to lie to yourself, make it more believable.

"Welcome to my family, Severu," my father concludes, without a single congratulation for me or word to me.

I do not care. My father isn't going to change and I'm past the point of ever expecting or wanting him to.

My gaze scans the rest of the guests and lands on my aunt and uncle. Zia Lora is smiling, as if delighted by this turn of events. Or she's putting on the appearance of being happy to keep up the façade. Zio Giovi isn't playing his role though. He's glaring at my father.

Is he upset by my father's subtle insults toward me in his toast? Or that I'm the sacrificial replacement bride? Zio Giovi would not be fooled, like everyone else, into believing this is some kind of unexpected love match.

There is a rustling from the other side of Severu. His mother, Aria, is standing. She wasn't supposed to give a toast, but she has her glass raised. The guests go silent in anticipation of what she has to say.

If I felt half as composed as she looks, I would be happy.

She smiles toward me. "My dear Catalina, while others may be surprised by my son's last-minute change of bride, I am not. A mother knows these things."

Again, there is laughter and this time my smile is effortless and genuine. It is easy to respond warmly to her words because they are so kind. Even if she is lying through her teeth. Is that a skill I want to learn? Maybe.

"You are such a good match for Severu, and I could not be happier to welcome you to our family. Thank you for joining us. It is my sincerest hope that you and my son will have a marriage as wonderful and blessed as the one I shared with his father. I wish you both only the best." She takes a sip of her champagne.

I pretend to follow suit, my eyes shining with gratitude I hope she can see.

After that, chatter resumes while the guests drink champagne and other beverages from the bar. Soft music begins to play in the background, signaling the time for dancing has come. Aria has not retaken her seat, but is now standing near Severu and I.

She leans down and says quietly, "We need to make some quick alterations to the skirt of your bride's gown, or she's going to end up tripping more than dancing."

Severu nods. I stand to follow Aria. Walking slowly, so I don't trip over the hem of my gown, she leads me from the ballroom and down a side corridor. The slow pace helps with the strain on my hip and I'm thankful.

What will happen when the don and his family learn of my infirmity? Will he feel deceived? It's hard to believe he won't care, but it's too late to worry about that now. For better, or worse, we are married.

CHAPTER 4

CATALINA

Aria opens the door to the ladies' room.

The outer chamber is luxurious, two walls lined with immaculate, tufted, white benches. A vanity and mirror stretch the entire length of the third wall. The fourth has the opening to the bathrooms. This room is large enough to accommodate at least a dozen women but there is only one. And she is clearly waiting for us.

Dressed to attend the wedding in a modest but elegant gown, the older woman's hands do not have the pampered softness of the other women here. Her grey hair is in a severe bun, and she doesn't wear any jewelry except a simple gold band on her wedding finger.

Aria smiles. "This is our housekeeper, Emilia. She has worked for our family since before I married Enzo. When she married, her husband also joined our staff."

I like that Emilia was invited to the wedding, and I extend my hand to her. "Thank you for coming."

"The pleasure is mine." Though the look on her face says she's holding her judgment in reserve as to whether she truly believes that, or not.

What she thought of Carlotta.

"Emilia is very good with a needle and thread," Aria says. "She will do a quick alteration to your gown."

"Oh, thank you," I say sincerely to Emilia. "I'd love to be able to walk without tripping. Right now, I don't know how I'm going to dance when I need both hands to hold up my skirt."

"Don't worry, Signora De Luca, I know just what to do."

"Catalina, please," I say automatically. I've always been uncomfortable with formality between myself and family staff.

Then I realize I might be overstepping and look to see how Aria has taken the invitation to call me by my first name. She is smiling. "Emilia will call you Catalina when it is just family, but like the rest of the staff will address you as Signora Severu to distinguish between you and myself when others are present."

Aria is instructing Emilia and myself and I appreciate it. I haven't spent the last three months having dinners at her home and figuring out how to behave as a don's wife like my sister has.

Emilia gets to work on my dress and a few minutes later, there's three sets of ruching on the front of the skirt, creating a scalloped hem that barely brushes the floor. The extra three inches on the back of the skirt is like a mini train I'll be able to manage.

"There, that looks like the skirt was meant to be that way." Aria's voice is filled with satisfied approval.

"Thank you so much, Emilia," I say with a relieved smile.

Aria examines my face. "Your makeup is holding," she pronounces.

"Good." I don't want to add more goop to my face, otherwise known as foundation. "I suppose I'll have to get used to wearing makeup now, but this feels so stifling, like my skin can't breathe."

"You'll be able to use a lighter foundation once your bruise heals and you can choose to wear minimal makeup, but I'm afraid you are right. You will have to get accustomed to wearing it daily." Aria's lips purse, her green eyes troubled. "I do not know what your father was thinking to strike you like that."

He was thinking that smacking and kicking me would get me to comply with his plans, but I don't say that. Aria is already distressed. I hope that means she's never witnessed that kind of violence in her home.

When I return to the ballroom, less than twenty minutes have passed. Severu is waiting for us. He puts his hand out to me and tugs me onto the dance floor. He pulls me into him, close enough that the silk of my dress brushes against his legs, and he settles his hands on my hips.

My hands land against his chest and I'm not sure how they got there, but I don't move them. I stare at the pulse beating in his throat and wish I could lean forward and place my lips against it.

The music changes to a pop ballad, one of the few things my sister showed any interest in choosing for her wedding day. The singer is one of her favorites, but I feel no connection to the lyrics.

"You didn't join in the toasts," Severu says quietly.

Pulled out of my fantasy of kissing his neck, I ask, "What do you mean?"

"You only pretended to drink. Why?"

Is he angry? I cannot tell. He's so self-contained.

"I do not respond well to opiates." I tell him the truth because I have nothing to hide. "I was already feeling nauseated and did not think adding alcohol to the mix would help."

"Why didn't you tell me you felt ill?" He makes his question sound like an accusation.

"What difference would it make? *What cannot be changed must be endured*." It was one of my mother's favorite quotes and has become one of mine.

She used to say it a lot, which makes sense, considering the life she had to endure with my father. I looked it up when I was a teen and discovered it was from *Lord of Chaos* by Robert Jordan. I've never read the book, but I've said the quote to myself over and over again.

"I would prefer you tell me you are feeling ill than to have you rushing off to throw up and leave our guests thinking that we had to get married because I got you pregnant."

So, not because he cared per se that I was nauseated, but so he could manage the situation with all of the facts.

"I guess it's a good thing I didn't do that then," I say, my tone sarcastic.

"Why are you angry? It's my job to watch for potential problems and deal with them."

I'm not angry. I'm hurt and I'm not about to admit that to my cold, emotionless husband. "I am doing my best. I didn't expect today to go the way it has, no matter what my father wants to believe."

"What does he believe?" Though we continue to dance there is an air of stillness about him as Severu waits for my answer.

"That I not only helped Carlotta to run, but that it was my idea." If there was a poor opinion to be formed about me, Papà was going to form it.

"Did you?"

My head jerks up and I find Severu looking down at me. I can see the ruthlessness he's known for in his stoic gaze, and I shiver.

"No," I say. "I did not. You can either believe me, or not. I have no proof either way."

He inclines his head, but he doesn't reply. Does he believe me, or my father's view of me? Would Severu have married me if he shared Papà's tendency to think the worst of me? If it meant protecting his image as the all-powerful Don, he might, I have to accede to myself.

We do not talk again for the rest of the dance. When it is over, Papà is standing there, ready for the father-daughter dance. I instinctively step back, in the other direction. I have no intention of participating in that mockery.

Severu's hand settles firmly against my back, stopping me from moving further way. "It is expected," he says. "I will be dancing with my mother."

Like that makes this any more palatable. I would rather dance with his mother than my father. He must realize that.

"I don't want to," I say in a low voice.

"What cannot be changed, must be endured," Severu says in an unbending tone. "It is only one dance."

My father puts his hand out imperiously. Severu pushes me toward him. My sense of safety in his presence vanishes. He is showing me that when it comes to a choice between my well-being and keeping up appearances, I will lose.

Squaring my shoulders, I step forward.

"Good girl," Severu says in an undertone.

More sickened than pleased by his approval, I allow my father to take me into a formal ballroom style dancing stance. The music playing is an orchestral waltz. I'm sure Papà had something to do with its selection. Carlotta would not have gainsaid him.

This is just another calculated scene in Severu's narrative for today. I don't blame him for pretending an affection he doesn't feel, or even that he's made it look like I was part of a "love" triangle and betrayed my sister. He is don and he cannot appear weak in any way. I get that.

Also, he promised to protect Carlotta and he cannot do that if her betrayal becomes known. I understand that too.

But this. Making me dance with my father. Forcing me to endure his touch while my body aches from the beating he gave me. This is taking that narrative too far. Severu could have prevented this.

A voice in my brain asks, "How?" but I ignore it.

Severu may not physically harm me, but he does not care if I am hurt. I am nothing to him but a means to an end. I am his wife to protect his pride, not because he craves me like I crave him.

He did not choose me.

"Smile," my father demands. "The guests are watching."

I ignore him, my gaze fixed over his shoulder. He squeezes me and I refuse to wince from the pain it causes my ribs. I do not look at him. I do not fake a smile.

"You think Severu will thank you for embarrassing him like this?" My father hisses the question.

I do not reply. I have my own narrative for today and in it my father is a monster who forced my 19-year-old sister to become engaged to a 35-year-old man for the sake of his own importance. Though I am twenty-five and well past the age when most mafia daughters marry, Papà never even considering putting me forth as potential wife to our Don.

Not for Carlotta's sake and certainly not for my own.

He leans down like he's saying something fatherly to me, but whispers so no one else can hear. "You're a stupid bitch just like your mother, refusing to do as you are told. At least try to be what is expected of you."

His words busts something open in my heart. My mother twisted herself into someone she probably didn't even recognize by the time he killed her, trying to be what my father expected.

I lean back so our eyes finally meet. I let him see my hatred.

He keeps his fake smile on his face, but his eyes show nothing but malice.

"I am like my mother," I say. "Too good for a disgusting monster like you."

I don't even care when his hand holding mine grips me so tightly, I know it will leave bruises. I refuse to show him my pain. But I let him see my disdain.

"You are so pathetic you have to hurt the women you know are better and smarter than you. We are stronger too. You could never have survived what you put mamma through." I don't know where the words are coming from. I've never spoken to my father like this before. But I am not done. "You are the weak little bitch, not me."

His grip on my hand tightens further and my bones grind together. I do not flinch. I do not cry out. I keep my gaze fixed on his, my head up, and my eyes silently defy him. I will not bend. Finally, the song ends.

Miceli is there to take me from my father as soon as it is over. "My turn."

My father is forced to release me. He does so with a mocking little bow toward me, never once letting his fake smile slip from his face.

My hand is throbbing now and the pain in my ribs is more acute. Any efficacy from the painkillers has worn off. Only the nausea is left behind.

I don't wait for Miceli to take my hand, but place both on his chest like I did with Severu. He looks like he doesn't know where to put his own hands. After long seconds, he settles them on my shoulders and he begins moving us to the slow beat of another pop ballad.

My sister's playlist. If only she was here to enjoy it and deal with Papà and everyone else.

My forbearance is stretched to the limit and though I never cry, it is all I can do to keep the tears at bay. Only a few hours ago, I thought this marriage might work out. That it wouldn't be so bad. That giving up my plans to run was worth it to save my sister, to keep my aunt and uncle in my life.

To be with Severu.

"Are you alright?" Miceli asks, his voice tinged with concern. "It didn't look like you were enjoying your father-daughter dance."

"I wasn't." My gaze drops to my hand where it rests against my brother-in-law's chest.

It is red and already swollen. I'm not sure how I'm supposed to hide it for the rest of the reception, but I know I will be the one held to blame if I don't.

Appearances.

"It must have been difficult to dance with him after what he did to you this morning. You're a strong woman, Catalina, stronger than I realized." He sounds admiring.

I do not care. Dancing with my father was not my choice. My strength, as he calls it, is born of necessity.

"I've had to be to survive living under his roof for twenty-five years." I wouldn't say this to anyone outside the family, but I won't hide what my life was like from the De Luca's.

They are my family now, too.

"It was that bad?" Miceli asks.

I lift my hand so he can see it. "Yes."

His dark eyes turn nearly black with fury. "He did that to you while you danced?"

"Yes." I put my hand back against his chest. "I'll need to ice it before the swelling gets too obvious to hide."

"Fuck."

My sentiments exactly. Though I've never said that word before in my life. Today might be a good day to start. Or not. After all, I am now the don's wife.

Miceli subtly guides us toward the edge of the dance floor and then drops his hands from my shoulders. He places one on my back and starts walking me toward the hallway I took earlier to reach the ladies' room. On the way, he catches the eye of one of his men, who immediately joins us.

"Get an icepack," Miceli instructs. "Fast."

The other man starts jogging down the hall. It must lead to the kitchens. Miceli does not stop at the ladies' room, but keeps going until we reach an empty room on the other side of the hallway. There are chairs stacked against one wall and round tables with their legs folded up on their sides near them. A storage room.

Miceli grabs a chair off the stack and puts it on the floor in the center of the room. I don't wait to be invited; I sit down. So grateful that at least the strain on my hip is lessened, my eyes sting with relief.

Miceli hits his palm with a fist. "That bastard."

Since I'm pretty sure he's talking about my father, I don't disagree.

"You should go back to the reception," I say to my brother-in-law. "We don't need gossip about us disappearing together. Not after everything else today."

"I'm not leaving you alone." But his expression says he knows my concern about the gossip is valid.

"I'll be fine," I say firmly. "Papà isn't going to track me down in here and your man will be back soon enough with an icepack."

"Severu would not be happy if I left you alone."

"Your brother will be downright furious if rumors start to circulate about what you and I were doing away from the ballroom so long together. You know people noticed us leaving, even if no one said anything."

Miceli shakes his head stubbornly.

I try for a smile I don't feel. "I am used to being alone. I will be fine. Please, Miceli. I cannot stand more of your brother's anger on top of everything else."

I don't like telling him that. I am not weak, but I am near the end of my tether.

Miceli must realize it because he finally nods. "Alright. Aldo will be back with the icepack, and I'll let Severu know where you are."

"You don't need to bother your brother. I'll ice my hand for fifteen minutes and then rejoin the reception."

Miceli just shakes his head and leaves.

CHAPTER 5

CATALINA

A knock sounds on the door only moments later. I get up and open it a crack to confirm it is Aldo, unsure what I plan to do if it is not. Relieved because it is him, I open the door wider, though not wide enough to let him in. The last thing I need is to be seen coming out of a storage room with one of Severu's men.

I put my right hand out for the icepack. He doesn't hesitate to give it to me.

I thank him and close the door before returning to my chair. Placing the ice pack against my sore hip, I set my hurt hand on top of it so it can do double duty. I am like that for about five minutes when the door slams open.

Severu storms inside, looking around, like he expects someone to be in here with me. I'm too exhausted to react. I simply stare at him in silence.

He shuts the door and turns back to face me, his expression stern.

"Your name fits you well. I wonder if you frowned a lot as an infant and your parents knew you would turn out to be like you are."

"What the hell are you talking about?"

"Your name. Severu. It means stern, strict, or severe." I looked it up. Why? I do not know.

"What happened?" he asks through gritted teeth.

"Since you are here, I assume Miceli talked to you, so you already know."

"I want you to tell me."

"My father hurt me. Again." I say the last word as a reminder to my husband that he'd pushed me into dancing with a man who had smacked me and kicked me in the ribs only this morning.

Not that I'd told him the extent of my father's violence, but he knew it was more than a slap because of my sore ribs.

Severu winces, like the arrow of my words hit their target. "Why?"

"Does it matter?" Does he think there's any justification for my father nearly breaking the bones in my hand while we danced?

"No." His features taut with fury, Severu's own hands fist at his sides.

Because he said it didn't matter, I tell him, "At first because I would not smile."

"What do you mean at first?"

"Just what it sounds like. He squeezed my hand hard enough to hurt. Then when I said some things he didn't like, he squeezed so hard I could feel my bones rubbing together."

"Fuck."

"That's what Miceli said."

"Don't make a joke out of this."

"You think I'm trying to be funny?" I ask, my voice rising. "You made me dance with a man you knew was not safe for me and he hurt me. Now I have to figure out a way to hide my swollen hand from the rest of the guests, while pretending to be happy I married you."

Severu stares at me like he's seeing me for the first time. "You are not happy to be married to me?"

"Considering how much you suck at protecting me, take a guess."

"I miscalculated your father's idiocy. You should have been safe dancing in front of hundreds of guests."

"Is that an apology? Only it didn't sound like one."

"I do not apologize."

"Neither does my father."

Severu doesn't like being compared to his consigliere. That is obvious. Though I'm not sure why. After all, he made me dance with Papà. I cannot forget that.

And he's not sorry.

He reaches out like he's going to touch me, but then his arm drops back to his side. "You will not return to the reception."

"How are we supposed to explain that? If you say I'm ill, everyone will think I'm pregnant like you pointed out earlier. The guests already think I'm some kind of slut who enticed my sister's fiancé away from him. I don't want them believing I had sex with you while you were engaged to her."

"What the hell are you talking about? No one thinks you are a slut."

I let my silence express my disagreement.

"You are stubborn."

"What I am is at the edge of my endurance." Only somehow arguing with Severu has invigorated me, rather than adding to my exhaustion.

"I do not believe it. I think you are stronger than a lot of made men."

His compliment makes me feel good until I remind myself that he didn't marry me because he wants me for his wife. He married me to salvage the disaster of his nonwedding to my sister.

And my belief he will protect me from my father has already been proven wrong.

"We need to get back to the reception," I say, fatigue pulling at me again as my adrenalin recedes.

"How is your hand?" Severu asks without agreeing.

"The ice is helping." I shrug and my ribs shift. I gasp from the pain. "I think I need more painkillers, but a regular analgesic, not a narcotic."

I do not want to be more nauseated than I already am.

He pulls out his phone and texts something. At least that's what I assume he's doing.

Slipping his phone back into his pocket, he looks at me. "We are leaving. Your injuries have gone long enough without being seen to."

"What? No, we need to cut the cake at least. I'll hide my hand in my skirt. It will be fine. I'm right-handed anyway."

He bends down and then scoops me up from the chair, so I'm cradled against his chest. Then he takes my place in the chair with me settled on his lap.

"We are going home, but don't worry. The guests won't wonder why we've gone."

"Wha—"

I'm cut off when his mouth lands over mine. Severu's lips are gentle and coaxing, not like our first kiss. He tastes like whiskey. I want more of that flavor. More of him. Darn ovaries. I open my mouth and taste his with the tip of my tongue.

He groans and the kiss goes from gentle to demanding in a heartbeat, though his hold on me never tightens. His tongue comes out to slide against mine, then thrust into my mouth and electric shocks zing straight to my core.

I try to shift, needing something, but that causes another sensation. One not nearly as pleasant. Pain.

I do not say anything but it's as if he knows, because he breaks the kiss to say, "Do not move, *mi dolce gatto*."

No one has ever shortened my name to Cat, not even at school. Now, Severu is calling me *my sweet cat*. Having him use such a personalized endearment is almost as arousing as his kisses.

Nodding my agreement not to move, I tilt toward his lips again, wanting more of his kisses. He gives them to me, his hand coming up to cup my nape.

His thumb brushes along my jaw and it feels so good, I shiver.

Severu lifts his mouth from mine again and gives me a stern look. "I said, no moving."

"I can't help shivering. That's an automatic response."

"No moving," he says again.

"I'll try."

"Good girl."

Ice water douses the desire heating up my insides.

That's what he said when he pushed me to dance with my father.

"What is it?" Severu asks, his gaze searching mine.

"I am not a *good girl*. I don't want to be one either when it means getting hurt."

He grimaces. "That should not have happened."

"But it did."

"It will never happen again."

Can I believe him?

I try to turn my head away, but he holds it in place, espresso brown eyes boring into mine. "I give you my vow. He will never touch you again."

"How can I trust you?" What is the vow of a made man worth when it is given to a woman, especially his wife? "You already broke the promise you made before God, the priest and our guests, to protect me."

Severu opens his mouth to speak, but I am not done. "My father spoke the same vows on his wedding day to my mother, but he broke them all."

He hadn't cherished or honored her, and he'd done the opposite of protect her.

"He hurt her too?" Severu's usually stoic tone reflects both shock and disbelief.

Had he really not known? Had his father been just as unaware?

"He killed her." It's the first time I've ever spoken the words aloud.

It is freeing and terrifying at the same time.

Will my husband believe me? My father is his consigliere, second in rank only to his brother, the underboss. Severu has been trusting my father to advise him since becoming don five years ago, and his father for two decades before that.

I have only been Severu's wife a matter of hours.

CHAPTER 6

SEVERU

My bride's claim that her father killed her mother is more shocking than when she said Francesco had abused his wife as well as his daughter.

How could my father have missed it? While we had rarely seen his daughters, Sara Jilani had accompanied her husband to dinners in our home. The Jilanis and my parents often attended social functions together.

My parents would have noticed if Francesco had been hurting Sara.

Catalina's assertion is the result of her resentment for her father's treatment of her. She's made him into the bogeyman to explain it to herself and to handle her own guilt.

When she was ten years old, my wife was running through the house, and she tripped her mother on the stairs. They both went tumbling. Sara Jilani died, her neck broken. Catalina was in the hospital for weeks with a broken leg.

Francesco was devastated. He tried not to, but he couldn't help blaming his daughter for the loss of his wife.

My father believed that was why he never tried to make a match for her despite the interest shown by other families. As the daughter of the Genovese consigliere, she had excellent prospects.

I loosen some of the pins from Catalina's hair, caramel curls tumbling down to give her a disheveled appearance. Her lips are swollen from my kisses and there is a pretty blush that goes from the top of her luscious curves to her neck.

She looks like I want her to look. A new bride who has been making out with her groom.

"Time to go." I stand and head to the door.

She makes a sound of disbelief. "You're not even going to ask me about it?"

"I know what happened," I tell her. I don't want to talk about it. I don't want to be the one to make her face her own culpability in her mother's death.

She had been a child. It was an accident.

"Really? Because he told you?" she asks, her voice laced with disgust when she says the word *he*.

What does she want me to say? "I saw how upset your father was by Sara's death."

"You mean like how happy he looked dancing with me tonight? We both know that was a lie, or I wouldn't have this." She holds up her hand that is still red and swollen, despite the ice.

I change my mind about meeting the doctor at my home. I'm taking Catalina to our private hospital. I want her hand and her ribs X-rayed.

"We don't have time to talk about this now."

Catalina does not reply. When we reach the ballroom, her body shifts and I look down. Suddenly, she's smiling and ducking her head like a shy bride being taken away for her wedding night by a husband she adores. There are good-natured cat calls and advice offered to us both on how to spend the rest of our wedding day, and night.

My personal security team peels away from their positions in the ballroom and two of them are ahead of us by the time we reach the doors that lead to the hotel proper. Everyone thinks we are staying here in the suite on the top floor.

My team leads us past the elevators and out a side entrance to the hotel. A convoy of four cars is waiting for us. One in front of my armored SUV, one behind it and one to the side, between it and the street beyond.

I settle Catalina inside, carefully shifting her to the other side so I can climb in after her. I reach across her and pull her seatbelt toward me, and clip it into place.

Her smile is gone, and she looks away from me to stare out the tinted window.

I tell the driver to take us to the hospital instead of my home as I'd previously instructed in the text I sent.

She does not respond to that, like it does not matter. We have been driving for about five minutes in silence when she asks, "Do you have men looking for Carlotta?"

"I do."

"Will they find her before my father's men?"

"Francesco has had no opportunity to order his men to search. His cell phone was confiscated and he has had a man on him from the moment he sat down in the cathedral."

"Oh. Too bad his guard couldn't stop him from hurting me."

An unfamiliar feeling makes something inside my chest tighten. Guilt?

I do not feel guilt. No remorse. No regret. Those are emotions a don cannot allow himself to feel.

"I'm worried about her," Catalina says.

"While it is obvious she does not have the same concern for you." I can only be grateful I did not end up married to a woman who so clearly was not suited to the role of don's wife.

"Carlotta isn't great at seeing the big picture."

I do not reply.

"Did you ever wonder why my father didn't use the mafia hospital for either myself, or my mother?" Catalina asks after another beat of silence.

"Sara didn't go to a hospital that day."

"But she went other times. Once with a broken arm. Once with a fractured cheek bone. Another time when she lost the baby that would have been born two years after my sister. He was a boy. Papà killed his own heir before my brother ever had a chance to be born."

"My father would have known if that had happened," I say, appalled by her words.

"Would he? You didn't know my father sent me to the hospital two years ago with a spiral fracture in my wrist. He didn't know about the time my father broke my ribs when I was thirteen."

Her words open up a hollow place inside me. If what she is saying is true, Francesco was a serial abuser and neither my father, nor I, realized it.

"You don't believe me?" she asks, still not looking at me. "The hospital records are easy enough to check."

She's right. They would be easier to check at our mafia sanctioned private hospital, but we can get what we need from the other hospitals in New York as well.

"What happened to your mother?" I ask, no longer sure I know the answer.

Finally, Catalina's head turns so her gaze meets mine. "He hit her and she started to fall down the stairs. I was at the bottom. I ran up, trying to catch her. I was desperate to save her, but I was too small. She knocked me down and we tumbled together. She died on impact and my hip was shattered."

"Your hip?" I ask, because her father had said it was her leg.

"Yes."

I remember Francesco's grief after his wife's death, but I do what my wife said to and examine that against the way he smiled throughout their father-daughter dance.

He had looked so proud and happy. All the while he had been hurting her and I had not realized it.

Then I think about how easily Catalina had slipped on the mask of shy, but happy bride while in pain and feeling anything but joy. Which of them should I believe?

"I wonder how many of your guests were fooled by my performance on the way out of the ballroom," she says as if she is reading my thoughts.

"I would say all of them."

"Your mother is much better at lying than I am, but I can pretend almost any emotion."

Her comment about my mother gives me pause, but she is right. Mamma has learned to lie to protect her position, my father, and even me. She is very good at it, as evidenced today.

"You are saying you get that ability from your father."

Revulsion crossed her lovely features already drawn with weariness. "I don't like to think so, but I cannot deny that he is a good actor and so am I. I definitely learned the skill because of him. Both as protection and to deprive him of his power. I stopped letting him see my fear the year after I finished at boarding school."

I am not a good man. I do not hesitate to kill for the good of *la famiglia*. I torture my enemies without remorse. I do not have nightmares or regrets.

Cruelty is just another tool I use to protect and strengthen Genovese interests.

And yet I am sickened to consider what Catalina would have gone through to teach her not to show her pain and fear to her father.

CATALINA

It is my first visit to the hospital used by most of *la famiglia*.

It looks like any other building in New York, but when our convoy of cars pull into the parking garage, a steel gate shuts behind us. We stop by a bank of elevators and hospital staff are waiting there with a gurney already.

Severu insists on lifting me out of the car and onto the gurney while his bevy of bodyguards surround us. The doctor starts asking questions and I answer, glad that the back of the gurney has been raised so I'm not lying flat on my back. It might feel better on my ribs, but it would have made talking awkward.

I am impressed that Severu is able to stop himself from interrupting. I can tell he wants to speak, but he doesn't.

Not until I've catalogued my injuries on the elevator ride up. Then he informs the doctor he expects a full scan done, regardless of the injuries I have listed and that he wants an orthopedic surgeon on standby in case my hand needs to be repaired.

"Do not worry, we will take good care of your wife." The doctor smiles at Severu as the elevator doors open.

My husband, clearly unimpressed with the assurance, glowers at the doctor.

Although he looks to be in his fifties and has to be used to treating mafia patients since he works at a mafia funded hospital, the doctor shrinks back.

I am wheeled into a corridor that looks more like a high end hotel space than any hospital I have been in. And I have been in a few. Papà took us to hospitals and clinics all over New York and Long Island to prevent an easy record keeping of the abuse injuries my mother and I suffered.

I mean, I assume he did the same for Mamma. I only know about a few of her trips, the ones I remember. I have no idea where he actually took her. I was bluffing when I asked Severu why my father never took my mother to this hospital or the mafia approved clinic on Long Island. His reaction confirmed my guess though.

We reach a set of double white paneled doors that look like they belong in my father's mansion. Both are open and I am wheeled through. The first room we come to is a sitting area, with a sofa and two armchairs, a mini bar and a big screen television. We pass a large desk clearly intended for the businessman who needs to work while waiting on treatment for a loved one.

The doctor looks at Severu. "If you and your men will wait in here."

"I will be staying with my wife," my husband, the don, says in a chilling tone.

"That is fine, but there is not room for your entire security detail in the treatment room. My team needs space to give your wife the best treatment possible."

Severu inclines his head. "Everyone but Aldo will wait here."

We go through another set of double doors and the smell of antiseptic, like any other hospital, hits me first. The walls are painted a soft peach color and the artwork looks like it could be in a museum. But there are all sorts of machines around the high-tech hospital bed in the center of the room and all the usual accoutrements for sanitization.

"We'll take your gown off before we transfer you to the treatment bed, Mrs. De Luca." The doctor nods at one of the nurses.

Severu steps forward before the male nurse can touch me. "I sent instructions for a female medical team. Why weren't they followed?"

"My team were the ones available. If you wish to wait for your wife's care, we can make the change." Apparently, the doctor has gotten over his fear because he eyes Severu coolly.

"You may proceed but you have exactly three minutes to get the rest of your team swapped out." With women. He doesn't say it, but no one in this room could possibly doubt Severu's meaning.

The doctor instructs the nurse to call for immediate replacements as he approaches my bed.

Once again Severu steps in the way. "I will do it."

The doctor puts his hands up and steps back. "By all means."

What the heck is going on? No way is the most powerful don in New York jealous at the thought of a medical professional removing my clothes.

Jealous, or not, he's definitely not going to allow it.

"Aldo, shut the doors and face them," Severu instructs the other man after the nurses leave.

I hear both doors shut with a quiet whoosh.

"Can you sit up a little?" Severu asks me, offering his arm to help me.

I grab it and pull myself into an upright position, but it hurts, and I don't try to hide my reaction. This is not the place for my acting skills.

Severu holds me up with one hand and lowers the zip on the side of my dress with the other. But it's too tight to pull off without stretching my arms and I give an embarrassing whimper when we try that.

He stops immediately and says, "This was not how I planned to undress you tonight."

CHAPTER 7

CATALINA

I don't know what he means until he pulls a knife from a sheath under his jacket.

"You were armed at the church?" I ask, shocked.

"I'm wearing a shoulder and ankle holster as well," he informs me, his voice amused, as he gently lets me settle back against the partially reclined gurney.

"I thought you weren't supposed to take guns into the cathedral." I was sure that a no weapons policy had been agreed to by the wedding planner.

"I make the rules, I do not abide by them."

I would have said something in rejoinder, but Severu places the tip of his knife at the center of the sweetheart neckline on my dress. I suck in a breath, but before I can get too worried, my husband cuts my dress right down the center of the bodice.

"We have scissors you can use for that," the doctor says, but it's already too late.

The wedding gown is in tatters around me. I am not wearing a bra because the one I had for my maid-of-honor dress hadn't been strapless and I am sure that is obvious even though only the valley between my breasts has been revealed.

"Turn around," Severu barks at the doctor.

I assume the man obeys because my husband makes several more cuts with that wickedly sharp knife until the silk is in tatters around me.

Severu looks down at my now bared breasts and something flares in his eyes. Despite my pain, that look heats my blood and makes my vaginal walls contract.

I should at least try to cover myself, but I don't. What is wrong with me?

Then Severu's eyes shift lower, and his expression takes on near demonic fury. "That piece of shit coward."

I look down and see the now dark purple bruises mottling my skin over my lower ribs. Even though it hurts, I force myself to take a deep breath and the pain remains a steady throb. Not broken. I was right.

Though I have no doubt Severu will insist on me being X-rayed regardless.

He takes several intentional deep breaths himself and the aura of rage around him becomes less pronounced. Then with two flicks of his wrist, his knife slices both sides of my blue lace panties. He pulls them off and despite the situation, my body reacts with a totally inappropriate wave of desire.

"I don't think those needed to go," I croak.

"Actually, for the X-rays and scans it would be best you were completely naked under your hospital gown," the doctor chimes in.

Severu ignores us both and lifts me, oh so carefully, away from the remains of my wedding dress and slides me over to the treatment bed. He grabs a sterile white sheet and lays it over the top of me.

It's soft and probably has a thread count higher than the sheets on my bed at home. "Alright?"

"Ye..." I clear my throat. "Yes."

"You need to remove your jewelry as well, Mrs. De Luca." The doctor may be speaking to me, but Severu reacts as if the words were meant for him.

First, he takes the tiara from my head and places it on the table. Then he removes the remaining pins from my hair and I'm sure I look like a bedraggled urchin wearing too much makeup rather than a bride right about now.

After that, he reaches behind my neck to unhook the clasp on the necklace. "It is a shame to take this off you. It makes you look like a queen."

He's not talking noble royalty, but a mafia queen. I've heard Severu referred to as King of New York. I guess that would make me his queen.

The thought is truly disconcerting. I have not yet considered all that will change in my life because I married Severu De Luca.

His fingertips brush my neck as he pulls the necklace away and I shiver.

"Do you need a blanket *mi dolce gatto*?" His knowing gaze says he knows exactly why I shivered, and it's got nothing to do with being cold.

But I would feel better with a blanket on top of the thin sheet covering my nudity and say so. He immediately demands one and then drapes it over the sheet.

He goes back to removing my jewelry, taking off my earrings and then my ring. Severu puts everything into a bag provided by the nurse. Seeing millions of dollars' worth of diamonds and gold in a drawstring plastic bag makes me want to laugh despite my pain.

Two women in scrubs arrive and one of them leaves the room with the gurney.

"I assume I can turn around now," the doctor says.

"Yes." Severu stands sentinel on one side of my bed.

With a look at Severu, the doctor approaches me. "I would like my nurse to remove your makeup to get a better idea of what damage was done to your face."

"Okay."

"I will do it," Severu says again.

Sheesh. Just how am I going to get X-rayed if no one else is allowed to touch me?

The nurse hands Severu a packet of cleansing wipes. It's the same brand Carlotta uses for makeup removal. How equipped is this place?

Severu takes one out and carefully wipes the makeup from my face. He uses a second one to make sure he's gotten it all without having to rub against my tender skin.

I put my good hand out, for the wipe. "I want to take off my eye makeup too."

He hands it to me, and I remove the last vestige of makeup from my face, feeling inexorably free after doing so. I really hate wearing the stuff.

The doctor reaches for my face under Severu's watchful eye and prods my cheek. Asking for pain levels, how certain pressures feel. I tell him and he seems satisfied my cheek is not broken.

The fact that there is no swelling is my first clue, but then I'm not a doctor.

"Now for your ribs." The doctor reaches for the top of the blanket and sheet, but stops when Severu barks, "I'll do it."

My husband arranges the bedding so the bruises over my left ribs are exposed and nothing else.

The initial physical exam confirms my belief that my ribs are not cracked, but as I thought Severu insists on X-rays being taken. A portable X-ray machine is brought in, and necessary safety measures are taken.

Severu does not like that he has to stand with everyone else behind a clear wall while the images are taken of first my ribs, then both my hands and forearms, though only one of them is hurt. The doctor takes an X-ray of my head as well, confirming there is no damage to my cheekbone.

"There is a hairline fracture on your pinky finger," he says to me when he is done. "But no other damage to bone, though I am sure you are aware that you have a remodeled break on your clavicle bone and two ribs."

I didn't know about the clavicle, but I did the ribs.

"Any others?" Severu has returned to my bedside and hovers like a gargoyle.

"At some point she suffered a spiral fracture in her right forearm."

Now, I understand why the doctor X-rayed both of my hands and arms. He didn't do any X-rays on my lower body, so he won't see the worst of the damage, which is the hip that shattered from the fall that killed my mother.

"You thought I was lying?" I ask Severu.

On the one hand, he barely knows me. On the other, he can see with his own eyes what my father is capable of.

"The spiral fractures are rare, but can indicate abuse as they occur from twisting or pulling a bone with great force. They almost never occur from a fall, or being hit with an object." The doctor's voice is clinical.

But these are not random medical facts to me. They are the story of my past.

"If we exhumed your mother's body, we would find all sorts of the same healed injuries, wouldn't we?" Severu asks me.

"No." I sigh. "My father had my mother cremated." Getting rid of the evidence.

"There was a casket at the funeral. It was buried in the Jilani family plot."

"It was empty except for an urn of ashes and whatever my father put inside to make it heavy so the pall bearers wouldn't notice."

"How do you know that? You were still in the hospital when she was buried."

"He taunted me with it."

SEVERU

I am so enraged, I want to tear Francesco Jilani limb from limb.

I already instructed Miceli to take him to the box. I had planned to punish the man and remove him from his position as my consigliere. Now, I know I will kill him.

My fury is not reserved for Francesco though. How could I allow the man to dance with my wife after what he did to her this morning? Am I so worried about what my syndicate thinks that I put her in the path of danger for the sake of appearances?

"Leave," I bark. "Everyone out."

"But we need to discuss treatment," the doctor says.

"After," I say.

Everyone leaves, even Aldo. Catalina is looking at me with confusion.

"I am sorry." It is the first time I have said those words since becoming a made man at fourteen.

Her eyes widen and her mouth drops open with a puff of air. "But I thought you never apologized."

"I have never done something I was willing to apologize for until now."

"You are sorry you made me dance with him?" she asks, like she wants to make sure.

"Yes. But I am also sorry that I did not know what he was doing to you."

"You couldn't have done anything. Not even the don can interfere in family matters."

"I could have removed him from his position."

"Yes, but that wouldn't have stopped him. It probably would have made him worse."

She is right and for only the second time in my life, I feel helpless. The first was when my father died of a heart attack. And now, as I look at the woman I married this morning and realize if I hadn't done so, she would have continued to be abused until she ended up like her mother.

Dead at her father's hand.

CHAPTER 8

SEVERU

I allow the doctor and Aldo back into the room.

"This is a compound of witch hazel, arnica, and other medicinal herbs." The doctor goes to hand a tube of cream to Catalina.

I put my hand out for it. He had to touch her for the exam; that was enough.

He doesn't hesitate to hand the tube to me instead, but keeps his attention on my wife's face. "It will help with the bruises and swelling on your hand and mitigate some of the pain. I also want you taking a staggered regimen of two different analgesics for at least three days. That will also help with the pain and swelling."

I put it in the pocket of my tuxedo jacket. I will apply it to Catalina's bruises when we are alone in our room later and no one else can see her body when I remove the clothing covering them.

"Alright," she says to the doctor.

"Do not skip doses and make sure you never take them on an empty stomach. They can wreak havoc with your stomach lining otherwise."

Catalina frowns. "If you say so."

"She will take every dose," I say, more for my wife's understanding than the doctor's.

She gives me a disgruntled look but doesn't argue.

"Apply ice packs to the affected areas several times a day for twenty minutes at a time. If you ice all three areas at the same time, you may get chilled, so make sure you have a blanket handy."

Catalina rolls her eyes at the doctor. "I think I can figure that out."

I feel a twitch in my lips that is almost a smile.

"Yes, well," the doctor says. "The bruising on your face and hand should heal within a matter of days, but your ribs will take four to six weeks."

"Will that hinder her ability to have sex?" I ask.

Catalina blushes violently, covering her face with her undamaged hand. "Did you have to ask that?"

"Yes," I assure her. I want her, but I will not take her if it will cause her further damage.

"She will do better with you above her until her ribs heal, either on her back or on all fours," the doctor says, showing no signs of reticence discussing this subject. "But do not allow your weight to rest on her in either position. No strenuous intercourse that shakes her body too much."

In other words, be gentle with my new wife. I am not a gentle lover, but if it means I get to sink my cock into her pussy without waiting six weeks, I can control my usual inclinations.

Catalina makes a strangled sound but doesn't lower her hand from her face. "Can we be finished talking about this?"

I look at the doctor. "Any other limitations?"

"No," he says.

Aldo coughs. Catalina's hand comes down and she glares past me at my head bodyguard. "Don't you laugh. And don't you dare repeat this conversation to anyone."

"Aldo would never repeat a private conversation between us," I tell her. The man is too smart to do something that stupid.

"It's not exactly private. The doctor and nurse are here. So is Aldo," she says in a tone that can only be described as grumpy.

Usually, I would chastise someone for talking to me like that, but my new wife amuses me. Most women are too afraid to talk to me with anything other than deference. My mother and sister being the two exceptions, but even they tread more lightly than Catalina has done since we met.

I still remember the way she lectured me about taking the time to get to know her sister to help alleviate Carlotta's fears before the wedding. No one else would have dared to take me to task like she did.

I'd done what she demanded too.

She has suffered abuse from her father for years and she should be afraid of her own shadow, but she is not afraid of me. The most terrifying man in all of New York.

Her lack of fear toward me gives me a strange sensation in my chest.

I ignore it.

"Focus on breathing deeply as often as you can, Mrs. De Luca," the doctor adds. "Consistent shallow breathing can lead to infections and even pneumonia."

From what she said earlier, my wife is already aware of this. Because of her previous bruised and broken ribs.

A wave of fury crashes through me, but I control it. I will vent my anger later, on the one who deserves it. Her father.

Catalina's brows draw together in a frown and I think she's going to get snarky with the doctor again, but she asks, "How am I going to get home?"

"The same way we came." Does she think I'm going to abandon her here?

"Are you going to carry me out of here wrapped up in a sheet? Someone sliced my dress into pieces, getting it off me."

I did not have a choice. Doing it any other way would have caused her unnecessary pain. "What size are you and what sort of clothes would be most comfortable for you right now?"

She tells me her size and then says, "Honestly? I wish I could just put on a nightgown, but I know that's not how the don's wife should be dressed outside of my bedroom."

"Our bedroom," I correct her before she starts getting ideas about having her own room. "So, a loose fitting dress?"

"Maybe a maxi dress with a princess waist. Something I don't need to wear a bra with."

I would prefer her to wear a bra whenever she is in public because her gorgeous breasts are mine alone to ogle. However, in this instance, an exception can be made.

Tomorrow, however, I will have my mother buy Catalina undergarments that will not constrict her ribs.

"Aldo, send one of the men to buy my wife a dress like she described and some kind of jacket or sweater to wear over it."

"Don't forget underwear." Catalina blushes again, as embarrassed by the request as she was me talking to the doctor about being able to have sex.

I nod to Aldo, to let him know to do as she says.

She gives me a testy glance. "Make it a lightweight jacket or sweater," Catalina instructs Aldo. "It's seventy-five degrees outside."

"The SUV will be colder from the aircon," I point out.

"If I get chilled, we can either turn it off," she says in a tone that borders on belligerence. "Or you can give me your jacket like a gentleman."

"You do remember that I am still your don." My own voice is not gentle.

She scowls at me.

What is wrong with her? I find her lack of fear of me refreshing, but this blatant antagonism in front of others is unacceptable.

"You are my husband first," she claims.

I do not argue because I am not sure if I agree or disagree with that statement and until I know, I will not say anything.

One thing I am sure about is that she must show me respect in front of others, and her attitude is anything but respectful right now. I let her see the displeasure in my expression.

Her eyes widen and she seems to realize what she has done. "I am sorry, Severu. I don't mean to be disrespectful. Of course your man should get me whatever kind of clothing you think best."

I don't like the lack of emotion in her tone, or the way she seems to stare through me rather than look at me. However, I have to set a precedent here. I cannot allow her disrespect to go unanswered.

I cannot show weakness.

My mouth set in a severe line, I acknowledge her apology with an inclination of my head. Then I snap my fingers at Aldo and he immediately starts texting on his phone.

CATALINA

Every time I let myself forget that I'm the consolation bride and start to think I somehow matter to my new husband, he says or does something to remind me of my place.

In the mafia there is a hierarchy for everything, but I always find myself at the bottom.

Don't forget your place.

Women in our world hear that phrase repeatedly before we are old enough to attend school. My father has certainly said it often enough to me, but my mother did too before her death. Zia Lora says it too. It's an attempt to protect me, but the words are something I will never say to my own children.

They'll hear it anyway. From Severu. From Aria. But not from me.

I'm so tired.

Turning my head away from Severu's penetrating gaze, I let my eyes close. I do not know how long I lay there in silence. At some point, I hear the doctor take his leave. I hear two sets of footsteps, one the hushed thuds of rubber soled shoes. The nurse. She is gone too.

Severu says something to Aldo about a box. They talk in low tones together and I don't try to hear what they are saying.

I'm doing my best to manage my pain. The pills Severu gave me earlier have long since worn off. The poking, prodding and shifting necessary for my examination has only made everything hurt more.

I hear the rustle of movement near me.

"I have pain relievers for Mrs. De Luca." It's the nurse.

Apparently, she noticed how my husband refuses to let anyone near enough to touch me now that the exam and X-rays are finished. Unlike the doctor, she speaks to Severu rather than to me, the patient.

So, I ignore her and do not bother to open my eyes.

"Catalina, I know you are not sleeping." Fingertips lightly touch my face and turn it toward the sound of Severu's voice.

I open my eyes and look at him. "I wasn't trying to pretend I was."

"Here are pills for you to take. They will help with the pain."

If he knows I wasn't sleeping, he knows I heard the nurse say they are painkillers. I frown, but don't call him out on stating the obvious. I'm not sure what's wrong with me right now that I would even be tempted to do that.

It's like the patience I usually extend to the world is all used up.

I see the small paper pill cup in his hand and the glass of water with a straw in his other one. Unlike other hospitals, it really is a glass, not a plastic cup, or the water bottle they give you when you're in overnight.

I reach for the pills, and he gives them to me. I toss them to the back of my throat and then reach for the water, but he holds onto it and brings the straw directly to my mouth.

I drink and swallow the pills.

"Drink more water," he instructs when I try to turn my head away again.

I refuse the offered straw. "I'm not thirsty."

"Drink."

"You are really bossy." And I'm not going to apologize for saying that either.

I'm tired. I am in pain. And I am fed up.

At least at home after my father hits me, I'm allowed to retreat to the quiet solitude of my room. This trip to the hospital has gained nothing but a destroyed wedding dress and confirmation of what I already told Severu. Nothing is broken.

Rather than giving me that disapproving glare he did before, my husband winks at me. "It comes with the job description."

He winked at me. Why?

I gulp down water because I don't know how else to respond.

"On a scale of one to ten how is your pain level?" The nurse looks at me expectantly.

Instead of answering, I ask, "What does it matter?"

"I need it for the chart. Then we can reassess in thirty minutes to see how effective the analgesics are. The doctor is willing to prescribe a few days of a mild opioid if necessary."

"I won't take them, so it makes no difference."

"Why are you refusing to tell the nurse how much pain you are in?" Severu asks me, like I'm being unreasonable.

I let my eyes slide shut and ignore them both.

"Fuck," Severus says under his breath. "You were asking for pain relievers back at the reception, before we left." He brushes his hand gently over my temple.

I can't stop the moisture from slipping out of the corner of my shut eyes.

"She is in a lot of fucking pain." Severu must be talking to the nurse. "Get out."

I hear the nurse leave.

"Aldo, stand on the other side of the door," Severu orders his bodyguard.

Then something cool and smooth is brushed onto my throbbing cheek.

"It's the cream from the doctor." Severu's voice is low and soothing.

I wouldn't have thought soothing was in his repertoire, but then I wouldn't have expected winking to be in it either.

CHAPTER 9

SEVERU

Of course, my wife is cranky as hell.

She's in pain and this is the first time we've done anything to address it since this morning. I feel like an idiot and that is not something I am used to.

I should have insisted she be given pain killers as soon as we arrived at the hospital, but I was too focused on finding out how serious her injuries are. Because I feel guilty for pushing her into dancing with her father and allowing him to add to them.

Catalina doesn't react to me spreading the cream on her bruised face, but when I tug the sheet and thin blanket down so I can do the same to her ribs, her eyes fly open.

Her arm comes up to try to cover the perfect round globes of her tits. "What are you doing?"

She didn't try to hide them from me earlier, but now she wants to. Why?

She is mine. I am going to look my fill and I'm going to play with them too. From the look on her face, it will be better if I don't tell her that right now.

"I want to put this on your bruises." I hold up the tube of cream.

"Earlier, with the doctor, you only uncovered that spot."

"Because he did not need see more of you."

"Neither do you."

"I am your husband," I remind her. "And you didn't mind me looking earlier."

"A gentleman wouldn't bring that up."

"I became a made man at fourteen, Catalina." She knows that means I made my first kill then. "I have never claimed to be a gentleman."

She reaches for the tube of lotion with her bruised hand. "I'll do it."

"No." I squeeze some of the cream onto my fingertips and start to apply it to the large bruise mottling her creamy skin over the left side of her ribcage. "Relax, wife."

"I..." She doesn't continue, like she doesn't remember what she was going to say. Her breathing grows ragged.

"Am I hurting you?"

"No." Then she thinks better of her answer and says, "It would be better if I did it for myself, so I don't press too hard."

"Too late, Catalina. You've already admitted I'm not hurting you."

"Severu."

"Yes, *mi dolce gatto*?"

"Why do you call me that?" She bites her lip and I realize I'm going to have to break her of that habit.

I press gently to remove it from her teeth, like I did before the wedding ceremony. "If you don't watch out, you're going to need an icepack for your lip as well as everything else."

"And then I might need *two* blankets to keep me warm." The humor in her voice, even if it is sarcastic amusement at the doctor's expense, is so much better than pain and exhaustion.

I let my fingers brush the underside of her breast as I apply more of the lotion.

She lets out a soft gasp, her eyes seeking mine. "What are you doing?"

"Trying to help you to feel better." Pleasure is a great antidote to pain as she will discover.

"I think there's enough lotion on those bruises," she says breathlessly.

"Are you sure?" I leave my hand resting where it is, barely touching her. She swallows and nods.

I lean down and kiss the bruise and then I kiss the top of each of her pretty tits, letting the tip of my tongue swipe along her smooth skin. The pulse in her throat flutters like a bird. Good. When I am done with her, her heartbeat will be running wild and her body will be filled with endorphins to combat the pain.

But first, I need to finish applying the cream. I put a dollop on her hand and gently massage it in. I make sure I spread it over each individual finger. Satisfaction fills me as goosebumps of arousal travel up her arm. My wife is so responsive.

When I am done with her hand, I carefully place it against the bed beside her and then lean down so I can kiss the other one that is trying to cover her generous mound. Plump flesh taunts me from between her spread fingers. I slide my tongue over it, licking her tit and the sides of her fingers.

"You can't do that here," she admonishes me, scandalized.

I almost laugh. I never laugh, but my sweet, courageous wife is so damn amusing. "I assure you, I can. Let me see your gorgeous tits, *mi dolce gatto*. Are your nipples hard for me?"

"I can't," she gasps out. "Not here."

"You let me see them earlier."

She blushes. "Stop reminding me. Besides, you're the one who cut my gown from my body."

"I cut something else off of you too." My hand brushes over the blanket at the apex of her thighs.

She jerks and then winces.

"No moving," I order. "You'll hurt yourself."

"I'm not the one doing all the inappropriate touching in a hospital room."

"It is not inappropriate to touch my wife," I growl. "You are mine. All of the time. Wherever we are." The sooner she realizes that, the better.

Her eyes widen and she goes to bite her damn lip again.

I let out a sound of displeasure and stop her teeth from sinking into her lip by placing my finger into her mouth up to the first knuckle. "Stop doing that. You're going to draw blood."

The tip of her tongue brushes against my finger, like she can't help herself. I almost groan with how good it feels, but right now isn't about me getting off, it's about giving my wife pleasure to combat the pain.

It has also become a chance to show her that she belongs entirely to me. Anytime. Anyplace.

CATALINA

"Now, move your arm." The dominance in Severu's tone sends a thrill through me.

His finger is still in my mouth, hard and solid, stopping me from biting my lip, or talking. How can I be so turned on with all the competing points of pain in my body? Not to mention knowing there are several of his men just on the other side of the double doors. Doors that do not lock.

My ovaries are exploding. Like my body has finally figured out why being touched by a man is so addictive for some women. I have a terrible feeling that if I don't watch out, I'm going to become obsessed with having Severu's hands on my skin.

Does any of that stop me from obeying him and letting my arm drop to my side? No.

He takes his finger from my mouth, sliding it along my lip as he pulls his hand away. "Very good, *bella ragazza*."

Beautiful girl. Warmth unfurls inside me. Does he really think I'm beautiful, or is this just sex talk?

"I like that better than *good girl*," I admit.

The latter will always be associated with him pushing me to do something I didn't want to, something that ended up hurting me.

Something flashes in his eyes, but he does not reply.

"Your nipples are such a pretty raspberry red." His dark gaze is locked on my breasts. "Do they taste as sweet as they look?"

Why do I feel like I want to arch my back and display myself for him?

"Remember, what I said?" he asks before kissing me. He lifts his head like he expects an answer.

I have none to give.

"Do not move," he reminds me in a tone that sends pleasure zinging along my nerve endings. Is it possible to orgasm from voice alone?

He kisses me and brushes his lips down my chin to my neck, where I can feel my heart beating a mile a minute. "I am going to give you pleasure, but if you move and hurt yourself, I will not be happy."

His teeth scrape over my pulse point. It is all I can do to remain still from that tiny bit of stimulation. He moves his mouth down my neck and over my collar bone. He kisses me there, laving the spot with his tongue before biting softly and then sucking.

I shiver, but I don't shift my body. At all. I don't arch toward his mouth like I want to, seeking more of that amazing sensation.

He lifts his head and meets my eyes. "You now wear my mark where he hurt you. When you look in the mirror and see it, you will be reminded that I will never allow him to hurt you again."

That's where the doctor said I had a remodeled fracture from a break that I hadn't even known about. I'd just thought the bone was bruised. It had taken nearly two months for the pain to go away completely.

Now my husband has turned the spot into a pleasure zone for me.

His mouth keeps moving downward, his teeth scraping over skin he sooths with his tongue afterward. I don't know how many love bites he puts on me between my collar bone and the top of my breasts, but my body is thrumming with a need that I have never known before.

I am twenty-five years old and though I know pain very well, I am almost totally ignorant about the pleasure my body is capable of feeling. I've tried touching myself, but my clitoris must be a dud, because I never got much out of it.

Only Severu's mouth against my skin is drawing forth sensation after sensation as ecstasy skitters along my neural pathways and sends moisture flooding to my vagina.

He cups both of my boobs with his big hands, kneading them. And it feels good. So good. His thumbs slide back and forth over my nipples, making them ache for more. They're swollen and tight, harder than they've ever gotten from the cold.

He pinches them and I arch with a cry. The pain in my ribs mixing with the pleasure of his touch.

Severu removes both hands, and then presses me back into the bed with careful pressure against my sternum only. "Do you want me to keep touching you?"

"Yes." I have no pride in this moment. Only an insistent thrum of irresistible desire.

"No moving."

"I can't help it." Tears spring to my eyes because I want what he's doing so much but I know I can't control my body. "Help me."

"You only had to ask, *mi bella ragazza.*"

Oh, goodness. I like that. Severu calling me *his* beautiful girl.

Wetness trickles down from my vajayjay, sliding between the cheeks of my bottom. It feels strange. New.

He maintains that gentle pressure between my breasts and cups one of my boobs with his other hand. I feel claimed and cocooned. He puts his mouth right on my nipple creating an arc of bliss between it and the bundle of nerves at the top of my nether lips.

He licks all over my nipple and aureole, his tongue first soft and flat and then hard and pointed. I want to lift toward his mouth, but his hand stops me and I relax into the pleasure, because I can do nothing else.

Then he sucks the hard peak sending another one of those shocking arcs of intense pleasure to my clit. I need more air. I'm sucking in as deep of breaths as my ribs will allow, but I can't get enough.

What is happening to me? Something knots low in my belly, a spring that coils tighter and tighter. Then the hand cupping my breast, slides down my body, until it reaches my mound.

He barely brushes the top of my pubic hair and I moan. That feels incredible. I didn't know hair could be sensitive. He presses down and his middle finger slides between the slick folds of my labia. He rubs first one side and then the other, tightening the coil of pleasure inside me until I want to scream. Then his finger dips inside my virgin opening and I can't help crying out his name.

"Severu," I say again in a tone I do not recognize. "Please."

The suction on my nipple increases and his finger presses deeper inside me. It stings a little, stretching me, but it feels good too. Right. Like having him inside me is what I was created for.

The initial sting morphs into nothing but pleasure and my vaginal walls contract around his finger, trying to draw him in deeper.

Then his thumb brushes over the knot of nerve endings that have never responded to my touch, and it feels like I've been jolted with a live electric wire. Severu makes a circular motion with his thumb. I try to tilt my pelvis to get more of the sensation and his big hand slides from my sternum to my belly, pressing my body down so once again, I cannot move.

Now, it is only pleasure building inside my body toward unimaginable ecstasy.

He slides his pointer finger inside me with his middle finger and I feel the sting of the stretch again. I welcome it and the pleasure that follows almost immediately. He thrusts in and out of me with his fingers, his thumb pressing against my clitoris with every push.

Everything but the pleasure he makes me feel recedes to nothingness.

There is no hospital room, there is no pain from my bruises. There is only this. Ecstasy that I have never felt before.

"Severu, please, I need..." I don't know what I need so I can't continue.

But he knows. He plays my body with the same passion and purpose I play the piano. He knows how to draw forth a melody of desire and delight.

He lets go of my nipple with a pop and then he's kissing me, thrusting his tongue into my mouth in a joint rhythm with his fingers pressing into my body.

The ecstasy detonates inside of me, and I scream into his mouth while my entire body goes rigid with pleasure that he draws out for second after second, moments that feel like a lifetime, until every muscle in my body relaxes and I go totally lax against the bed in utter bliss.

He withdraws his hand from between my thighs and raises his fingers to his mouth, licking my essence off of them while trapping my gaze with his own.

My lips part, a sigh escaping as I watch the most erotic thing I have ever seen in my life. His eyes are dark with lust, color darkening his chiseled cheekbones.

He removes his fingers from his mouth and then slides them inside my own mouth. "Suck. Taste yourself."

I'm not sure why I feel compelled to do as he says, but I let my tongue swirl around his fingers. I taste my own excitement, tart and strange, and the salt of his skin. I suck on his fingers and watch his pupils dilate, his jaw go granite hard.

He likes that.

He lets me suck on his fingers for several seconds before gently withdrawing them from my mouth. Then he pulls the bedding up and covers me once again with the sheet and blanket. "You'll get more later."

"I didn't ask for more." Soft and filled with want, my voice is not at all convincing.

"You will," he promises me in a dark voice. "You will beg for it."

CHAPTER 10

SEVERU

Catalina came so beautifully on my fingers. She is *mi perfetta bellezza,* perfect for me and beautiful in her passion. She loves sucking my fingers; I cannot wait to feel her mouth around my cock.

Later, I tell myself. *Later.*

"Do you feel better?" I ask her.

She blushes, like she wasn't just begging for my touch. So innocent. She's twenty-five, so I do not expect her to be a virgin, but her reactions are too untried for her to have much experience. The primitive part of me is very happy about that.

"Yes, thank you," she says primly.

For the second time in less than an hour, I want to laugh. I shake my head instead. "Do not thank me for touching you. It is my pleasure."

"But you didn't—" She breaks off, obviously too uncomfortable to continue.

My wife is such a contradiction. Her body responds like a Siren, but she blushes like a virgin.

"I will. Later," I promise her.

"Oh." Her face is fire engine red, but the look in her eyes is more interest than embarrassment. "I did not realize that doing that could make my pain go away."

"You have never given yourself a climax to take the edge off of your pain?" I understand her not doing so as a child, but teenage girls masturbate, don't they?

"No."

"Have you ever masturbated?" I ask, curious.

She glares at me. "How is that any of your business?"

"I am your husband. There is no place for false modesty between us."

"My modesty is not false, believe me," she says in a strangled tone.

Not wanting to undo the good I did with her orgasm, I don't press the matter since it is clearly causing her stress. I did not pleasure my wife and end up with a rock hard cock in my pants just to have her tensing up with pain again.

I call Aldo back in and he is carrying a bag from a nearby boutique. He holds it up. "Clothes for Signora Severu."

The staff and my men already refer to my mother as Signora De Luca. I like this name for my wife. It feels more personal. Like she belongs to me, not my family.

Catalina chokes out a, "Thank you." She's blushing again and cannot meet Aldo's eyes.

Does it bother her that he knows I gave her pleasure? She'd better get used to it. Our bodyguards are around almost all of the time. Unless I want to limit our sex life to after we have retired to our room for the night, which is not going to happen, there will inevitably be times they are aware we are fucking.

Wetting a washcloth with warm water, I approach Catalina.

"What's that for?" she asks.

Rather than answer, I push the blanket and sheet up her body until the pretty caramel curls covering her mound are exposed.

She shrieks. "Severu! What are you doing?"

At this point it should be obvious. I push on one thigh. "Let me in."

"What? No! Aldo is right there."

"And his back is to us. Do you want your panties soaked before we even reach the SUV?" It is a reasonable question.

She looks like she thinks I've got a screw loose.

Not waiting for her to get onboard with the program, I push her legs apart and then clean her juices from her inner thighs, pussy, and ass crack.

"I could have done that."

"But why deprive me of the enjoyment of taking care of you?" I slide her panties up her legs. They are white lace. Very bridal. I will enjoy removing them again once we reach our home.

She doesn't try to argue when I help her into her dress. It is exactly what she asked for, made in a flowy, slick fabric with a pattern over a cream background by one of my sister's favorite designers.

Catalina's eyes light up when she sees it. "That won't hurt to wear," she says with approval.

So, it's not the designer she is excited about but the style of the dress and it reminds me how much pain she was in before I touched her.

"What number would you have rated your pain before?" I ask her.

"Before what? Oh," she says, her expression shy. "That. Um...it was a seven, maybe an eight."

What would she consider a nine, much less a ten? My bride would withstand torture better than some of my made men. Not that I will ever allow her to be in that position, but I can't help admiring her pain threshold.

"And now?" I prompt.

"It's much better."

"Give me a number," I insist.

She goes to bite her lip, gives me a look and licks it instead. "Maybe a three? The pain relievers have metabolized, and the cream helped too."

"And the orgasm?"

She glares at me.

"Did it help?" I demand.

"You know it did." Her gaze slides to Aldo and then back to me. "I'm not comfortable talking about this in front of your bodyguard."

"He is now your bodyguard," I tell her, informing Aldo of his change in position at the same time.

"Oh, well the discomfort still applies."

"Get over it and answer my question."

Her glare intensifies. "No."

"No?" I repeat as a question.

She scans my face with her hazel gaze. "I can't just stop being embarrassed."

"But you can answer when I ask you something."

"Fine," she says with an attitude bordering on insolent.

My wife needs to learn her place, but for some reason I feel disinclined to tell her so. I merely wait in silence for her answer.

"The pain went away entirely during my, uh..." She trails off.

I help her out. "Your climax."

"Uh, yes."

"And afterward?"

"It was better."

"But not now?"

She rolls her eyes. At me. "Now I'm stressed having to talk about it which makes me tense and that makes my pain worse."

I nod. Then I kiss her.

She startles at first, and is unresponsive. But then her lips soften and finally her body relaxes completely. I keep my mouth against hers, gently eating at her lips and slipping my tongue inside her mouth leisurely until I feel my own sexual urgency rise.

Then I break the kiss and stand straight. "And now?"

She looks at me in confusion and then understanding dawns on her beautiful face. "Better. Is that why you kissed me?"

"The only reason I will ever kiss you is because I want to," I inform her. "If it has the added benefit of relaxing you, that might influence the timing."

"Oh." She is back to looking confused, but not unhappy.

The nurse chooses that moment to return. She asks my wife about her pain level again. This time, Catalina answers and offers that it was between a seven and an eight when the nurse asked her before. Looking pleased to be able to tick her boxes, the nurse inputs the information on her tablet.

"The doctor said your wife can leave once I go over her homecare instructions with you," the nurse informs me.

"He did not think it necessary to return and inform me of that himself?"

"He didn't mean to offend you," the nurse hastily assures me. "But an emergency patient came in and he didn't want you to have to wait until after he treated him."

"When my wife is in this hospital, there is no patient more important, no emergency that supersedes her care," I inform the nurse in a tone that causes made men to squirm.

The nurse blanches and stutters out, "Of c-course. I am so sorry. I will get the doctor immediately."

"Severu," my wife says my name softly.

"What?" I ask, letting her see with my expression I will not tolerate another bit of disrespect from her, or anyone else.

"Please, I do not want to wait. I am tired." She looks it, the dark shadows under her eyes like more bruises against her pale skin. "Please," she says again. "I want to go home. Maybe you could call the doctor later and yell at him then."

There is only one time I want to hear that word from Catalina. When I am fucking her. She should never have to beg otherwise.

She needs to learn her place.

While it is under me, it is not less than me and it damn sure is not less than anyone else.

"Get on with the homecare instructions," I growl at the nurse.

The nurse appears to hear both the threat and the impatience in my voice because she rushes through the instructions.

"That's all stuff the doctor said before. Why the hell did my wife have to wait through you going over it again?" I demand.

"I'm s-so s-orry," the nurse stutters out. "It's hospital policy, Mr. De Luca."

"Get another tube of that arnica shit. My wife says it helps and I don't want to run out."

The nurse nods and runs from the room.

CATALINA

After he finishes terrorizing the nurse, Severu pulls a shawl out of the bag and drapes it around my shoulders, and then lifts me from the bed.

It's soft and I rub the material between my thumb and forefinger. It will cover as Severu wanted, though the dress itself is an opaque fabric that will not reveal my braless state. If I'm warm, I can wear the shawl bunched up, exposing my arms. If I get cold in the air conditioning of the car, I can cover my arms and wrap up in it.

Did Aldo instruct the guy who went shopping to find the perfect compromise to make both Severu and me happy? I kind of hope he did because then I would feel like I'm not so alone in my unexpected and new situation. That my voice is heard.

Severu settles me in a wheelchair. I don't even try to insist I can walk, because that would mean reminding my husband about my shoeless state. I don't want to put the heels back on, much less try to walk in them.

I don't have to worry. Severu has no intention of allowing me to walk at all. When we reach the parking garage, his SUV is parked right by the bank of elevators. My husband lifts me from the wheelchair and carries me to the car. He puts me in the backseat and does up my seatbelt, before going around to the other side and climbing in beside me.

He spends the ride to his home on his phone and rather than feeling ignored, I'm appreciative of the chance to retreat into my own thoughts.

I cannot believe I am married to Severu. The most powerful don in New York. I'm still a little stunned that he touched me like that in the hospital room too. If his fingers feel that good, what will it be like to have his sex inside my body?

I shiver at the thought.

"Are you cold?" he asks without looking up from his phone.

"I'm fine." I let the shawl spread down my arms and hold it to myself.

"Turn off the A/C," he barks out. Then he's back to texting, or maybe writing an email. Something where his thumbs are busily tapping away on the screen of his smartphone.

The order leaves me feeling almost as stunned as him touching me so intimately at the hospital. When I suggested that solution if I was chilly, he gave me a look like I'd thumbed my nose at him and flipped him the bird at the same time. I'd apologized for goodness' sake.

My husband confuses me. Like a lot. He also intrigues me, and I can't stop stealing glances at his harsh profile. He can be cruel and domineering. Yet he seems to care about my comfort. I think he's ignoring me, but he notices when I shiver.

He's a big man and strong, which should frighten me after my experience with my father. Only, when his muscles rippled against my side when he carried me, it excited me. The fact he didn't so much as take an extra breath doing it was also a turn on.

CHAPTER 11

CATALINA

I am surprised when we pull into yet another parking garage. This one is underneath a U-shaped art deco building.

"Where are we?"

"Our home."

From the way Carlotta talked, he lived with his family in a mansion. "I thought you had a house."

"We do. In the Hamptons. But we live here."

"Uh. Okay."

"What?" he asks as he pulls me out of the car and lifts me against his chest for the umpteenth time today.

"From the way Carlotta talked, it sounded like you lived in a mansion even bigger than my father's."

"Our home comprises the top two floors of the building as well as exclusive access to the rooftop. The floor below is made up of apartments for our staff."

Remembering how large the building had looked when we arrived, I now understand what my sister was talking about. The De Luca home is more than twice the size of my father's house. The central part of the building is about the same size and it has both a left and right wing that are easily fifty feet long. If you add the floor with their staff apartments, It's over three times the square footage of my family's mansion.

Are all the family bedrooms in the same wing, or even on the same floor? I wish my sister had paid closer attention and shared what she saw.

Severu carries me into the elevator. We are accompanied by half of his bodyguards. The other half cut away from us.

"Where are they going?" I ask, wanting to confirm we will have fewer bodyguards when we are in his home.

"They will take the freight elevator. Taking all our security in one elevator puts us at too high of a risk. The whole family never travels in the main elevator together either."

"That's a pretty cautious protocol. Don't you have security in the building already?"

"Yes." He doesn't elaborate.

I decide not to ask him to because we're almost to our floor. When the doors slide open to a massive foyer, my eyes try to take in everything at once. There is a life size statue of a woman wearing an evening gown done in the same art deco style of the building in the center of the foyer. This era of art, architecture, and style is one of my favorites.

"That is a sculpture of my 2nd great-grandmother." Severu's chest rumbles against me as he speaks. "The De Luca's have lived here for the past hundred years."

I look at the carved marble more closely. "She was beautiful."

"Yes, she was. She was sent over from Sicily to marry my great-grandfather when she was 18. He was 38."

"That is quite the age gap."

"Not so uncommon in those days."

I am glad Severu is only ten years older than me instead of having an entire generation separate us. Our perspectives on life are different enough.

Yes, we were both raised as part of the mafia family, but him being a male and future don meant he had an entirely different upbringing than mine. He was trained to fight and handle weapons. He became a made man by killing someone before he was legally an adult.

While I attended an all-girls boarding school in my teen years and the only violence that touched my life was my father's temper. Severu went to Harvard University and everything I have learned since high school has been via online courses and lectures, documentaries, and reading.

Not wanting to focus on our differences, which will only increase my nerves, I take in the living room, visible through an open archway. It is decorated with a mix of modern furnishings and 1920s art deco pieces. It's amazing. Even the gorgeous room cannot keep my attention when I am in Severu's arms though.

I look up at him only to find him staring back at me, like he was waiting for me. "Welcome to our home, Catalina."

The words roll through me in an inexorable wave, breaking down walls I've built up over decades. How does this man get to me so quickly? So easily?

He's not perfect. He messed up making me dance with my father. He's arrogant and bossy. But he's careful with me too. He gave me amazing pleasure to dull my pain. He carries me around like he likes it, not because he has to.

"You confuse me," I say to him.

"Do I?" he asks.

I nod. "You can put me down now." I can walk barefoot now that we are in his...our home.

"I don't think I will. There is still one threshold to carry you over."

He's talking about the bedroom. The idea of going directly to our bedroom fills me with excitement. I want more of his touch. I want to touch him too. I want to see him naked. It's only fair. He's already seen my body.

He carries me across the foyer to the right and then down a hallway. When we reach a set of double doors, he leans down and opens one without jostling me.

His strength makes me feel safe.

Severu kicks the door shut behind him and then carries me through a private sitting room to the bedroom, once again shutting the door behind us with his foot. Only then does he lower me to my feet.

I look around. The room is massive, with a huge bed in the center of one wall. I suppose a man as tall as him needs a large bed, but this one is like an island. All the furniture is in dark wood tones, the rich paneling on the walls a lighter shade that adds warmth to the room. Floor to ceiling drapes cover massive windows on one wall. Is there a terrace outside them?

It's the scent of sandalwood and masculine cologne that permeates the room I like best though. It's him.

I inhale, reveling in the knowledge that this is now my inner sanctum too. That I have a right to be here because I am Severu's wife.

I am Severu's wife.

I have gone from believing I would leave the mafia behind forever to making a lifelong commitment to the man who *is* the mafia in New York.

The snick of a lock has me turning to face him. Severu watches me with a predatory glint in his dark eyes.

"Are you ready to consummate our marriage, *mi dolce gatto*?"

With no thought of trying to prevaricate, I nod.

I'm nervous, but I want him so much. The entire three months I helped my sister prepare for her wedding, I fought my intense and inexplicable desire for the don. I had believed that leaving New York was not only necessary to keep me safe from my father, but to stop me from making a fool of myself over the man who I thought was going to be my sister's husband.

Now, he's mine.

"Good." He shrugs off his jacket and then tugs the bow out of his tie so the black ends fall on either side of his tuxedo shirt's white collar.

I move toward him wanting to help, to unwrap him like a present. He is my gift, the one I never thought to have.

But he shakes his head. "This time, I will undress both of us."

Because of my injuries? Or because of something else?

The possessive, dominant expression on his face says it might be simply because that's the way he wants to do it.

He unbuttons his shirt, exposing a tight sleeveless white undershirt that clings to his muscular chest. He removes the crisp white fabric and the dangling tie, dropping them on the floor, before peeling off his undershirt to reveal dark chest hair. His upper body is on full display.

Drawn by an irresistible force, I step up to him and trail my fingers over his abs. I cannot help myself. He has an eight pack. "I thought that was a myth."

"What?"

My answer is to brush each bulge of his ab muscles until I've counted all eight with my fingertip. His face is almost frightening as dark, animalistic desire takes it over.

He likes when I touch him.

But he shrugs, like his amazing physique and the desire I see on his handsome face are no big deal. "I have to be stronger, faster, smarter and more ruthless than any other man in New York."

"Because you are don?"

He nods.

"Other dons are not like you."

"Some are. Some aren't." His tone makes it clear what he thinks of the dons that rely on their men to do all their fighting.

He unclasps his watch and then turns to drop it on the dresser.

I gasp. His entire back is covered in a tattoo done in black ink. I'm not sure why I'm so shocked. It's common practice for mafia men to wear tattoos that symbolize important events in their lives. This one is a ferocious lion standing on a hill, roaring his power for all to hear. There is a gravestone in the background. I'm sure the date tattooed on it is when his father passed.

Once again unable to control my urge, I reach out to trace the lines of the lion's body. Severu shudders and my body responds with a flood of wetness between my legs.

"This is beautiful." I don't know why I whisper.

"I got it right after my father died."

As I guessed. "When you became don."

"Yes."

He lets me touch until I've run my fingers over every line. Then he turns to face me, his expression ferocious with its violent need.

But I'm not frightened. I'm excited. And intrigued. His male nipples are hard points in the center of dark, coin sized discs. Would he enjoy me touching them like I enjoyed him playing with mine? Curious, I circle one with a fingertip and then brush over it. He sucks in a harsh breath.

The way his chest rises and falls under my hand fills me with pleasure and a sense of power. I can arouse him like he does me. "You like it too," I observe.

"Yes."

"Will you like this as well?" I lean forward and gently tug on one tiny nipple with my teeth.

He groans and puts his hand behind my head, holding me in place. An image of him doing that, his hands buried in my hair, when his hard sex is in my mouth flashes through my brain. I want that, but I know if I try to drop to my knees, I'll regret the exertion.

Pulling my head away so I can look up at him, I tell him. "When I can kneel, I want to take you in my mouth."

"Fuck." He steps back and jerks the rest of his clothes off with rapid movements.

His penis juts out from his body, engorged and darker than the skin on his thighs, it sends a frisson of sensual fear through me. It's much bigger than I expected it to be.

One of the limits of learning on my computer has been that my father had parental controls on both my sister's and my laptops. Which I hate because I haven't been a child for a long time, but it wasn't a fight worth waging with him. I wasn't going to win regardless.

So, no porn sites. No sites with naked bodies at all. Carlotta and I used to complain to each other, but that's as far as it went. Complaining.

I've seen a hard penis before, only because one of the girls at school bought a sex magazine with male models. It was illuminating, but nothing like seeing Severu in the flesh now.

I don't know how something that big is supposed to fit inside me. I have to use the smallest tampons during my monthly, which means changing them more often, but the bigger ones aren't comfortable.

"Can I touch?" I look up at him to see his face when he answers.

His expression is feral, and I feel an answering atavistic reaction in my own body. This thing we are about to do, it is as old as humanity and as natural as the earth itself.

"Yes," he growls out.

I reach out and wrap my fingers around him. They don't quite touch, but that doesn't stop me moving my hand to learn his shape. The skin of his sex is like the softest velvet, but his dick is hard like steel.

"You are so warm." I lick my suddenly dry lips. "I like it."

"You're taking me to the brink, *mi dolce gatto*," he rasps.

CHAPTER 12

CATALINA

"If you come, will you get hard again?" Should I stop touching him?

"Can you doubt it?" he growls. "But I don't want to come until I am inside you."

I bite my lip. "I don't think you are going to fit," I tell him, though my vagina is pulsing with the need for him to try.

He growls and tugs my lip from my teeth. "I told you to stop that."

I shift my gaze from his sex to his handsome face again. "If I don't, what are you going to do?" I'm not sure where this daring sensual woman is coming from, but I like her.

"What do you want me to do?"

"Kiss me?"

"That's hardly a punishment."

I give him a teasing look. "Are you sure?"

"Yes, wife. The way you respond to my kisses tells me you enjoy them very much."

I can't deny it. Nor do I want to. "True."

"Maybe I'll *stop* kissing you. One day of no kisses for every time you bite your lips."

I drop my gaze, feeling like my daring has backfired on me. I don't want that. It's hard enough knowing that for him this is just sex, that I'm not his first choice. For him, our touching is not intimate like it is for me. It's just a bodily urge for Severu. It doesn't connect his soul to mine.

With no kissing, I cannot ignore that lack of intimacy. I cannot pretend. "No."

"No?" he asks, his voice silky.

"I am not a child, and you are my husband, not my father. It is not your job to punish me."

He tips my head up so I can see his face. His eyes are calm, no anger in them like I expect. "I was teasing you, *mi dolce gatto*. I enjoy kissing you too much to give it up for a single day, much less the number of times you abuse that poor lip of yours."

"Oh."

He growls and suddenly he's kissing me, but his lips are not gentle. He devours my mouth, imprinting me with his power and his possession. My knees are weak and I'm panting when he pulls away.

"Time to undress you," he rumbles in a low voice.

I nod and drop the shawl.

He helps me out of my dress without raising my hands above my head. Past experience has taught me that won't hurt so much in a couple of days, but right now I appreciate his consideration.

He kneels in front of me and leans forward to inhale the scent of my feminine core, making a noise of approval. I never imagined him doing this. It's earthy and turns me on even more. My hips tilt forward of their own accord. He exhales against me; his breath sends sensation I do not expect.

Severu rubs his fingers along the crotch of my panties. "You're soaked."

"I can't help it."

"Why would I want you to?" he asks, like it's a rhetorical question.

I guess maybe it is. Getting wet enough for intercourse is a necessary part of lovemaking. I'm not so naïve I don't know that. Still, it embarrasses me a little. He presses his mouth against the apex of my thighs and breathes for long, enticing seconds, sending zings of sensation to my core.

Then without warning, he rips my panties down my legs.

I squeak, but can't jump like I instinctively want to because he has clamped his arm around my thighs. He kisses my mound and then dips his tongue between my nether lips, touching my clitoris and sending pleasure skyrocketing through my body.

"Spread your legs."

I do, though it's hard to stand.

He alternates between laving my folds and sucking on them. His tongue dips lower and he growls against my vulva. "Delicious."

My knees want to buckle, but he still has a muscular arm around my hips, holding me in place. His finger presses against my opening and I feel like I'm going to drown in sensation. He owns my body in a way no other man ever will.

He suckles on my clit. A keening cry sounds and I know it is me.

Severu pulls his head back and looks up at me. I cannot look away from his gaze.

"I want you lying down for this."

I nod, unable to form even a single word of assent.

My husband stands and tugs me over to the bed where he rips the duvet and top sheet off, before picking me up and depositing me in the middle of the vast mattress.

He stands at the end of the bed, his handsome features cast in lines of brutal arousal. "Spread your legs, I want to see your pretty pink pussy."

I make an embarrassing meep noise, but after a couple of seconds, I separate my legs a few inches.

"More," he demands.

Lifting my knees to make it less difficult on my hip, I do what he tells me, only realizing how much more open this position makes my body to him when his dark eyes turn nearly black with lust.

I may not have been his first choice, but he wants me. He's not picturing anyone else while he touches me, his gaze is too intent, too focused on me.

Once again, wetness weeps out of my most intimate place to slide down between my separated buttocks. Only this time, he can see it.

"Look at that sweet little pussy. You are drenched for me." He climbs onto the bed, right between my splayed thighs. "I cannot wait to taste it."

I feel so exposed, but the way he looks at me makes me hot too.

He reaches down and dips his finger inside me to the first knuckle. It's uncomfortable, but before I can decide if I like it, or not, his hand is gone.

He brings it to his mouth and sucks my juices off his fingertip. He hums with pleasure.

His smile is pure sex as he reaches down and swipes more of my cream with his finger. Then he traces it over my lips before pressing against the seam. "Taste."

With no thought of disobeying, I open my mouth and let him push his finger inside. I swirl my tongue, tasting myself again.

"Suck it."

I do, hollowing my cheeks.

"Such a good, obedient wife."

Even in my intensely aroused state, I notice that he doesn't call me a *good girl* again and it warms something deep in my soul that has been cold for too long. He remembered what I said about it.

"Catalina."

"Mmm?"

"You do not have to be on your knees to suck my cock."

I stare up at him, instantly craving the taste of his sex in my mouth, but he shakes his head. "Another time."

He tugs his hand back and my lips make a pop as his finger leaves my mouth because I'm still sucking.

"You are so fucking sexy, wife." Severu leans forward to run his tongue over my lips, licking until I'm sure he's gotten every bit of my juices he rubbed on them. Then he kisses me with fierce intensity.

I tilt my pelvis upward, seeking some kind of friction, but his hand presses me back to the bed and he breaks the kiss. "Stay still."

"I don't want to."

"If you want me to keep touching you, you won't move."

He's protecting me from pain, but it's so hard to keep my body still when he's kissing or touching me. Nevertheless, I nod agreement.

"Good."

He shifts back so he's once again kneeling between my legs. "I want to pleasure you with both of my hands, but that means you have to control yourself. Can you do that, *my dolce gatto*?

"I'll try." I can't promise.

"Good," he says again and warmth unfurls in me at his approval.

I'm determined to keep my hips still because that is what he wants.

Severu runs one forefinger along my labia, up and down, up and down, spreading the wetness from my vagina all over my most intimate flesh.

He dips the middle finger of his other hand inside me, going deeper than before and stretching my sensitive flesh.

My husband groans. "So damn tight."

All I can do is agree. "Uh huh."

The finger rubbing along my folds with such enticing rhythm slides up to press against my clitoris and I want to arch, but I hold myself in place. A strange sound comes out of my mouth. A wordless whine.

"You're doing so well, but perhaps you need some help, hmm?"

"Yes," I breathe out.

He nods and grabs a pillow. Then he slides it under my hips, tilting them upward without putting any strain on my torso muscles. Or my damaged hip.

Severu shifts his body so he's laying between my thighs, his face right *there*. I can feel his breath on me without the barrier of my panties. It's warm and scintillating. I fist my hands in the sheet, needing something to hold onto to tether me to reality. It feels like I'll float away on the incredible pleasure buffeting my body otherwise.

He places one big hand right over my lower abdomen, holding me firmly in place and then his tongue touches me. He licks me from the opening of my vagina, up my labia and then over my clit.

I make a strangled sound and he does it again. And again. And again.

It feels amazing and intimate, but it's not enough. One incredible sensation builds on top of another, but that coil of ecstasy inside me doesn't spring, it just grows tighter and tighter until I feel like I'm going to scream.

"Severu," I gasp. A plea and an acknowledgement of what he is making me feel.

"Patience, *mi dolce bellezza*. I've got you." He kisses my clit, his lips pressing against it enticingly. The tip of his tongue swirls around it and then he nips me right on my nub of pleasure.

I cry out, the ecstasy ratcheting higher inside me. "I can't stand it, Severu, it's too much!"

"You will take what I give you," he tells me in a voice dark with control.

Oh, yikes, why does his domineering bossy side turn me on so much right now?

Using both of his hands, my husband pushes my legs impossibly wide and for once my hip doesn't even twinge. His hands remain on my inner thighs, but they are so big, his thumbs press on either side of my clit. He massages up and down, sometimes sliding over the bundle of nerves with one thumb, sometimes with the other.

His tongue spears into my vagina pressing my sensitized flesh open for his claim. No one else will ever know me this way.

That thought sends me over. I scream, trying to arch off the bed, but his hold on my thighs won't let me. Even in the midst of my ecstasy, he is controlling me, protecting me from pain.

He licks and touches me until the aftershocks are no longer shaking my body and I collapse into boneless satiation.

CHAPTER 13

CATALINA

Severu lifts his head, his beard glistening with my juices and renewed arousal twinges through my exhausted body. He swipes at his mouth with the back of his hand and then comes down over me to kiss me.

I taste myself on him again, this time it feels even more profound as his tongue that was just inside my vagina plunders my mouth, forcing my own tongue to engage in a deeply intimate kiss.

The blunt tip of his erection presses against me, encountering resistance from my tight opening. I crave this act and want nothing more than for him to be inside me, but atavistic dread washes over me.

He's so big, not just his sex, but all over. His body dwarfs mine completely.

This is my first time and as much as my ovaries are exploding right now, a primal part of me fears this act and what it will mean. The claim he will make not only on my flesh, but on my heart.

For him, this is a purely physical act. How could it be anything else? I'm the consolation bride. And he hadn't even shown tender feelings for my sister, the woman he had *chosen* to be his wife.

Reminding myself that it was my beautiful sister he wanted in his bed tonight doesn't stop the emotions washing over me like a tsunami as my body experiences sensual pleasure. At *his* touch.

It isn't just my emotional vulnerability to this man that scares me. Some of the girls at school said it hurt like heck the first time, others said it was no big deal.

With how tight I am and how oversized his erection is, it's going to hurt. A lot. And I *still* crave both the physical connection and the emotional one my heart will make.

He breaks his mouth away from mine, and curses. Like he doesn't want to stop kissing me. "Are you on birth control?" he asks in a strained voice.

Why on earth would I be? I had no idea I would be getting married today. "No."

"You know I need children."

Not he *wants* children, much less with me. He *needs* them. But I do know. For the security of *la famiglia*.

"Yes."

"We haven't talked about it though, whether you are ready for me to plant my baby in your womb."

Near barbaric delight courses through me at the way he says it. I can only answer one way. "I am."

I had hoped that someday, after I ran from the mafia, I would find a man to love and who would also love me and want to build a family, but part of me believed I would never have that. Never know the joy of motherhood.

I want it though. Almost as much as I want Severu.

He nods, but I cannot tell if my agreement has pleased him or not. "I'm clean, Catalina. I don't want to use a condom."

I don't want any barriers between us either. "Then don't."

His body jerks forward, the head of his hardon breaching my vagina. My flesh stretches almost painfully around him.

He stops moving again and grimaces. "Are you clean?"

"I showered this morning." Why does he care about my bathing habits right now?

Is he a germaphobe, or something? Only he already had his tongue inside me, why would he be more worried about putting his penis there?

"Damn it, Catalina, when was the last time you got tested?"

"Tested for what?" I'm starting to feel dirty, like there's something wrong with me.

"Are you serious right now?" he asks with a humorless laugh. "You've never been tested for STDs?"

"Why would I be?" You have to have sex to get a sexually transmitted disease and I'd never even kissed a man before Severu.

"You're twenty-five."

"So?" What does my age have to do with anything? And when can we get back to the touching and kissing?

This is all starting to feel really clinical and I don't like it. I'm nervous enough as it is. I don't need him turning into my gynecologist. Not that I've ever actually seen one of those. Papà isn't keen on yearly physicals, much less his daughters seeing that kind of specialist.

"You don't have a boyfriend."

It's not a question, but I answer anyway and I'm feeling testy. "First off, if I had a boyfriend, don't you think I would have mentioned that before I agreed to marry you? Secondly, where would I meet this mythical creature? In my back yard?"

Regardless of mafia culture, I'm not against sex outside of marriage. Maybe because my father makes such a big deal about keeping Carlotta and me *pure*. Anything important to him is suspect in my eyes.

But when would I have had the chance? I lived as a practical prisoner in my father's house and have since finishing boarding school.

"Your father has men."

What the heck is my husband implying? I shove against Severu's chest, wanting him off of me. He doesn't budge.

I glare up at him. "So, your sister dated your father's men, did she?"

He looks furious I would dare suggest such a thing. "Of course not."

"Why would you think I would do it then?" I demand with equal pique.

"My sister was promised at twelve and engaged at sixteen."

"And married at twenty-two. What is your point?"

"She knew her future husband and would never have cheated on him."

"So, because I was never promised, I was so desperate I went looking for a man among the guards who never once lifted a hand to help me or my mother when my father hurt us?" I am so angry, I could spit. The arrogance of this man.

"I did not mean to insult you."

"Don't try. You've got it locked down without any effort." Suddenly I'm saying whatever is coming into my head and I don't even care if it makes sense. "Sure, I'm so pathetic and sex starved, I've been to bed with at least a half a dozen of my father's men, even though most of them are almost as old as he is. I guess I have daddy issues. They taught me everything I know, so you can thank them later."

Severu's eyes fill with rage and his big body goes rigid above me. "I want names." He sounds like a demon and he kind of looks like one now too.

Because of my sarcastic claim to have past lovers? He makes no sense. He's the one who thinks I slept around with my father's men.

"Would you get real? I am a virgin, you...you *numbskull*."

He stares at me like he's trying to tell if I'm lying.

"I wish I had slept around," I grouse. "You don't deserve to know you're the only man who has ever touched me."

He's completely still above me and he doesn't look like a demon anymore, but he still looks frightening.

He's got that primal expression that says he wants to claim every last inch of me again.

CHAPTER 14

SEVERU

My wife just called me a numbskull. I cannot let that pass.

But she also told me that I was the only man who had ever touched her.

I lever myself up on my arms, so I can see her face better. She's sweaty from passion, her caramel hair sticking to her temples and forehead, but her expression is anything but passionate. She's frowning and I should not find that cute, but hell, the way her lip pouts the tiniest bit is adorable.

"Do you mean you have never had sex before, or are you saying you have never been touched in any way by another man?" Holding my breath, I wait for her answer.

"I said what I meant." Her pout morphs to a full on frown on her kiss swollen lips; her tone is definitely irritated.

I do not know what this unfamiliar warmth is, but I do know the possessive, dark beast that lives inside of me, the one that asserts ownership of New York and my mafia, the one that now wants to imprint my claim on Catalina in a very physical way, is very pleased.

I lean down and press a hard kiss against her lips. "So, you have never been kissed by anyone else?"

"No." She doesn't sound so cranky now; she's breathless.

She reacts so well to my kiss, to my touch.

I almost feel like smiling. "No other man has handled your beautiful tits?" Balancing myself on one arm, I cup her breast and then pinch the nipple with my free hand.

Catalina moans. "No."

"And I am the only one to feel the wet, silky folds of your pussy?" Reaching down, I circle her clit with my thumb. "And this?" I let my thumb press against her entrance.

Her *yes* is long and drawn out; her breath is coming in pants now.

"I am the only person to touch you here?" I slide my hand lower until I can tap against her tight sphincter.

She yelps. "Yes!"

I circle the nerve rich opening, but don't press my fingertip inside. I will save that bit of her virginity for another time. Tonight, my beautiful, untouched wife will bleed on my cock when I break her virgin barrier with it.

I am the first man to taste her, to hear her breathy moans, to feel her pebbled nipples. Fuck, I've never been so close to coming from just my thoughts alone.

"You're the first person to give me an orgasm too. Do you like knowing that?" Catalina asks in a throaty voice.

My wife has realized how her innocence turns me on.

Wait. That can't be right though. "You've never touched yourself?"

"I tried. It didn't work. I thought my clitoris was defective."

I don't laugh because she's so damned earnest, but I can't help saying, "It's not."

Satisfaction feeds that possessive beast more as I realize I'm the one to show her that ultimate pleasure.

"I guess not." She wraps her arm around my neck and gives me that sweet Siren's smile. "Maybe it was operator error."

Laughter bursts out of me. This woman.

"Severu?"

"*Sì, mi dolce bellezza?*"

"Do you want to play operator some more?"

This time my laugh ends in a groan as my cock shifts a just a little bit deeper into her virgin pussy. I am about to say that I'll play more later when I realize that my completely untried wife probably needs more preparation before I bury myself in her tight channel.

Tight not because it had been a while for her, like I thought, but because she'd never had fingers, much less a cock inside of her.

I groan.

But I am no adolescent to lose control. I start by kissing her because Catalina melts when my lips touch hers. Then I worship her body all over again with my lips, teeth and tongue, showing her how erotic a teasing bite on her nape can be, on the inside of her wrist, on the inside of her elbow, on the flesh of her inner thigh. I knead her beautiful tits and she moans when I suck her nipples.

She keeps trying to arch and it turns my crank that I have to hold her still to protect her from straining her ribs.

"Stay still," I remind her.

"You're bossy," she says but her body stops moving.

Even after her ribs are healed, this enforced stillness will be part of our sex life. It feeds my lust. Every time she arches even a little, I stop touching her, waiting in silence for her obedience. And my cock gets harder.

"More," she begs, tears of passion making her hazel eyes glisten.

By the time I put my mouth back on her pussy, Catalina is moaning and desperate for relief. I slide one finger all the way inside her and she jerks, like it hurts. I let her get used to the sensation before I start gently finger fucking her. When she's close to losing it, I pull out.

"Severu!"

"You are very tight, *mi dolce gatto*. Let me prepare you."

"Do it," she orders me.

I smile against her clit before sliding my forefinger and middle finger inside of her. I don't go too deep because I don't want to break that barrier with anything but my cock. She tries to jerk away from the intrusion, but I've got a hold of her thigh and she's not going anywhere.

"I...Severu...it's too much," she gasps out.

"No, wife, it is not enough." Because it is not my cock.

Scissoring my fingers inside her, I alternately nip, suck and lick at her clit and slick folds. As I bring her to another climax, I stretch her so her tight channel can receive my cock. I've never had sex with a virgin before. If it were anyone but this woman, I would not have the patience to make it good for them.

Not when I'm aching with the need to thrust my steel-hard cock deep into her pussy and claim her as mine.

But the primitive need to claim her fully and make her mine fights with the need to protect her. I cannot hurt her. Not that I'm a violent lover, but this concern for her wellbeing is something new. Something more.

I suck on her clit, and she screams, cream squirting around my fingers as her inner muscles clench tight. I rub up against the spot on the front of her pussy walls until she's given me every bit of pleasure she can and her body has gone boneless on the bed.

Only then do I slide my fingers out of her. I suck every bit of her delicious cum off of them, but force myself not to lap at the cream glistening at her pussy opening.

Her untried channel needs to be extra slippery for what comes next.

I shift over her until my cock is once again in place to penetrate her most intimate flesh. "You ready, Catalina?"

She's pleasure drunk and manages only a wobbly nod, but it's enough.

Pressing my head into her, I feel how tight she still is, but I keep going. She whimpers. I force myself to stop and wait for her body to adjust. My muscles shake with tension and the need to move. But I don't. Not until she relaxes under me.

We continue at this excruciatingly slow pace until I have about two inches inside her, with at least six more to go.

I am losing my damn mind with the need to thrust deeper. I don't know if it would be better to finish breaching her with one powerful thrust, or to keep pressing forward a little bit at a time.

"I knew you weren't going to fit." She sounds on the verge of tears.

Something about those words call to the beast inside me. Of course, I will fucking fit. She was made for my cock.

"This is going to hurt, but it will get better." I hope.

She looks at me with trusting hazel eyes, still glistening with moisture that could be from pain or pleasure. "Even if it doesn't, I want it. I want you inside me, Severu."

Damn it. My control evaporates. I thrust forward, pushing the tight walls of her virgin pussy to accommodate my girth and length. I feel the barrier, but I shove through it, going deeper until I'm fully seated and my balls brush against her.

She's biting her lip again, tears running down her temples into her hair. And I realize that with everything that has happened today, this is the first time I have seen her cry.

I should probably feel bad about that. I don't. I feel primal satisfaction. Those tears belong to me.

Her hazel eyes might be drenched, but the expression in them says she still wants this. She still wants me. Wants this.

I will not ruin her first time with my impatience.

I grit my teeth and once again force myself into stillness as I wait for her body to adjust to having me inside. Finally, her vaginal walls relax a little and I can pull back before thrusting forward again.

She cries out.

"Pleasure or pain?" I demand, not sure if I can stop if it's the latter.

"Both. Oh, it's both, Severu."

I reach to slide my hand between our bodies, pressing my thumb against her clit so it shifts with every thrust of my hips.

"Ohhh..." Her eyes go wide. "That feels so good." She sounds surprised.

"It's supposed to." I kiss her, moving my hips in short thrusts, my tip pressing against her cervix with every single one.

"I like that." She groans. "How it feels inside. It hurts a little, but it's like a jolt of pleasure every time too."

My innocent wife enjoys a little pain with her pleasure.

She's so fucking perfect for me. I kiss her and Catalina's tongue tangles with mine, the passion between us building. Is my virgin wife going to cum her first time being penetrated by my cock?

Bit by bit, I elongate my thrusts until I am pulling almost all the way out and slamming back in with each one.

"Yes, Severu, yes!" Catalina cries.

And then I feel it, her body tightens around me, and she screams trying to surge up to meet my hips. I don't allow it. And it's not just to protect her ribs. That dark beast inside me needs to control her pleasure and I let him.

I'm hammering into her pressing my thumb into her clit on each downward thrust, my hand holding her pelvis in place.

She begs, "More...no...stop...please...oh god...*don't stop.*"

I don't make her tell me which she wants, for me to stop, or keep going, because there is only one choice. I keep fucking her until her mouth opens to scream, but the pleasure is so intense no sound comes out.

I let my own climax take me, emptying my seed deep inside her while shouting the one word playing over and over again inside my head. "*Mine!*"

CHAPTER 15

CATALINA

I lay under Severu, so drunk on pleasure, my head is spinning. It hurt. Oh, goodness, did it hurt, but then it felt good. Better than good. It felt intimate and real and *blissful*.

I don't know how many times I came, but my body is a wet noodle.

My husband stays inside me for long minutes after his own shouted climax nearly pops my eardrums. He's breathing hard and shifting his hips so residual waves of pleasure roll through me, and him I assume.

"That was amazing," I say when I can finally make words.

"You are very responsive."

"My clitoris is definitely not defective."

"None of you is defective, Catalina."

Even if he only means the sex stuff, his words warm the cold places in my heart that crave the approval that has been in such short supply in my life.

My hands reflexively grab for my husband as he lifts his big body away from me, but I cannot hold him.

He climbs off of me and the bed.

"Where are you going?" I want him to hold me, but I would be mortified to say so.

"I need a shower."

I stuff down my disappointment, not wanting to look like a clinging bride. After all, it's not as if this is a love match. I'm not even the one he chose to marry. No matter how earth-shattering the sex, I can't let myself start thinking there are any tender emotions between us.

At least not on his side. Whatever I'm feeling can just stay buried.

But my heart hurts as I hear the water come on in the shower. Why didn't he ask me to join him? Is it because of my injuries, or is he just...done with me for the night?

He comes out twenty minutes later, dressed in one of his bespoke suits and putting on his watch. Or *a* watch rather because the one he wore to the wedding is still sitting on the dresser.

"I ran you a bath. I'll help you get into it and then I'll instruct Emilia to come up in a half an hour to help you get out, dried off and ready for bed."

Stunned, I ask. "Where are you going?"

"I have business I need to take care of." He bends down and lifts me in his arms.

"On your wedding night?" Would he have had business if he'd married Carlotta today instead of me?

"I'm not only the don, but I run a multinational corporation, Catalina. You need to be prepared for me working all hours." His words are said coldly, like he's talking to a stranger, not the woman he just made insensate with ecstasy.

He carries me into the bathroom, and I barely notice the luxurious space because I'm trying so hard not to yell at my insensitive husband.

"Our wedding night is not a normal workday," I say as calmly as I can manage.

He places me in the tub, the scent of lavender, peppermint, and something delicious I can't quite place wafting up from the water. I can't imagine that the flowery scent is his usual thing. He probably bought special salts in preparation for his wedding night with my sister.

Thinking like this is not helping my heart, but I can't seem to help myself.

The hot water does feel good, and I moan a little as I relax into the deep tub.

Flaring with lust and desire, his eyes rake over my nudity. "Soak until Emilia comes for you. You'll be glad you did."

"Like you know."

"Believe it, or not, sweet wife, I am not a god, but a mortal man. I strain muscles, I get beat up in training. Soaking helps."

"You're saying you use these oils yourself?" I ask in disbelief.

"Yes. But it's not bath oil." He scoops up water and lets it pour down over my shoulders and the tops of my breasts that are not fully submerged. "It's lavender, peppermint and frankincense oil infused Epsom salts. All are anti-inflammatory."

"Oh. Um...thank you."

"You're welcome." He cups my boob, his thumb rubbing over the sensitized nipple. "So beautiful." He shakes his head and stands, like he has to force himself to do it.

That's something I suppose. Maybe he doesn't want to leave, but has no choice? At least I know the bath salts were not meant for Carlotta, but he did think of me and my comfort when he put them in the water, of the bath he ran for me, even while he was busy getting ready to leave.

Those thoughts are cold comfort when Emilia helps me into bed, where I lay alone, the vast space on his side empty. The bath did help and so do the pain relievers the housekeeper insists I take on Severu's instructions, but I still have to lie on my back because of my ribs.

"If you need anything press this button."

I tilt my head up to see she is pointing at a brass plate in the wall near the headboard. It has two buttons. One black and one white.

"If you press the white button, you will connect to my receiver. If you press the black one, it will connect you to the security detail. It works like a walkie-talkie, so you need to keep the button pressed when you want to speak and release it so I can reply."

Neither of them would connect me to Severu, which is who I really want to speak to right now, but I murmur my thanks before settling my head at a less awkward angle against my pillow.

"I will return to give you your next dose of pain relievers in a few hours."

"Just leave them on the bedside table. I can set an alarm to take them." I already noticed a carafe of water on the table with a glass beside it.

"Oh, no, Signora Severu. I could not do that."

"I insist," I say firmly.

I'm tired and I don't want to argue, but I'm not letting this kind woman lose sleep just to hand me two pills I can just as easily take myself.

Emilia nods. Then she pours water from the carafe into the glass and opens the bedside drawer to pull out a bottle of pain relievers. She shakes out the pills and places them beside the glass of water before putting the bottle back.

"Thank you," I say sincerely. I'm not used to being fussed over and I much prefer this arrangement.

The housekeeper hands me my phone. "So you can set your alarm."

I take it and set the alarm before reaching to put the phone on the table, but far enough away from the painkillers, I won't accidentally knock them off when I'm fumbling in the dark to turn off the alarm.

"If you need anything, please call for me."

I nod. Though I can't think what I could need that I would call someone else to get me.

"Don Severu does not want you going to the bathroom by yourself," Emilia informs me.

"Hmm," I answer noncommittally. If Severu thinks I'm going to wake up someone else to take me pee, he's delusional.

With a nod, Emilia moves to turn out the lights before she leaves and closes the door behind her.

SEVERU

Leaving Catalina to her bath is for the best. Her pussy can't withstand another session so soon after her first time. If I stay, I won't be able to keep my hands off of her, much less my dick out of her.

Besides, I have business that cannot wait until tomorrow.

Francesco Jilani.

Letting him wait in the box until tomorrow would be good psychological torture, but my need to get my hands on him and make him pay for what he did to my wife at our reception overrides strategic rationale.

Her remodeled fractures tell the story of long time abuse, even if she hadn't been as candid with me as she was in the car. My former consigliere did not just hurt what is mine; he broke faith with both my father and me. He lied to his don.

When I arrive at our front building, Miceli and my head enforcer, Angelo, are waiting for me. We go down to the hidden level below the parking garage together. I leave my security detail guarding the elevator doors.

Angelo uses his code and the retinal scan to access the outer room and then the box. When the wall that hides the box slides to the side, I find Francesco dozing, his head lolling forward. The sturdy metal chair we use for most interrogations has been attached to the floor. His ankles and wrists are bound with zip ties to the chair legs and arms.

He's naked. That was a detail Miceli left out in his update to me while Catalina's injuries were being seen to in the hospital.

I look at my brother with a raised eyebrow.

"You would have been pissed at me if I knocked him around for what he did to your wife, so I did this instead."

Yes, all the pain that Francesco would suffer over the coming hours would be my honor to inflict. I start by backhanding him to wake him up. My blow knocks the older man's head back and to the side.

He wakes with a start, jerking his head upright. "What the hell! Severu, what is the meaning of this?"

"The meaning?" I ask. Then I look over at Angelo. "Does being in that chair have any existential meaning?"

"Nope. It's just a good place to dole out pain."

"Cut the shit, Severu. You can't treat me like this. I'm a made man. I'm loyal. I've got rights within *la famiglia*."

I look at the cockroach that called himself my consigliere. He's kept himself in shape, which will make the coming hours more satisfying. He will last longer than a man with no stamina.

I spit in his face.

He shouts curses at me.

"Trust a lawyer to go on about rights," Miceli says. "At least his own."

"You have no rights," I bark. "You betrayed me, your don, like you betrayed my father before me. You are nothing in *la famiglia* now."

"I didn't betray either of you!"

I punch Francesco in the stomach. I want it to hurt, but I don't want this to go too fast. His pain is going to last.

"The hell you didn't. My father had the same policy I do. No capos, no underbosses, no head enforcers, *no consiglieres*," I stress. "Who beat their wives or children."

"That's bullshit. You got no right to interfere with my personal family. They are not mafia business."

"I have every right to get rid of a consigliere who is untrustworthy." I backhand the other side of his face, harder this time.

"I am trustworthy," he slurs a little. "I have spent the last 25 years serving you and your father. That's got to count for something."

"You lied to my father."

"Your father owed me. He had no right to take what was mine."

"He took nothing from you," I say harshly. "You gave your honor away for free."

"You knew if our father discovered that you abused your wife and then your daughter, he would remove you as his consigliere." Miceli's tone is nearly as chilling as mine.

He's furious on my wife's behalf, but even more so on our father's. He trusted this piece of shit and Francesco played him for the fool.

"How I chose to treat my dead wife or discipline my daughter was none of your father's business and it isn't yours either." Francesco sounds like he still thinks he has an argument he can make.

Must be his training as a lawyer. Unfortunately for him, I trained to be a don. A man who can dole out punishment better than any other.

"You want to talk discipline?" I ask, sounding reasonable, though murderous rage boils in my blood.

"Let's talk about how I plan to punish you for your dishonesty. Should I cut out your tongue because you didn't use it to tell me the truth?" I do a spinning kick that lands against his right ribs.

The smell of urine rises strong and pungent. The pissant pissed himself.

"How did you even become a made man? Knock off some old guy in an alley who couldn't fight back?" Miceli mocks.

"Should I cut off your hands because you used them to harm what is mine?" I tie a tourniquet on each arm in preparation.

Francesco sobs and begs me not to do it.

"I thought you had more pride."

"He only knows how to be strong when he's beating a woman half his size." Angelo's voice is filled with contempt, his eyes that are usually dead are burning with disgust.

My head enforcer has his own demons from the past. Demons that give him a personal hatred for domestic violence.

"Maybe I should cut off your ears because you never fucking listened when my father or I told you what we expected from our consigliere." I box both ears, knowing it will hurt and make them ring, but not ready for him to lose his hearing. I have more to say.

"I listened," he lies.

"If you listened, then you know, because we both fucking told you, that my father and I expect you to be above reproach. No man who cannot control his temper with his family will sit in the top ranks and wield power under my authority."

CHAPTER 16

SEVERU

I turn to my brother. "Get the capos and their underbosses here. My men need a reminder that I don't tolerate dishonor."

Miceli nods and heads out of the room. There's no cell reception on this sublevel or the one above.

Before he exits the outer room, I call out to him. "Miceli, tell Domenico to get the treatment records from all area hospitals for Sara and Catalina Jilani going back to the year Sara married this piece of shit."

I don't bother to give instruction to search under Sara's maiden name and other variants Francesco might have used when getting his wife and daughter treatment when he'd gone too far. Domenico is my capo over online gambling and money laundering. His team also oversees our digital security and has some of the best hackers in the country.

They'll know exactly what to look for.

I watch my wife's asshole father while I'm talking to my brother and am satisfied to see his face leach of color. He knows what Domenico is going to find. Evidence of his coverups.

"You're going to fire me as your consigliere in front of everyone, while I'm tied naked to a chair sitting in my own piss?" There's no mistaking Francesco's foolish wish that is all I'm going to do, no matter how he tries to make it sound like that's a fate worse than death.

I burst his bubble of hope without a qualm. "We are beyond firing."

"You can't just kill me," he says, like he believes it.

"I won't *just* kill you. You will pay in pain before I give you death."

He manages some bravado and glares at me. "You'll lose the respect of your capos."

"Even though you would deserve it for beating your wife and daughter, you might be right. Our traditions don't allow me to interfere in your family that way, but the fact you did it in secret so you could remain in your position as consigliere? That's betrayal of your don."

Punishable by death.

"*La famiglia* won't see it that way."

Again, he's living in a fantasy land of wishes. "I am don and none of my men will blame me for killing the consigliere who disrespected me and tried to betray me. Too many of them are witnesses to your dishonor."

"What are you talking about?" But his shifty gaze tells me he knows.

I spell it out for him anyway. "The minute you knew Carlotta had run, you should have told me. Instead, you tried to trick me. You sent Catalina down that aisle wearing her sister's wedding dress and you left her veil on when you should have removed it. Did you think I wouldn't notice the difference?"

The look on Francesco's face said that was exactly what he thought.

"That's fucking offensive," Miceli says, returning faster than I expected. "My brother isn't a fool and the two sisters look nothing alike."

"I know you wanted to marry a beautiful woman," Francesco says like he's latched onto an argument that might save him. "Not damaged goods like my oldest, but I needed to buy time to find Carlotta. I was trying to protect your reputation as much as my own."

Miceli laughs.

I don't. "The only damage to my wife was inflicted by you." I keep seeing that mark on Catalina's cheek, the bruises on her ribs. How many times had she worn similar?

"You weren't trying to protect your don," Miceli says snidely. "The whole family saw you try to dupe Severu into marrying your oldest daughter while thinking it was your youngest."

Furious all over again, I nod. "That's a betrayal no Don would stand for."

"But you made everyone think it was your idea," Francesco whines. "That you discarded Carlotta in favor of Catalina."

"That was for the sake of our guests from outside the Genovese family." It was an easy impression to make when I'd craved Catalina from that first dinner with the Jilani family three months ago.

"You did marry her, even knowing who it was, though." Francesco sounds like he finds that both unbelievable and distasteful.

"Because she has a hell of a lot more honor than you do." Catalina didn't try to pretend to be her sister for even a second longer than she had to in order to get away from her father.

"Domenico is taking care of contacting everyone. They should be here within the next hour," Miceli informs me. "He said he's got access to the major health networks already, so he'll have the records you want by then too."

"There's a lot we can do in an hour that won't spoil the main event," Angelo says.

He's right. I loosen the tourniquets from Francesco's arms and pull them off. They've done their job. Preparing Francesco mentally for what is to come. The puddle of piss around his chair is testament to that.

The threat to cut off his hands and ears is effective psychological torture, I won't be doing that. Because then we would have to dispose of the body in the chemical bath under the floor of the box.

That is not the most expedient path for a well-known lawyer. A car accident that ends in a superheated fire can account for broken bones, but not severed one. There won't be any soft tissue left to attest to what we will do in the next hour either.

Besides, I don't want him to bleed out. I want him to feel my hands on his skin when he dies, to know his don took his life. I lean forward and speak right into my former consigliere's ear. "Like I said, everyone will think I'm killing you because of your disrespect, but that's not why."

"Then why?"

"Because you dared to touch what is mine. You hurt my wife and that is an unforgivable offense."

"She was being disrespectful. I squeezed her hand a little. She deserved worse."

I punch him so hard it knocks him out. I wait until he comes around before I start in on his fingernails. "Who did you leak information about *la famiglia* to?"

We know we've got a rat, but even my best men haven't been able to figure out who it is. Because it is my consigliere? A man who before now had been considered above reproach.

"No one." He's not screaming yet, but he looks like I gutted him asking that question. "I'm loyal to our cause."

"Bullshit," Miceli spits. "You betrayed your don. Who did you betray the rest of *la famiglia* to?"

By the time my first capo arrives, I've removed all ten of Francesco's fingernails and both of his big toenails. Slowly.

I let Angelo and Miceli have some fun too. Angelo punches the hell out of Francesco's groin and Miceli slices several shallow cuts into our victim's skin. Then Angelo pours a salt based solution that stings like hell over the cuts.

Francesco maintains he's not the rat the whole time.

His voice is hoarse from screaming and he can barely get sound out when the capos and their underbosses are gathered. We kept the wall between the outer room and the box recessed so everyone can see the spectacle that is my former consigliere.

"Does anyone need an explanation of why Francesco Jilani is here?" I ask the men.

I see several heads shaking and not a single face shows confusion. They know what he tried to do.

"I want you all here for this little reminder of what happens to traitors. Francesco didn't just try to trick me this morning, he's been secretly abusing his daughter for fifteen years and did the same to her mother before he murdered her and blamed the fall down the stairs on Catalina."

I nod to Domenico. He holds up a bigger stack of printed papers than I want to see. It represents all the times Sara Jilani and Catalina ended up in the hospital because of Francesco's abuse.

"If anyone needs proof of the abuse, or the cover up, it's right here." Domenico pounds the papers with his fist. "Francesco Jilani checked his wife and daughter into hospitals all over the New York metropolitan area under different versions of their own names which meant they didn't get flagged in the system."

Some of the capos and underbosses mutter together.

"He never used our hospital or clinic so Don Enzo and Don Severu would not find out about it." There is nothing but disgust in Domenico's tone.

"That's not an offense punishable by death," Lorenzo Ricci says.

I grind my teeth, but I answer him because even though no one else voiced the thought that doesn't mean no one else had it.

"How he treated his wife and daughter is despicable, but you're right Lorenzo, if that was all he'd done, he wouldn't be dying a very slow and painful death tonight. He didn't just do that, though, did he? He hid it because he wanted to keep his position as consigliere. You all know the rules my father set for his capos, the same rules I reiterated with each of you after taking over as don."

There are nods and murmurs of agreement.

"Francesco lied to my father and to me." I'm so furious, I stop talking to let those words sink in. "If anyone questions how untrustworthy that made him, you only have to look at this morning's actions to know that a man who will lie to his don about one thing, will lie about another."

I meet the eyes of every man there, letting them see my rage, my disdain for the cowardice and dishonor of this man.

"We have a leak and every bit of information that has caused us loss of shipments, product and business in the past year came across this man's desk." I don't know if he's the rat.

After the last hour, I'm inclined to believe he's not, but only time will tell.

If the leaks of information stop, we'll know it was him. If they don't, then it wasn't. Either way, he's going to die tonight. And I'm not so complacent I won't keep looking for who is behind the attacks.

But I can tell that even suggesting it has a lot of the capos and their underbosses uncomfortable. That a consigliere could be a rat is unbelievable, but then who would have believed he would be arrogant enough to try what he did this morning? This is what I want them thinking.

I start his punishment in earnest. First, I punch him in the face. "I am not a patsy you can dupe."

Then I grab a mallet from the tool wall and bring it back so he can see what I hold.

Francesco shakes his head. "Please."

Did he ever listen to his wife's pleas? To Catalina's? She's too stubborn to plead with him now, but this shit started when she was a little girl.

Just thinking of my wife small and helpless in the face of her father's temper has my own arm swinging high. I bring the mallet down on his right forearm. I give him a few seconds to feel that pain before I do the same to his left.

They aren't spiral fractures, but they'll do.

"Uncuff him."

Angelo does it and, grabbing his bicep, jerks Francesco into a standing position. Then I kick my former consigliere in the ribs, over and over. "We're still missing something aren't we?" I muse.

He can only groan in pain.

"That's right. You fucking shattered her hip bone when you knocked your wife down the stairs and killed her. *You*. Not Catalina, you bastard." Knowing he lied and convinced my father that an innocent child was the cause of her mother's death and not her abusive husband adds to the cauldron of rage that boils inside me.

My roundhouse kick lands exactly where I want it to and the crunch of shattering bones sounds just before more of Francesco's hoarse screams as he falls back to the chair, unable to stand up.

Convenient.

"Miceli, get the pliers."

My brother grabs them from the tool wall and brings them over. He knows what to do. I don't even have to force Francesco's jaw open because he's still trying to scream from the pain he's already in.

I look back at my men. "You lie to your don, this is what you get."

"This is for my father." I slice right through Francesco's tongue with my father's knife.

I brought it for this purpose. Miceli recognizes it and nods to me.

"Remember who didn't lie to me. You all saw Catalina lift her veil. She was no party to her father's deception. I chose to marry her and now she is my queen." My wife will not pay the price for her family's treachery.

If anyone treats her with less than the honor she is due, they will pay in blood for their mistake.

"Pick him up."

Angelo and my brother each take an arm and lift Francesco to standing again.

I go around so I'm standing behind him and facing the rest of *la famiglia's* high ranking made men. I position my hands and he knows what's coming.

"This is for my wife," I say so only he can hear and then I snap his neck.

"Make it look like a car accident," I order. "Make sure our ME is the one called to the scene. I don't want any blowback from this."

I look toward my uncle, Big Sal De Luca. He's currently capo over our clubs. "Uncle Sal, I need a new consigliere."

The big man steps forward, his expression grim. He was my father's brother and learning how the dead man at my feet betrayed him has been a blow. "It would be an honor, Severu."

I nod and then look at my cousin. "Salvatore, you've been your father's underboss for ten years." Since he was twenty. "You are ready to become capo."

Salvatore jerks his head in affirmation. "I will never betray you or *la famiglia.*"

"I believe you." I look around the now silent room. "Each of you is in the position you are because I trust you. We are all better off after getting rid of this cancer in our midst."

No one disagrees, not even fucking Lorenzo Ricci.

I hear one of the underbosses tell his capo that Francesco was an idiot to try to trick me into marrying his older daughter so he could keep the beautiful one to get a higher bride price. I don't tell them it's bullshit.

The rumor will protect Carlotta. Something, I promised Catalina I would do. But really? They think she's of more value than her older sister?

Fools.

I take a shower and change my clothes, putting the ones I wore to torture Francesco in the building incinerator. I will not return to my wife with her father's blood on my skin.

CHAPTER 17

CATALINA

My alarm goes off, waking me from a deep sleep and I groan. I reach out blindly to tap the phone to turn off the obnoxious noise. I'm tempted to go back to sleep, but if I don't take my pain meds, I'll regret it in the morning. Also, I don't want Emilia getting in trouble for not administering them.

I gingerly roll to my side and push myself up into a sitting position. I touch the base of the lamp on the bedside table and soft light illuminates the room. I grab the pills and toss them to the back of my throat. Then I pick up the water and gulp some down so I can swallow the pain relievers.

The need to pee has me standing and walking gingerly toward the bathroom. I'm making my way slowly back to bed when the door to the outer room opens.

Severu crosses the floor before I can even get a greeting out. His hand comes around my waist. "What are you doing walking by yourself?"

"I had to use the bathroom."

"You were supposed to call Emilia."

"Don't be ridiculous, Severu. I've been much worse than this and made it to the bathroom on my own."

He tenses beside me. Then he says, "Your father was in an accident on his way home from the reception. He did not survive the crash."

What? No. That wasn't possible. Then I realize what Severu is trying to tell me. "Did you kill him?"

"What do you think, Catalina?"

"I think that's where you went when you left me here."

He doesn't confirm or deny my supposition.

"Will you have trouble with the other made men over this?" I ask, worried.

"He tried to dupe me in front of representatives of all Five Families and the rest of the Cosa Nostra. The insult could not go unpunished."

In other words, no. Only, Severu went to a lot of effort to create the impression that it had been him who changed his mind at the last minute. I can't help worrying his men won't be nearly as accepting as he thinks.

Unless he told them. "Did you tell your capos that my sister ran away?"

If they knew, their wives would know. Maybe they wouldn't all talk, but it would only take one before they all knew. Carlotta's reputation would be shredded.

"They know that your father tried to trick me. They do not know it is because Carlotta ran."

"But they can guess. Why else would he do it?"

"Some assume Francesco was trying to get more money for *the most beautiful mafia princess* in this generation."

I feel an unfamiliar spark of jealousy when Severu uses that title. Even if the whole Five Families consider my sister that, I don't like that my husband agrees. Carlotta couldn't be more well known if she'd been named Miss New York. Whereas there are plenty of people in the Genovese *famiglia* that don't even know I exist.

My father saw to that.

Regardless. "My father would have had to be unforgivably foolish to have done something like that."

"You mean as unforgivably idiotic as what he did this morning?" Severu shakes his head. "His betrayal cost him his life. That is all they need to know."

"I need to tell my aunt and uncle about his death. Can you have someone take me to the house in the morning?" I can get some of my things as well.

"That will not be necessary. My new consigliere will inform Lora and Giovi of Francesco's accident and instruct them on how we are handling your sister's disappearance."

I don't argue. My aunt will cry and expect me to grieve my father's death, but I can't. "How are we handling it?"

"They are to tell anyone that asks that she has been sent away for a while to minimize gossip over the change in brides."

"But there will be gossip, speculation that she ran."

"As long as it is not confirmed, it will remain speculation. If my men suspect it is because she ran, they will not talk about it." Severu sounds so sure.

"Your men might not, but their wives and daughters will."

He shrugs, like that doesn't matter. Maybe it doesn't to him. It will to Carlotta though, when she finally comes back. She thinks it's only a matter of our father getting over his anger. She hasn't considered what her actions will do to her standing among *la famiglia*.

Heck, if she'd been thinking at all, she never would have left. She's such a babe in the woods. She has no idea how dangerous the world outside our family cocoon is. Does she even have money for a hotel?

"Stop worrying about your sister."

"How did you know that's what I was thinking about?"

"You are too tenderhearted for the family you come from, Catalina. Your sister abandoned you to your father's wrath."

"Not on purpose." Though part of me knows it really was. Then something else occurs to me. "I never needed to marry you to protect Carlotta. You had no intention of allowing my father to live once he'd betrayed you."

Severu gets me back in bed before he answers. His movements are careful, but his expression is that of an executioner. "You are wrong, Catalina. Your father is dead, but I am still alive, and your sister betrayed me as much as she did your father."

Fear rolls through me like a wave. I never asked him to promise not to punish her. I just assumed he wouldn't. What kind of naïve fool am I?

"Stop looking like that, wife." He tucks some of my hair, messy from sleep, behind my ear. "You did marry me and that will naturally influence the severity of the punishment I have planned for your sister."

"What are you going to do?" I ask, not sure I want to know.

"You may be there when I tell Carlotta after she is found. But make no mistake, I expect you to stand with me, not your sister."

"Just tell me this, will it make me hate you?"

His dark gaze probes mine for several silent seconds. Then he shakes his head. "No, but it won't be easy on her."

"How can you be sure I'll approve?" I ask, his nearness making me want to forget talking about my sister, which makes me feel guilty.

"I do not need your approval."

Lord save me from bossy, arrogant men. "Fine. But you said I won't hate you for it."

"You want what is best for her." He sounds so sure.

And he's right, but that doesn't mean I think any punishment he devises will be that. "How can a punishment be best for her?"

"You will have to trust me." His face is granite now, his tone not in the least conciliatory. More like demanding.

I consider his rule about men in positions like my father not abusing their wives or children and how he has treated me since this morning. I remember how he reacted to my phone call demanding he do some wooing of my sister. And I nod.

He might hurt me with unthinking comments, or just plain disinterest, but he reserves his physical cruelty for mafia business. Neither do I think he would hurt me emotionally *on purpose*.

"Good. Now close your eyes and get some sleep." He starts undressing.

I'm not about to forego the pleasure of watching my husband take his clothes off. My eyes stay open.

His lips quirk. "You're not very obedient."

"I can be obedient when I want." Like when we're making love and he tells me to stay still.

That was so hot. Just the memory has moisture collecting between my legs. Okay, maybe the memory and the sight of my husband's body.

He turns off the light and walks around the bed in the dark to climb onto his side. I wish he would hold me, but he doesn't move closer.

I lay there wishing and thinking and definitely not sleeping, so I ask, "Why did you ask me about birth control when you know you need to have children?"

"I wasn't going to take the choice away from you. The timing of your pregnancies is not just my decision."

I accept that I am expected to have children as soon as possible but that does not mean I accept that any man, even my husband the don, has the right to demand it of me. I am surprised he didn't do that. His whole question about birth control threw me for a loop. But now that I've had time to think about it, I also like that he asked.

Not that he followed it up with a question about STDs though.

Still, it gives me hope for a more equal marriage than my parents had. We're already ahead because he won't physically harm me. I can't help feeling that despite that fact, our situation parallels my parents one significant way. Severu expected to marry the beauty of our generation and instead, he got me.

Does he know that my father was supposed to marry his mother but ended up marrying my mom instead?

"Some women might say that the timing of my pregnancies aren't your decision at all."

"It is a moot point. You may already be pregnant."

"After only one time? Does that happen?"

"It does. Now can we please stop talking about making babies? Or I'm going to forget how sore you must be from your first time and fuck you until you can't walk tomorrow."

I want to say that I'm not that sore, but it would be a lie. "Maybe I won't be so sore in the morning," I suggest before letting my eyes slide shut against the dark.

"Fuck."

That's the last thing either of us says before I fall back asleep, glad my new husband is lying beside me, even if he isn't holding me.

CHAPTER 18

SEVERU

I wake as soon as Catalina shifts in the bed. She rolls over and stands up in a way that says she's trying not to disturb me.

Sitting up, I say, "You're not supposed to walk to the bathroom alone, wife."

"Oh, Severu, you are awake. I'm feeling much better this morning."

"Good, then my mother can take you shopping as planned today for clothes."

Catalina makes a face, like she can't think of anything she'd rather do less.

Her attitude surprises me. "I thought every woman dreamed of shopping for clothes with an unlimited budget."

Her expression doesn't change at the mention of an unlimited budget. "Sexist much? Shopping for clothes is not my favorite thing."

"Calling me names again?" I ask, realizing this is a good time to bring up her calling me a numbskull the night before.

"Making an observation," she says, clearly unrepentant.

I don't want to come down too heavy on her. Adjusting to a role she didn't expect to have will be a challenge for her, but Catalina will have to learn what is expected of a don's wife.

"A proper wife would never call her husband a numbskull. Especially if he is the don."

"And a proper husband would not accuse his virgin wife of acting the whore for her father's men. Which do you think is worse?" She shakes her head, heading into the bathroom. "Never mind. I already know what you think. Your unquestioned authority as a don is what's most important to you. Slicing into my heart with your words is no sin in your eyes, I'm sure."

Incensed at the accusation, I jump out of bed to follow her. "I did not call you a whore."

"If you say so."

"I do."

"Fine."

Clearly it is not fine. Her anger at me the night before was justified. I made assumptions based on nothing but her age. Asking a virgin about STDs was not my finest moment.

"I did not intend to imply I believed you were a whore."

"Just a woman with loose morals." She shakes her head. "Regardless of what I think of the double standard for men and women in the mafia in regard to sex, and I think it stinks by the way, I know that men like you expect a woman to remain a virgin until her wedding night."

"What do you mean men like me?"

"I'm sure you expected your sister to go to her marriage a virgin, even though she went to university before getting married. You expected it of Carlotta. Why would you assume I was not as chaste as my sister?"

What is Catalina doing to me? I have never acknowledged wrongdoing before. I do not regret actions that cannot be changed, but damned if I don't want to apologize for the second time to her in less than 24 hours.

Enough is enough.

I'm a hard man who does not worry about how my words affect others. If she is going to thrive as my wife, she'll have to come to terms with that. This is not about hurt feelings. It is about Catalina showing proper respect to her husband the don.

"I will not tolerate disrespect." I let the authority of my position bleed into my voice.

Showing not the slightest bit of fear or acknowledgement of wrongdoing, Catalina lifts her chin. "Neither will I."

If she were a man, I would crush her in this moment. If she were any other woman, I would do the same. But this is my wife. I want Catalina to rule in strength at my side. I am King of New York and she is Queen.

I will not apologize again, but I will acknowledge her place in my life. "More than any other woman, you deserve for me to treat you with respect, Catalina. You are my wife."

Her mouth drops open, like my words have shocked her. They surprised me too, but I'm not going to let her see that.

"That's good to know. Now please show some of that respect and leave me in peace to use the bathroom."

"You are my wife, Catalina."

"I think we've established that."

"You do not need to be embarrassed to pee in front of me."

"In what world, Severu?"

"Ours."

She stares at me. "Are you saying it wouldn't bother you to pee in front of me?"

Actions speak louder than words. I go around her, drop my boxers and piss in the toilet.

She squeaks and turns her back. "What are you doing?"

"I think that is self-evident."

"If you needed the bathroom, you could have asked me to leave, or let me tend to myself in privacy and then come in here."

"There will be no part of your life I do not have access to," I assure her.

"There are parts of your life I don't want access to."

"Really?"

"Yes. I don't want to know details about last night, though I'm glad you told me what you did."

I did not in fact tell her. She inferred from the fact her father was dead. I shake off my cock and step out of my boxers.

Is she still too sore?

Stepping back, I jerk my head toward the toilet. "Tend to your needs," I repeat her modest words back to her.

She glares. "Please, leave."

"That is not going to happen."

She does not want access to every part of my life and I am glad for that, because I cannot give it to her. Mafia business is off limits to her. She never needs to see the monster who rules my men with an iron fist.

But just like those men, she is mine. Every part of her.

Catalina jiggles a little, making her tits shift enticingly. "I mean it, Severu, I need to go."

"Then go."

"Why are you doing this?"

"I told you."

"Because you don't want me keeping secrets from you. I won't, but peeing isn't a secret. It's a bodily function." She presses her legs together and moans a little. "Please, Severu."

"I would prefer to hear you pleading for my cock."

"After this? Good luck with that."

I take that as the challenge it is meant to be. But first things first. I step forward, yank up her nighty and set her on the toilet.

There is the sound of liquid splashing into the bowl almost immediately.

I kiss her chastely. "That wasn't so hard, was it?"

"You are a control freak," she accuses.

That is one name I own. "You think any other type of man could command the New York Cosa Nostra?"

"I don't want to be commanded," she says grumpily.

"That's not true, Catalina. You enjoyed being commanded in bed last night very much."

"Out of bed," she clarifies.

Her honesty pleases me so much, I leave her to finish up without my presence. Unfortunately for my strong-willed wife, though she is my queen, she still must obey me. Even out of the bedroom.

I have no intention of curbing her freedoms unless it comes to her safety, but there are things she will have to do simply because she is the don's wife.

Fetching the dress she wore yesterday, along with a fresh pair of underwear because my soldier had enough foresight to buy multiple pairs, I carry the clothes back into the bathroom.

Catalina is staring at herself in the mirror, her expression troubled.

"What is wrong?" I ask.

"I'm supposed to wear makeup, but I don't have any. And I don't like it. Only I don't want to be seen in public with your mom with this bruise on my cheek showing."

I like the way she catalogues her thoughts without a filter.

Luckily the bruise on her cheek isn't as big as the red handprint was yesterday. Only a small spot just over her cheekbone is showing discoloration. "My sister can help you with your makeup today."

"Okay, but what about tomorrow?"

"I'm sure my sister will teach you."

"Never mind that. I know how to learn what I don't know. YouTube is awesome for tutorials."

"Then what did you mean?"

"I still don't have any makeup and the stuff I have at h...back in my old room is pretty sparse. Some mascara and a couple tubes of lipstick."

"Buy some while you are shopping for clothes today."

"I suppose." She frowns.

"My mother and sister will help you find what you need."

Catalina nods, her expression lightening. "I'm sure you are right."

"What is this really about, Catalina?" I don't believe she's this worried about something so small.

She sighs. "It's just hitting me what I signed up for."

"When you signed the marriage certificate you mean?"

"Yes."

"You are my wife."

"And you are a not only a made man, but you are the don. It's a lot."

"You were raised in the mafia lifestyle."

"Sort of. After he killed my mother, my father kept me on the periphery. My aunt and uncle were better, but I never received some of the training and mentorship Carlotta did. No one expected me to marry."

"Why not?"

"My father made it clear from the time I might have been promised that he wasn't going to look for a husband for me. He claimed it was because he could never forgive me for causing my mother's death. He wouldn't saddle an honorable man with a killer for a wife."

"He said that to you?" I want to bring the bastard back to life and torture him all over again.

"Yes, but I knew it was a lie. Just like he did. He couldn't risk letting me marry a good man because I might spill his secrets and he would be removed from his position as consigliere."

"That would have only been the first thing he had to worry about. At the very least, my father or I would have cut his tongue out for deceiving us."

"Oh. Is that what you did?"

"I thought you didn't want details."

"I don't. Not all of them, but I like the idea of his tongue being cut out for hiding what he did to my mother."

My wife is so perfect for me. She is innocent and kind, but with a streak of ruthlessness she'll need to stand by my side for the next fifty years, or more. "I did it for lying about you both."

"Good."

"Why didn't your father marry you off to someone like him?" As much as I despise the weakness my men show by being that way, there are a lot of made men in the mafia who bring violence home with them.

"If a man was like my father, then telling him the truth would have given him leverage over papà."

"So, you were trapped in Francesco's home, subject to his abuse."

"That's what he thought, yes."

"You had plans?" I ask, believing easily that even living as a prisoner in her father's house, Catalina had been plotting some kind of escape.

"I did."

"Marrying me wasn't one of them."

"No, it wasn't." She laughs softly. "Not even in my wildest imaginings."

"I'd like to hear about these plans sometime, but right now I have a more pressing question."

She turns away from the mirror and faces me. "What is that?"

"Are you too sore?"

She shakes her head.

"Are you sure?"

"Yes, Severu, I'm sure."

I'm already naked and my cock has been hard throughout this conversation, the result of standing so close to my delectable wife wearing nothing but a borrowed nightgown. I slide the straps of the gown that is just a little too big over her shoulders and it falls to a puddle on the floor at her feet.

Her nipples harden immediately when they are exposed to the air and I brush them with my thumbs before squeezing her tits. Fuck, she turns me on.

CHAPTER 19

CATALINA

Severu touches my body like he knows exactly what will excite me the most. I love when he grabs my breasts like that, while abrading my nipples with his thumbs. I'm still sensitive from last night and the rough skin of his thumbs brings pleasure bordering on pain.

I'm still a little sore, but not too sore.

I want this, as much or more than I did the first time. Because now I know how it feels when my husband brings me to orgasm. Indescribable pleasure that he draws out until I am completely spent.

Reaching down, I grasp his erection. It's thick and big and now that I know it fits inside me...barely...not nearly as intimidating. "How can you stay hard so long? Is that normal?"

He started getting hard when we were *discussing* marital privacy boundaries, of which he apparently thinks there shouldn't be any. He's been aroused ever since.

"It's something you're going to have to get used to," he says. "You excite the hell out of me."

"I do?"

"Can you doubt it?"

"But you were going to marry my sister."

"I was, but I wanted you from the first touch."

He can't mean that the way it sounds. "Yesterday, when you touched me in the hospital you mean?"

"No, *mi dolce bellezza*. When I shook your hand that first time and your pulse went crazy."

"You noticed?" I want to be embarrassed, but the intensity in his eyes makes it impossible.

The attraction was never one sided.

"Yes, and it turned me on."

"But you got engaged to Carlotta." Even after he knew he wanted me. "Did you want her too?"

"Not even a little."

"But she's beautiful."

"So are you."

I shake my head. Him calling me *his sweet beauty* doesn't change reality. It's just a term of endearment anyway. "My looks are nothing special."

"That is a lie."

"I don't lie to you." I hate lying at all, but you learn deception in a home where it can be the difference between going to bed with bruises, or not.

"Then it is a lie you believe. You..." He kisses the top of my left breast. "Are..." He does the same to my right. "Beautiful..." His lips press against my collar bone, making me shiver with delight. "And..." His mouth moves up my neck. "Sexy." He takes my mouth with claim staking intensity.

When he lifts his lips from mine his espresso eyes are nearly black with desire. "I want you."

"I don't understand." He'd wanted me like I wanted him. He had *not* wanted my sister, but he was still going to marry her. "It makes no sense."

"I'd given my word."

"Until the engagement was announced, you could have changed your mind, especially if it meant marrying another woman from the same family." Even after really. As the don, he could have changed his mind without repercussions.

As yesterday and his created narrative showed.

"Letting the others believe I'd rejected your sister for you was necessary; It was the lesser of two evils."

That's not what I meant. He's referring to our wedding. I was referring to his choice to marry Carlotta despite knowing he wanted me and that I wanted him. My heart hurts.

Which makes me sarcastic when I reply to his comment. "Right, because the big, bad, macho mafia don couldn't be humiliated by a runaway bride."

I'm blisteringly angry and I'm not even sure why. I don't get angry. I cannot allow myself to give into negative emotions. It's not safe. Or it *wasn't* safe while I lived with my father.

But I'm furious now. Because despite wanting me, he *hadn't* rejected Carlotta for me. He'd left me to my father's mercy, or lack thereof. He'd been prepared to consign my sister to not only a loveless, but also a passionless marriage.

Maybe his cruelty isn't reserved for his role as don of the mafia.

"It wasn't about being humiliated. It was about showing strength, cementing my power in their minds. If I couldn't control my fiancée, then maybe I couldn't control my Cosa Nostra *famiglia*? Maybe we are vulnerable to encroachment and attack."

"A weak don is a dead don." I'd heard that phrase often enough.

"Exactly."

"You knew you wanted me before the announcement of the engagement. You could have become engaged to me instead. My father couldn't have denied you."

Severu was the one man in all of the Cosa Nostra that could have forced my father to let him marry me.

"I did not want to."

Savage hurt claws at my heart. Whether he wanted me, or not, I wasn't worth making the effort for.

"Do not look at me like that."

Unable to change my feelings, I turn my head so he can't see them on my face.

But he cups my cheeks with both his hands and lifts my head so our eyes meet. "Carlotta was safe. I knew you weren't."

"What do you mean safe?"

"I didn't want to marry, but I recognized it needed to be done for the good of *la famiglia*. I definitely didn't want a wife that would haunt my every waking moment and even my dreams."

Is he saying that I do?

"I wanted someone I could ignore," he continues. "Someone who wouldn't cause any upheaval in my routine. A woman who would look pretty on my arm, give me children and would not impact my life much otherwise."

The very thought of my sister trapped in such a marriage makes me sick. "That's terrible."

He shrugs. "It's like a lot of marriages in our world."

That might be true. I personally wouldn't know. My parents' marriage was toxic, but my aunt and uncle are happy together. They don't ignore each other. Even though they've never been able to have children, my uncle treats my aunt like a queen.

"You're heartless," I tell him.

"It's good that you realize that."

"Why? You want me to hate you?"

"No. But loving me will only hurt you."

"Because you won't love me back." I don't say *can't* because I don't believe that. He loves his family. I've seen it.

If he doesn't care about me, it's because he chooses not to.

"I can't afford that kind of weakness, Catalina."

"But unbridled lust is okay?" I ask sarcastically.

Something shifts in his eyes and it's almost frightening. "Yes."

Then he's kissing me again and this time, he's holding nothing back. He storms my mouth like a conqueror, sliding his tongue in and out like he did his dick in my body last night.

His arms come around me, pulling me flush against him. It hurts my ribs, but not enough for me to protest, or ask him to stop. Because the way my nipples rub against his hairy chest feels so good. The harshness of his hold excites me, sending wetness gushing from my core.

Breaking the kiss, he spins me around and then lifts me. We move and then he's leaning back on the counter and I'm on his lap, my legs dangling to either side of his hips. One of his hands delves between my legs, his fingers sliding between my already slick folds, the heel of his hand pressing against my clit.

My breathing is erratic and my heart feels like it's going to burst out of my chest. All I can do is feel.

He mauls my boobs with his free hand, squeezing and playing with them, pinching my nipples.

"Open your eyes. Watch what I do to you," he demands. He squeezes my breast a little harder than he has been. "Do it."

Why does his rough treatment make me only want more? He's not hurting me, but it's not gentle like the night before either.

"Look at what I am, what we are together," he orders.

Finally, I open my eyes and focus on the image in the mirror opposite.

There is no tenderness in Severu's handsome face; it is stark with lust and his eyes burn with sexual need. His hands on my body are both obscene and incredibly sensual.

To be wanted this much fills me with a sense of power. He might never love me, but the man in that mirror is as controlled by his craving for my body as I am by mine for his. He might have planned to marry my sister, but now that I am his wife, he'll never let me go.

He manipulates the tender flesh between my thighs, driving my desire into the realm of critical need. I feel my climax building and just as all my muscles contract with ecstasy, he shifts my body up and thrusts himself into me. There is no careful advance and retreat, but he plunges his erection as deep as he can go in a single stab into my tender body.

I shatter, screaming my pleasure, but he is nowhere near done.

Thrusting in and out, he keeps his hands where they are, forcing me to build toward another orgasm almost immediately. It's too much, but I can't get my voice to work to say so.

And maybe I don't really want to.

We are two primordial beings caught in a battle not against each other, but against anything that would attempt to separate us before we find the ultimate pleasure together. Even our own bodies. His muscles strain from staying upright, my vagina is so swollen, it clings to his sex as he pulls back and presses against it as he pushes deeper again.

I lock my arms around his neck. His pace turns brutally fast and my climax takes me by surprise, making my core clench and dragging another uncontrolled scream out of me.

"Mine!" he shouts as he releases inside me.

A memory surfaces from the night before. He'd yelled the same thing when he came then too.

He might not love me, but he wants to own me.

How long before he realizes that in taking possession of my body, he's claiming my heart and my soul as well?

CHAPTER 20

SEVERU

Her eyes heavy-lidded with exhaustion, Catalina is docile as I finally lead her to the shower.

I wore her out.

A kinder man would have waited at least another day before fucking her again. I am not that man.

The shopping trip with my mother and sister will have to wait though. Catalina's things can be collected from the Jilani mansion, and she will have to make do.

My wife needs more rest to heal.

And to keep up with my craving for her body.

She was a virgin last night, but Catalina didn't protest once about how roughly I just took her. She was with me all the way, right up to when she screamed out her orgasm.

Even now, her nipples bead under my hands as I wash her body. As tempted as I am to take her again, I also see the way she winces when she shifts the wrong way.

Not wanting her to have to raise her hands above her head, I wash her hair. I'm surprised that I like taking care of her this way. Does she enjoy it as well? I massage her scalp as I work in the shampoo.

My wife groans. "That feels good."

An odd sense of pride fills me. "Tip your head back so I can rinse you without the soapy water getting in your eyes."

She obeys and I like that too.

After I'm done rinsing away the shampoo, I start to wash my own body. She reaches for the bottle of conditioner, and I take it from her.

"I need it, Severu. My hair will look like a lion's mane after it dries otherwise."

"I'll do it." I work conditioner into her hair and leave it while I quickly wash my own hair. Then I finish rinsing my wife before turning off the water.

When we step out, I use a towel to soak up every droplet of moisture from my wife's sexy body, letting my own start to air dry. I make a mess of her hair trying to squeeze the water out of it with another towel.

She looks up at me with curiosity. "Can I expect this kind of treatment all the time, or is it because I'm wounded?"

"I don't know," I say honestly.

I want to do it, so I do. If I think about it, I'll have to ask myself why, so I don't. "Stay there."

She doesn't ask why. I go into the bedroom and return with her pain meds and the lotion from the hospital. After she takes the pills, I gently rub the lotion into her bruises and her hand.

"Is it still sore?" I ask her.

"Only a little."

I nod and finish rubbing the lotion in.

"Thank you," she says softly when I am done.

Still delightfully naked, she sits down on the stool in front of the vanity mirror and picks up a brush from the drawer beside it. When she reaches up to swipe it through her now tangled hair, she winces.

I take the brush from her and carefully run it through, working out the tangles carefully.

"I'll need to blow-dry it before I go anywhere."

"I'll do it." But first I have to call down to Emilia to get a blow dryer.

"I need to put defrizzing product in my hair, or I'll end up looking like a mad scientist despite the conditioner. Not the look your mom is hoping for when she takes me shopping, I'm sure."

I don't tell her I have decided to put the shopping trip off for a couple of days because I'm busy using the intercom system to call Emilia.

"*Sì*, Don Severu?" she answers.

"My wife needs a blow dryer and defrizzing product." Whatever that is.

"Does she have a preferred brand?"

I look questioningly at my wife. She shakes her head.

"No."

"Then I can have both items delivered to your rooms in a few minutes."

"Good."

I step away from the bathroom intercom and finish drying off.

"Aren't you going to tell her thank you?" my wife asks me.

"No."

Catalina frowns. "Why not? Emilia is doing us a favor."

"She's doing her job. She does not thank me every day for keeping her and her family safe."

"Sheesh, it's not the same. I don't imagine you thank her every day for keeping your house running smoothly either."

"If you want to thank her, then do it."

"I'll get dressed so I can meet her at the door."

"It won't be her at the door, but a maid."

"Oh. Well, at least I can thank her."

"I don't want you to get dressed yet."

She ignores me and stands up.

"Catalina," I warn her.

She turns, her expression set in stubborn lines. "Listen, Severu, you can boss me around during sex. Weirdly enough, I like it. Since this isn't about sex or my safety, you need to back off."

I don't think anyone has ever told me to back off. Not even my father.

My wife is so damn strong. How does her family not realize it? Her aunt and uncle act like she needs to be protected. Her father didn't see her value at all. And even her sister treats Catalina like a prop to her life, not the astounding woman that she is.

I step in front of her, putting my hands on her naked shoulders. "Who says the sex is over?"

"I do." She blushes. "I can't...not again. I'm really tender and swollen down there."

"Let me see."

"What? No!"

I shake my head. She's still putting up unnecessary barriers between us.

"I really must insist, *mi dolce bellezza*." Without waiting for her answer, I pick her up with one hand under her knees and another behind her back.

She wraps her arms around my neck and sighs. "I suppose you don't know if this is going to become a habit with you either?"

That I have an answer for. I like carrying her and that won't change once her ribs heal. "It definitely is."

"I don't want you examining me like a gynecologist."

"Have you ever seen one? Your medical records didn't show a visit with any specialists." Not even after her hip was shattered. Had her father hired a physical therapist under the table?

"When did you read my medical records? How did you read them?"

"Last night. One of my guys has access to the major medical databases."

"I'm impressed."

"I gave you jewelry worth twenty million dollars yesterday and that's what impresses you."

"What? Those aren't mine. You bought them for Carlotta."

"I bought them for my bride. Which you were. They are yours."

"I can't keep them."

"On the contrary, you will keep them. This is not negotiable, wife."

"Have you noticed you call me *wife* when you are being particularly bossy?"

"A don is not bossy."

"What is he then?"

"In charge."

"You really have a thing for control."

With her? Absolutely.

I lay my wife down on our bed and then notice her pebbled nipples. "Arousal or cold?" I ask her.

She blushes. "Both."

Catalina is so damn honest with me, it is addictive.

I grab a soft cashmere throw blanket and drape it over her, but leave her legs exposed. "Lift your knees, Catalina, open yourself for me."

"You can't be serious. Severu, the maid is going to be here any minute with the blow dryer and product for my hair."

"She will leave it in the sitting room. The staff know better than to disturb us in the bedroom if the door is closed."

"But you called them."

Rather than argue further, I walk over and lock the door to the bedroom and then return to my sexy little wife. "Now, Catalina." I don't repeat what I want her to do. She already knows.

"Are you always going to be this bossy?"

"Yes."

She smiles, her pretty eyes lighting with humor. "Well, at least you're honest."

"So are you."

"I wasn't always, but here I can be."

Her admission makes something in my chest constrict. I ignore the odd feeling and caress her thigh. "You are safe here."

"I know."

"Good."

She raises her knees, opening her thighs so I can see her pussy. Slick cream glistens on her folds.

"Wider."

"I think it's a good thing I do yoga," she grumbles, but she obeys me, revealing her opening to my gaze.

I press my finger into it and feel how hot and swollen her flesh is. I also feel how her pussy continuously weeps moisture.

I want to taste those juices.

CATALINA

"You're very swollen here." My husband pushes his finger deeper into my channel.

It stings a little, but it also feels intensely good. I don't think I could accommodate his sex, but I want him to keep his finger right where it is. What is happening to me?

Before I met Severu, I thought I wasn't a sexual being. I'd never had a climax before our wedding day. Now, I can't get enough of the ecstasy he gives me.

He draws his finger back, but not out of me, and then presses forward again. "My finger barely fits."

"I told you."

"Do you like this?" he asks, sliding that single finger in and out of me again.

"Yes." I sigh with the pleasure, no longer even remotely embarrassed to have him between my legs, looking at my most intimate flesh.

"Then you are going to love this." He leans down and his tongue replaces his finger inside me.

"Oh...oh...Severu..."

He's right. His tongue is slick against my over sensitized flesh and gives only pleasure as he mimics how he takes me with his giant dick. He does that thing with his hands he did last night, holding my hips in place and spreading them wide so his thumbs brush up on either side of my clitoris.

It feels amazing and pleasure starts to spiral through me again, when five minutes ago, I would have said I couldn't climax again any time soon.

I would have been wrong.

My phone buzzes on the bedside table. Someone is calling. It could be Carlotta. I don't want to answer, but I can't ignore it in case it's her.

"Severu, my phone."

He lifts his head, his eyes so incredibly dark. "Ignore it."

"What if it is Carlotta?"

"She'll call again."

"She could need help." I give him a beseeching look. "Please."

He surges to his feet and stalks over to my phone. "It is your aunt. She can wait."

Maybe I'm being selfish, but I agree. Zia Lora will want to talk about my father, about funeral arrangements. I'd prefer not to have to attend the funeral at all, much less have to help plan it. I will call her later, but now? I want to revel in the way my husband makes me feel.

Severu settles between my legs again, and his hands go back to the way they were, both holding my thighs immobile and his thumbs on either side of my clitoris.

His penetrating gaze sends a shiver of anticipation through me. "Play with your tits, wife."

The order jolts me with a zing of arousal. "I..." I've never done that, but I want to. For him.

And for me.

"Cup them with both of your hands, *mi dolce bellezza*."

I do what he says, marveling at how soft my own skin feels to me. My breasts are heavy in my palms and spill over my fingers.

"Yes, just like that," he says, his thumbs keeping up their steady rhythm on my clitoris. "Now squeeze."

I do and it's not exactly like when he does it. His hands are bigger, his fingers firmer, but I still enjoy it.

"Perfect." He watches me squeeze and release my boobs rhythmically for several seconds, then says, "Now pluck at your nipples."

I pinch both my nipples, not hard, but enough to feel it and moan a little. Then I pull and release. Oh, gosh, that is good. I do it again and again.

"You've got me so damn hard, Catalina."

I tilt my head so I can see and gasp. His penis is jutting straight out from his body, red with the blood rushing through it.

"Keep playing with yourself," he demands and then his head is back between my legs and his tongue thrusts deep.

He thrusts in and out of me, my swollen, over sensitized flesh clinging to the slippery appendage. When he pulls out and swipes his tongue up my labia and over my clitoris, the ecstasy shatters inside me.

I cry out his name, "Severu!"

He coaxes me through aftershocks that should be measured on the Richter scale until I can't take any more and my body jolts with every caress of his tongue against my clit.

Severu lifts his face, but doesn't move his hand. "Good?"

I nod, too pleasure addled to speak.

His thumb swipes over my too sensitive bud and I cry out. He smiles and does it with the other one.

"Please, Severu."

"Who do you belong to, Catalina?"

"You. I belong to you."

"You are my wife."

"And you are my husband." It goes both ways, even if he is the dominant partner in the bedroom.

"I am."

Hearing him confirm what I know to be true sends another zing of bliss through me. He finally moves his hands, using them to lower my legs to the bed.

He shifts up my body and I am so spent, I can do nothing but lie there, waiting for what comes next. But he doesn't lower himself over me. He moves until his knees are on either side of my shoulders, his erection nearly touching my face.

CHAPTER 21

CATALINA

"I told you that you don't have to be on your knees to take me in your mouth." Severu goes down on all fours above me and the head of his sex presses against my slightly open mouth.

There is a bead of moisture on the tip and I dart my tongue out to taste before I even think of what I am doing. It's a little salty, but mostly sweet. Will his cum taste the same? Soon, I will find out.

"Open wider, *mi dolce bellezza*. Let me in."

With no thought to deny him, I open as wide as I can, and he presses himself into my waiting mouth. I move my tongue around his shaft, exploring his shape in a new way and taking in the taste of him.

"Cover your teeth with your lips."

I do, but it takes me a second to figure it out with his erection already in my mouth. He pulls back, drawing the wetness from my mouth over my lips with his dick. He pushes back inside and continues this shallow thrusting until my lips are slick with my spit.

"Suck me," he orders, his tone tense and dark.

I want to. I want to feel him lose it in my mouth like he just took me to ecstasy with his. So, I suck and he keeps moving, sometimes hitting the back of my throat. I gag a little, but he doesn't stop and I don't try to pull my head away.

"I'm close, wife, swallow when I press against the back of your throat. Let me in."

I try. The first time, I just gag harder, but I grip his buttocks to stop him pulling out and try again. This time, his head slips into my throat. I wanted to control him with pleasure but he's the one controlling my body. I feel completely owned.

He thrusts only a couple more times before he shouts my name. "*Catalina.*" He pushes deeper, stretching my throat as he shoots warm viscous fluid into me. "*Mine.*"

His big body shakes, his breath bellowing in and out. I don't say the word, but I think it. He is mine too. I own him, if only in this moment.

I'm getting lightheaded but Severu pulls back allowing me to draw in air through my nose. I suck on his softening shaft, licking the remains of his spend.

He shifts to lie down beside me and places one big hand on my stomach. It's not exactly cuddling, but it is better than him going to his own space like he did last night.

"I guess it's time to blow dry your hair now."

I just want to sleep but his mom and sister are expecting to take me shopping.

"Okay," I say, trying to lever myself into a sitting position.

"Maybe a nap. You are still healing."

I hope his mom and sister don't mind moving our shopping trip to the afternoon, but right now? I really want to sleep and if Severu isn't pushing me to get up, I'm not going to.

Moments later, I find myself tucked under the duvet, a towel on my pillow to soak the moisture from my still wet hair.

My husband leans over me and kisses my swollen lips. "Sleep, now."

"Are you leaving?"

"If I don't, you won't sleep."

The man with ultimate control, is challenged enough he has to leave the room, so he won't initiate sex again. And he's willing to do that so I will get the rest he thinks I need. It's not love, but it is something.

I smile and close my eyes.

SEVERU

My wife falls asleep between one breath and the next, a sweet smile still on her lips. If I don't get out of here, I'm going to take her in her sleep, regardless of her sore pussy.

I dress quickly and head for the sitting room but stop and turn back to the bed. Leaning down, I kiss Catalina's lips. Even in her sleep, she responds. So, I kiss her again, but then I force myself to straighten and turn away.

My gaze lands on her phone. I don't trust her aunt not to call again and wake her. And if Carlotta does, I want to be the one to speak to the little runaway. I grab the phone and shove it in my pocket.

As I walk out of the sitting room, I pull my own phone out and text Aldo to meet me in the study.

He arrives a few seconds after I do. "Yes, boss?"

"You will be Catalina's primary bodyguard."

"I'll protect her with my life."

"I know. Pick five men you trust implicitly to join you guarding my wife. She is never to leave the house without all six of you. When she is home, one of you is to be with her at all times. Preferably you, but that won't always be possible. Make sure she always has a guard with her who has had training with Niccolò's crew."

Niccolò is ex special forces and his crew is too. They train other enforcers for the family as well as running special ops for me.

Aldo nods. "Consider it done."

"When she goes to the rooftop there are two of you. She is not to remain up there if a helicopter is within striking distance." The entire rooftop garden and living area is surrounded by bullet proof plexiglass, but that can't protect her from threats from above.

"I'd feel better if I had seven men," Aldo says, showing initiative and that he's already thinking about what will keep my wife safest. "Three should be trained by Niccolò's team, so there are always at least two of us with specialized training with her."

I consider the request.

It makes sense to have extra guards to move in and out of rotation. "Make It nine. There will be times we are on high alert she'll need a convoy and a ten-man team to leave the building."

"We could draw from the family security teams for those times."

My mother has four guards assigned to her and there is another team of four that rotate guarding the two floors of our home.

"Add two more to the house team, or to my wife's team, but I want them available at a moment's notice."

"On it, boss."

"And Aldo?"

He inclines his head like he's waiting for me to speak.

"Not a single fucking one that might flirt with her or get ideas in their head about anything more. I prefer not to have to torture and kill my own men."

But I'll do it, just like I showed my capos and their underbosses last night.

~ ~ ~

I take notes on the company purchase proposal I am reading. It has potential benefits for both our legitimate business under the umbrella of Oscuro Enterprises and laundering money from our less legal endeavors. It's a good investment opportunity and I take note of who put the proposal together.

The phone in my pocket buzzes as I finish the email to my procurement manager greenlighting the purchase.

Pulling it out, I see that it is Catalina's aunt. I consider letting it go to voicemail, but there are things I want to discuss with Francesco's sister when my wife is not around to hear what I have to say.

I swipe to answer. "Hello."

"Oh," she sounds uncertain. "This is Lora Revello. I was calling to speak to my niece."

"She is resting."

"If you could get her?" she asks politely enough.

"No."

"I know you are newly married, but it is not as if..." She lets her voice trail off, clearly uncomfortable. "Regardless, there are plans we need to make for my brother's funeral." Lora's voice is choking with tears when she says the last.

I have no sympathy. I do not say I am sorry for her loss because I am not. She lived in that house. She knew what Francesco did to Catalina. She could have come to me, she did not.

"We spent two hours at the hospital yesterday seeing to injuries inflicted by your brother on my wife."

"What? I...that doesn't make sense. Why would he hurt her before the wedding?"

So, she knows Catalina was unharmed before arriving at the church. "Are you saying he needed a reason to hurt her?"

"What has she been telling you?" Lora asks, aghast.

"Something he should have admitted to long ago. You are aware that I do not place or keep men in positions of authority within *la famiglia* when they visit violence on their families."

"I'd heard something like that," she says cautiously.

"And yet you never told me, your don, that your brother was violent with your niece."

"No."

"Were you aware that he beat his wife as well?"

"What? No. He didn't. Did Catalina say that? She lies sometimes."

"To protect herself from her father." She'd already implied as much. "Not about this."

"Don De Luca, please, believe me, my brother was not a bad man. He had his reasons for treating Catalina the way he did. I never agreed with it, but it didn't happen very often, and he never touched Carlotta. He did not beat Sara. He grieved her death until the day he died."

"That is a lie."

"What? No, despite her not being the woman he was originally promised, he fell for Sara after she gave him their first child."

"Is that what he told you?"

"Yes."

"He lied."

"How can you say that?"

"I have Sara's medical records. They show a pattern of abuse spanning the entirety of their marriage."

"That can't be right."

"He took her to different hospitals and used different versions of her name to hide his base behavior. My father would have demoted him to foot soldier if he had known." I had killed him.

I wasn't telling her that though. Her husband wasn't one of my men, though he lived in my territory, he remained loyal to the Detroit don.

"I don't think so," Lora said. "Your father owed Francesco. He never forgot that."

"What do you think he owed him?"

"Your mother."

What the hell was she talking about?

"Your mother was promised to my brother when they were both young. Then when she grew into such a beauty, your father decided he wanted her. His father arranged it, promising Sara to Francesco instead. That was why he was promoted to consigliere at such a young age. Your father appreciated my brother's loyalty."

"There is no loyalty in deception."

"You must be wrong about Sara. Francesco never complained about the change in brides."

I will ask my own mother about this, but it is clear that Lora has an idealized vision of her dead brother.

"I am not wrong. You saw for yourself what he did to Catalina."

"As I said, he had his reasons. It wasn't right, but he resented her for causing Sara's death."

I will not let this lie stand. It sickens me even more now than the first time I realized how Francesco had blamed his own cruelty on his innocent daughter. "Catalina didn't put Sara in the hospital a dozen times over the life of her marriage and she did not shove her mother down the stairs the day she died. Francesco did that and Catalina tried to save her mother but fell down with her instead."

"No, that's not right. Why would Catalina lie like this? My brother is dead. Speaking ill of him is just wrong."

I am done with this woman. "After the funeral, you and Giovi will return to Detroit. You no longer have a place in the New York *famiglia*. My mother will make the arrangements for the funeral and you will be informed its time and place."

I hang up to her squawks of protest.

Catalina believes her aunt and uncle love her. I'm furious with Lora for being so deluded about her brother. She justified his treatment of Catalina because he blamed her for Sara Jilani's death. Even if it were true, nothing could excuse a grown man beating a defenseless child.

The fact that it is a lie only makes it worse.

I call Luigi and instruct him to have Catalina's things retrieved from her room in the Jilani home. She is never going back to that place. I text my mother and tell her that under no circumstances do I want Lora or Giovi Revello to be alone with my wife.

I then text Aldo with the same instructions and add that I want whatever guard is with my wife to interfere by whatever means necessary if Lora begins speaking to Catalina about her mother, her father, or her sister.

I will not allow her to be hurt by her aunt's fantasy view of Francesco.

CHAPTER 22

SEVERU

I return to our suite to wake my wife.

Emilia offered to have one of the maids style Catalina's hair. I declined. Undoubtedly, the maid's ability will be useful before my wife's injuries heal completely, but today I want no one to touch Catalina except me.

Dark possessiveness rolls through me, and I make no attempt to force it to abate. *She is mine.*

I run her a bath, putting some of the anti-inflammatory Epsom salts into the water. I add bath oil so her delicate skin will not dry out before I return to the bedroom. I pull the duvet and sheet back, surprised when she does not stir. Lifting her into my arms, I revel in the feel of her soft naked body against me.

I'm still wearing the suit I put on earlier. Holding her naked while I am dressed sends a sexual thrill straight to my cock. I picture myself fucking her exactly like this, only unzipping my slacks and pulling my cock out to make it possible.

I force myself to save that fantasy for another time and carry her into the bathroom. I shake her a little, "Catalina, wake up."

She mumbles something and turns her face into my chest. She's so damn sweet.

I release her legs, letting them drop down, but I don't trust them to hold her up when she's like this, so I keep one arm around her. I manage to get my jacket, my tie and my shirt off before she stiffens like she's finally waking up.

"Severu? What are you doing?"

"Getting you in the bath." And trying to do it without dunking my bespoke suit.

"We showered earlier."

"You need to soak." I lift her legs again and take the final step to reach the jetted tub that is large enough for me to recline in. It's practically a swimming pool for her.

I lower her into the hot water.

She sighs. "Mmm, that feels good."

"Do not go back to sleep," I warn her. "You will slide right under the water."

Not that I'm leaving her here to bathe herself.

She blinks sleepily at me but keeps her eyes open. I don't start washing her because I want her to soak for a while. As her eyelids slide down again, I realize that sitting beside the tub will not be enough. I'm going to have to join her.

Since deciding to marry her yesterday, I have exercised almost no self-control where she is concerned. However, even her delectable body will not tempt me to take her when it could mean hurting her.

Despite evidence to the contrary, I am too well disciplined for that.

My training to follow in my father's footsteps was overseen by a former Army Ranger and one of the world's best assassins. Those lessons only augmented what my father started with me before I learned to walk.

I never played a game as a child that did not prepare either my mind or my body for my future. Trying to catch my father's hands enhanced the speed of my reflexes. Playing hide-and-seek was an exercise in stealth and tracking. Chess taught me strategy and the ability to think several steps ahead to the outcome of any action.

Success was rewarded; failure was punished.

Failure here will punish my wife. That I will not allow.

I finish stripping and get into the tub, maneuvering Catalina in front of me. Her silky skin slides against mine in the oil softened water. The scent of the bath salts is familiar, but different now. I'll never associate it again with my post workout. It now makes me think of Catalina floating naked in our tub.

My hardon presses against her back. She doesn't react to it; she's completely relaxed.

Like she trusts me absolutely to take care of her. This woman who has so little reason to trust powerful men, has no physical reticence with me.

It is a heady truth to acknowledge. I have had the responsibility of the entire New York *famiglia* since becoming don five years ago, and yet this moment is more profound than any I have felt.

We lie in the water together for thirty minutes. Any longer will have little extra benefit and any less will not be the maximum benefit achieved.

Though I mentally track the time, I allow myself to relax like I never do. My inner clock tells me when the half hour has passed, and I begin washing my wife's body with moisturizing bodywash that Emilia must have left for my future bride.

I lather my hands and wash her shoulders and then her breasts, forcing myself not to stop there and play. It is harder than it should be. I swirl water between her legs rather than touch her there and be tempted to do more.

"You're pretty attentive for a man who didn't want to bother with his wife."

"I did not say that."

"As good as."

"Marriage to you was never going to be the same as marriage to your sister."

She is silent for several seconds, and then says quietly, "A week ago, I would have assumed you meant I could never measure up."

"The opposite is true." Carlotta would never have tested my resolve like Catalina, *mi dolce bellezza*, does.

"I'm still finding it hard to believe you were going to marry her feeling that way." Catalina sounds disgruntled, but it's tinged with something else. Sadness? "You would have hurt both of us."

I do not know if she means herself and her sister, or herself and me, but it doesn't matter. "Emotions cannot control the decisions a good don makes."

Even when it hurts someone important to him. My father drilled that into me. He rarely had to make that call, but when he did? I never saw him hesitate.

"I don't know if I could do that." Catalina runs her hands along my forearms, sparking a conflagration of need such a simple touch should not be able to.

"What?" I force myself to ask, when I just want to flip her body and kiss her senseless.

"Ignore my feelings when making a decision." She places her hands over mine, inserting her fingers between my own.

Her hands are so much smaller than mine. Perfect, unblemished skin beside my scars and rough ridged knuckles. I may dress like a billionaire off Wall Street but my body tells the true story. I have risen to the top of the criminal world through a life bathed in violence.

And yet for all the softness that is my wife, she has a core of steel to match my own. "You are stronger than you know, Catalina. If you had to, you could."

Her fingers tighten convulsively. "Here's hoping I never have to."

"You already have."

"What are you talking about?"

"You ignored your desire for me when you demanded I take your sister on dates to make the wedding a less frightening prospect for her."

Catalina helped plan the wedding despite her own longings and desires. Because she has so much honor, she would never give into weakness and let her sister down. Unlike Carlotta, who left her older sister to face their father's fury when she ran.

Marrying the younger sister would have been a huge mistake on my part. Not something I like admitting, even if only to myself.

"You ignored your fear of your father when you learned to shoot a gun." She'd saved her and her sister's lives with that skill a mere month ago.

"Tio Giovi made that possible."

"You still took the risk, Catalina. You did it again yesterday morning to protect your sister." This woman's courage amazes me. "You lived for years with the knowledge that your father had killed your mother and still, you stood up to him."

I'm not sure my intrepid wife has ever let the emotion of fear dictate a single one of her decisions, or actions. She might be tiny next to me, but she has the spirit of a ten-foot-tall warrior.

"How do you know I did?" she asks.

"Because you've done so with me and I'm a hell of a lot scarier."

"Not to me, but you're right. I did."

"My queen is already tempered steel." I say it with satisfaction. Because one thing her sister would never have been, was a queen to stand by my side. I cannot imagine Catalina in any other place.

"I'm not sure I would go that far."

She will learn to see herself as she is and not the warped vision created in the reflection of her family's toxic fun house mirror.

She shifts like she's going to get out of the bath. "I'm going to have to French braid my hair." There is no enthusiasm for the idea in her tone.

How will braiding it be any easier on her than using the blow dryer? Both require her lifting her hands above her head for long periods of time and that will pull against her bruised ribs. Not acceptable.

"Get it wet and I'll blow dry it for you, like we planned."

She turns now to face me, floating in the water, though her tits press against my chest. "Are you sure?" She's biting her lip again. "Emilia would probably do it if we asked nicely."

I gently tug her lip from her teeth and she blushes as if just now realizing she was doing it. "Emilia already offered the services of one of the maids," I tell my wife. "I declined."

"Why?" Her brows are drawn together in confusion.

I am not ashamed of the truth. "I don't want anyone else touching you right now."

"That's a little obsessive, don't you think?"

"No."

She laughs but doesn't argue further. I pour water from the faucet over her hair, using my cupped hands, as the tub drains. When her hair is soaked, I help her stand and then lift her from the tub.

Catalina stands docilely while I dry her, but when I'm done, she grabs another towel from the heating rack and starts to dry me with it. I let her do everything that doesn't require bending or reaching.

When we are both dry, I take the bottle of pain pills I left on the counter and shake two out. She's supposed to stagger the two analgesics and I'm going to make sure she gets every dose. I give them to her along with a glass of water from the carafe near the sink. She swallows the pills down and I administer the healing cream to her injuries again.

Neither of us speaks. She barely breathes as I touch her carefully, seeking to help relieve her pain. This strange hush between us feels intensely intimate and neither of us seeks to break it.

She sits in the chair in front of the vanity mirror, like she did earlier. Only this time, I work the product through her hair that is supposed to prevent it from getting frizzy.

This is a whole different world for me. I wash my hair and let it dry naturally after I comb it into place.

"Use your fingers to separate my hair when the blow dryer is pointed at that section," she instructs me, finally breaking the silence. "It will dry faster. Don't start using the paddle brush to smooth it until it's at least half dry."

It sounds complicated, but I do what she says and find myself relaxing from the rhythmic movements.

My wife watches me intently through the mirror, looking away when I catch her eye. But then her gaze is back on mine a moment later. Eventually she stops looking away and I continue what I'm doing until her hair is dry and falls like a smooth caramel curtain around her shoulders.

"It's like silk." I lift it over her shoulders.

"You did a great job." She frowns at herself in the mirror.

"What is it?"

"Besides that awful bruise on my face? I just wish my hair wasn't so mousy brown. Maybe I should get highlights."

"Do not fucking dare."

Her eyes widen. "That's a strong reaction."

"Your hair is not mousy. It is like rich caramel. If you ruin it with highlights, I'll..." I try to think of a threat that would actually dissuade my strong-willed wife that I would be willing to follow through on. "I will invite the nosiest wives in *la famiglia* over to visit you every day until it grows out."

"All you had to do was say you like it this way," she says with a laugh. "I mean, if I really wanted highlights, I'd get them. But it was just a passing thought. I'm not big on spending a lot of time at the salon."

"Good. You don't need it."

"Even your compliments are bossy."

"Part of my charm."

"Okay, Prince Charming, as much as I enjoy being naked with you." Her eyes sparkle like she's proud of saying that. "We both need to get some clothes on so we can have lunch with your family. I guess I'll have to wear the dress from yesterday."

"Since it does a good job of hiding your braless state, you may wear it without the shawl."

Catalina opens her mouth like she's going to say something, but then closes it and her eyes, which are sparking with feisty resolve. When she opens them, her expression is tranquil. Even so, she inhales a deep breath and lets it out slowly.

She's showing circumspection.

I should be glad, but part of me wants to know what she intended to say.

CHAPTER 23

CATALINA

I want to tell Severu what he can do with his *permission* to wear the dress I came home from the hospital in, but I manage to bite the words back. My mom used to say, "Pick your battles, Catalina."

I had a tendency to mouth off to my father because I resented the way he treated my beloved mother, and I ended up in trouble most days because of it. That trouble didn't lead to him striking me until after her death. The first time he smacked me because he was angry at Carlotta, I wondered how many punishments my mother took because of my sass.

Knowing she took any is one of the reasons I refused to become the cowed creature my father wanted me to be. If Mamma could take pain for the sake of my character, so could I.

Remembering Severu's plans for me to go shopping with his mother and sister later, I decide that is a battle I'm willing to fight. No matter how much I learned to enjoy both women's company during my sister's engagement, I *hate* shopping.

"I don't need to go shopping," I tell Severu. "I have clothes at home."

And I have my ballet flats by a designer that specializes in comfort. As well as a generic shoe insert I ordered online to help, at least a little bit, with the inch difference in the length of my legs.

"This is your home now."

So not the point. "My former home then."

"You don't need to go today. You still need to heal, but my mother wants to equip you with a wardrobe that suits your position as my wife. The sooner the better."

They'd already talked about it? When? We just got married yesterday.

While I was napping? No. He brought the shopping trip up this morning before pleasure left me exhausted. Did they talk during the reception? They must have. His mother thinks it's such a drastic need she brought it up during the reception.

The parallel I drew yesterday between mine and Severu's marriage and that of my parents comes back to haunt me. I guarantee that if he'd married Carlotta neither he nor Aria would believe today's shopping trip necessary. It doesn't make me feel any better to realize that my sister would not balk at going either.

He might physically desire me more than my sister, but that doesn't mean he sees me as a good candidate for don's wife. If he had, he wouldn't have announced his engagement to her.

I grimace when I have to slip my feet into the shoes I wore for the wedding. They are the only ones I have here, but I hate wearing heels. I wish I could go to lunch barefoot, but Zia Lora would be apoplectic if she knew I was even considering it. And I'm sure Severu's family would not be impressed if I showed up to the table with my bare toes peeking out from beneath my dress.

I really need my things.

~ ~ ~

Severu helps me into a chair, like the gentleman he sometimes pretends to be, before taking his own seat at the head of the table. He's put me to his right.

His mother sits at the other end and though technically that should be my chair as his wife, I do not mind. I like that my husband has placed me close to him.

Aria gives a rueful laugh and stands. "I am sorry, *cara*. This is your seat now."

She starts to take another seat, but Severu stops her. "Catalina is fine right here, mother."

"Severu, it is her right."

I don't want mother and son arguing over something so inconsequential. Especially as I like this arrangement. "I prefer to sit here."

"I liked that seat when my husband was alive as well," Aria says with a satisfied smile as she returns to her original chair.

Heat climbs my cheek at her words, because they imply an affection I'm not comfortable voicing. However, I remind myself that this seating arrangement was Severu's idea. So, apparently, he would rather me sit near him as well. That knowledge has heat settling in other places besides my face.

Miceli sits across from me and examines my face with his dark gaze so like his brother's. "Hello, Catalina. Survive your unexpected wedding alright?"

"I'll admit the last thing I expected yesterday morning was to end up married to your brother and moving into your family's home by the end of the day." Not that I am actually moved in, with a single dress and a pair of shoes, that are too big for me, my only current wardrobe.

"How are you feeling?" Aria asks me.

I smile. "Good, thank you. Nothing broken."

"That's not a very high bar to set," Guilia says with a concerned look for me. "Are you in pain? Should you be in bed? You could have eaten on a tray."

The thought had never occurred to me. "I wanted to come to lunch. You'll be leaving New York soon."

"I would have come to your room and visited you there," Giulia says, sincerity ringing in her voice.

This family. They are so different from my own.

"I am doing much better today," I reassure her. "Severu is making sure I take my pain meds and putting the anti-inflammatory cream on my bruises."

"Is he?" Miceli gives his brother a strange look. "I've never known Sev to play nursemaid."

"Your brother now has a wife. Taking care of her is not only his responsibility, but his privilege," Raffaele Mancini says with a smile for Severu's sister that somehow encompasses me as well.

Guilia smiles back at her husband, her eyes glowing with emotion.

Their marriage wasn't a love match, but it's obvious that affection has developed between them.

I doubt Severu shares Raffaele's sentiment about caring for me though. He's more patient than I expected, but that's not the same as feeling it's a privilege to take care of me.

After giving me a long, unfathomable look, my husband says, "She is mine."

The words resonate in my heart, though they have nothing to do with emotion. Why do I find his possessiveness so utterly entrancing? Is it because no one has claimed responsibility for me since my mother died?

Belonging is as heady as any drug to someone who has gone so long without it.

"Thank you for taking such good care of me," I say to him with a smile, feeling unaccountably shy.

He gets an arrested look on his face, but then he shakes his head and very deliberately turns to talk to his brother. They discuss business as the food is served and I have an acute understanding of how my sister could have shared so many dinners with this man and told me she had not gotten to know him at all.

Her complaints about his boring business talk at the dinners she attended in his home were what prompted me to call him and tell him he needed to court her.

Unlike Carlotta, however, I'm interested in what they are talking about. It sounds like there have been several attacks on the New York Cosa Nostra in the past eight months. Only a couple of them successful.

Severu must trust his brother-in-law, talking New York mafia business in front of the Las Vegas Cosa Nostra underboss.

"You think it is the Irish?" I ask when there is a pause in the conversation.

Miceli frowns. "Someone wants us to think it is."

"But you don't?" I ask him, including my husband in the question.

"We cannot be sure, but Shaughnessy isn't sloppy." Severu frowns, like he doesn't like admitting this. "If he attacked one of our warehouses it would be ashes on the ground."

"He claims he's had similar incidents and there has been an effort to make it seem like Italians are responsible," Miceli adds.

They answer my questions so easily, I don't hesitate to dig further.

"But he doesn't believe it either?" I want to confirm, because if the Irish mob boss in New York believes the Cosa Nostra is infringing on his territory, that means war.

The thought of Severu going to war against another powerful syndicate sends icy dread through me.

"He says he doesn't," Severu replies.

"Because he knows that if our men were responsible, they wouldn't leave a calling card, nor would they fail," I guess.

Severu nods, approval glittering in his espresso gaze. For a moment, I am lost in his eyes and do not hear what Miceli says.

I force myself to look away from my husband. "I'm sorry, what did you say?"

"The attacks were sporadic for a while, but they have picked up in the last month. Ever since the attempt to kidnap you and your sister."

"So, it was an attempted kidnapping?" I remember how it felt to shoot that man and mentally shake off the horror that comes with the memory.

I might not be a made man, but I will protect my family in any way I can.

"Francesco didn't tell you?" my husband asks, his eyes narrowed.

"He never discussed business with the family." Not even Zio Giovi, who used to be a capo in Detroit.

"But he should have at least told you that the men wanted to kidnap, not kill you," Giulia says spiritedly. "You were his daughter."

It strikes me that none of the De Lucas have expressed sympathy for my loss. It's as if they realize that I'm not grieving my father's death and they don't want to be fake with me. There will be enough of that at the funeral.

I smile wryly at her. "Mafia business was not *our* business according to him."

It sounds like she says, "What a tool," under her breath, but I pretend not to hear. Not because I don't agree, but because I don't want to draw attention to her comment in case the men around the table would be offended by it.

In my family, women do not criticize made men. Full stop. Period.

"They were going to hold us for ransom?" I ask.

"They were going to ransom Carlotta, but they were going to s—"

"Shut it," Severu barks at his brother before Miceli can finish his sentence.

But Miceli said enough. "They were going to sell me?" I ask faintly, feeling sick. We all know what that means and it's not an arranged marriage.

I cannot help the shudder of revulsion as terror engulfs me. I am safe. I am here. But if I had not been able to defend myself, I wouldn't be. That ability should make me feel confident, but the knowledge that I could have so easily ended up a victim of human trafficking rolls through me.

Carlotta crying. The bodyguards yelling. Blood on the road. Unmoving bodies. The sound of gun fire. Glass shards glittering in the spring sun. The smell of burnt rubber. Blood spreading out over a man's chest.

The man I shot would have sold me. I feel my lips moving. Did I say that out loud?

"Severu would never have let that happen," Giulia says to me, but it sounds like her voice is coming through a tunnel.

I nod, but the ice I felt earlier spreads through my veins until I'm shivering uncontrollably from the chill.

Everyone is looking at me. I don't like it. Earlier when everyone talked to me and showed concern for my wellbeing, I felt cherished. Now I just feel like a bug on the end of a pin. I try to make myself smaller in my chair, but wince when curling in on myself hurts my ribs.

Someone whimpers like a wounded animal. It's me. I'm that wounded animal.

I need to get control of myself, but I can't get enough air. I can't stop the movie from that day playing over in my mind. The feel of the gun in my hands when I pull the trigger. It's so loud.

Aria is saying something, but I can only hear the gunshot.

CHAPTER 24

CATALINA

What happens next seems to shock every person at the table. Severu shoves his chair back, stands up, and lifts me into his arms before sitting down with me in his lap.

At the dining room table.

In front of his entire family.

"You are safe, and you will stay that way." Severu's voice cuts through the cacophony in my head.

His scent casts the remembered smells of that day into the background. He rubs his hands up and down my arm. "Shh...*mi dolce gatto*. I will keep you safe."

I nod. Because I believe him.

The cold dissipates as my entire body flushes with embarrassment-tinged pleasure. Because my unemotional husband is holding me and comforting me with no regard for where we are, or our audience.

He pulls my plate near and gives me a bite of the flaky and moist tilapia, as if there is nothing out of the ordinary about holding me on his lap and feeding me during lunch. "You need to eat."

I don't reply, too busy chewing.

"That's one way to keep her safe," Miceli says with a laugh.

No one else comments on the odd seating arrangement, but when I chance a glance up at my husband's face, I know why. His expression is more than forbidding. He looks like he wants to kill someone.

My body relaxes into his of its own volition and I sigh. "I guess I should have stayed in bed."

Only I've never coddled myself after Papà hurt me; I've certainly never been coddled by others.

"Yesterday was taxing on you," Aria says sympathetically.

I flick my gaze to her and notice the worried expression on her perfectly made up features and it does something funny to my heart. Tears prick at my eyes and I blink them away. I do not cry.

"Not the first one," Giulia says. "From what I can tell. If your father weren't dead, I'd be tempted to shoot him myself."

I probably should have asked to borrow makeup from her. I'm sure the bruise on my cheek isn't helping anyone's appetite. And I hate seeing Severu's sweet sister so upset.

"*Amore mio!*" Raffaele sounds scandalized.

Giulia gives her husband a challenging stare. "Tell me you don't feel the same. She was kept a practical prisoner for years in that awful man's home while he beat her so badly she had to be treated at the hospital nearly a dozen times. All the while we welcomed him into our home and at our table. Papà and Sev trusted his advice. I hate it."

My heart cracks right down the center. My own family spent years ignoring how my father treated me. And this woman I barely know is genuinely upset. On my behalf.

"The only place he'll be welcomed now is hell," Severu says, his voice chilling.

"You told your family everything," I say to him.

"I did," Miceli says. And he doesn't sound like he regrets it. "We don't keep secrets in this house."

Can that be true? Do they really tell each other everything? They are a mafia family. Even outsiders have secrets in their families. Don't they?

Does this mean they talk mafia business in front of the women? They certainly don't seem to mind discussing the recent attacks. However, last night, Severu had been careful to avoid admitting he had killed my father.

Navigating this new life of mine will be even more challenging than I expected.

"I'm glad he did. You're one of us now," Giulia says.

Aria looks at me with sadness. "I wish I had known, Catalina."

I can only shake my head. How could I have said anything? Until yesterday morning, I had no inkling *I* would ever become part of this amazing family.

"Your clothes will be brought over from your old home this afternoon," Severu says calmly as he feeds me another bite of food.

"Thank you," I say after I swallow my asparagus. "You can let me up now. My meltdown is over." I try to shift off his thighs.

But his arm comes around my hips like a steel band. "You are fine where you are."

"But..." I indicate the others at the table.

"We all understand," Giulia says.

They do? Because I don't. I never fall apart like this. And allowing my husband to feed me like a child should be awkward at the very least, not make me feel comforted and cared for.

Giulia gives Severu a cheeky grin. "Though I have to say this more tender side of my brother is something of a surprise."

I'm not sure tender is the right word. Possessive more like.

When the maid comes in to take away the plates, I force down my embarrassment at being found on my husband's lap and shoot for a look of equanimity.

"Wow, you've got the aura of mafia queen down," the irrepressible Giulia says. "I don't know how you manage to look regal sitting on my brother's knees, but you've done it."

That makes me blush which earns me a wink from Raffaele and that only makes me blush harder.

The growl that sounds from my husband sends a shiver of arousal through me and garners a laugh from both of his siblings. Why?

"I meant no offense," Raffaele says. "She is my sister now, though, is she not?"

And I realize the growl was in response to the other man's wink.

I look up at my husband. "Possessive, much?"

"You like me that way," he says.

I cannot deny it. I sigh. "I'd like to continue discussing these attacks if you don't mind."

I wait to see how Severu and Miceli react to this.

Surprise flares in Severu's espresso gaze, but he nods. "We will adjourn to the living room though."

Aria excuses herself to make some phone calls, but Giulia, Raffaele and Miceli join us.

SEVERU

I carry my wife into the living room, and she doesn't even try to convince me to let her walk. Which is a good thing.

Because although I have put on a calm façade, rage is a consuming fire inside me. Seeing her succumb to the memories, her skin going pasty, her beautiful hazel eyes filled with horror caused a feeling I have no experience with. Helplessness.

Putting her in my lap was the only way I was going to control the murderous fury exploding through me.

Her father is already dead, but the men who worked for him still breathe. His head of security should have had a detail of at least six men on her and her sister when they travelled to and from their mansion on Long Island to the City. Her aunt and uncle, who were complicit in her father's abuse through their silence, still live.

Catalina will be devastated if I kill them though. Damn it to hell.

"You have a ferocious expression on your face." She brushes my face with her small hand. "What are you thinking about?"

"Our enemies." It is not a lie. I consider every adult in that household who stood back and did nothing while my wife was subjected to Francesco's violence my enemy.

I sit down in my favorite armchair and settle Catalina sideways on my lap so I can see her face.

"What do you want to know about the attacks?" I ask her, fully aware that I cannot share certain details, including the fact I tortured a man we believed a member of the Irish mob for information when he tried to burn down one of our warehouses.

"We'll get to that, but first I want to make an observation."

"Yes?"

"We know that my father valued my sister more than me and was unlikely to pay a ransom to get me back, but how did the kidnappers know that?"

"It's possible your father was the rat." I don't mention that whoever hired the Albanians considered her to be unimportant and told the thugs to leave her.

"You think there's an informant working with our enemies?" she asks.

Miceli says, "These attacks show inside knowledge to our operations."

"And you think my father leaked *la famiglia's* secrets to an enemy?" she asks, her voice drenched with disbelief. "Nothing was more important to him than the Cosa Nostra."

"You forget that he betrayed his don." He was a rat, even if he wasn't the informant.

"I don't," she says immediately. "But that was his arrogance, not a lack of loyalty. At least he would never have seen it that way. But selling the Cosa Nostra's secrets?" She shakes her head.

"You said it yourself, the would-be kidnappers knew that he did not value you as much as he did Carlotta." Which only shows just how deluded Francesco was.

"Which means either someone who did know that is the rat, or that the instructions were to leave me behind and the men who attacked us decided to take advantage of an opportunity."

I should not be surprised she guessed the facts of the situation, but my wife never ceases to amaze me.

"That's what the Albanian said."

"I thought the attacks were being staged to look like the Irish mob are behind them. Do you think the attempted kidnapping is separate from the other attacks on the business?"

I tell her, "The Albanians were hired anonymously."

"Hmm..." She's silent for several seconds and then frowns. "Looking at this objectively, it's a no win situation for the Shaughnessy's mob. They control about the same number of boroughs as the Genovese mafia, but we have some unique businesses. So do they. Going to war with the Cosa Nostra would cost them more than they could hope to gain."

"I thought you said your father never talked business with the family."

"I listened at doors and his men weren't nearly as reticent talking about business around me. I was a nonentity in that house."

"It could be the bratva, trying to stir trouble between us and the Irish."

But she shakes her head. "No. Just because a bratva family in Detroit double crossed the Irish doesn't mean any of the bratva families in New York are looking to risk their people trying to steal territory. They don't have to use New York to bring in their cargo. They have family connections in port towns on Canada's East Coast, not to mention Boston."

"Don't tell me you overheard that listening in on conversations between your father's men."

She grins. "Nope. It's the result of intense intelligence gathering."

What the hell is she talking about?

"Once I came home from boarding school I had very little to do except learn and research things that interested me. My father liked to say I'm stupid and ignorant. Useless. Knowing more than he did about the Cosa Nostra made me feel powerful. It was my way of proving him wrong."

Impressed by my wife's determination and intelligence, I point out, "The bratva are not the Cosa Nostra."

"Well, no, but researching the Cosa Nostra naturally led me to accumulating information on all the major syndicates in the Cosa Nostra's five territories."

"How?" my sister asks, sounding fascinated.

"Yes, how?" My brother-in-law seems far less trusting. He thinks my wife is talking out of her ass.

I know better. I don't underestimate the woman in my arms.

"How can you know they aren't the same bratva family?" Miceli asks. He wants specifics related to our current situation.

"Surnames. I track all the family and syndicate connections via the news, social media, public arrest records and government reports which are often published in easily accessible places."

"Fucking hell." That is Raffaele. "Where do you keep this information?"

"It's analog. My father might have found it on my computer, or God forbid, law enforcement with a warrant for the household computers. A written document can't be hacked and it's unlikely that any warrant would cover my personal possessions since I have nothing to do with the business. Even so, I took pains to hide all the information I have accumulated. In the wrong hands it could undermine *la famiglia*."

"You got that right," Miceli says explosively.

I tilt Catalina's head up with my knuckles under her chin. I want to kiss her, but I ask instead, "Where is it?"

"In my bedroom at the mansion."

"We need to get it now," Miceli says, a rare urgency to his tone.

I nod. "Call Luigi. He's there retrieving Catalina's personal things."

"I might need to go to the house to get it. I'm not sure Luigi will be able to figure out the mechanism for the entrance to the secret room. It's complicated."

Chapter 25

SEVERU

"Secret room?" I ask, stunned.

"I know it looks newer, but that's because the original house has been added onto and doesn't show in the outer façade of the mansion it has become. I don't think Papa would have bought it otherwise."

I'm sure she's right. Appearances were important to Francesco.

"My bedroom is part of the original house. My father wasn't interested in its history, but I was. I learned it was built by a Mason over one hundred and fifty years ago. That's how I found the secret room."

"I don't want you going back there."

She rubs her face against my knuckles. I'm not sure she's even aware she's doing it. "Why?"

She needs to ask?

"It was my home. I never want to live there again, but I'll want to visit my aunt and uncle sometimes."

"They won't be there. They're moving to Detroit after the funeral."

"That will make my uncle happy. I don't think he ever thought of Long Island as home."

I don't care if her uncle is happy. I just don't want them anywhere near Catalina. They had their chance to be decent family to her and they blew it. They're damn lucky I'm not going to kill them.

"I can try to explain the unlocking mechanism to Luigi, but I think you should see the information I have compiled before leaving it to a soldier to pack up and move."

She's right. Damn it. "Tell me how to open the room."

"I want to go with you. It's my research."

I nod grudgingly and then I text Luigi and tell him I want the mansion cleared when we arrive.

I don't want Candilora and Giovi there and I can't trust Francesco's men until Big Sal has a chance to vet them and decide who he's keeping on his crew. He'll be there when we arrive though. He's going through Francesco's files already and will be moving what he needs to his office. The rest will be disposed of.

After texting Luigi, I send a message to Aldo:

Full team of Catalina's guards. Going to Long Island. Have cars and men ready in 10 min.

"I should probably put some makeup on before we leave," Catalina says as she stands up.

"I'll do your face," my sister offers.

My wife smiles, but it doesn't reach her eyes. "Thank you. That would be great. I'm not used to wearing it." The small downward twist to her lips says she doesn't like it either.

"If you don't want to wear makeup, don't," I tell her.

Giulia gives me a pitying glance. "Isn't that just like a man. Do you want people thinking your wife is unsophisticated? She's a don's wife. She can't afford to make a bad impression."

My mother and sister love their makeup and spa treatments, but that's not Catalina.

"The only impression she needs to make is on her left finger." Speaking of, I need to get her an engagement ring to wear with her wedding ring. Something big that will leave no one doubting that she is taken.

"I don't want anyone thinking you gave me this bruise," Catalina says firmly. "I will not allow you to be tarred with the brush that belongs only to my father."

What is that weird feeling? I thump my chest to dislodge it.

"Your wife sure is protective of you," Miceli says after the women leave.

Raffaele nods. "Considering she's a stand in for her sister, that's unexpected."

"She's no stand in." I move menacingly toward my brother-in-law. "She is my queen."

"No argument here, brother." Raffaele puts both hands up, but he's not afraid of me.

He never has been, which is one of the reasons I consider him a good match for my sister. Even his father, the current Don of Las Vegas Cosa Nostra, is more cautious around me.

"This stays between us," I say to Miceli and Raffaele.

Both nod.

"Not even your father knows, Raffaele. We'll share information, but no one can know where you get it."

Raffaele shows no reservation when he agrees. "No one else. Knowledge is power and having access to this knowledge strengthens my power base."

I never thought that way with my own father, but the Don of Las Vegas is a different man than my father was.

"What do you think we'll find in her files?" Miceli asks.

"Even if it's only a list of family names and their connections in the different Cosa Nostra territories, it will be a damn good resource."

Both my brother and brother-in-law agree.

Catalina returns and I cannot see the bruise, but my sister hasn't overdone the rest of her makeup. I nod my approval. *Mi dolce bellezza* does not need artificial enhancement to her natural loveliness.

Giulia gives me an exasperated look, but she doesn't say anything.

Catalina nearly trips as we approach the elevator. I grab her arm. "What is it? Are you feeling dizzy?" Damn it, maybe we should put this off.

But if she has documented even half of what she implied earlier, that information is too sensitive to leave in the Jilani mansion. Even in a secret room.

"I'm fine. It's these shoes. They're a size too big and don't want to stay on my feet."

"You should have said something," Guilia admonishes Catalina. "What size shoe do you wear?"

When Catalina tells her, my sister frowns in disappointment. "You're a size smaller than me."

"Take them off," I say to my wife.

"I can't leave the house barefoot."

"Fine." I pick her up again.

"Severu." She slaps my chest. "I can walk. I just need to put some more tissue in the toes."

She stops protesting once we are in the elevator.

The men and SUVs are ready as we step off the elevator in the parking garage.

"Carlo, you and Aldo in the Cayenne with Catalina and Me."

The lead SUV is a Hummer, equipped with military grade weapons that slide out of their hidden compartments when necessary. It will be followed by Miceli in his McLaren Speedtail. It is not armored, but the tires are bullet proof as is the glass. He refuses to have the body reinforced because it would impact the speed and maneuverability of the car. A second SUV will be between my brother's car and the Cayenne. The final truck in the convoy is another weaponized Hummer.

I promised Catalina she would be safe, and I will keep that promise.

"It's like traveling with the president," Catalina says with a small laugh. "Will it always be like this when we go places together?"

"When our security alert status is green, you will have one extra SUV with three guards and three in your armored car. When it is yellow, you will have a second SUV traveling behind you with four additional guards."

"And when it's red?" she asks, her eyes wide.

"You will either be in the apartment with an army of guards or a safe house out of state."

She swallows. "It *is* like being married to the president."

"You are married to the King of New York," I remind her.

"I'm not sure I'm queen material."

"You are my wife."

She laughs. "Things are pretty basic for you, aren't they? I am your wife and therefore I *am* a queen. Doesn't matter if I know how to put on my own makeup or schmooze other mafia wives."

"Other mafia wives will be honored to be in your company. No schmoozing necessary."

"Good to know." But she rolls her eyes.

"You've got an irreverent streak in your nature."

"It's a good thing you aren't God then, isn't it?"

I unbuckle her seatbelt, pull her to the center seat and buckle her in again.

"Why did you do that?" she asks, sounding a little breathless.

My touch does that to her.

"So I can do this." I kiss her, exploring her sweet mouth with my tongue.

I snap my fingers and hear the whir of the privacy glass sliding into place between us and the front. Then I reach behind my wife and unzip her dress, sliding it down to reveal her luscious tits. I play with them until she's writhing on the seat and mewling against my lips.

Only then do I slide my hand up under her dress all the way to her soaked panties. I slide a finger inside and groan myself when I feel her satin slick folds. My mouth waters to taste her, but I settle for slipping my finger inside her pussy, rubbing her swollen walls. Her hips cant toward my hand and maneuver my thumb under her panties so I can reach her clit. I press against it and then slide my thumb back and forth, repeating the pattern until she screams her climax into my mouth.

I pet her until I've wrung every aftershock from her I can and then I withdraw my hand and suck the flavor of my wife off my fingers.

She stares at me with glazed eyes, her mouth slightly open, her face and tits flushed with pleasure.

"What about you?" she asks after long moments of silence.

"I can wait." I'm hard as stone, but my pleasure in her ecstasy is strangely satisfying.

CATALINA

I'm still reeling from the bliss Severu's touch gives me when we arrive at the mansion.

His men exit from the other cars and create a wall around us as we get out of my husband's Cayenne.

"I cleared the house after I sent the Rivellos, the staff and the soldiers away." I think the man speaking is named Luigi. He was part of the entourage yesterday.

Why did they send everyone away? Maybe Severu doesn't want to risk anyone finding out about the information I've compiled. I'm disappointed because I'd hoped to see Zia Lora and Zio Giovi.

But part of me is relieved too. So much has happened in the last two days that I don't want to talk about. Me marrying the don. My father's death.

Carlotta running away. Especially when she hasn't been found yet. Worry for her plays a constant discordant note in the back of my mind. Except when Severu is touching me, or I am sleeping.

Severu inclines his head. "Good. Does Big Sal have any men with him?"

"He brought four. He doesn't trust Jilani's men yet and they know it."

"What is your take on the Jilani Soldiers?"

Luigi frowns. "I don't like the look of a couple of them."

"You tell Big Sal?"

"Yep. He was already looking at them."

My husband nods, like he's satisfied.

We go up the steps and into the mansion. Walking into the foyer, it's familiar but also feels like it's part of a different life. How can only two days make so much difference? But this does not feel like home.

Though, it really hasn't been much a home since my mother's death, has it?

After Severu has a word with Big Sal in my father's office, I lead the way. We go up the stairs to the second floor and walk all the way to the end of the hall. As we progress, men from the entourage peel off to take up security positions along the way. It's all so well-orchestrated. No hesitation, no questions about where to stand. Each of them is alert, their stance military tight.

My bedroom door is open. When I step inside, I see that there are half packed open boxes on the floor. Some with clothes, some with books. Purposefully avoiding even glancing at the books, though I do note with relief that my bookcase is almost empty, I kick off the too big pumps and make a beeline for my wardrobe.

My shoes are sitting in a neat line across the floor. I don't have that many pairs. Just one in each basic color. Other than a single pair of low heels in nude Zia Lora insisted I wear to my cousin's wedding three year's ago, the rest are flats. Satisfaction floods me as I slide on a pair of tan ballet flats with the insert already in the right shoe.

Only then do I head for the fireplace, original to the house. I pause, unable to start the sequence that will open the door hidden in the wall.

CHAPTER 26

CATALINA

"What is wrong, Catalina?" Severu asks me.

I shake my head. "Nothing. Not really. It's just the first time I've ever opened the secret room with anyone else here."

"You do not need a secret room any longer, Catalina," my husband says like he knows that the room is where the real Catalina has lived for the past eleven years.

I found it when I was fourteen, my first summer home after going away to boarding school. It had been so hard to settle back into life in the mansion after living like other girls at school, with no threat of violence and verbal cruelty hanging over my head every day.

The masonic symbol on the fireplace made me curious and I researched what it might mean. When a book I read said the symbol could indicate a hidey hole in the fireplace, I started searching for other clues. I found the bricks with the three dots. I spent almost the entire summer figuring out what they meant. When I discovered a secret room rather than a hidey hole, I was elated.

Knowing I have no choice but to expose this part of myself I've kept hidden so well for so long, I nod.

I'm comforted to see that the only people in my bedroom now are Severu and Miceli. Even Aldo and Luigi have left. The bedroom door to the hallway is closed.

I like that Severu listened to me and took my suggestion not to let anyone else see my files before he got a look at them.

I push one side of nine bricks in the fireplace marked with a tiny masonic symbol in one corner. Then I grab the little step stool I found in the attic years ago when exploring. I keep it near my bookcase, like it's there so I can reach the top shelf. Although it has been years since I needed it for that as I can reach the books by standing on my tiptoes.

I put the step near the fireplace and get on it to reach up to press the same side of a brick in the chimney. Following the pattern it took me weeks to figure out from both research and trial and error, I press each of the nine bricks in groups of three. Three on the right side, three in the center, three on the left side.

When I push against the last brick, the wall to the left of the fireplace swings out silently revealing a narrow opening into the room beyond.

"There's not a lot of space to move around," I warn Severu.

The room runs the entire width of my bedroom, but it's only about four feet deep. It's never presented a challenge for me, but Severu and Miceli are both big men. Trying to get by one another is going to present a challenge.

Stepping inside, first I disable my failsafe and then I flip the switch on the battery operated lights I hung a few years ago. I recharge one battery set each night so that there is always power. The batteries match those I use for the digital camera Carlotta passed on to me when she stopped using it in favor of her smartphone.

"Fuck me." That's Miceli.

Other than the table and chair I found in the room when I first discovered it, there is no furniture. But I have covered the long wall with boxes stacked up like storage cubes. I check the recyclables weekly for boxes of the right size. Most are from food deliveries to the kitchen.

Feeding a family of five, a half a dozen staff and ten mafia soldiers requires buying food staples in bulk.

"What is all this?" Severu asks.

The boxes aren't full, but all of them have something in them. Composition books filled with my notes, papers I've printed off my computer on the printer I saved from being recycled when a newer model was purchased. It uses the same ink cartridges as the old one and I'm careful, so I don't use more than two cartridges a year. There are books, magazines and pictures related to each box's subject when I can come by them.

"Those are the boxes dedicated to my research into the syndicates." I point to two stacks of boxes five high at the right farthest end of the room. One for each Cosa Nostra territory and the others hold miscellaneous information gleaned about related crime organizations in other states and countries.

Severu and Miceli stride quickly to where I'm pointing. My husband grabs one of the composition books from the top box. It is for New York and is almost full.

He flips through the pages and then looks up at me. "This is more detailed than I expected."

I shrug. "I had a lot of time on my hands."

"The FEDs would shit themselves for this kind of info." Miceli frowns.

He's right. "You see why I had to keep it analog and in a secret room."

Both men nod, but go back to skimming my notes.

"This is about when you took over as don, Severu. She notes the alliances father formed, those you are likely to keep and those you will probably build. Damned if she isn't right about every single one." Miceli sounds astounded and impressed.

"Let me see," Severu says, tucking the composition book he's holding under one arm.

Miceli hands him the one from five years ago. Some books have multiple years, but some only cover a single year. It depends on what information I gathered and how many important events happened.

Severu looks up from reading, his dark gaze intent on me. "These are amazing, Catalina. Thank you for telling me about them."

"You are my husband." And I trust him.

I would have never shown my research to my father.

Scooting past both Severu and Miceli, I pull a file from one of the boxes on the right. "I think this will interest you."

Severu tucks the second composition book with the first and then takes the thick file from me.

"You can spread it out on the table," I suggest.

He does just that and silently reads through the news articles, social media posts and highlighted portions of the government reports on organized crime I found related to the pattern I found.

When he curses long and volubly, I know he's seen it too.

Miceli is reading over his shoulder and grows more and more tense as he flips one article after another. "You think the Gutierrez Cartel is behind the attacks on both the Irish mob and us."

"Yes. They did it in three port cities on the East Coast already."

"Pitting two big syndicates against each other and moving in to reap the spoils of the massive conflicts." Severu's big body is rigid with fury.

Miceli whistles. "You think they're financing the bratva family in Detroit."

"They need those routes to move drugs and people." I despise the Gutierrez Cartel because it is one of the main players in human trafficking. "I don't know why they're trying for New York. Like the bratva, they have access to other ports."

That's the part that doesn't make sense to me. The cartel knows exactly what they want and how to get it, whether it's using a bratva family to take over territory they want or coming in hot on their own and securing a port that they need.

New York crime families are entrenched and have been for generations. Severu is not a weak don like Russo in Detroit. There's no way he's losing a war, even against the Irish.

"I can't figure out what the cartel hopes to get out of a conflict between us and the Irish. Even if we are in a full-scale war..." Which I hate the idea of. So many would die. "Unless they are bringing in a huge contingent of their soldiers, which you and Brogan Shaughnessy would notice, they can't hope to take territory from either of you."

"It fits with what they've done in other states, but then again, it doesn't," Severu says, his tone cold and calculated.

Right now, he's the don. The Genovese. Nothing of the passion we have shared shows. No inkling of the man who could rub cream into my bruises so gently.

"What else is here?" Miceli asks, indicating the many boxes beyond those he and Severu have been looking at.

"Nothing that would be of interest or help to *la famiglia*," I say with a shrug.

Miceli nods, like he believes me. "All of this..." He waves at the 12 boxes filled with information about organized crime players. "Will have to be moved to the vault."

"Yes," Severu says before I can respond.

They are right, but it's *my* information. I spent years compiling it. Only it's not safe now that people know about the secret room, even if those people are only my husband and his family. Secrets that are shared get out.

And I won't be living in the mansion to watch over my hoard of information any longer.

Severu is crouched down and looking at something in the bottom box beside the table and nearest the doorway. "What is this?"

"An incendiary device. If I don't deactivate it upon entering, it will go off one minute after the door opens. If my calculations are correct..." I spent two whole months studying incendiary devices, so I'm certain they are. "Everything in this room will burn within two minutes. The fire will erupt in such a way that whoever is coming inside will be forced to leave or risk being burned alive."

The material closest to the door will burn first, leaving no time to grab it and get out.

"Who are you?" Miceli's voice is tinged with awe. "Mata Hari?"

"Not even close. She used seduction to infiltrate her enemies. I'm just an information junkie who doesn't want my notes falling into the wrong hands."

"You realize the whole mansion could burn down along with the room?" Severu asks me.

"The mansion is equipped with a state-of-the-art fire suppression system. Besides this room is made entirely of brick. Even the floor. It might spread through the open door to my room, but wouldn't have the chance to spread further."

"It was too damn big a risk," Severu says, his jaw taut. "You could have died."

"I could have died at my father's hand too. I chose to live to the fullest extent I could manage."

"While planning to leave."

Miceli jerks at that. "You were going to run away? Like your sister?"

"No, not like my sister." I'd had no plans to leave someone else to face Papà's wrath on my behalf. He would have been glad to see the back of me. "No one would have come after me."

Severu growls and I'm not sure what that means, so I don't respond to it.

He faces his brother. "Have the documents in these boxes moved to the vault and the others packed up and delivered to our home. Put them in one of the empty guest rooms on the main floor."

I assume the main floor is the one with the communal living spaces and our bedroom.

"Will do." Miceli pulls out his phone and starts texting.

"Are your family's bedrooms on the main floor?" I ask Severu after a minute of pensive silence on his part.

He shakes his head. "The only bedrooms on our floor are ours and guest rooms that eventually will belong to our children. Miceli and our mother have rooms on the floor below. There are also four more guest rooms. One that my sister uses whenever she and Raffaele are in town."

"That seems like a big space for six bedrooms."

"Three of the bedrooms are suites. There is also a smaller kitchen, dining and living room for entertaining, and it houses the gym, movie room and my mother's office."

"She has an office?"

"Being a don's wife and mother is as much a job as a role."

"Oh. Will I need an office?" The idea of having my own space in the De Luca home is tantalizing.

"Yes."

I don't ask anything else because Severu has turned away and is leaving the secret room. I follow him and Miceli comes with us.

"Show Miceli the sequence again so he can get back into the room," Severu says to me.

It takes a couple of times before my brother-in-law is confident he can release the hidden entry.

Afterward, Severu opens the door and ushers Luigi and Aldo back in. "Finish packing my wife's clothes and put them in the Cayenne's cargo space,"

"Come back tomorrow to pack the rest of her things."

"Yes, boss."

I have to bite back my instinct to argue. I want the books brought with us now, but if I draw attention to them, my husband will realize the secret room wasn't my only silent rebellion against my father. And I'm not ready to share the other one. Not yet.

Today I have revealed enough.

CHAPTER 27

CATALINA

"I need to talk to Big Sal again before we go back to the City." Severu leaves the room without telling me if he wants me to accompany him.

Since he didn't tell me *not* to, I follow.

Big Sal is going through files in my father's office. He looks up when we come in. His face is set in grim lines, and he shakes his head. "Francesco's idea of security was to have locking filing cabinets. I could have picked those locks when I was three."

Severu looks around the office. "I always assumed the more sensitive documents were kept somewhere else. That isn't the case?"

"Nope. He's got stuff in those files that could sink us if the FEDs ever raided his place."

"Fuck."

"My father was an arrogant man," I say. "He assumed no one would ever breach his inner sanctum and that he was too smart to be caught by any level of law enforcement."

"I'm not a trusting man, and yet I put too much trust in him," Severu snarls.

He's so angry, I find myself taking a step backward. But then I remind myself that his anger is not my enemy. He is not like my father, and I force myself to move further into the room, away from the door.

Severu pins me with a dark glare. "How did you get my phone number when you called me that time to bust my balls about Carlotta?"

"I wasn't busting your balls," I say, indignant. "I was only pointing out that a few dates might help ease my sister's worries."

"It didn't work," he says, sardonically.

"I'm not sure anything would have. Not if she was determined to run. I know Carlotta was good at playing the part of the submissive daughter, but she was even better at getting what she wanted."

Which I never minded. Women in our world have few weapons at our disposal. One of Carlotta's was manipulation. I cannot judge her for using it. In the end, she'd had to run away to gain the freedom she wanted, which means the two of us aren't so different after all. Because that was my final planned move on the chessboard too.

I won't run now because I don't need to. I'm safe. Deeper feelings than lust for my new husband don't come into it, I tell myself.

"How did you get my number?" he asks me again. "I thought you asked your father for it."

But now he knows how unlikely that would have been. Both for me to ask and for my father to actually hand the number over.

"I snuck into his phone while he was in the shower."

"You knew his passcode?"

"I knew a lot of things my father thought I didn't," I acknowledge.

Severu and Big Sal are both giving me speculative looks and fear makes my hands clammy while a flush prickles over my skin. "I'm not the rat," I say loudly.

Severu frowns. "I never said you were."

But Big Sal, who must be the new consigliere, is still looking at me like he's trying to see into my head.

"Why would I work with the Gutierrez Cartel?" I ask them.

"You think that's who is behind the attacks?" Big Sal asks my husband. "Since when?"

"Since my wife pointed out that they've done something similar in two other port cities on the East Coast and are behind the bratva double cross in Detroit."

"You did?" Big Sal asks me. He doesn't sound impressed; he sounds suspicious.

I don't know if Severu wants him to know about my research, so I don't mention it. I just say, "It was in the news. Anyone could have noticed the similarities."

The fact that none of my husband's men in charge of gathering intel did feels like a victory though.

"She's not the rat, Sal. If she were do you think she would have pointed to her co-conspirators?" Severu asks his new consigliere.

"If the cartel are the ones behind what has been happening, no." Which means he thinks it could be someone else.

Who?

"Domenico's team will have to do some more digging to confirm the connections," my husband says. "But now that we have a place to start, Domenico should have no trouble finding what we need."

"Someone in this house could be the leak," Big Sal says, his face set in stubborn lines. "Francesco's files are too accessible. We swept the office for bugs, but it's clean. His phone is in the safe until our guys can look at it and see if it was compromised."

"You think the rat is a member of my family?" I ask, feeling lightheaded. It can't be.

"Or one of your father's men, or even one of the staff," Big Sal says. "Your father's security measures were shit."

So, he's not assuming it's me, but he's not assuming it's not either.

What about Carlotta? Her running is going to make her look guilty. Or will it? If she was leaking information, she would have jumped at the chance to gain access to the De Lucas, not run from it. I just hope Severu and his men see the logic in that.

~ ~ ~

Severu is busy on his phone while we drive back into the City. I'm tired and despite all my whirling thoughts, I fall asleep. I wake up when the Cayenne stops moving.

My eyes open and I blink, taking in my surroundings. We are home. Well, the parking garage anyway. I can't help noticing how differently I respond to arriving here than the mansion I was raised in. Peace settles over me, a feeling of safety.

Severu is still on his phone, but now he is talking.

I don't try to interrupt him to say goodbye when Aldo opens my door. My husband makes no move to unbuckle his seatbelt and I assume he's not coming up to the apartment.

Aldo and three other bodyguards surround me as we walk to the elevator. Aldo in front, one on each side of me and one behind me. We step onto the elevator, and the guard behind me shifts to my left while that man moves to stand with Aldo in front of me. It's all very precise and practiced.

Like they've done this a hundred times before.

"Do you all guard Aria as well?" I ask.

Aldo replies, "No. You are our primary."

"Oh, you're all so organized, like you've been doing this for years."

"The don would never allow you to be guarded by untrained men," Aldo says.

"I don't think any of my father's men are as well trained as you all."

"They're Big Sal's men now," the man to my right says.

I nod. "Of course." I ask him his name and he tells me. Then I ask all their names and when we arrive at the foyer to the main floor of the De Luca home, they are still answering my questions.

I want to know if they are married, or have other family. How long they've been working for Severu. Aldo has been with him the longest. He and another man had specialized training with Niccolo's team. I learn that I have ten guards assigned to me, though.

"I thought I only needed ten guards when we are on high alert."

"That is true. The extra men allow for rotation so your security detail is always fresh. Two will cycle into rotation for security here in the house or with other family members, when needed."

I find it odd that they refer to the two levels of the apartment building as a house, but the family does as well. No wonder Carlotta gave the impression they lived in a mansion.

"I'm glad to have met you all," I say to the men still standing around me. "Thank you for telling me about yourselves and I hope you will allow me to get to know you better as we spend more time together."

The men all reply in different ways, but all of them in the affirmative. Then Aldo tells the other three that they can go.

"You're staying with me?" I ask.

"I will be with you from after breakfast until dinner six days a week."

"That means you'll work nine to ten hours a day with only one day off a week. Isn't that against labor laws, or something?"

He laughs. "I'm a made man, not a corporate drone. We have our own laws in the mafia."

"But what about when you get married? Your wife won't want you working so much. Even if you are a made man."

"When things get serious enough for me to ask a woman to marry me, I'll be removed as the lead on your security detail."

"What?" I don't like the sound of that. "Why?"

Change is not a big part of my life, or at least it hasn't been until now. And I already know it's not something I'm going to embrace when it comes to the people I spend a lot of time with.

"Your primary bodyguard needs to be able to put your life above anyone else's. Even the don's."

"What about your vow?"

"I would die for Don Severu, but I would not place his life above yours because my vow to him means I execute the duties he gives me without failing."

"And he assigned you to keep me alive."

"Yes."

"Is it the same for all dons' wives?" I wonder out loud.

"If they are assigned a personal bodyguard, yes. But usually only one bodyguard is tasked with that level of loyalty to their charge. Your husband has tasked everyone on the team with your personal safety."

"You said they'll guard the house and Aria sometimes."

"Regardless of where they are working, if it is a choice between your life and anyone else's, yours comes first."

My heart is racing and I'm finding it difficult to breathe. I don't know why. All of this talk of death? Or is it that I know there are ten people assigned specifically to protect me when I have spent the last fifteen years without a single person I could trust to do that?

"Are you alright, Signora Severu?"

"Please call me Catalina," I gasp out. "I'm fine." But it's a lie.

"Do you need to lie down?" he asks.

I shake my head. Then through the archway into the living room I see the edge of the piano I noticed this afternoon when we were in there talking. I head towards it.

Situated near the windows in a section of the room that is raised above the rest, the white lacquer Steinway grand piano is a beacon. Playing has always helped me deal with the chaos of emotion.

I climb the two steps and cross the floor before settling myself on the tufted velvet piano bench. There is a harp to one side and chairs similar to those in the lower area of the living room arranged in three conversational groupings. It's like a music room, but made part of the main living space.

Someone in the De Luca family tree loved music like I do.

Right now, I don't care who that was. I just want to play.

Running my fingers lightly over the keys, I play a scale to check if the piano is tuned. It is and my tight muscles relax just a little, my heart beating not quite so fast. I begin with the song I always do with *La Campanella*. It sooths me and I can feel my breaths even out, my heart rate settle and the tension leave my shoulders.

Then, because the only one here is Aldo, I allow myself to indulge in one of the songs I composed.

When I am finished, I let my fingers rest softly on the keys.

"That was beautiful, but I do not recognize it," Aria says from behind me.

Startled, my fingers come down on the keys in a discordant note. I turn to face my mother-in-law. "Um...thank you."

When had she arrived? Had she been standing there very long?

She smiles at me, her green eyes gentle on me. "What is that song called?"

"I call it Peace."

"You call it? Did you write it?"

I've never put the notes onto paper, but that's not really what my mother-in-law is asking.

"I composed it. It's nothing special." Just a song that helps me get my thoughts in order and my emotions under control.

"It's beautiful." Aria smiles. "Do you mind if I sit and listen to you play?"

"Not at all." And I find I am speaking the truth.

I usually prefer to play without an audience, but Aria's presence does not feel like an intrusion. If I'd known she was there while I played Peace, I probably would have stopped, but now that I'm a little calmer, it's fine.

"This is your home," I tell her.

"It is the family home," she agrees. "However, Catalina, this floor belongs to you and my son. If you don't want company, you only have to say so."

CHAPTER 28

CATALINA

I'm back to feeling out of my depth. It's too much. All of this kindness. The implications that I am important in a way I have not been for all of my twenty-five years of life.

I just shake my head and start playing again.

Out of the periphery of my eye, I see that Aria has taken a seat. Aldo is standing guard somewhere close by. Willing myself to forget them both, I seek solace in the music and allow my brain to process the last two days.

What is happening with Carlotta? Is she alright? How is she surviving on the outside? She has very little money, if any, and that worries me. Though if she uses her credit card to pay for lodging and food, it should make it easier for Severu's men to find her.

My sister is so naïve though. Anything could happen. She doesn't know the first thing about life as an outsider. I hope they find her soon.

Who else, besides Big Sal, thinks the rat might be a part of my father's household? Does Severu suspect me? He says not, but he's wily. He wouldn't let me know if he suspected me.

I change the song I'm playing from a fast-paced folksong keeping time with my whirling thoughts, to a slow, meditative piece as I play through my memories, looking for suspicious activity on the part of my father's men, or the staff. I'm sure I saw more than I was meant to because in my father's house, I *always* did my best not to draw attention.

And most of his men saw me as unimportant. No threat. Which I wasn't, but that doesn't mean I didn't watch and listen. Even the staff would gossip in my presence about things they would never have mentioned in front of my aunt or sister.

There was the time I saw Fausto, the head of father's soldiers, coming out of Papà's study. Not unusual, but this time he'd looked like he didn't want to be seen there, checking the hall before coming out and closing the door softly behind him, before hurrying off. He didn't notice me. He rarely noticed me, and I was glad.

Because the few times he did, he could be as cruel and threatening as my father.

I'd seen staff in parts of the house they had no business being, but that didn't mean they were spying. I know of at least one maid who is in a relationship with one of the soldiers. My father frowned on that kind of fraternization, so they both were sometimes places they wouldn't otherwise be.

Should I tell Severu about the anomalous and sometimes sneaky behavior? I don't want to. I know how the mafia extracts information and I don't want to be responsible for an innocent person being subjected to torture. Not even Fausto. But I'm not living in the mansion any longer. I can't gather further information to make a more educated determination whether someone should be questioned, or not.

Even more than I don't want to have an innocent tortured, I don't want to be party to a rat going free and further harming *la famiglia*. I don't want to let Severu down.

With his image playing in my head like a slide reel of all our moments of interaction between our first meeting to our wedding night and then today, my fingers slide into a different tune. It's soft jazz, a song that always makes me feel longing for something.

Now I know what that something is. Or rather that someone. My husband, don of the Genovese family.

SEVERU

While Miceli personally sees to the removal of the boxes from my wife's secret room before anyone from Francesco's former household is allowed to return to the mansion, I meet with Domenico and Angelo.

I want Domenico to confirm Catalina's research so that when I talk to Shaughnessy, I will have sources for him that will not reveal my wife's knowledge or penchant for gathering intelligence. And I want Angelo to work with Big Sal vetting the men that used to belong to Francesco.

"Catalina noticed some news reports that could point to who is behind the attacks on us and the Irish mob." Big Sal knows she brought the idea up because I refuse not to give her any credit. However, I have to make sure the nature and depth of her research stays strictly in family. "I want you to look into it and any activity of the Gutierrez Cartel in New York."

"You got it, boss," Domenico says. He shares a look with Angelo and then says, "There's something you need to see. Go to YouTube on your laptop."

I flip open my computer and do what he says.

"Now type Stellina into the search."

When I do that, a channel and several videos populate the right side of the screen. They're of a woman playing a piano. She looks a lot like Catalina. I press play on the one featured.

After I click past the ad, the sound of piano music filters from my computer's speakers. The woman doesn't look like my wife, she *is* my wife.

What the hell? Francesco would never have approved of this. Did she do it in one of her quiet acts of rebellion?

My gut churns as I continue to watch her play. The music is haunting, even soul-wrenching. No wonder the number of views is over a million.

"It's a monetized account, boss."

I want to hit something. This is how my clever wife intended to finance her new life after running away. I hate that anyone else is seeing her this way. That she would let them. Her every emotion is exposed in a way she would never allow me to see.

"I don't think she knows she's being recorded," Domenico says, cutting through my furious thoughts. "Look at a couple more and you'll see what I mean."

As much as I feel compelled to watch the video to its completion, I don't have time. I fast forward and watch bits before doing the same to several more uploads.

Catalina's eyes are almost always closed. Sometimes her lovely face reflects peace, but sometimes it's agony. Sometimes longing. The emotions are too raw, too intimate for her to share this way.

My wife, who doesn't want to share her pain level on a number scale with a medical professional, would never allow another person to see her like this. She would not post it to social media for a following the size of the one on this channel.

"I've watched all the videos," Domenico says. "Your wife never once looks at the camera."

Because she doesn't know it's there. My gut tells me that this is not Catalina's account. The name of the owner is in the name of the channel. Stellina. The endearment Francesco used for Carlotta.

Her fucking sister, using Catalina again. The first video was posted three years ago, when Carlotta was sixteen.

Domenico points at the screen. "There are a lot of comments trying to figure out who she really is. The owner is meticulous about deleting spam and that shit posted by trolls, but she leaves those up."

"They probably increase the popularity of the channel." Angelo frowns. "The public loves a mystery."

He's right, damn it.

Domenico nods. "I'm surprised no one from that boarding school she attended recognized her and posted her name. If they did, the owner deleted the comment."

"Carlotta took a chance," I growl. "Both with her sister's safety and the privacy of *la famiglia*."

At sixteen she might have been forgiven for thinking she didn't need to worry that her sister would be recognized, because her father had basically kept her a prisoner in her own home. But in three years, hasn't she grown any wiser? Her recent actions are evidence to the contrary.

"You think it's Carlotta?" Angelo asks, no inflection in his tone.

"I would bet my favorite knife on it." I've had that knife since I became a made man. It was a gift from my father.

"We'll know soon enough," Domenico says with satisfaction. "I've got a tracer on the account. The next time she signs in to monitor comments, we'll get her IP address."

And then my men will know where to look for Carlotta.

"Good. After, I want a copy of all the videos and then I want the channel taken down. Scrub the net for any bootlegged copies," I instruct Domenico.

"Planned on it, boss."

CHAPTER 29

SEVERU

Catalina is tired and preoccupied over dinner, only speaking when conversation is directed at her. Today was rough on her. That secret room was her haven and now it's gone.

"Your grandmother's piano is finally getting some use." Mamma sends a smile toward my wife. "Catalina played this evening, before dinner."

"I got to hear a little after I put my little monster in bed," Giulia says, "You play beautifully, Catalina. I took lessons, but I never got much past Chop Sticks."

My sister isn't exaggerating. Much. She hated her piano lessons.

Catalina smiles wanly and suddenly it hits me. "Did you remember to take your pain meds when you got back?" I ask her.

She shakes her head.

"On a scale of one to ten?" I ask her.

She looks around the table, clearly uncomfortable with answering in front of my family. Tough.

I repeat the question.

She sighs. "Five, maybe six."

Which means six, maybe seven. I'm learning to read my wife. I stand up and don't bother to excuse myself, walking swiftly to our room. I return a minute later with her pills and hand them to her.

She stares down at the green gelcaps. "I'm afraid if I take them, I'll fall asleep at the table."

"I will carry you to bed then. Take the pain meds."

She does, swallowing them with a gulp of water.

Twenty minutes later, her eyelids are drooping and she's listing to one side. I lift her up from the chair, ignoring the comments from the peanut gallery. I can see to my wife's welfare if I want to.

She is *my* wife.

She does not belong to the millions of people who have watched those Stellina videos.

~ ~ ~

After tucking Catalina into bed, I meet my brother and Big Sal in the study.

"Angelo is going to help you vet the men," I tell Big Sal.

My new consigliere looks pleased. "Just having him there will garner some telling reactions."

Sometimes, the way Big Sal talks reminds me that I'm not the only made man with an Ivy league education. His son, Salvatore, went to the West Coast for college. Stanford's not Ivy League, but it's as good as.

"I think you should ask Catalina what she thinks of the men and the staff," Miceli says. "She is observant."

That's one way of putting it. "I'll talk to her."

"I'd like to be there," Big Sal says. "I have some of my own questions for her."

"No one is interrogating my wife." I glare at the older man.

Miceli coughs, like he's stifling a laugh and I turn my sulfuric look on him. "You got something to say?"

"Nope."

"I don't want to interrogate her, but we can't dismiss the possibility that she's the source of the leaks, whether knowingly or unwittingly."

"How could she do it unwittingly?" Miceli asks.

"Social media. Talking with friends from school."

Catalina has access to social media, because she uses it for her research, but using it to post about her own life? That I don't see. Still, it's possible.

"If she has any friends left from school, I don't know about them," I say, realizing even as I speak the words that they don't mean much.

I married the woman only the day before and spent very little time in her company prior to that. Because I wanted her, and she wasn't the woman

I was going to marry. Unlike Carlotta, Francesco never talked about his oldest daughter.

Miceli frowns. "I like Catalina."

"And?"

"I don't like saying this, but she's got motive for selling our secrets."

"The hell she does."

"Her dad kept her a prisoner in that house, and he abused her." Miceli gives me a knowing look. "She was getting ready to run. That means she needed money."

"One thing I've already found out is that there was no love lost between father and daughter. I doubt she felt any particular loyalty to him." Big Sal rubs his chin thoughtfully.

I want to deny it, but Catalina didn't grieve her father's death. She was relieved by it. Which I liked. I don't want her hurting over that son of a bitch's death. There's a ruthless streak in her character that I admire. It could also be what makes it possible for her to sell our secrets.

Did she do it? I doubt it.

Even if she did, do I think she would do it now that she's married to me? Absolutely not.

Is that just my ego talking? Or even my damn cock? Which loves being buried in her hot pussy.

Hell. I said no one was interrogating my wife, but I should have said no one but me. I have to find out if she's the leak. To protect her as much as *la famiglia*.

"She married me to protect her sister," I point out. "That's not the action of a woman lacking in loyalty."

"Does she feel that loyalty towards you?" Miceli asks. "We know she didn't toward Francesco, not that he deserved it."

But if she equated her father with the Cosa Nostra, my wife might have seen selling secrets as a way to get the money she needed to run, like my brother suggested.

Hell.

"What better way to spy for our enemies than from inside the don's own family?" Big Sal asks.

"She's good at gathering information," Miceli points out.

I tell him to shut it with my eyes, but he's not saying anything else anyway. He's made his point.

After dismissing the other men, I go to find my wife. Waking her from sleep should make her easier to question. She'll find it harder to lie and keep track of her lies if she's tired. Even though they are only analgesics, the pain meds will help too.

I've already seen how strongly she reacts to them. Which makes me think she's not used to taking painkillers after one of her father's beatings.

Shoving down guilt that has never bothered me before when doing my business as don, I go straight to our bedroom and shake my wife awake.

CATALINA

Someone is shaking my shoulder. I try to push the hand away, but it's insistent.

"Catalina, wake up. I need to talk to you."

"Can't it wait for tomorrow?" I mumble.

"No."

His tone forces me awake more than the repeated jiggling of my shoulder. When I open my eyes, he's sitting in a chair beside the bed close to my head. I don't remember it being there before. I blink and then blink again.

"Sit up." He's leaning forward and literally lifting me into a sitting position with his hands under my armpits.

He shoves some pillows behind me so I'm not leaning forward and putting pressure on my ribs. Then he pulls away, sitting back in the chair and crossing his arms over his chest.

Severu's expression is grim, his gaze boring into me without a trace of emotion. I am facing the don again, not my lover, not the man who insisted I take pain medication and get some rest.

This man wants something, but I don't know what and I'm too muzzy headed from sleep and pain meds to even guess at it.

"Would you betray me, Catalina?" he asks with an aura of dark menace.

I can't make sense of the question at first, but then my sluggish mind catches up and I am horrified. "No. You know I wouldn't."

"That's the problem, wife. I don't know. I know I like your pussy, but I barely know *you* at all."

How can he say that? I've revealed more of myself to Severu than any other person in my life.

"Big Sal has been talking to you, hasn't he?" I ask, trying to figure out how my husband went from the concerned man at dinner to this.

"Why do you say that?"

"Earlier today. He suspected me." I rub at my eyes, trying to wake up. Trying to think more clearly.

"He has reason to, don't you think?"

"No." That much I am sure of.

There is no reason to suspect me because I haven't done anything wrong. Though I can't make my mouth form all those words, so I stick with the simple denial.

"You admitted yourself that you spied on your father."

I can't believe he's using what I told him against me. "You know why," I say.

"I know what you told me. Maybe it's even true."

Maybe? And maybe all the remodeled broken bones the doctor saw on the X-rays at the hospital were just shadows on the film.

"Your father's abuse only makes your need to get out of his house more urgent. You had to figure out a way to get the money you needed for your escape from him."

He stares at me like I'm supposed to say something. I keep my lips pressed tightly together.

"Maybe you figured out a way to get money with that information. Maybe it even felt like poetic justice."

"Maybe you're an asshole." Only there's no *maybe* about it. Anger is jump starting the synapses in my brain. "Betraying the mafia's secrets is not poetic justice. It's a death wish."

"I agree, but a woman raised the way you were, sheltered from the brutality of our life, might not really believe that."

"You think I was sheltered from brutality?" I ask, feeling sick and wanting to scream at the same time. "Me?" I emphasize. "The one my father whipped with cruel words? I was *so* sheltered by his fists and feet. All my bruises and broken bones were my armor?"

I'm getting hysterical and I don't care. I trusted Severu. I showed him my true self. My secret room. The Catalina no one else knows.

And now he's using that knowledge as a basis for these horrible accusations.

"Tell me this, genius," I say, my eyes burning, my throat raw. "If I was so *fucking* sheltered how did I come into contact with someone to sell my secrets to? Huh? Is this like the mythical men that were supposed to be my lovers while I was trapped in my father's home?"

"You left the house. You went shopping with your sister and aunt."

"Yes, I did. And you think I ran into someone from the Gutierrez Cartel at Saks? Or maybe you think I contacted them some other way. Because we both know I know how to find out names. I'm smart enough to leverage those names into contacts." What am I doing? I'm making his case for him.

But I'm so furious, I don't care. I'm so hurt, I want him to believe me. Maybe I want him to hurt me, so I'll know once and for all that all men are bastards. Under the skin, they're all violent brutes.

He's staring at me like he doesn't know me. Because he doesn't. He said it himself. He knows he likes having sex with me, but he doesn't know *me*.

He didn't look in my room and see *me*. He saw the intel I gathered. He didn't see the woman desperate to prove to herself that she wasn't stupid, wasn't worthless, wasn't all the awful names my father called me.

"You were going to run away," he says like that's an indictment.

But he doesn't react to my claim that I could have contacted the cartel if I'd wanted to.

"You blame me for that?" I swipe at the wetness on my cheeks. I will not cry. Not now. Not for him. "Knowing what you know?"

"You could have come to me."

Even when my father beat me, I never wanted to hit him back. I just wanted him to stop. Right now, I want to hit Severu with a baseball bat. In the nuts. I have never been so angry. Not ever.

"Wrong. Coming to you would have only put me more at risk," I say scathingly. "Sure, you would have fired your consigliere and that would have solved *your* problem, but how do you think my father would have reacted to losing his position because of me?"

A flicker of uncertainty shows in Severu's brown eyes. It's not enough. He should have doubted this whole stupid scenario from the beginning.

"If I was the rat, then why put myself at risk of being shot with that attempted kidnapping?"

"We only assume it's related to the other attacks. Maybe it's not."

"You've got an answer for everything."

"No, I fucking do not have an answer for everything." Severu explodes up from the chair and looms over me. "You just sit there telling me how you could have done it when I'm looking for reasons to believe you didn't."

Because he married me. He doesn't want his wife to be a mole. It would look bad for him. Way worse than a runaway fiancée.

I refuse to cower away from him. "Go ahead, hit me. I can't stop you."

"Fuck." He rubs his hands over his face, and he sits back in the chair with a thump. "I'm not ever going to hit you."

"You think my father's fists hurt me the most? You think when he kicked me, he left the worst damage? Newsflash, he didn't. Broken bones mend. Words leave wounds that don't heal. You've just flayed me with his whip. Congratulations."

Severu leans forward, his head in his hands. He just keeps saying fuck over and over again. And then he goes silent.

We sit like that, neither speaking for a long time. All I can hear is my own harsh breathing and his.

"If I'm the rat, you may not hit me, but you'll have to let someone interrogate me. Someone who will." I say it like it doesn't matter to me, but my heart is shattering into bits around me.

CHAPTER 30

CATALINA

He looks up, his dark eyes filled with fury. "No one will ever harm you that way again."

"You can't promise that."

"I can, because we both know you aren't the leak."

I don't believe him, and I let my silence tell him that.

"Damn it, I never thought it was you."

"Right? That's why you woke me out of a sound sleep to interrogate me." Now that I'm more alert, I know exactly what he was doing. "You probably thought the pain meds would make me more truthful. Less able to hold a lie together."

He already knew I got sleepy when I took them.

Something flashes in his expression, and I know I'm right.

"Is that why you insisted I take them?"

"I gave them to you because you were in pain. Yes, when I realized I had to talk to you, I knew it would make the questioning easier. I didn't expect you to play devil's advocate against yourself though."

Neither had I. "I am angry."

"I know." He laughs bitterly.

What does he have to be bitter about? I didn't accuse him of betraying me. He actually did it.

And I'm so furious all over again I can't stand it. "I trusted you."

"You did." He sounds like he wishes I hadn't.

Well, so do I.

"You never would have shown us the secret room," he says, no inflection in his tone. "Much less told me that you used to spy on your father, or that you planned to run, if you were the mole."

"You don't think?" He couldn't have figured this out before scourging me with his lack of trust?

"I had to question you." His eyes hold no remorse. "I am the don. You are my wife, no one else could do it."

"Why question me at all?"

"Because you had motive and opportunity."

"You sound like a cop."

He doesn't look amused.

Well, neither am I.

"You need to see something."

"What?" Does he have some proof that makes me look guilty?

"Grab your phone."

I do and he takes my hand and unlocks the phone with my fingerprint before taking it from me. I sit without moving, my entire body flushing with heat from that touch. Stupid body.

The sound of piano music comes from my phone. It takes me a little while, but suddenly I realize the person playing is me. I grab my phone, expecting to see that he's playing an audio file and wanting to know who recorded me.

It's not though; it's a video and it's up on YouTube. I stare down at the screen in horror as my body goes first hot and then cold. It's me at the piano in my father's music room. Someone filmed me playing and I never even knew. Then they posted it online.

The video has over a million views. I'm going to be sick.

All of those people witnessed an intensely personal moment of vulnerability.

"I wasn't playing for an audience." That was supposed to be private. I'd waited to go to the piano until I knew none of the rest of the family was in the house.

"I know." He's got his don face on, all stoic and unfeeling, but I know he's furious.

That rage is vibrating between us.

If I can know him like this, after such a short time, and he's about as revealing as a smoke bomb, why doesn't he know me better? I opened a vein for him and it's like he just stepped right through the blood without noticing.

How had the recording been taken? One of the staff? One of my father's men? And why post it online? What did they have to gain from it?

"Over a million people have seen this." They saw my pain, my attempt at emotional healing because that's what playing the piano that day was for me. A chance to release feelings too heavy to carry, to let go of pain I had no other outlet for.

"But none of them know you."

I look up at him. "What do you mean?"

"It's not in context, *mi dolce bellezza*. They don't know you're working through your hurt, that you're finding the one small bit of peace you can in a home that is filled with torment for you."

How can he understand me so well? "You said you don't know me."

"I lied. It's an interrogation technique."

Smart ass. I don't say it out loud this time. I already got away with calling him an asshole; I'm not going to push my luck. "You said you only know that you like having sex with me."

"If you believed me maybe I'm not the only *genius* in this marriage."

So, he heard the sarcasm when I called him genius. And somehow, I got away with that too.

"You let me call you an asshole." I need to know why.

"I am aware." And he doesn't sound happy about it.

"You didn't yell at me or go all Don of New York on me. Why?"

"Because you are you."

He didn't say because I was his wife. He said it was because I was myself. Catalina De Luca. What does that mean?

"In case you are wondering, I don't want you to do it again."

"I wasn't." That's a given.

"I've cut men's fingers off for less."

I shiver at the visual although taking a finger is a don's prerogative when punishing his men. "I'm not one of your enemies, or your made men."

"Neither are my sister or mother, but they would never disrespect me that way." His tone implies he would deal with it if they did.

I don't know how, but I'm sure it's not the same way my father would have.

I can't say I didn't mean to disrespect him. I did. He hurt me and my heart is still smarting. "Not even if you were being a hurtful, untrusting jerk?"

Oops. There I go again.

Am I still pushing him, still trying to see if he'll retaliate with his fists? *I am.* And I don't like what that says about where my mind is at.

"They would not consider me doing my job as don in those terms," he says through gritted teeth.

So not so calm about the name calling after all. "Lucky them." I just keep pushing. I need to shut up.

He sighs. "I am sorry, Catalina. I did not mean to hurt you."

Okay, that is seriously not the response I expected. "I thought you said you don't apologize."

"Apparently, you are the exception."

"Why?"

He just looks at me and I can hear the words between us even though they go unsaid. *Because I am me.*

And somehow that is special? I don't understand this man.

I look down and notice the phone in my hand. How did I forget? Distress rolls over me in an icy wave, leaving me nauseated.

"Who posted the video?" I ask.

Does he think I did? Is that why he thought I might be the leak? But what does one have to do with the other?

"Videos," he says. "There's a whole channel and it's monetized."

"What does that mean?"

"It means your sister has been making money off of your talent for three years." He almost looks like he feels sorry for me.

I don't need his pity. I am a survivor, but three years? My sister? My *sister?* Carlotta wouldn't do that, would she?

"How many videos?" I ask faintly.

"Thirty-two."

I'm really feeling sick now. "I think I need the bathroom."

Severu doesn't ask. He just swoops me up in his arms and carries me to the en suite where I proceed to retch over the sink. I don't actually throw up, but the retching hurts my ribs. Like really, really.

He has a glass of water and goes to try to help me drink it. I take the glass from him and gulp down half of it. It sloshes in my queasy stomach.

He grabs the tube of cream we got from the hospital from the counter because we've been applying it in here.

I think of all the times he's spread it so carefully over my bruises. "How can you be so careful with me one minute and so unfeeling the next?"

"It's a gift."

Was that a joke?

I frown, in no mood to laugh. When he opens the tube, I put my hand out for it. He hesitates.

"Give it to me. I can do it myself." I'm not getting lulled into a false sense of intimacy with this man again.

Because even more than the sex, the way he's been taking care of me has had me creating fantasies in my head about feelings and some kind of relationship that we *don't* have.

He looks like he wants to argue. I glare at him, with my hand out. I've been taking care of myself for years. I don't need him, or anybody else, coddling me. I take the tube from him and put cream on my bruises, using more on my ribs than my face. My hand doesn't need it anymore.

I head back into the bedroom, my boobs swaying, and it's only then that it hits me. We've had this entire conversation while I was naked. Gah!

I should be embarrassed, but I'm not. He's seen it all. He's touched it all. It would be ridiculous to put a nightgown on now, so I don't. I arrange my pillows and climb into bed.

After a minute of silence from the bathroom, Severu makes a sound between disgust and frustration. Then he storms back into the room and starts undressing on his side of the bed with jerky movements.

"What are you doing?"

"Getting ready for bed."

"You're sleeping here?"

"This is our room. Where else would I sleep?"

Our room. Our bed. Our life. A life I can't just walk away from, no matter how angry I am. I am a don's wife and there is no divorce in the mafia. Which isn't strictly true, but it's close enough.

If my mom had tried to leave my father and filed for divorce, her death wouldn't have been an accident because he hit her too hard and sent her tumbling down the stairs. He would have murdered her on purpose.

"That's it?" I still find myself asking. "You accuse me of betraying *la famiglia* and now we're just supposed to sleep together?" As in sleep. Not sex. That is so off the table right now.

"Call it my penance."

"How is it penance?"

"Because this." He shucks out of his boxers and his erection springs free. "And there's no way you're going to let me touch you tonight."

He's got that right. No matter how tempting the idea of drowning pain in pleasure is. He showed me at the hospital how easy it is to do and I'm pretty sure it will work on emotional pain too. Only afterward, the cuts on my heart would be deeper, not healed.

Severu gets into bed, shifting until his naked body is right next to mine under the covers.

"Don't get any ideas," I mutter.

"Not getting ideas," he says with too much frustrated sincerity to be lying.

I don't look at him. I don't need the temptation. "How do you know my sister is the one who put up those videos?"

"She named the channel Stellina."

"That's hardly incontrovertible proof."

"We're tracking the IP address of the owner. If it's not her, we'll know."

I hope against hope it isn't my sister, but something inside me tells me it is. There are a limited number of people with access to the mansion. Of them, only one is known as *stellina*.

"Even if it is Carlotta, that doesn't make her the mole either."

"You don't think?"

"Don't forget, they were going to kidnap Carlotta. She wouldn't have done that to herself."

"She could have staged it as a way to get away from New York," he says, though his voice lacks conviction.

"Not going to mention again that the attempted kidnapping isn't necessarily connected to the other leaks?" I taunt.

"No. That would mean we've got two rats and that's a coincidence I don't buy."

Well, that's something.

"She might be young, but she's not stupid," I tell him. "They shot at us, Severu. Either of us could have died that day, or both. Besides, where would she get the money to pay them? Our father kept even his favorite daughter on a tight leash financially."

I don't ask where I would have gotten the money because I know I've been adding to my escape fund since I was twelve years old.

"The YouTube channel."

"You think she got enough off of it to pay for a team of Albanian kidnappers?" That would mean that more than one video had gone viral.

I hate that thought so much I shove it to the back of my mind. "Are you going to get the channel taken down?"

"Yes. Domenico will scrub the Internet of the videos."

"He can do that?"

"Not quickly. Finding bootleg copies and deleting them will take time, maybe even years."

"But you're going to have him do it?" I ask anxiously.

"Yes."

"Thank you." It's grudging, but sincere. I don't want those videos out there.

"You are my wife."

We lay side by side in silence after that. I should be able to sleep. I'm still tired, but my mind won't shut off. Severu turns toward me; I'm on my back looking up at the ceiling.

He brushes his fingers up and down my arm. It makes me tingle, but it also relaxes me. So, I go with it and let my body melt into the bed.

"What about Candilora and Giovi?" he asks.

"What about them?"

"Would either of them betray *la famiglia*?"

"No. My uncle was a capo in Detroit. He's above reproach."

"I thought my consigliere was above reproach too, but I was wrong. Maybe Giovi resented having to step down as capo to move here with his wife after your mother died."

"He would have had to step down at some point. They never had any children."

I must fall asleep soon after that because I don't remember anything else until I wake up the next morning.

CHAPTER 31

SEVERU

Last night was a total clusterfuck. If I'd listened to my gut, I would not have woken my wife to interrogate her. I would have waited until this morning to ask her about the rest of the Jilani household.

Instead, I treated her like a suspect. It hurt her and I don't like it.

She's my wife and it's my job to protect her. Just like I take care of and protect *la famiglia*.

I need to do something to make up for it. Something that shows her that I do trust her. She trusted me with her deepest secrets, and I shit all over that.

I do not feel shame for the men I've hurt, tortured, or killed. I don't feel guilty for running a criminal enterprise. I like the look of fear I see in a politician's eyes when I single him, or her, out at a fundraiser. It does not bother me that my men know I will kill them for betrayal and sometimes for failure.

I was born to this life and will die in it.

But I felt shame when Catalina taunted me, daring me to hit her. Because I could see beyond the anger in her hazel eyes. I saw the uncertainty, the hopeless belief that I might do it.

I never want to see that look again.

And I don't want her to look at me like a pile of shit when I want to touch her. She didn't let me put the cream on her bruises again this morning and when I went to carry her into the bathroom for our shower, she slapped my hands away.

"I climbed up and down the stairs in the mansion with broken ribs. I can walk to the bathroom with bruised ones."

Fuck.

CATALINA

Aria, Guilia and little Neri are still at the table when I come into the dining room for breakfast. It took me a little longer to get ready this morning because I refused to let Severu do anything for me. Including blow-drying my hair.

I'm not surprised he isn't at the table. He was in a foul mood when he left our bedroom. Neither Raffaele, nor Miceli, are here either. They're probably having a meeting to try to figure out which of my family is the rat, or discussing the likelihood that I am.

Have they told Giulia and Aria their suspicions about me?

Neither woman seems perturbed to see me. Both smile when I sit down, but that doesn't mean anything. We were all taught to hide our true feelings when necessary.

I'm not going to dwell on what might be. As long as they treat me the same, I'll do likewise. I enjoy breakfast, mostly because of Neri. I'd only seen him at the wedding. This is the first time I've seen him at the table.

When I mention that to Giulia, she says, "My brother didn't want to risk Neri being in one of his boisterous moods yesterday and maybe bumping you."

It's hard to believe I only got married a couple of days ago. So much has happened since.

I see what she means about Neri's rambunctiousness, but his antics make me smile. Giulia doesn't seem to mind them either.

Neri falls off his chair and starts to cry. Giulia jumps up and comforts him. It's a beautiful sight.

Once Neri is back in his seat and munching on a piece of bacon, Aria gives her daughter a pointed look. "He's going to be don one day. He needs to learn self-control."

"He's only three, Mamma. There's plenty of time to train him to be stoic."

"Severu knew how to suppress his tears by this age." Aria looks unhappily at her grandson. "I wish it wasn't necessary, but you know it is. A don cannot show weakness."

"But a little boy can. Enough, Mamma."

In the mafia, we all eventually learn to control our tears when necessary, but three seems awfully young. What else did Severu learn to repress at such a young age?

Clearly done with the conversation, Giulia smiles at me. "How did you sleep last night?"

Other than her brother waking me to grill me about being a spy for the mafia's enemies? "Fine."

"Good. Are you up to shopping today?" Aria asks.

"I would prefer to go tomorrow." I'd rather not go at all, but I know that's not an option. "Today I want to meet the staff and learn the layout of my new home."

Giulia gives me a commiserating look. "How are your ribs?"

"Manageable." I shrug and manage not to wince.

"That's good to hear," Aria says. "I'll introduce you to the kitchen staff after breakfast."

I nod, but Emilia comes into the dining room just as I finish eating. "There is a Giovi Revello to see Signora Severu." The housekeeper looks at Aria.

"It is my uncle. Let him up." I don't wait for my mother-in-law to answer. She told me yesterday that this was my home, and that this level in particular was mine and Severu's.

A surge of longing for the familiar washes over me. Zio Giovi would never suspect me of being a traitor. And he won't expect me to pretend a grief about Papa's death I do not feel.

Zia Lora is probably shopping in the City and Zio Giovi is using the time for a visit. Excited to see him, I jump up and hurry to the foyer to wait for his arrival.

But the moment he sees me, my uncle's face fills with fury. "That god dammed bastard. I knew he forced you to take the spoiled princess's place."

His words halt me in my dash forward to give him a hug. I'm not used to Zio Giovi being angry. In fact, I don't ever remember seeing this dark, dangerous expression on his face before.

"Come into the living room." I lead the way, not surprised that Aldo follows, but so does another bodyguard.

Is it because I have a guest, or because that guest is from my family?

I go to sit on the sofa and change my mind at the last second, taking an armchair.

Zio Giovi sits at the end of the couch nearest me. "I'm so sorry, Catalina."

"What are you sorry for?"

"I should have realized you were getting married under duress and stopped it. Your bruise didn't show at the wedding."

Self-conscious, I put my hand to my cheek. "Papà didn't force me." I can't say I wasn't under duress without lying.

And I don't want to lie to my uncle. I never want to have to lie again.

"I'm not your aunt." Zio Giovi's eyes spark with fury. "He may be dead, but you can speak the truth about your father to me."

I knew he wouldn't need me to pretend to be sad. I just didn't realize how angry he is.

"Papà did try to make me pretend to be Carlotta, but I wasn't going to try to trick our don."

"He would have killed you once he realized."

I don't think so, but I doubt I can convince my uncle of that. Anyway, it doesn't matter. "I married Severu because I wanted to."

Which is not a lie. He may have coerced me with the threat of my sister's safety, but I wanted the man. I still do, even though right now I'm so angry with him, I could cheerfully shred his favorite suit. Or maybe even, all of them.

"You don't have to lie to me, *tesorina*." Zio Giovi looks at the two guards stationed discreetly nearby and shakes his head. "I understand."

He's not listening to me and now he thinks the bodyguards are there to spy on what I say. I explain, "Severu has a thing about safety."

"More like he has a thing about control. He's probably afraid you're going to run like your sister."

"How did you know she ran?" Had my father told him?

"Francesco told Lora and I at the reception. He was furious. That's probably why he was driving himself home from the reception and lost control of the car. He was in a rage with no one to take it out on."

I don't reply.

Misunderstanding my silence, Zio Giovi reaches to pat my hand. "I am sorry, *tesorina*. You do not need reminders of the past."

"You and Zia Lora haven't told anyone else, have you? About Carlotta running away?"

"No, of course not."

"Not even the staff? Or one of the soldiers?"

"Lora would cut out her own tongue before besmirching the Jilani name." Zio sounds bitter.

Which is understandable. Zia Lora has always shown more loyalty to the family she came from than the one she married into.

After that, we talk about everything and nothing, just like we used to. He wants to know if I will keep up my target practice. I ask if he's going to buy the new car he talked about. He tells me stories from the news he thinks I'll find interesting. They're always positive stories, like my uncle needs me to know there is good in the world.

We don't talk about his upcoming move back to Detroit. Me, because I don't want to think about losing the last of my family. I don't know why he doesn't bring it up, unless Severu has not told my aunt and uncle they are moving yet? Perhaps my husband will reconsider.

Though that is a selfish thought. Zio deserves to return to the city he loves so much. He has a huge family there and he misses them.

When it's time for him to go, I hug him for a long time.

He pats my back and tells me, "You are the best of all of us, *tesorina*."

SEVERU

Aldo texts me a transcript of Catalina's discussion with her uncle, explaining that he did not interfere because the uncle was not being unkind to Catalina. My soldier also thought it was important to find out what the Revellos knew about Carlotta's no show at the wedding.

I'm not surprised Francesco found a way to tell them at the reception. Nor am I surprised that Lora Revello isn't about to spread gossip about her niece's disappearance. What does surprise me is how much Giovi seems to resent Francesco's treatment of Catalina.

CATALINA

As promised, Aria takes me to meet the kitchen staff. I spend so long learning about the division of cooking responsibilities between the morning cook and the chef who prepares lunches and dinners, plus getting to know everyone, we only have time to tour the main floor of my new home.

We don't go into the study or Miceli's office, but Aria shows me an amazing library which I know I will spend a lot of time in. There are five bedrooms on this level, including the master. One is already kitted out as a nursery.

My hand automatically rests against my lower stomach. One day I will have Severu's baby. If it is a boy, will he force him to learn to control his tears before he's old enough for preschool?

Pushing that depressing thought away, I return to our room and get ready for dinner.

I have to admit that I need more clothes. I'm so used to no one noticing if I wear the same thing to dinner every night for a week, it's a shock to realize that I don't want to wear the same navy skirt I wore the night I met the De Lucas for the first time.

Even so, I manage to put the shopping trip off until the day before the funeral. No one questions my need to heal. Even Severu hasn't tried to have sex with me since our argument.

Whether it is because he realizes my body needs the rest, or he's respecting the distance I have put between us, I'm grateful for the respite.

I need time to build up barriers around my heart before giving him my body again.

CHAPTER 32

CATALINA

I'm doubly glad I took the extra time to recuperate when I realize what power shoppers both Aria and Giulia are.

Giulia has stayed in New York so she can attend my father's funeral, but her husband and son returned to Las Vegas two days ago. I can tell she's missing them both and looking forward to the shopping trip as a diversion, so I do my best not to spoil it with my decided lack of enthusiasm.

At first, it's clear Aria wants me to buy clothes similar to what she wears, but though I am a don's wife, I am only twenty-five, not in my fifties.

I gravitate toward long denim skirts and outfits in citrus colors. Aria tries to gently steer me away and after the third outfit is nixed, I'm frustrated and feeling helpless. Only I'm not helpless.

No matter how hard my father tried to make me think I was, I never believed him. I had my quiet rebellions, but the time has come for me to rebel out loud.

I have a choice. I can allow Aria to do to me what my father did to my mother, and try to turn me into another mimic of herself, or I can stand up for myself and find my own style.

No I am not the slave to fashion that my sister is, but that doesn't mean I don't know anything about it. And even I know that dressing like my mother-in-law is more likely to have me mocked than admired.

"Excuse me, Aria," I say and turn back to the acid green sheer top and long skirt. I wave to the attendant who has been hovering in the background. "I would like to try this on."

She already knows my size. All of the stores we are shopping at today have been prepped ahead of time with our sizes and preferences. Only they don't have my preferences because no one asked me what they were.

"Oh, Catalina, I don't think—"

I don't let Aria finish. "My mother spent almost eleven years trying to emulate you for my father's sake. I'm not going to do that."

Giulia is trying on a dress she saw when we first came in, so this conversation is just between Aria and me.

The older woman's green eyes widen, shock filling them and then horror. "I don't know what you mean."

"I think you do." She was old enough to know who she was promised to and who she ended up married to.

Aria nods, her kind features cast in sadness. "I noticed the change in Sara's hair color, but it only became truly concerning when she started wearing those colored contacts. I tried to be her friend, but she never confided in me about what Francesco was doing to her."

"I believe you." I clasp Aria's hand and squeeze. "As much as I like you, I don't want to be a shorter, younger version of you."

"But neon green?" she asks.

"It's acid green and it's trending this season."

After that, Aria only gives her opinion when I ask her and that's usually regarding formalwear because I have attended so few occasions that require dressing up.

I ask Giulia for her advice on the types of clothes to wear to family dinners, since it seems everyone dresses for them. Though, regardless of time of day, Severu is always in a bespoke or tailored designer suit. So is Miceli.

When we get to the shoe department, both Aria and Giulia are adamant. I must wear heels.

"I don't wear heels." I don't tell them why.

After how revealing my true self to Severu and Miceli resulted in me being accused of turning spy and traitor, I'm not about to admit to the challenges my hip presents.

What if the De Lucas think I deceived them in some way by not telling them about my limitations before agreeing to the marriage?

Aria pats my arm. "I know you never expected to be a don's wife and of course you must dress as a young woman in your position, not your mother-in-law." She winks. "But there are certain expectations, regardless of your age."

"I'm glad you finally figured that out, Mamma, some of those outfits you wanted Catalina to try on were awful." Guilia shakes her head at her mother and then she looks at me apologetically. "But she's right about the expectations."

"And wearing high heels is one of them?" I ask.

The fact that both Aria and Giulia are wearing heels and I've never seen either in a pair of flats, not even at the house, answers my question before Aria opens her mouth. Though I can't help hoping one of them will say no.

Only they both nod.

"It's a matter of looking put together at all times," Aria says.

Giulia nods with a grimace. "I know it seems silly, but heels are a part of the uniform. Just like wearing designer dresses and even workout gear."

"The smallest thing can make you vulnerable and thereby reflect badly on your husband," Aria adds.

Appearances.

Determined to do my best, I look for the lowest heels I can get away with.

I flat out refuse to try anything above two inches. "Tripping and falling on my face isn't going to enhance the family image."

Giulia laughs. "I guess not."

Even Aria smiles and goes looking for yet another pair of low heels, this time boots that will look great with my denim skirt, or so the sales attendant assures us.

As the day wears on, I find it more and more difficult to return those smiles.

Not because I don't enjoy Aria and Giulia's company, but because I am in pain. My hip is acting up something fierce. It's the tiled floors of the stores coupled with walking between them on cement sidewalks. The other women eschew getting into the car to walk only a couple of blocks.

And as much as I know it's my own fault for not telling them I'd rather do just that, I still can't admit to my weakness. So, I limp when no one is looking and sit down whenever I get the chance.

Lunch provides a welcome respite, but it only gives my shopping partners a second wind. We don't head back to the De Luca home until late afternoon.

By then, I'm cursing myself for being so stubborn and New York city blocks for being so long.

"I am glad Severu married you," Aria says in the car on the way back. "I prayed for a miracle right up to the day of the wedding and then it came when it was you at the front of the church and not your sister."

Her words shock me into alertness despite my exhaustion. "You didn't want Severu to marry Carlotta?"

"She has a lot of maturing to do."

"But you said you were a year younger when you married."

"Even from the first meeting, I did not hold the indifference toward Enzo that Carlotta exhibited for my son. Without a desire to be a good don's wife, what was the likelihood that she could be one?"

"You wouldn't have to take her shopping for clothes."

"External appearances are easy to change, but you cannot paper over the cracks of character."

"Carlotta has character. Not wanting to be traded into marriage like a commodity doesn't make her a bad person."

"No, but neither does lying and pretending an intention to go through with the marriage make her a good one."

SEVERU

I arrive in the parking garage at the same time as my wife, sister and mother return from their shopping trip.

Working from home is sometimes more efficient with fewer interruptions. If I left my office when I learned they were headed home, that does not mean I cannot keep away from Catalina. Or that I am missing her.

We see each other every day for dinner and sleep in the same bed, but that is all we do in it. She turns away from me at night even though I see her watching me with hunger in her beautiful hazel eyes.

I do not apologize for anything and yet I've said that I am sorry three times now to my wife. It is not enough for her. A man of action, I have plans that will get me back into her good graces. I will reveal them after her father's funeral.

They will show her that I trust her, and that she did not make a mistake trusting me.

I've never been in this situation before. If I had married Carlotta, I never would have been, but even the thought of that makes me more furious than being at this temporary impasse with my strong-willed wife.

Catalina is my equal which I never expected to have in my wife. It is not a man-woman thing. Since my father's death, I have never considered another person as my equal. Not even my brother. Because ultimately, he still has to defer to me.

So does my wife and yet...behind closed doors, whether in the bedroom or out of it. That is not true, but shouldn't it be? I am Don of New York.

I despise this confusion.

My mother and sister exit the car, but Aldo reaches down to help my wife out with a hand around her waist.

I'm going to kill him.

I'm across the distance between us before I realize I am moving and I jerk Aldo's hand away from Catalina. "You don't need to touch my wife to guard her."

Aldo's mouth tightens and his eyes narrow, but he steps away from Catalina. I don't expect this reaction. Aldo is loyal and one of my best trained men. What the hell is going on?

"Hello, Severu," Catalina gives me a tight smile and then looks at her head bodyguard. "Thank you, Aldo. Will someone bring the bags up?"

"Of course, Signora Severu."

She nods and turns to go. My wife walks away without another word for me, but for once I'm not watching her. My gaze is fixed on Aldo.

I grab him by the throat and shove him up against the armored SUV. "What the hell, Aldo?"

His eyes narrow and he stares at me in a way he never has before. Like he's pissed at me. "Maybe the shopping trip could have waited until your wife was fully healed."

She is *my* wife and Aldo needs to remember that. She's had nearly a week to recover and she told me she was fine with going this morning when I asked her.

I shove Aldo away from me, letting go of his neck so he falls against the hood of the SUV.

"She said she was feeling up to it." I can't believe I'm justifying myself to my Soldier.

Aldo straightens his tie and collar. He doesn't say anything in reply, but his expression says he wants to.

"Are you implying my wife lied to me?" I ask.

My concern for Catalina is overriding my anger. A first for me. Hell.

"No." Aldo's vehemence shows he is already loyal to Catalina.

Does it indicate something else? Something more?

"What then?" I demand.

"She has been limping on and off since lunch."

Something inside me tenses. "Did she fall?"

"No, I was with her the entire day except when she was in the changing rooms. She seemed to be trying to hide her limping from your mother and sister."

"Did she?"

"Neither asked about it, so I would say yes."

Fuck. Why was my wife limping? And why hide it from my family?

I'm going to find her and demand an explanation, but my phone rings and it's Brogan fucking Shaughnessy. I take the call.

I don't waste time with pleasantries. "We think it's the Gutierrez Cartel behind the attacks."

"They've got a toehold in Florida," he replies. "But they aren't coming all the way to New York."

So, his intel is as inadequate as mine was. Before Catalina showed us her research.

"They're behind the takeover of mafia businesses in Detroit and they've already done this same shit in two port cities here on the East Coast. Those times they got rival gangs to go at each other. When the gang wars were over, they moved in on the weakened territories."

"And they think they can do the same thing here?" Shaughnessy sounds as pissed as I feel.

"You need to find out who your leak is. I'm working on pinning my rat down." And it's not my wife.

Big Sal has an idea about who it might be, but I hope he's wrong. He sure as hell was to doubt Catalina.

"I'll find my mole. Don't worry about it."

I'm glad I don't have to try too hard to convince the Irish mob boss that the cartel is behind the attacks. I don't have the patience. If he gave me a raft of shit, we could end up at war even if he's not the one that ordered the latest hijacking of one of our shipments.

"Your people are good, I'll give you that, De Luca."

My wife is a marvel, but I'm not telling him that. "They are."

Shaughnessy will confirm the intel with his own people regardless.

"You want to coordinate hitting back?" he asks.

"An alliance?" We haven't had an actual alliance with the Irish in generations.

"I've got an idea about that."

"You find your mole and we'll talk." I'm not agreeing to an alliance with any boss who can't control his people.

I ignore the fact we haven't identified our own rat. We will. It's just a matter of time.

CHAPTER 33

SEVERU

Catalina isn't limping when she comes to dinner, but she is walking slowly, and her expression is not open toward my mom and sister like it usually is. She's wearing a mask and I don't like it.

She's not exactly quiet over dinner, but she doesn't start conversations either. She looks like she needs to sleep about ten hours.

After dinner, I sweep her up into my arms before my mother can suggest Catalina join her and Guilia in the living room.

"Put me down. I can walk." Her tone is all frost, but her body is so damn warm against me.

I don't bother to reply. I'm watching out for what is mine. Even if Catalina would rather I left her alone.

Mamma gives my wife a concerned look. "I think today took a lot out of her. She needs some rest, son."

I nod and carry *mi dolce bellezza* toward our suite.

Knowing that if I go into the bedroom with her my craving for her will override my good intentions, I put Catalina down in the sitting room. She's made herself present in this space. Her Yoga mat is spread out beside the window. There is a vase of spring flowers on the table between the armchairs. Eliana's doing, I'm sure.

My wife has lived here for a week and already the staff adore her, according to my mother. Aldo's reports reflect the same loyalty toward Catalina from her security team. I'm still equally pissed and appreciative of how Aldo implied criticism of my encouragement for today's shopping trip.

Looking at my beautiful wife standing in front of me almost asleep on her feet, I am angry I didn't consider having a personal shopper bring her a selection of clothing. She said it herself, just because my mother loves shopping doesn't mean my wife does.

Although looking at the results of her excursion incites all sorts of thoughts she doesn't need in the moment. She's wearing a yellow silk top, alternating horizontal stripes of sheer and opaque fabric. She's got on a nude bra, no camisole, which makes her look naked underneath the top.

Knowing that's not true does nothing to control my unruly dick.

Catalina's straight denim skirt reaches her ankles, but the slit up one side ends mid-thigh, giving a tantalizing glimpse of her gorgeous leg. All through dinner, I wanted to pull her into my lap and slide my hand up that slit until I could feel her panties and the sweet flesh beneath them.

Fuck. It has been too long since I felt her sweet body around my cock.

But she needs her rest.

"Go to bed, *mi dolce gatto*," I grit out, controlling my desire to join her. "I've got some work to do."

My wife's lovely face softens. "You haven't called me that lately."

"You barely talk to me. When would I?" I work long hours but my wife is adept at avoiding being alone with me.

She still hasn't forgiven me for interrogating her and when she finds out who needs to be questioned next, she's going to hate me.

Catalina's expression shutters. "Goodnight, Severu."

Her easy agreement to go to bed early says more about how tired she is than the lines of strain around her eyes.

"I'll be up later." Much later. The longer I stay away, the more sleep she will get. Because I do not like my chances of leaving my beautiful wife unmolested once I join her in our bed tonight.

But this state of celibacy between us ends tonight.

CATALINA

I teeter between dreams and wakefulness, my body hot with need. My vaginal walls clench, and my hips arch up, chasing something. It's Severu's tongue.

I've been wearing a nightgown and panties since that night he woke me only to grill me about being a traitor. Both are gone.

His big hands press my thighs apart and his mouth devours my feminine flesh. He spears me with his tongue and I groan, his hands sliding up my body to squeeze and play with my breasts. Pleasure travels my neural highway directly from my now hard nipples to my vagina.

Why did I think avoiding sexual intimacy was a good thing?

This pleasure is too good to give up because my husband proved himself to be as ruthless as I knew him to be.

Too turned on to be shy, I grab his head and hold his mouth to me as I arch toward him. My ribs twinge. So does my hip. I don't care. Pleasure trumps pain tenfold.

He nuzzles my clitoris and then runs his tongue all along my labia, sucking on my nether lips before returning to my sensitive nub. He's so darn good at this.

Rockets are going off in my core and all I want is more.

"Yes, oh, Severu, please!" I need this.

I need him, even if it's nothing more than physical connection. I need that with him.

He thrusts two fingers into my aching vagina, curling them so they rub against that spot inside that sets off sparklers to go with the fireworks.

Excitement builds inside me with the intensity of a volcano. I yank on his hair, silently demanding more. He gives it to me, and pleasure erupts through my body, every muscle contracting in the rictus of ecstasy before bliss flows through my veins like lava.

My husband's big body surges up like a god rising from the sea. He comes down over me and thrusts his big erection deep into my molten core.

A flash of pain sparks when his blunt head bangs against my cervix, but then the discomfort turns into sparks of pleasure and my greedy sex sucks him in just that much deeper.

His mouth comes down on mine, the kiss voracious, his tongue emulating in my mouth the thrusts of his sex inside my tender flesh.

My fingers curl into his shoulders, my nails digging into his skin.

He growls and savagely pistons his hips against me.

Pleasure explodes inside me again, but he doesn't slow down and he's not content with the two climaxes he's already wrung out of me. Severu twists his hips on every downward thrust, pressing himself into my clit over and over again.

I gasp. I strain against him, but I cannot move. His big body is holding me in place. And I revel in his strength.

He pulls his mouth from mine. "Come for me!"

"I can't." It's too much.

"You can." His tone is forceful, and his body does not slow down.

My nipples abrade against his chest hair, my thighs rub against his hips. "Now, wife, come with me," he demands.

His penis grows impossibly big and hard, stretching my sensitized vaginal walls. "Now," he says again, in a tone I cannot deny.

And stars explode behind my eyelids, my body shuddering with ecstasy I cannot hold in. I don't want to. I want to share this intimate moment with him.

In this second, in our bed, no one else exists. Not the mafia. Not my family. Not anything but him and me.

Hot fluid fills me and sends aftershocks of bliss through me.

But he is not done. Still hard, he rolls off me and then turns me and lifts me onto my knees. Sliding right back inside my body, he starts it all over again.

This time he plays with my body, using my nipples and featherlight caresses to my clit to force another orgasm. I'm mindless with pleasure and not sure how many times I've come when he erupts for the second time inside me.

He does not try to talk after we are done. He pulls out and settles us on the bed. Me beside him, his arm possessively over my waist. The silent message is loud and clear.

Neither of us is leaving this bed.

I don't want to. The scent of our combined passion is proof of what we just did. Did we make a baby? A child that will bind us together as no contract could do.

I am sliding back into sleep when his hands start roaming over my skin again.

He does not love me. I don't even know if he trusts me, but he craves me as I crave him.

~ ~ ~

My father's funeral mass is in three hours.

There was no viewing of the body beforehand because the fire destroyed too much. The casket will be closed at the church as well.

Is something wrong with me that I feel no grief today? Carlotta will grieve his death and it hurts more to think about her missing the funeral than to think of his demise.

I'm restless though and I want to run my hands over my books, to seek comfort I should not need since I am not grieving. Why does the prospect of burying the man who tormented me make me want to be sure of my ability to run if I have to?

Over breakfast, the urgency to hold my books and thumb through the pages to assure myself they are as they should be grows.

However, I've looked in every room on the main floor except Severu and Miceli's offices. If my things had ended up in either place mistakenly, they would have told me, or at the very least had them brought to the suite I share with Severu.

Luigi must have put my things in a guest room on the lower level by mistake.

I have hesitated to tour those rooms because it is the primary living space for Aria and Miceli. And Aria has not offered to take me. She's been busy I know. Her social calendar is frighteningly full.

One day soon I will be expected to participate in the seemingly endless luncheons, charity organizer and board meetings, and coffees with the capo's wives. I've been given leeway because of my recovery and lack of appropriate clothing.

The bruise on my face is nearly gone and doesn't show through the light makeup I prefer to wear. That cream the hospital gave me is amazing.

Now that we've been shopping, I have outfits for every possible occasion, as well as a full complement of makeup.

I feel increasingly trapped in my new role and I need my things. The reminder that I have options because I made them. I am not useless. I am capable. I can do this. I can be this.

Aldo and the rest of the security detail are in a meeting with Severu and Miceli. A mafia funeral is a logistical challenge and an inevitable security risk. Having the don with so many high-ranking made men in one place is a temptation for our enemies.

Because the rest are in that meeting, there are only two guards watching Aria, Guilia and me. Neither notice when I take the stairs down to the floor below. I'm not worried about it. The house is secure. No one can come up the elevators without the family's approval. The staff elevator is locked.

I only peek briefly into rooms that are clearly occupied. I don't want to snoop; I just want to find my things. I've found an empty kitchen and living area, the gym, which has a great set up. I'll start doing my Yoga down here instead of the floor of mine and Severu's sitting room.

I'm in the east wing of this floor when I hear several deep voices. I recognize all of them. Severu, Miceli and Big Sal.

The habit of years kicks in and I edge closer to the open door.

"We can't just let him go back to Detroit," Big Sal says.

"I agree." Miceli's voice is grim. "He'll find it too easy to disappear from his home stomping ground."

"We'll pick him up after the funeral," Severu says, his voice cold. "Angelo can question him tonight."

Angelo is one of Severu's top men. But who are they talking about picking up?

I only know of one man who is supposed to move to Detroit soon. Zio Giovi.

But why would Severu want him questioned?

My stomach starts to churn. They can't think he's the mole. Zio would never betray the Cosa Nostra. Besides he doesn't have access to sensitive information. My father always saw him as an outsider because he wasn't from New York.

He never told Zio anything.

Big Sal's voice saying how bad my father's security system was replays in my head. No. I won't believe it. Not my uncle. Zio is a good man. He never hurt me. He's the only person to see me as a treasure since Mamma was killed.

I realize the men are going to come out of the room any second. All thought of tracking down my things gone, I rush to the stairs. I rip my shoes off and carry them in one hand while grabbing the stair rail with the other and going up as quickly and silently as I can.

I don't know what Severu would do if he found me spying on him and I don't want to find out.

Lucky for me I make it to the guest bathroom before anyone noticed me or the men return to mine and Severu's floor. I sit on the closed toilet lid and catch my breath for several seconds before I put my shoes back on. I flush the unused toilet and wash my hands and then open the door.

Aldo is standing on the other side. "No one knew where you were," he says.

I frown. "Am I expected to announce when I need to use the bathroom in my own home?"

It hasn't been an issue until now because I always have a bodyguard with me, usually Aldo.

"In the unlikely event that you do not have one of us with you, yes. You need to tell the house security detail where you will be."

"No."

He looks at me like I've just spoken Latin. "It is a matter of your safety. If you need to be evacuated, my men cannot waste time looking for you."

"Then put a tracker on me but I'm not going to ask for permission to use the restroom like a child in school."

"I will speak to don about it," Aldo replies stiffly.

He's upset with me. I can't make myself care.

I'm terrified for my uncle. I know what *being questioned* means in the mafia. Severu plans to have the one person who sees me as a treasure tortured.

My bodyguard says, "The don wants to talk to you in his study."

Is Severu going to tell me about Zio Giovi? How will I react to it if he does? At least then, I could plead my uncle's case, but if Severu knows I know, he'll be watching to make sure I don't warn Zio.

Would I do that? I wish I knew. I am no traitor, but family is family and Zio is my true family.

CHAPTER 34

SEVERU

Catalina is tense when Aldo brings her into the study.

She stands before me in a black dress with diaphanous sleeves. It nips in at the waist and falls in a full skirt around her calves. Her shoes are simple black pumps. She wears no jewelry and has her hair pulled into a low chignon at the back of her head.

She looks every inch the don's wife, and I am proud of her, though I prefer her hair down. Hell, I would rather see her naked than wearing this forced mourning when she has more reason to celebrate than grieve.

Though I doubt she sees it that way. She is not grieving the loss of her father, but that does not mean she is glad for his death either.

She's biting her lip and I cannot deny she is under stress. We will bury her father today. Whatever their relationship, this will be hard for her. If for no other reason than for the sorrow so many others will express to her and expect her to share.

"What is it, Severu?" she asks, her tone tense.

"Carlotta will be at the funeral mass today. If she behaves, she will be allowed to attend the graveside service as well and go to the mansion afterward for the gathering of the mourners." I would keep her locked in the safehouse until I'm ready to deal with her except for the optics.

Her attendance at the funeral will dampen gossip about her disappearance.

Catalina's mouth drops in astonishment. "You found her?"

I nod. "Yesterday."

"How?"

"The YouTube channel." I am surprised she does not ask why I did not inform her as soon as her sister was found.

My wife winces. "So, it was her. I'd hoped..."

She doesn't have to spell it out. Catalina hates the idea that her sister violated her privacy so badly.

"Is she alright?" Catalina asks after a moment of utter silence. "I should have probably led with that."

"Do not." I grab my wife and pull her close, needing to touch her. "You will not feel guilty for anything. Your sister made her own choices. She will now live with them."

"You said she would be allowed to go to the cemetery if she behaves. Is she not being reasonable about returning home?"

"She is not returning home, but we will discuss that later."

"Oh. Okay." The easy acquiescence bothers me.

Something is wrong, but I do not know what.

"Your sister is unsurprisingly shocked and devastated that Francesco is dead. I hope I do not have to tell you that neither she, nor your other family can be told how he really died."

"Of course not," Catalina says with vehemence. "Not only would it not be safe for you and the other made men that were there that night, but it would hurt her to know the truth. She saw our father very differently than I did."

"His treatment of you was disparate." Francesco had spoiled Carlotta and been a monster to my wife.

"Yes." Catalina bites her lip again.

I cannot stifle my growl of displeasure and make no effort to stop myself tugging her lip from her teeth.

"Um...was there anything else you wanted to tell me?"

I want to tell her about her uncle, to ask her what she thinks of the fact that when he was a capo he had a relationship with the Gutierrez Cartel. He'd been in charge of the clubs in Detroit and used the cartel to source designer drugs for his customers.

The nephew that took over from him shifted to another source.

Even if Giovi is not the rat, he needs to be questioned for intel on the cartel. I will not burden my wife with this reality. She has enough on her plate as it is.

"Do you want to know where we found your sister?"

Guilt flashes in Catalina's eyes again and I wish I had not asked. She nods though.

So, I have to tell her. "She thought she was slumming in a chain motel with room service."

"What do you mean she thought she was slumming?"

"Your sister acted like she'd been living in poverty for a lifetime, not a moderately priced hotel for a week."

"Did you go to get her?"

"She's not important enough for me to see to personally. I sent a team with Luigi. He reported back." Catalina needs to understand that she's the only member of that family that matters to me.

Giovi never swore loyalty to my father, or me, keeping his affiliation with *la famiglia* in Detroit. Lora is his wife, therefore still Don Russo's responsibility. And Carlotta is only still alive because Catalina loves her.

Unaware of my harsh thoughts, Catalina smiles a little. "I'm glad you found her before she ran out of money."

"She should be too. She's not equipped to survive on the outside."

"Most mafia princesses aren't."

"You could."

"I'm not a princess."

"You were a princess, now you are a queen."

My wife looks so lost when I say that, I have to kiss her. I am happy to see that she looks more turned on than upset when I finally lift my head.

I cup her cheek. "Beautiful."

"Time to go, boss." It's Carlo.

He and Aldo will be our point bodyguards today.

I take Catalina's hand and walk with her to the elevator. Before we step on, I lean down. "You do not need to pretend a grief you do not feel."

I will not have her feeling obligated to mourn the death of the man who caused her so much harm.

CATALINA

I spend most of the mass chewing over the problem of Zio Giovi. He is sitting next to Zia Lora, his arm around her shaking shoulders. She sobs quietly throughout the service.

She adored my father. Carlotta is sitting next to her and she's crying too. They both expected me to sit with them, but I am next to Severu, his mother on my other side. Exactly where I want to be.

My eyes are dry, my expression as stoic as I can make it.

It remains that way as Severu speaks about my father. His words are appropriate, but he does not lie once. He says things like, "Francesco Jilani served as consigliere for my father and myself." But without a modifier. No loyally, or well, or even to the best of his abilities. Severu mentions loyalty only once, saying that Francesco was loyal to his ideals, not the Costra Nostra's ideals, much less his don's.

My aunt and sister do not seem to notice, but I see the grim looks on the faces of the capos. They know my father betrayed their don. They are here for appearance's sake. There can be no question that my father died in an accident. No hint that he was not in good standing with *la famiglia.*

Not today.

Closure. That is what I feel when I throw a handful of dirt onto my father's casket at the cemetery. My sister falls to her knees and cries after tossing hers. My aunt leans heavily against my uncle.

I just feel closure. That time in my life is over. Francesco Jilani can never hurt me again. My husband made sure of it.

I take his hand and squeeze it in thanks. He does not look down at me. Public displays of affection are not at all the thing for the Don of New York. But he doesn't pull his hand away and he returns my pressure briefly.

Comforted, I manage to hold onto my emotionless mask.

~ ~ ~

I'm trying to figure out how to get Zio Giovi alone so I can talk to him, when Zia Lora grabs my arm. "You could show a little grief, Catalina. I know you aren't an emotional girl, but people are starting to talk."

Turning to face my aunt, the shifting of my body pulls my arm from her hold. "I know today is very hard for you, Zia Lora."

"Yes." Her chin wobbles but she takes in a breath and manages not to start crying. "He was my brother. I should have made the funeral arrangements."

I didn't realize she hadn't.

She doesn't need me to respond, going on to say, "Your husband shut me out. He had no right. It's shameful."

"My husband is also your don," I remind her, looking around to make sure no one overheard her disrespect.

Aldo is near but he's talking to someone on the phone, his eyes are trained on me though and he raises his brows like questioning if I'm okay. I give him a small nod to say everything is fine.

"And Francesco, was your father. Did you even pick out the flowers?" my aunt demands, like that should have been the least I did.

Fifteen years of pretense drops away in a moment.

"He was my jailer and my tormentor," I say bluntly, done completely with my family's attempt to pretend ignorance of how Francesco Jilani treated me.

He was my biological father, but he never earned the title, much less Papà. Why do I still give it to him? From now on, I won't.

Zia Lora's face pales, her expression scandalized. "You should not speak ill of the dead. Your father was a good man."

"Then I cannot speak of him at all," I tell my aunt.

I don't want to argue with her because I recognize that she *is* hurting and I do not want to add to that, but neither will I ever agree that my father was a good man. He was a wife and child beater. A murderer.

Zia Lora sighs. "You know I love you, Catalina."

I always thought she did. She adored my father though. She was kind to me, but never at the expense of her relationship with her brother.

Still, Zia Lora treated me better than her brother did. She taught me to cook. She praised my ability on the piano. She hugged me and often tried to point out my good qualities to Francesco.

A sudden rush of appreciation for her rolls through me. "I know, Zia."

"You need to talk to your husband," Zia Lora says to me appealingly. "He wants to send me and Giovi back to Detroit."

I want to blurt out that Severu isn't going to let Zio Giovi go anywhere, but of course I can't. So, I say, "I think Zio would enjoy that."

"He's no longer capo. It won't be the same. He won't have any standing." Her gaze goes distant. "It was so different when we were first married. He was a big man in Detroit. He ran the clubs, did you know that?"

I shake my head. Zio Giovi talks about his family back in Detroit. His favorite restaurants. But never his time as capo.

"There were parties every weekend." She shakes her head. "Important people came to our clubs. Beautiful people. He had connections everywhere. With the Irish, the Colombians, even the local gangs. Your uncle was good at networking. It all changed though. We didn't have children."

And somehow that translated to Zio Giovi passing his role onto his nephew and moving to Long Island. It had to have been hard for both of them.

"He has no standing here," I remind my aunt. "At least there, he would be a soldier. He would have his family."

He'd given it all up so Zia Lora could keep the Jilani home running and take care of my sister and me. But Francesco wanted it and what he wanted, he got.

Until Severu made sure he didn't.

"A soldier?" Zia asks, shocked. "I did not marry a mere soldier. I married a capo."

This isn't about Zio Giovi at all. It's about Zia Lora and *her* standing. Here she is the sister of the former consigliere. Francesco's position gave her clout, and she believes it will continue to do so.

She doesn't know that the capos are aware of how Francesco tried to dupe Severu into marrying me thinking I was Carlotta. But what the capos know, their women will eventually know. They won't learn about how my father really died, but they'll all believe the car accident was the result of his frame of mind after his don discovered his duplicity.

It won't be any time at all before Zia finds herself on the outside of the society she's currently a leading lady in. I pity her, knowing how devastating that will be for her. If her husband turns out to be the rat, her life will be all but over.

If only I could protect her and my uncle, but that is not within my power.

CHAPTER 35

CATALINA

The long day and the press of people begins to get to me. Aldo takes another call and I text him, telling him I'm going to be in Francesco's office. I'd rather go to my old bedroom, but I'm not up to climbing the steps in my heels.

There. Bodyguard alerted to my plans.

The computer is still on the desk. The room was never messy, so it doesn't look like anything has changed, though I know that Big Sal has emptied the filing cabinets and drawers of the desk. Did he find all the secret compartments?

I sit down and idly press the piece of molding that pops the hidden gun storage in the center down. The Glock is still there along with a silencer.

My conversation with my aunt plays over in my head, adding sympathy to my worry for my uncle. Then something she said takes on additional meaning. Zio Giovi had connections with the Colombians. The Gutierrez Cartel is based out of Colombia.

Nausea climbs up my throat and I lift the lid of the laptop. Pulling up my aunt's social media I search for images she would have posted before coming to Long Island. It takes a long time, but I finally find photos from back then. There are several pictures of my uncle with a man I recognize. He was not then what he is now, but the younger man in those photos is now the head of the Gutierrez Cartel.

Oh, God. I'm really going to throw up.

This is no coincidence. Is it why Severu wants to question Zio Giovi? Did someone remember that he had the connection to the cartel back in Detroit?

"I thought I saw you come in here. I know how you hate crowds, *tesorina*. You should never have been forced to marry the don."

Looking up at my uncle, my heart hurts under the genuine concern reflected in his caring gaze, his tone first understanding and then angry. I feel the inevitable rushing toward us with the power and destruction of a crazed tiger.

"Zio." It is all I can say.

He notices immediately that I am upset and steps toward me. "Are you alright, *tesorina*? I did not think you would grieve your father, but you have such a tender heart."

"Oh, Zio." Tears burn the back of my eyes.

I do grieve my father, but not the one who donated his sperm to create my life. I am grieving the loss of the man in front of me. The only man to ever treat me like a beloved daughter.

I feel no grief for the loss of Francesco Jilani but I'm breaking apart inside at the prospect of what is going to happen to Zio.

Pressing the OS-Alt-Letter combo, I turn the computer so Zio can see the screen. It takes a moment before his eyes focus on it instead of my face. When they do, he gasps and stumbles backward, sitting with a heavy thud into one of the chairs that used to be in front of my father's desk. They are now pushed against the wall to my right.

"Zio tell me you're not the rat." I cannot get my voice above a whisper, but he hears me.

The look he gives me. So much pain.

"Thirty-six years ago, Enzo De Luca decided he wanted Aria Bianchi, but she was already promised to your father."

I nod. I know this.

"Francesco agreed to give up his claim on the most beautiful mafia princess of that generation. But that meant he needed a new bride for himself."

"My mother."

Zio nods, looking as if he has aged a decade in the past minutes. "Your mother. Sara Russo. But she was also promised. To me."

Shock courses through me.

"Her father, the don, made a trade with Enzo's father. Madonna Candilora would become my wife and my sweet Sara would become Francesco's wife. He didn't even bother to marry her until she'd suffered years of humiliation remaining single when all her friends were marrying around her."

"I hated watching her languish, waiting for Francesco to marry her. Of course, if I had known he would treat her like he did, that she would die here...I want you to know that I never blamed you, *tesorina*."

"My father hit her, and she fell down the stairs. I tried to stop her falling and ended up going down with her."

Fury fills my uncle's features, but it goes away as quickly as it came. "Just one more thing to blame the Jilanis for."

"What do you mean?"

"Your aunt had meningitis as a child. It left her infertile. Her parents knew, but they hid it so she could make a good match."

"Because you didn't have children, your don didn't fight removing you as capo and sending you here to live," I say, so ashamed of my family, I can barely stand it. "You never mistreated her because of it."

Another way that my uncle is superior to the man I once called father.

"No. She was as innocent in all the scheming as your mother."

My father wasn't innocent though. I bet he knew the truth about his sister. My grandparents weren't innocent. Even Don Enzo wasn't innocent. His desire for Aria caused so much fall out for two other families.

"You know, I always suspected your mother's death didn't happen the way Francesco claimed, after seeing the way he treated you."

"You never asked about it."

"I thought if you wanted to talk about it, you would. You were just a child. None of this was your burden to carry."

And yet it has been a weight around my neck since I was ten years old.

"I tried so hard to think of a way to get you out of this house, but Francesco would not hear of arranging a marriage for you. Your aunt always believed that as much as he could not forgive you for killing your mother..." He grimaces, like he doesn't like repeating the lie. "Francesco could not bear to let you leave because you were a living reminder of her."

Zia Lora has never seen her brother in a clear light.

"You do look so much like her, *tesorina*," Zio Giovi says.

"She was beautiful," I say fiercely.

"Yes. I hated my brother-in-law for stealing my life, first my bride and then my role as capo. The one good thing about coming here was you. You are the daughter I never had. The daughter I was meant to have with Sara."

Tears clog my throat and burn at the back of my eyes. He loves me and I am going to lose him as sure as I lost Mamma.

"When Eduardo approached me about the plans he had for Detroit, I had just found out about Candilora's infertility. I was raging." He shakes his head. "It was too easy to tell him what he needed to know to orchestrate the takeover through the bratva and the Irish."

"Betrayal was easy?" I ask, every word like ground glass coming out of my throat.

"They betrayed me first, *tesorina*. My don. My father-in-law. Francesco."

"But now?"

"A year ago, Eduardo contacted me again. He wants territory in New York. He'd orchestrated campaigns in two other cities successfully. This time, I was desperate to get you out of here. Timing..." He shakes his head.

"What do you mean?"

"Your father had broken your arm again. You walked around this house like a ghost and I could not stand it. I considered going to Don Severu, but what good would it have done? He would have fired Francesco."

"But that would have only made him want to take the humiliation out on me."

"Yes. I wanted to take you and run away, but I needed a way to keep you safe. Eduardo offered it. He was going to make me a captain with the cartel. I already have a house in Colombia where I was going to take you and your aunt."

"But how many of *la famiglia* would have died if war was declared with the Irish?"

"I did not care. I still don't, unless you were one of them. When you married Severu De Luca, I knew my plans didn't matter. Even if Eduardo managed to incite war between the mafia and the mob, you would be impossible to get out of New York. It was all for nothing. My daughter was lost to me."

I'm crying now, hot tears running down my cheeks and I do not care.

The father of my heart is lost to me too.

"Will you tell me what you know about the cartel and their plans here in New York?" I force myself to ask and then listen as he does, silent sobs wracking my body.

He names the conspirators that are here in the US. He tells me how they contacted each other, who they got to work with them. He names the leak in the Irish mob.

Finally, he stops talking and just stares at me like he's memorizing my face.

I want to hug him, but if I do, I'll lose the courage I need to save him. I'm running out of time. Whether it is Aldo or Severu, someone will come looking for me soon and I have to save my uncle the only way I know how.

Because he did it for me.

He was trying to save me.

"I can't let them torture you, Zio. You're the only real Papà I ever had." I lift the gun and screw the silencer onto it.

Tears wash into his eyes along with understanding. Even gratitude.

We both know he's going to die. That his dream of becoming a captain in the cartel and living in South America will never happen. Even if he ran now, Severu would find him. The only thing I can do is prevent Zio from experiencing the living hell of torture before his death. He doesn't just have information the mafia wants; he's a traitor.

The pain of loss splinters inside me.

"I love you *tesorina*."

"I know." I lift the gun with the silencer attached and aim, but he's a blur through my tears. "I love you too, Papà."

My hand is shaking so hard, I have to wrap my other hand around it to steady the Glock.

He nods, giving me permission.

I sob, my finger squeezing the trigger.

But I hear the hiss of another shot and mine goes wide as I jerk in surprise. A red hole blooms in Zio's forehead though.

He falls forward, tumbling to the floor in a heap.

A keening wail fills the air. It goes on and on. Why won't it stop?

CHAPTER 36

SEVERU

Aldo nods to the door of the office, "She's in there. Giovi Revello is with her."

Grabbing my Baretta from my shoulder holster, I put a silencer on it. We don't need anyone to come running if they hear gunshots. I open the door cautiously. If Giovi is the leak, my wife is in danger. What I hear as I step inside the room stuns me.

Giovi is telling Catalina the name of the leak in the Irish mob.

Catalina's body shakes with silent sobs as her uncle talks. My wife never cries. The sight hits me with gut wrenching force.

Neither she, nor Giovi, notice when I open the door to the office. They are so intent on each other.

She lifts a Glock from her lap and attaches a silencer, her words as shocking as her actions. She wants to save him from being tortured and she's prepared to kill him to do it.

I make a split-second decision. Stop Catalina from killing her uncle and take Giovi for further interrogation, or kill him myself?

He is a rat. He sold us out and broke his vow to the Cosa Nostra. He deserves time in the box, but if I take him, it will break her. I can see that.

Her bastard father wasn't able to break her with fifteen years of abuse. I'm sure as hell not going to be the reason she breaks now. I can't let Revello go, and I sure as hell can't let her kill him.

It would destroy her.

I silently slide the safety off my Baretta and pull the trigger. My bullet hits where I aim, slamming Giovi's head backward. Another bullet lodges in the wall to the right of the now dead man, proof that I acted in the nick of time.

He topples forward.

My wife makes the sound of a wounded animal, sobs wracking her small body.

I hate that she watched him die.

Furious, I snap at Aldo, "Where did my wife get that gun?"

"I don't know, boss. She didn't have it earlier. It must have been in here."

Big Sal cleared the room out, but Francesco must have had the gun hidden in here somewhere. Of course, Catalina knew about it. She made it her business to know as much as she could just for the power of holding that knowledge.

She drops the Glock without warning and launches herself across the room, throwing herself over the back of her slumped uncle's figure.

I hand the gun I just used to kill Giovi Revello to Miceli. "Take care of this."

"I'm sorry Zio," Catalina sobs over and over again.

The blood from the exit wound in the back of his head smears her arms and face. She doesn't seem to notice.

He was a traitor, but he loved her. And she loved him.

Dropping to my knees beside her, I try to pull her away from the body. She fights me. "No, I can't leave him alone."

"Fuck," my brother says with feeling.

"I killed him," she sobs and then she throws herself into my arms.

I hold her tight. "No. It was my bullet that killed him."

"But I interrogated him instead of telling him to run. I knew he needed to run, but he knew too much. He couldn't go to the cartel." She breaks down again, her tears soaking my shirt.

"You protected *la famiglia*."

"At what cost?"

His life. Her peace.

"He was going to be my children's grandfather."

Over my fucking dead body was a traitor going to be grandfather to my children. I don't say it though. She doesn't need the truth rubbed in her face.

Her grief is a living, breathing thing between us. "He started this in motion five years ago." I don't know if he told her about Detroit, but I'm sure he played a role in the Russo losing his territory.

"They all betrayed him, Severu. Your father, my grandfather, Francesco. They took everything from him. He deserved so much better."

I cannot say what I think, that a traitor doesn't deserve jack shit. She sees him as a victim, and she loves him. Even in death. And still she put *la famiglia* first.

She is one of the strongest people I have ever known. Her integrity is titanium threads running through her soul.

"I'll need you to tell me what he said, but not right now." It would be better to get it out of her immediately, but I cannot make myself question her in this state.

My wife shakes her head. Something tightens in my gut. Can I force her if she refuses me? My brother's expression reflects the doubt I feel.

She points to the computer. "It's all on there. I recorded it."

I see the red light that indicates the computer is still recording. I meet my brother's eyes and then nod toward the laptop. He will take care of it.

I need to take care of my wife.

"Lock this room and bring in a cleanup team after the mansion clears out," I tell my brother. "Send Carlotta back to the safe house now though."

"What about Lora Revello?"

She's a loose end but I don't want to dispose of her. Catalina has lost enough.

"The Jilanis have connected family in Italy. Relocate her there with a team of bodyguards who can keep her under surveillance." If she becomes a problem, they'll be in a position to take her out.

"We need to get you cleaned up then I'm taking you home." I pick Catalina up and she lets me, clinging to my neck.

I feel a tightness in my chest. I'll have to make an appointment with my doctor. These pains in my heart are happening more and more often.

I carry her into the office en suite and set her on the counter. I can't do anything about the blood on her dress but it's black, so the blood shouldn't show. She's not going to be mingling with any mourners on the way to the car.

I wet a towel and then carefully wipe away the blood from her face and neck. She never stops crying, but the tears are silent now. I help her wash her hands. As bloody water swirls in the porcelain sink she starts to sob in earnest again.

"I'm sorry he had to die," I tell her.

I am not sorry he is dead. I cannot be. His collusion with the cartel could have cost the Cosa Nostra dozens if not hundreds of lives. Good men. Loyal men.

She doesn't reply and remains silent and docile as I guide her out of the office, down the hall, through the foyer and out the door. No one approaches us. I glare murder at anyone who looks like they are going to try.

CHAPTER 37

CATALINA

I have a headache from crying when Severu follows me into the master suite's bathroom. The sobs have finally stopped, but my sorrow is still choking me. Zio Giovi is gone.

"Thank you," I say to my husband. "You showed him mercy."

What kind of world do we live in that I feel gratitude for my husband killing my uncle instead of torturing him? But I do.

And I'm thankful that it wasn't my bullet that ended Zio's life. I don't know how I would have lived with that.

"I showed *you* mercy." Severu's enigmatic gaze is fixed on my face.

"Yes, you did."

"We should take a shower."

I nod, but I make no move to undress. My husband doesn't wait for me to, but unzips my dress and then takes it off of me without jarring my still healing ribs. They're much better than they were, but it will be a couple of weeks before they stop twinging when I reach too far. He removes my bra and panties too.

I stand there, totally naked my arms wrapped protectively around my-self.

He turns on the water, letting it heat, before peeling off his own clothing. Then he ushers me into the shower. I let the hot water fall over me, refusing to look at our feet where I know blood will turn the water pink.

He lathers his hands and then washes my body.

"Here, let's take this down." He's talking about my bun.

Although my hair is already wet, he doesn't seem to have any trouble removing the pins holding the chignon in place. He opens the shower door and tosses them onto the floor near our clothes.

Will a maid take the clothes away?

My dress soaked in my uncle's blood.

A sob snakes up out of my throat and I find myself held firmly against my husband's muscular body. His heat seeps into me and blankets the cold that comes from somewhere deep in my soul.

I tilt my head up. He's looking down at me, his dark eyes unreadable.

"Death is pressing in on me. I can't breathe. Make me feel alive."

He kisses me and my lungs expand. He caresses my body and the oppressive weight of death begins to lift.

Severu takes me against the wall in the shower and then again on our bed. I fall asleep, but wake with a nightmare. It happens throughout the night and every time, Severu is there to soothe and to drown my pain with pleasure. He brings me to climaxes with his hands and his mouth and his gorgeous sex. Sometime near morning, I finally fall into a deep sleep wrapped in my husband's ruthless arms.

He showed mercy to *me*. The thought chases me into slumber.

SEVERU

The weeks after Francesco's funeral and Giovi's death are busy. Watching the video Catalina made of her and her uncle in the office, we learn the names of the cartel members in New York. Tracking them down is a lot harder than it was finding her naïve sister.

These men and women know how to hide and cover their tracks, but I will not rest until they are all dead. Until my people are safe. Until my wife is safe.

Catalina accompanies my mother to her many social engagements. She hides the bruises of exhaustion under her eyes with makeup, but I know they are there. I do not know what to do about them.

She does not ask about Carlotta. She never mentions the things we brought from her bedroom and the attached secret room in the mansion. I want to show her what I did with them, but not right now.

Not when mafia business keeps me away from our home from before she wakes until after she's gone to sleep at night, with the exception of dinner.

While I can't be there every night and neither can Miceli, we both try to eat dinner with our mother and my wife as often as we can.

Despite the shroud of grief surrounding my wife, I am getting to know her better every day. She is such an intriguing woman. She holds her own in discussions whether about finance, family or politics. Day by day, she is less reticent to share her opinions and I like it.

I don't like how wan she looks, but I've had the doctor by to check her out and he gave her a clean bill of health. She's not pregnant. Yet.

Catalina still wakes with nightmares and can't sleep until I've exhausted her body with pleasure. I'm a greedy bastard, because I'm more than willing to drown my own stress in her beautiful curves. And eventually, I will plant a baby in her womb.

Shaughnessy called me with the news he'd identified his own mole before I could tell him who it was. He suggested an alliance cemented in blood.

A marriage between my brother and his niece that will result in children that carry both our family's blood legacies.

His men and mine are working together to scour the city and eradicate the Gutierrez Cartel from our streets.

Three weeks later, we've killed the last cartel infiltrator.

But it's not enough for me or Shaughnessy. I contact Don Russo and tell him if he retires in favor of his son, that I will help them regain their businesses and territory now in the bratva hands.

Shaughnessy negotiates an alliance between the Cosa Nostra in Detroit and the Irish mob that got double crossed by the bratva. The Gutierrez Cartel will lose their allies in Detroit.

We have plans to go after the port cities they took over territory in too. Shaughnessy's mob and my family have been doing business in this country for over a hundred years. We have contacts and allies the cartel can't match. When we are done with them, they won't have business in any territory we have influence or allies.

The Gutierrez Cartel will never threaten my territory or my family again.

I spend more time at home after the hunt, while we put our other plans into motion. I notice that Catalina waits until my mother leaves the main floor to play the piano. It's often late and probably accounts for her lack of sleep. She's going to bed much later than I thought she was.

I tell Mamma that I want my wife to get more rest and she needs to go back to her floor after dinner. I'm surprised when my mother does not argue, but she's worried about Catalina too.

That first night, Catalina's eyes widen in surprise when Mamma doesn't join us in the living room. She does not go directly to the piano though, so I tell her I have work to do in the office. There is always work to do.

Minutes later when I hear the haunting notes of the piano echoing down the hall and through the open door of the study, I nod with satisfaction.

A few days later, the music no longer sounds like a funeral dirge, even if sometimes it starts that way. Catalina has begun playing songs that are more upbeat. She's working through her grief.

The next morning at breakfast she asks about Carlotta. "Is Carlotta living with Zia Lora at the mansion?" My wife's pretty lips twist in a half-frown. "I should have asked before."

"No, you shouldn't." I hate that she feels like the weight of both her family and mine are on her shoulders.

Carrying that burden is my job.

"I'm surprised neither of them have called me, to tell you the truth."

"Carlotta does not have a cell phone and your aunt has a new one to go with her new life in Italy."

Surprise flickers in Catalina's eyes. "Zia Lora moved to Italy?"

"She needed a fresh start." And I needed her out of New York.

"Life here wasn't going to be easy for her. Thank you for arranging that." "My pleasure."

"Why doesn't Carlotta have a phone?"

"I don't trust her."

"What's she going to do, call the FEDs?" Catalina jokes.

But I don't smile. "It's a possibility. She took your father's death hard."

"That doesn't mean she'd turn snitch."

"If it gets her what she wants?"

Catalina sighs. "I don't want to believe it, but maybe. What are you going to do with her?"

"I'll have her brought to dinner tonight so we can talk about that."

The smile my wife gives me is small, but genuine. "I'd like that, thank you."

"Your family is my family now, *mi dolce bellezza*. I will take care of all of you."

"I wish you didn't have to, but I'm glad you are."

My beautiful wife really is incredibly sweet.

I stand and swoop her off her chair and into my arms.

She gasps. "You haven't carried me like this in a while."

"Text my mother and tell her you won't be doing whatever it is you both have planned for today."

"Why? What will I be doing instead?"

"Me."

CHAPTER 38

CATALINA

Carlotta arrives for dinner and our visit with a bodyguard. A woman who looks like she could break my sister in half. She doesn't smile and she doesn't say goodbye to Carlotta when Severu dismisses her to have dinner with the rest of the staff.

My sister runs to me and gives me a hug. "I've missed you so much, *soru*. I've been all alone."

I hug her back, my heart squeezing with love for my little sister. But then I remember the videos and I pull away. She's been alone because Severu doesn't trust her and won't allow her to stay in our home.

"Severu won't even let me have a phone. I wanted to call you so many times."

"You will address me as Don De Luca." My husband walks into the living room. He wants to get the discussion of Carlotta's future out of the way before Aria and Miceli arrive for dinner.

"You're my brother-in-law."

Severu doesn't reply, simply staring Carlotta down.

She looks away from him. "Fine, I'll call you Don. Alright?"

"You do not have a phone because you cannot be trusted with electronic devices."

"Is this about the Stellina thing?" my sister asks, her tone implying Severu is being unreasonable.

"The account has been shut down, but millions of people saw your sister's private moments because of you."

"She was playing the piano, not bathing."

My sister's callous attitude hurts. It also makes me angry. "You knew why I played, and it was selfish of you to use my pain for your own benefit."

I sit down on one of the sofas but Severu doesn't allow my sister to join me, taking the seat beside me and man spreading so she has to sit elsewhere.

With a frown for him, she plops down into a nearby armchair. "Some posts did better than others. The ones after..." She lets her voice trail off. "Well they went viral. Your emotion was so raw in them."

"My emotions. *Mine*. You had no right to share those moments of catharsis with strangers."

"If Sev...I mean the don hadn't told you about it, you would never have known."

"What I don't know can't hurt me?" I ask, shaking my head "No wonder my husband doesn't trust you with a phone."

"That's not fair. I needed money to pay for culinary school and there was no other way."

"So, you weren't saving up to run away?" Severu asks.

"Oh, no. I thought if I had the money to pay, Papà would see how serious I was about going, and he would let me. I never thought he'd arrange a marriage for me at nineteen. Catalina is twenty-five and he hadn't arranged one for her yet."

Nonplussed, I turn my head to meet my husband's eyes. My sister has no regret for her actions. None at all. His concern that she might go to the FEDs if she thinks it will get her what she wants is more valid than I wanted to believe.

Carlotta is not a bad person, but she is selfish and short-sighted.

"What are you going to do?" I ask my husband.

Two months ago I would have been scared he was going to marry my sister off to one of his made men, but he knows that would hurt me and he doesn't like me being hurt. My heart wants me to believe that means something it doesn't, so I ignore the pitter-patter in my chest and wait for him to reply.

"She will go to culinary school."

Carlotta lets out a squeal. "Oh, thank you, thank you. Which one?"

I have no doubts there will be restrictions, but I'm not surprised this is part of his answer for her future. His own sister was allowed to get a bachelor's degree at university before marrying Raffaele.

Severu names a school and Carlotta's expression turns confused. "I've never heard of them."

"It is small, but you will learn most of the same cooking techniques you would at the Culinary Institute."

The size must make it easier to keep her safe while she's attending classes.

"But I want to go to a school that is taught by top chefs in the industry."

He ignores her and says, "While you are attending the school, you will be living with the family of one of my low-ranking soldiers. They know not to give you special treatment. You will be expected to pull your weight in the household just like any other member."

"What does that mean?" Carlotta is starting to look worried.

"I believe you will learn to do chores like washing dishes and cleaning toilets."

My sister gasps and opens her mouth to say something, but Severu puts his hand up. "Do not interrupt me again," he says harshly.

She snaps her mouth shut and stares at my husband like he's a gargoyle.

"Your grades at the school will be dependent on *your* effort alone, not your family connections. When you graduate, if you graduate, you will be given a job as a prep cook in one of our restaurants."

"Prep cook?" Carlotta practically screeches. "That's menial labor."

"It's honest work that requires an education or experience to get the position in one of our kitchens. You will work for a minimum of two years. Whether you advance in the kitchen will depend entirely on your work ethic and talent. Be aware that your job is not guaranteed. If the chef does not think you are up to the task, you will be put to work washing dishes for the remainder of your two years."

Severu is outlining a future that is both fulfillment of my sister's dreams and punishment.

"I never wanted to work. That wasn't my plan," Carlotta says.

"How did you think you were going to survive away from your father's house?" Severu asks, not sounding even mildly interested in the reply.

It's more like a rhetorical question.

She answers anyway. "I didn't plan to stay away from my home. I couldn't know Papà would die in a car accident. I was going to come home after his temper had a chance to cool off."

"Or after he'd vented it on your sister." The chill in Severus voice tells me exactly why he thinks my sister needs to learn a lesson.

Not because she abandoned him at the altar. But because she left me to face the fallout from her choices.

Carlotta's guilty look says it all. That *had* been part of her plan. "I didn't want to marry you, but no one would listen to me."

"Who is everyone?" Severu asks with bite. "Who did you tell that you did not want to marry me? Not me. Not my mother."

"I told *soru*."

Anger snaps in his dark eyes, his big body going rigid with lethal intent. "The one person in your house you knew had no power to change your fate."

"I couldn't tell Papà. He would have been too angry, and he wouldn't have listened anyway."

"She is right. Our father would not have listened." I put my hand on Severu's thigh, hoping it will help dispel his anger.

He is furious with my sister for putting me at risk.

"You did not try," Severu's voice is filled with judgment. "Instead, you played the part of the perfectly demur daughter, who would never think of disappointing her parent. You lied with your words. You lied with your actions."

Instead of being cowed by his condemnation, my sister glares at her don. "What else was I supposed to do? You don't know what it was like with Papà. Yes, I saw how he treated *soru*. Do you think I wanted him to hit me too?"

"You could have told me, or my mother."

"If you cancelled the engagement, Papà would have blamed me."

"You didn't think he was going to blame you for running away?" I ask with disbelief. At least if she'd told Severu, *he* wouldn't have a grievance against her.

"I knew he'd be mad at first, but he would have gotten over it. He always did."

Not before he found an outlet for that rage. It wasn't always me, but it was often enough. Carlotta had expected our father to vent his anger on me before she returned home.

It hurts, but I can't blame her. Anyone who isn't raised in a house with violence cannot understand. The fear is ever present, even for the child that is never beaten. Every day Carlotta had to wonder if that would be the day it changed for her.

Seeing what he did to me traumatized her too. She loves me and she loved our father. Her loyalties were constantly divided.

There is a tick in Severu's jaw.

I squeeze his thigh needing him to listen. "Growing up in that house damaged her too."

"You are too damn compassionate." The gentle brush of his hand on my cheek belies his angry words.

I shake my head. "I lived it. I know."

"I'm sorry. I'm sorry, *soru*." My sister starts to cry.

Part of me wants to go to her and comfort her, but the other part of me isn't there yet. Because although I understand, that doesn't make her betrayal hurt any less.

"I would like to add one condition to your plans for Carlotta."

My sister's head jerks up, hope lighting her gaze.

"What is it, *mi dolce bellezza*?"

Carlotta's eyes widen at the endearment.

Ignoring her surprise, I say, "I would like Carlotta to get therapy to help her process our childhood."

My sister gasps, her expression indicating that is not what she expected me to say. "I don't need to see a shrink."

"Do you want to go to culinary school?" Severu asks.

"You know I do."

"Then you will also see a therapist once a week and that therapist will be giving me reports, so you will do the work you have to. Despite your selfishness, your sister wants the best for you."

"I am selfish," Carlotta admits. "But I love you *soru*. I always will."

"I love you too." It is easy to say, sitting beside Severu and knowing I am safe from the abuse of my past. "Your don is giving you a chance at the life you said you wanted. It will mean you learning to take responsibility and work for your dreams, but I believe you can do it."

"In other words, don't look a gift horse in the mouth."

I smile. "Exactly." Severu could have meted out a much harsher punishment for my sister's lies and betrayal.

He's not the most compassionate man.

He is hard and ruthless, but he is showing her mercy and even the stipulations are an extension of that. They will give my sister the chance to grow strong. To *grow up* before she herself marries one day. If that is her future.

Once again, I get the impression that Severu's mercy is directed at me and not my sister though.

CHAPTER 39

CATALINA

Severu calls for my sister's bodyguard after dinner.

Carlotta and I hug, and she tells me she loves me again.

"I love you, too. I don't trust you though. Learn to be a person both your sister and your don can trust."

She nods. "You're a much better match for him than I ever was. I don't know why Papà didn't arrange the marriage between you two to begin with."

"Because he didn't think I was worthy." I'd determined weeks ago that I wasn't pretending with my family anymore.

Carlotta doesn't try to argue. She just nods again. "He was wrong. He never saw you for who you are, but we all knew how good, how strong, you are."

By *all* she means herself, Zia Lora and Zio Giovi. Thinking of him hurts, and it probably always will. I will never grieve Francesco's death but there will always be a wound in my heart for Giovi's.

I tell Carlotta goodbye as she steps into the elevator with her bodyguard.

The doors close and Severu sweeps me up into his arms.

"It's been a while since you let your caveman tendencies out. What's going on?" I ask breathlessly, expecting him to carry me to our bedroom.

But he goes toward the other wing. "I have something to show you."

He pushes open the door to Miceli's office, but his brother isn't here. Severu sets me on my feet.

"Why are we in Miceli's office?" I ask.

"We moved my brother's office downstairs."

"When?"

"A few weeks ago."

So, he and his men were talking in my brother-in-law's office the morning of Francesco's funeral. That explains why they were on that floor, but not why Miceli moved his office.

"Why?"

"Because I wanted this room for you."

Stunned, I stare up at him. "I don't understand."

"You need your own space."

It's something I want, but I haven't said anything. Not even to Aria. But Severu realized it anyway. My ruthless husband who takes such good care of me.

"That look." He shakes his head and then his mouth descends on mine.

I fall into the kiss like I always do, my body molding to his. Sliding my hands inside his suit jacket, I revel in the feel of his hard muscles. He is the epitome of masculine perfection to me.

When the kiss ends, he has me wrapped tightly against him and we are both breathing heavily.

"You tempt me, wife, but there is more to see."

I force myself to pull away from him and take in the room around me. It is narrow and long just like the study and the library. I'm surprised that the family never moved the library so they could enlarge the study, which serves as my husband's home office. But this space is just right for me, a precious gift from my thoughtful husband.

"This is really my office?" I can't help asking.

He smiles. "Yes. Do you like it?"

There are Art Deco wooden cubbies that look like they have always been here on the back wall. However, they are set up similar to my cardboard boxes in the secret room. There aren't as many, but that is okay. There is still lots of space to add to my library of information.

I rush across the room and pull out one of the composition books as if the material inside might have disappeared. It's still there, of course.

Everything is still there, except the data about the syndicates.

A stack of brand-new composition books rests in the topmost right cubby. I run my fingers over them.

I turn and see that a state of the art laptop sits atop an Art Deco style desk with a feminine flair. "That's not mine."

"It is now. One of Domenico's guys transferred everything from your old laptop to this one. It doesn't have parental controls." Severu frowns.

"Francesco never acknowledged that I was an adult woman."

"Whereas I am thrilled you are exactly that." The way my husband looks at me is anything but childlike.

Blushing, I break my gaze away from the heated look in his eyes.

A few feet behind the desk, there is a table similar in size to the one in the secret room. A single violet tufted velvet straight-back chair is situated behind it. The desk chair is covered in the same dark shade of purple velvet, but it is on a wooden base with castors. Two armchairs in a lighter shade of lavender are set up as a conversational grouping in front of the desk.

"This room was my great-great-grandmother's office," Severu says. "But her son had it assigned to his underboss and the don's wife's office moved to the floor below. It has been that way ever since."

It's certainly not an underboss's office now. I can't imagine anyone loving this space as much as I do.

Bookcases line the wall to my right and some of them are already filled. With the books from my bedroom. My heart skips a beat and relief washes over me. They're all here.

There is a painting of a woman wearing a glamourous 1920s style evening gown leaning on a grand piano just like the one in the living room. She looks a little like me. Where did my husband find this piece of art?

He notices me staring at the painting.

"That is my great-grandmother. This was her office originally. I thought you would like having her portrait in here."

"I do." I love it, actually. "I'm surprised you had time to create this room for me. It's perfect."

Maybe he had Aria oversee the transformation.

"You were worth the time." He moves to take me in his arms again. "Do you like it? Did I get it right?"

I can't believe he's asking. "It's beautiful." I smile so hard my cheeks hurt. "You thought of everything."

"Good. Miceli thought I should let Mamma help, but it is *my* wedding gift to you," he says with his usual possessiveness.

"It means a lot to me that you did it," I assure him.

I don't know which of us initiates the kiss, but I'm lost in the pleasure of my husband's lips for long minutes. I'm starting to wonder what sex on top of a desk would be like when Severu pulls away. This time he steps back like I present too great a temptation.

"There is one last thing I want to show you."

I look around trying to figure out what it could be.

He grins and it transforms his face. For a moment, the cold don is gone completely and the mischievous boy who might have existed if he'd been allowed a real childhood shines from his dark eyes. "Did you know criminals were just as likely to build their homes with secret passages as the Masons?"

"You have a secret passage?" Excitement and curiosity burn inside me.

He nods and then with a flourish, he waves me toward the wall with the painting. Severu presses against one of the carved squares that connects the sections of wainscoting.

A panel shifts to the side to reveal a modern biometric scanner. "My family had these installed when the technology was first developed," he tells me. "We've kept them up to date ever since."

What's in the secret passage they are so careful to protect? He puts his hand on the pad, it is scanned and then he types a code into the keypad beside the scanner. He types into the keypad again and says, "Put your hand on the scanner."

I do and a laser travels the length of my hand.

"Now you can open it. The keycode changes weekly. I'll give you the new combination every Sunday."

Wow. "Okay."

"Only three people have access to this passage. Myself, Miceli and now you."

Not even his mother? Something stirs in my chest. He's telling me that he trusts me. Like a lot.

Part of the wall swings inward, and we enter an elegant, if narrow, hallway. No dank, or barren wood passages for this mafia family. It looks empty, but Severu stops in the middle of the wall and goes through the same process as before, having me scan my hand a second time.

Afterward, the wall slides open and reveals a steel vault door. This is the vault he mentioned to Miceli back at the mansion? Is my research data on the syndicates inside?

Excitement burbles through me.

The biometric scanner on the vault door requires an eye scan and another code typed in. Then a clank sounds and Severu pulls it open.

Inside is an area about eight feet deep and easily fifteen feet wide. The wall to my left is lined in shelves filled with ledgers. Some look really old, some look fairly new. The wall to my right is made up of drawers and the back wall has a series of cabinets. Everything is dark wood, the handles on the cabinets and drawers brass fittings like they had in banks back in the 1920s.

There's a six-foot table in the center with two straight backed chairs.

Now I understand why the study, library and my office are designed the way they are. The narrow rooms seem longer than they really are, providing space for the passage and the vault behind them. If I remember the layout of this floor, this hidden vault lies between the kitchen pantry and the closet of the empty guest room to the right of my new office.

He points to a column of drawers. "This is where Miceli stored your research. You can add information to it, or access it any time you like, but it will remain here for safekeeping."

And I have access through my office. He's showing me a level of trust that humbles me. What does Miceli think of me taking over his office and having access to the vault? He hasn't shown any resentment toward me. Does that mean he's okay with it?

"I'm surprised it's all wood." It's easier to comment on that than to let myself think about what Severu showing this means to me.

"The vault is lined with concrete and steel plates, which means no internet or phone access. There is power, so air-gapped computers can be used. There are also sealed spaces above and below lined with more concrete and steel plates. Their entire purpose is to stop anyone from getting to our vault from above or below and to create a fire barrier."

That must be why the vault's ceiling is only seven feet when the rest of the home has 12 foot ceilings.

He pulls open a cabinet to reveal a set of leather bound volumes on one of the shelves. "These contain the history of the De Luca family in New York."

Severu hands the one from the far left to me.

I open it and carefully thumb through the pages. It's handwritten. Some pages just have dates and events. Some show family lines and others have entries like a journal. It's all from the late 1800s, before this building was even built.

"The journals are added to by every generation and then passed on to the next." He's giving me access to a hidden history, to information about his family that no one else knows. "The De Lucas were one of the first families to swear allegiance to The Genovese, but my grandfather was the first De Luca don. He was a behind the scenes player who could step in when the top men went to prison on RICO charges."

An unknown made man with a long history in the family would have been the perfect choice for don when the Cosa Nostra in America had to return to their incognito roots.

"You don't mind if I read them?" I run my hands reverently over the journals.

"They are as much yours as mine now, Catalina."

"I guess you don't think I'm the mole anymore."

His beautiful face goes hard. "I never did."

He'd said that before, but I hadn't believed him.

"If you didn't think it was me, why that whole scene?" If he is and was telling the truth about never believing it was me, it reframes that night.

"Because I am me." His lips quirk in a sexy, teasing smile. "According to you that means an asshole and not very smart."

Heat climbs into my cheeks. He remembers that. "I shouldn't have said those things." Even if I thought them.

"I should not have woken you out of a deep sleep to grill you. It was an asshole move toward my wife and reflected a definite lack of higher cognitive reasoning on my part."

"True."

He laughs. "You will keep me on my toes, won't you, *mi dolce bellezza*?"

"I'll do my best."

"Your secret room was filled with information about so many subjects." He gives me a quizzical look. "Why?"

I don't mind the shift in subject. The whole trust thing is doing my head in and my heart too, if I'm honest.

"I wanted to go to college like your sister. But that was never going to happen. I was determined to learn though, so I studied anything I wanted to and could find information on. Despite its restrictions, my computer made so much of that learning possible." I smile at the memory of the day I realized there were university level classes I could audit online. For free.

"I took courses in psychology, ancient history, economics, world history, and even counter interrogation techniques."

"What is your favorite?"

"I don't know if I have one, but I enjoy studying politics because of the real world application."

"You're that invested in who wins elections?" he asks.

"Sometimes, but it's another way of gathering data on the Cosa Nostra and other crime syndicates."

"Politics?" He sounds disbelieving.

I nod. "Definitely. I could tell you which politicians are in your pocket."

"I doubt that very much."

"Want to make a bet?" I ask, feeling daring.

Learning he took the time to make a place that is all my own in this home and having him give me access to this vault, that only he and Miceli even know about? It's done something to me. Made me look at my place in Severu's life differently.

"What are we betting for?" he asks, sounding intrigued.

I like that, so I'm not about to pick something as mundane as money. "If I'm right, you pleasure me with your mouth. If I'm wrong, I'll do the same for you."

His eyes darken with passion. "It sounds like I win either way."

Could he be any sexier? My ovaries don't think so. They are dancing the macarena.

"I guess we both do," I sass.

He makes that growling sound he does sometimes. He's seconds away from forgetting about the bet and taking me on the table.

I rush to start listing names. "I don't think you have the senator in your pocket, but I think you donate a lot of money to his campaigns. He doesn't seem like the type of person who can be bought, but he can be influenced."

Before he says a word, I can tell by the growing look of surprise in his eyes that I'm right. "It looks like I'm going to be eating out that pretty pink pussy."

The way he talks. My breathing goes shallow, and my heart starts to beat wildly in my chest in anticipation.

"But first tell me about the counter interrogation techniques."

Wait. What?

I glare. "Are you serious?"

"Absolutely."

It's just another way of teasing me. Putting off the pleasure to make it bigger.

However, this is one topic that's guaranteed to douse my ovaries with ice water. "That was a specialized course Zio Giovi got me for my 18th birthday. He thought it would help me deal with Francesco since I was home from boarding school and in his sights more often."

"Did it?" Severu asks, pulling my body into his, like he wants to protect me from my past.

"Yes. I couldn't stop him from hurting me, but I could stop from losing myself in the process."

"Why didn't Giovi come to my dad or me?"

I can only guess, but I'm sure I'm right. "He thought like I did. You might demote Francesco, but that wouldn't have protected me, or even Zio Giovi. My father would have been free to keep abusing me and filled with resentment and hatred for me costing him his position. I also think Zia Lora told him not to, she might have even threatened to tell the don that her husband was lying. I never realized how important her status was to her until we talked at the funeral."

"She might have been kinder to you, but she and Francesco were cut from the same cloth."

I nod, but I'm done talking about depressing subjects. "Enough talk about the past. You owe me an orgasm."

"Just one? I'm hurt you have so little faith in my oral skills."

And just like that, arousal surges through me.

I learn just how incredible it feels to be eaten out while lying on a table, my knees raised and my feminine core open completely to him, as he proves that his oral skills are more than up to the challenge of sending my body spasming with multiple orgasms.

He's carrying me to our room after and I realize what this tight and then expansive feeling in my chest is.

I have fallen completely and irrevocably in love with my mafia don husband.

CHAPTER 40

CATALINA

I don't know why, but I somehow expected the whirlwind of social engagements Aria insists I need to attend as the don's wife to taper off. Eventually.

They haven't. This fundraiser today is so not my thing. Yoga? Yes. Walking a 5K on city streets? Not so much.

"Why can't we just donate the money?" I ask her, trying not to whine and not entirely sure I'm succeeding. "Isn't a walk-a-thon beneath the dignity of a don's wife and mother?"

"Don't be silly, *cara*. I've been doing this fundraiser for ten years. Trust me, it's important. It sends a positive message. And it's fun."

"Most important being that I can protect my family and am not afraid for them to be in public." Severu bends down to kiss his mother's cheek as he joins us at the breakfast table.

I don't usually see him for breakfast, but the 5K starts at a godawful 7:30 AM. Any later and it would be too hot. Summertime in New York city is no joke.

"Not that we won't have guards. Some will be on the walk with us, others on the sidelines, following us." Aria smiles up at her son. "Severu will always keep us safe."

I don't reply but I do return Severu's kiss when he places one on my lips.

"So, you want me to do this?" I ask him when he sits down.

He nods. "Yes."

Because it sends an important message. I stifle my sigh and force a smile for Aria. "I'm looking forward to it."

My hip is aching by the end of the 5K, but I take some analgesics, drink an espresso to counteract how they make me sleepy, and hope for the best.

Because afterward, there is a reception for the biggest donors. Which of course includes Aria and me. At least I get to sit down for most of it.

Unfortunately, this evening happens to be a cocktail party being hosted by Big Sal's wife as well. It is a way to cement his place as the new consigliere in the minds of *la famiglia*. No matter how much I wish I could stay home and soak in a hot bath after an extra session of Yoga, I cannot miss it. It would look like I resent him taking Francesco's place.

I take a dose of the higher dose ibuprofen left over from the hospital after dinner with an energy drink, while Severu is putting on his tuxedo.

I put off sliding my feet into my heels until the last minute. I'm wearing a dark green cocktail dress that clings to all my curves. It has a high neck with a keyhole cut right over my cleavage. Emilia sent a maid to help me style my hair and I'm grateful. I've barely got the energy to put on a light layer of makeup.

Once I'm ready, I meet my husband in our private sitting room. He's on his phone, but he puts it away when he hears me come in.

Savage desire casts a near cruel look over Severu's handsome features as he takes in my outfit. "I like that dress."

"Your sister picked it out."

"I'm not sure if I want anyone else to see you in it though."

I laugh. He always talks like other men find me as irresistible as he does.

He shakes his head. "You think I am joking?"

"Teasing, or not, we don't have time for me to change and I'm not risking messing up my hair to do it anyway." The maid put it up in a soft updo with a few tendrils falling around my face.

"I have something for you to wear."

"I'm not putting on a sweater. It's eighty degrees out there, Severu."

He hands me a recognizable small red box with gold accents. Jewelry.

"What's this for?" I ask as I open the box.

"Because I wanted to."

My breath catches when I see the pair of earrings inside. They are platinum infinity hoops with diamond accents.

"They're beautiful."

"Not nearly as beautiful as you, wife."

He calls me that almost as often as he does *mi dolce bellezza* now, and not just when he's being bossy. I like it.

I put the earrings on and take my husband's arm.

My heart sinks when we arrive at the rooftop venue for Ilaria De Luca's party. Tall, circular tables covered with elegant white tablecloths that reach the floor are strategically placed throughout the space. There are no chairs or benches. I've got at least two hours of standing on heels to look forward to.

I don't think even a prescription dose of ibuprofen is going to be enough to get through tonight.

And I'm right.

I don't drink any wine, but even after the caffeine shot of the energy drink earlier, I'm fighting to hide my weariness the entire time we are there.

By the time we leave to go home, I'm done. I don't wait for my husband, or even say goodnight to my in-laws. I go straight to our room and strip out of my dress, leaving it where it falls on the floor. Stepping out of the hated heels, I take out my beautiful new earrings and manage to place them on my nightstand before climbing into bed.

Fatigue battles pain and I hope exhaustion wins as I try to relax and breathe out the pain.

CHAPTER 41

CATALINA

I wake from a fitful doze when Severu's hand lands on my shoulder. He tugs me onto my back, leaning over to kiss me. His lips taste and feel so good, but I turn my head away.

There is no way I can handle sex right now. Yoga keeps me limber, but when the pain flares like this, any movement is too much.

"What is wrong?"

"I can't right now."

"Is it that time of month? Is that why you were so tired earlier?" Concern fills his voice. "Do you have cramps? Should I get you something?"

"It's not that."

"Then what is it?"

"It hurts too much right now. I can't spread my legs." If I try to walk right now, I think my leg would give away. I only hope I can go the night without needing to pee, because I'd probably have to crawl to get to the bathroom.

"What hurts?" Severu asks, sounding worried. "Was I too rough with you last night?"

The night before we'd made love with me up against the wall before we went to bed, where Severu had seduced me into another round of lovemaking. He'd been voracious for some reason and had woken me twice more to join our bodies.

Come to think of it, the lack of sleep probably did contribute to my exhaustion, but he wasn't too rough. It's never too rough, no matter how out of control he gets sometimes. I like it hard or gentle. With him it is always perfect.

"No. It's not that. It's my hip."

He sits up and turns on a light. "Did something happen to your hip? Do you need a doctor?"

"A doctor can't fix what was broken fifteen years ago."

"You weren't hurting like this yesterday."

"I always hurt, but it's usually manageable."

He frowned at that. "What made it unmanageable today?"

"Walking in a 5K. Your mom is no slouch in the fitness department," I try to joke and then I sigh and offer truth that it pains me to admit because it's about more than a once-a-year event. It's about every day. "It didn't help that it was followed by a reception when I probably should have taken some time for Yoga. The two hours spent on my feet in high heels tonight really did me in."

"Wearing high heels hurts you?" There's something in his voice that I can't place. "Why the hell do you wear them then?"

"They're part of the uniform of a don's wife. Your mother and sister agree on that." And I have to admit, all the capos wives wear heels as well.

"When you went shopping with her and Giulia, Aldo said you were limping."

"I didn't know he noticed." I'd done my best to hide my pain that day. "Your mom and sister are tireless shoppers."

"Marathon shopping, walking 5Ks and wearing heels? That's what makes you hurt the most?"

"I don't love going up and down long flights of stairs either." Might as well tell him everything. "But I can wear heels."

"How long can you normally wear a pair of heels before your hip starts hurting?"

I sigh. "About half an hour. Longer if I can sit down, of course." I force a smile. "What cannot be changed, must be endured."

He nods, like he understands and then, his gorgeous face cast in grim lines, Severu gets off the bed. Is he leaving? Going to call a doctor? But he doesn't go toward the door to the hall, he goes to the walk-in closet.

A few seconds later, shoes start flying out and landing with thumps on the bedroom carpet. Every single pair of heels I own ends up in the melee on the floor. He comes out of the closet wearing a t-shirt and sweatpants

I've never seen him in. I mean he has to wear something besides a suit to work out, but I've never seen it.

Severu makes sure the bedding is covering me up to my chin and then he goes through the sitting room, and I hear the door leading to the hall open. My husband barks something in a furious tone. Carlo comes into the room with Severu a few seconds later. It's the first time one of the security team has come into the inner sanctum of our bedroom.

I'm so confused. And a little embarrassed, but I'm in too much pain to give much concern to the fact he's seeing me in bed. It explains why Severu made sure I was covered to my chin though.

"Get rid of these. All of them."

"No, wait, Severu. I need them."

My husband just glares at Carlo, who immediately starts picking up my shoes. It takes a couple of trips but soon all the heels are gone. While he's doing this, Severu is on his phone.

"The doctor will be here shortly." My husband drops on his knees beside the bed so he can meet my gaze. "I need you to make me a promise."

"What?"

"If something causes you pain, you tell me. No more enduring."

"I didn't want you to know Francesco broke me." I didn't want to give my sperm donor that power, but neither did I want Severu to look at me as less than.

"You are not broken. That is not a word you get to use referring to yourself." He's scary serious.

Only my husband doesn't scare me. Not in any way. Little tendrils of happiness unfurl inside me.

"No more heels," he says, like maybe I didn't get the memo when he had Carlo take them all away.

His mom isn't going to be pleased. "Wearing heels is important. It's what people expect of your wife."

"Fuck what anyone else expects. I expect you not to hurt yourself and that's all that should matter to you. My wife does not put herself in pain to fit some goddamned stereotype of what a mafia wife looks like."

"What about what a mafia wife acts like?"

"Explain."

"Your mom is a very social person."

He nods. "She's an extreme extrovert."

"I'm not."

"Few people crave social interaction as much as my mother."

"I want to be a good don's wife, but I miss having time to study new things and do my syndicate research."

"You are perfect as you are. You are my wife. That makes you a good don's wife."

"You're so arrogant."

"Am I wrong?"

"I hope not because all this people-ing is exhausting me."

"Good, because I would like you to go back to your research as well. And I would like you available to meet with Miceli and I at least once a week."

"You would? For what?"

"Your insight. Catalina, you have an amazing brain."

Despite the ache in my hip, the pleasure of knowing my husband thinks so highly of me washes over me in warm waves.

"I will speak to my mother."

"Thank you." I hate the thought of disappointing Aria, but not as much as I hate the idea of spending the rest of my life in an unending social whirl.

The doctor I met at the hospital on my wedding day arrives. He asks tons of questions about the pain, what causes it, when it is most acute, how long I've been dealing with it and when he finds out about the fall down the stairs fifteen years before wants to know all about follow-up care.

There wasn't any.

"I thought Francesco had hired a physical therapist under the table. I should have known better," Severu says, sounding guilty.

Severu is so upset about the pain I'm in, he doesn't complain when the doctor says he'd like to do a physical examination. However, he does make sure every part of my body other than my hip area is covered.

"I'd like to have X-rays taken of this area as well as an MRI," the doctor says when he's done.

"Set it up for tomorrow at our hospital," my husband demands.

The doctor nods and then looks at me. "Do you use a chiropractor?"

"No. I do Yoga."

"That is probably why you are as mobile as you are, but either a chiropractor or a physical therapist would be beneficial. You might try acupuncture as an alternative to taking pain meds every day."

"I don't take them every day." Only when the pain gets too bad to manage. "And I rarely take a prescription level dose of ibuprofen either."

The doctor nods.

Severu pulls the blankets back up, covering my nudity. "Would an acupuncturist help her tonight?" he asks.

"It would be worth trying."

I'm kind of shocked that a traditional doctor would suggest alternative medicine and say so.

He grimaces. "I see a lot of patients with recurring injuries. Prescribing opiates every time is a recipe for addiction."

And made men cannot be controlled by anything that would make them a risk to the organization.

"That's why you had that cream on hand at the hospital."

"Yes." He looks at my husband and then back to me. "Bruises are a common ramification of certain jobs within your husband's organization. As are broken bones."

"Call an acupuncturist," my husband instructs the doctor, who nods.

Then he gets up and goes into the other room to make the call.

"You want me to let someone stick needles into my hip?" I ask.

He looks at me like I'm precious to him. "Whatever it takes to diminish your pain."

I'm surprised to discover that mitigating the pain in my hip requires needles in several parts of my body. Even more shocking is how it relaxes me. I fall asleep before the needles are removed.

CHAPTER 42

CATALINA

W hen I wake, it is morning and I'm almost entirely pain free.

I turn to find Severu watching me. He's still in bed. Wow.

"How are you feeling?" he asks.

"Much better."

"Good. Your X-rays and MRI are scheduled for later this morning."

"Do you really think they'll be able to do something to fix my hip?" Wouldn't they have done it fifteen years ago if they could?

"We'll know later today. Regardless, it looks like acupuncture helped."

"It really did. It put me to sleep too."

"I noticed."

I reach for Severu, but he grabs my hand. "No. I'm not hurting you."

"How many times have we had sex since we got married?" I demand.

My husband's jaw goes taut. "That's not the point."

"It is exactly the point. You said I can't call myself broken. You can't look at me like I'm broken either. Last night was not the norm and making love does not hurt me, but it might kill me if you stopped doing it."

He still looks unconvinced.

"I'm in less pain than I have been in a long time."

"You will have regular sessions with the acupuncturist."

"Okay." I lean forward and kiss Severu's chest. "But right now, I want a session with you."

He pushes me on my back and kisses me for long, glorious minutes. But then he pulls away and says, "Later."

I grab his hand and put it between my legs. "Feel how wet I am for you. Please, Severu, don't treat me like I'm broken."

It's the second time I've said it, but this time the words seem to penetrate.

His fingers slide back and forth between my slick folds. "I've wanted to be inside you since I saw you in that green dress last night." He huffs out a laugh. "Who am I kidding? I always want to be inside you."

His words and the way his body presses into mine soothe the jagged edges in my heart. I hated telling him about my injury, but he doesn't make me feel like I am less than. Only like he wants to protect me.

Is it any wonder I love this man?

Pushing against his shoulder, I get him to lie on his back. I climb on top of him and rub my vulva over the hard length of his cock.

"You feel so good." I press down so my clit is stimulated with each thrust of my hips.

He cups my breasts, kneading and playing with them, stimulating my nipples. "You are so fucking beautiful, wife."

I shift so his hardness presses against my opening, but suddenly his hands are on my hips and he's flipping us. "Not yet."

I reach for his shoulders to stop him, but he moves too quickly, climbing off the bed. He opens his bedside table and grabs something from the drawer. He tosses it on the bed by my legs.

"Open yourself for me."

Dark need shudders through me. I love when he gets like this. Without hesitation, I lift my knees and let my thighs fall open until I'm in a modified lotus position with my feet close to my buttocks.

I am completely open to him.

He makes an approving rumble. "Such a pretty little pussy. So wet and ready for me."

But it's not his sex he presses into me. It's his fingers, and he leans down to put his mouth on my tender flesh. He eats me like he's starving. I climax almost immediately.

He doesn't stop though. Of course, he doesn't. When does he ever stop after giving me just one orgasm?

I cant my hips, but he lifts his head. "Stay still."

I love this game and I try. So hard.

As everything inside me explodes in a second burst of cataclysmic bliss, I feel something slick and hard press at my other hole. He's touched me here before, even slipped a finger inside me while claiming my vaginal channel with his hardon.

So when he slides his finger inside me, it doesn't shock me. I've already discovered that my tissue there is nerve rich, and it feels amazing when he plays with this forbidden opening to my body.

But he doesn't stop with one finger. Seconds later, he's sliding another one inside me one slow knuckle at a time until I'm stretched around both of his thick fingers. It stings a little, but it feels good too. And he hasn't stopped using his mouth to pleasure me.

He scissors his fingers inside me and suddenly I know that he's not going to stop at playing. He wants to put himself *there*.

I tense up, my knees trying to come together. "You're too big."

I don't know how he fits in my vagina, but that oversized piece of manhood is never going to fit where his fingers are.

He lifts his head and his dark gaze traps mine. "Do you trust me, Catalina?"

There can only be one answer to that. "I do."

"You are mine."

"Yes." I lick my lips. "But you are mine too."

If he ever tries to take a mistress, I'll show them both just how good of a shot I am.

"There is a feral look in your eyes I like very much, *mi dolce bellezza*."

"Say it."

"Ahh." His smile is smug. "I am yours."

Something settles inside me. "I trust you," I tell him again.

He slides his fingers out and then he puts more lube on them before pressing three fingers into me. *There.* "Every part of your body is mine."

"Yes."

"I will fuck you here." He spreads those three fingers, stretching me again. "Tell me yes."

"Yes." It scares me, but I want it. And the way it feels with him moving inside me there. It's incredible. I feel full and possessed and strangely cared for.

Am I losing touch with reality?

The answer has to be *yes* when his mouth goes back to work on my lady parts. Severu drives my pleasure higher and higher. It feels different, like it's deeper inside me and when I climax, it's so intense I scream as tears run down my temples.

Only when I am completely limp does he pull away from me and gently maneuver my limbs and body so I am on my stomach with my knees up by my ribs.

The blunt head of his erection presses against my stretched hole. "Are you ready for me?"

"Yes," I sigh out.

He pushes inside and it hurts. His steel hard penis is much bigger than his three fingers. But he doesn't shove forward. Rocking his hips, he claims my final virginity an increment at a time.

I can hear how labored his breathing is, the only indication of how difficult this slow pace is for him. Sweat droplets fall onto my back and my hands curl into the sheet.

My body tries to tense up, but his inexorable movement does not stop and I go limp again as he claims me completely.

While he holds himself above me with the hand he'd been using to prepare me, his other one slides around my pelvis and his fingers find my over-stimulated clitoris. His touch is featherlight, but every soft touch sends sparks of ecstasy through me.

Unbelievably, that storm of pleasure rises inside me again and it is only fed by the dark delight of having him inside me in such a primal, intimate way.

"I'm going to fill you up," he says.

I don't know how much of his massive erection he's gotten inside me, but I nod against the bed, wanting all of him.

He surges forward with a strong thrust and I cry out with the pain of the invasion, but as he pulls back that pain morphs to intense pleasure that radiates deep inside me. He makes love to me, his body not just blanketing me but filling and surrounding me until I do not know where I end and he begins.

Maybe we don't. Maybe right now, we are truly one entity.

When my orgasm hits his shout is ringing in my ears and we come together. Joined. One. Fully inundated with the ecstasy only we share.

CHAPTER 43

CATALINA

My body is registering nothing but the pleasure and connection I felt with my husband when we arrive in the dining room for breakfast.

Miceli and Aria are both at the table and give me near identical looks of concern.

The bubble of bliss around me is penetrated by their worry as I realize that Severu must have told them about my weakness last night.

"I'm fine," I assure them. Still too floaty from what we did before showering to work up much censure, I ask my husband, "Did you have to tell them?"

"Yes."

The morning cook comes in and serves us our breakfast herself, telling me she made the French Toast just for me.

After she leaves, I look around the table. "Which one of you told her?"

Aria grimaces. "The staff adore you. Of course, they all knew a doctor was called last night. She'd worked herself into a state thinking you were seriously ill."

I don't know what to say. I have never had so many people concerned about my wellbeing before. My eyes burn with happy tears that I blink away.

~ ~ ~

I am playing the piano after my X-rays and MRI. My bum is a little sore, but I have my suspicions about why my husband decided to introduce me to that kind of intimacy this morning.

He'd had the hospital run a pregnancy test on me when we went in and when it came back negative, he'd immediately started talking about birth control. He doesn't want anything stopping me from having corrective surgery on my hip.

Not even pregnancy with his heir.

My fingers dance over the piano keys as my brain tries to make sense of everything that has happened since the morning Carlotta ran from her wedding.

Severu wanted me, not my sister.

And he married me.

He trusts me with the most closely guarded secrets of his family. He hates me being in pain. He killed my uncle for me, to protect me. He should have stopped me and taken my uncle to interrogate him further. But because he knew how devastated I would be if he tortured Zio Giovi, even if he was a traitor, Severu had given my uncle an easy death.

My husband is the head of a century old criminal organization. He kills as easily as he breathes. And feels no remorse for it. He is not a good man, but he is good to me. Better than good. He treats me like the queen he calls me.

Does he love me?

For the first time since we said our vows, I think it is possible. Maybe even probable.

"That's a joyful song, *cara*."

I stop playing, and turn to smile at my mother-in-law. "I was thinking happy thoughts."

"I am glad. Do you have a moment?"

"Yes, of course."

I stand up.

"Can we go to your office? Severu wouldn't let anyone else see it until after you did."

"It's beautiful. Perfect for me." I lead Aria to the room that belongs to me and me alone.

My mother-in-law takes her time admiring the room. "Oh, he's done a wonderful job in here."

We sit down in the chairs in front of my desk.

She takes my hands in hers. "*Cara*, I owe you an apology."

"No. You've done nothing wrong. You've been nothing but kind to me."

"I wish that were true, but last night..." she shakes her head, her green eyes growing wet. "So much of that was my fault."

"I never said anything."

"You may not have said anything specific about the challenges your hip presents for you, but you told me you don't wear heels. I didn't ask why. I just assumed you would grow used to them. When you told me you preferred Yoga to going for long walks, I laughed. But it wasn't a joke and I think somewhere deep inside I knew it."

"Please, Aria, you can't feel guilty for what I would not say."

"I noticed how drawn you were looking, how strained your smile had become."

I can't deny either. I've been wearing an extra layer of concealer under my eyes to hide the dark circles.

"This is the life that I love," Aria continues. "However, I have ignored the truth that we are different people. There *are* social engagements you must attend, but far less than I've been dragging you to."

"From now on, I only want to go to those," I say with alacrity. "I trust you to guide me, Aria, but I need to stop trying to *be* you."

"I hope you know Severu doesn't want you to be anyone else."

"What about you?" I ask, unable to hide my worry.

"Oh, *cara*. I adore you just as you are." She leans forward and hugs me. "Part of the reason I've been dragging you all over the city is because I'm so proud of you I want to show you off."

"That's a kind thing to say."

"I'm not being kind. I'm being truthful. The other reason is entirely selfish. I find such delight in your company."

"I enjoy spending time with you too."

"I hope one day you will see me as your mamma as much as I am to my other children. Until then, know that I consider you my daughter."

I'm so touched, I hug her again. And if we both cry? For once I'm not bothered by my own tears.

We go over our combined social calendar and begin taking items off mine. It is such a relief that I'm grinning by the time we're done.

"That's the smile I miss," Aria says as she stands to go. "Please know that I think you are the perfect wife for my son, which makes you the perfect don's wife."

It's so much like something Severu said that I laugh.

She's smiling when she leaves my office.

For a minute I simply stand there, wallowing in my joy that this space is all mine. Every piece of furniture was chosen with me in mind. It's such a thoughtful and romantic gesture, it leaves me breathless.

Now that I am alone though, I cannot stop from going to the books filling the two top shelves of one of the bookcases. The books my father taunted me with, the only gifts he ever gave me while lavishing Carlotta with everything a mafia princess could desire.

One each birthday and Christmas since I was ten. They are all written in Latin. It was his way of rubbing in my supposed ignorance.

They became my secret rebellion. First, as a place to safely hide the money in my runaway fund, and later as a source of pride in my own accomplishment. He couldn't read the books, but eventually, I could.

He never knew I learned to read Latin, auditing the class at boarding school so it didn't show up on my transcripts. I took my education beyond that with personal study until I could read every single one. Books by Cattulus, Augustine of Hippo, Virgil, Ovid, Horatio, Petronius and the rest.

My hands shaking, though I don't know why, I pull one of them off the shelf. Simply holding it gives me a sense of peace, of agency over my own life. Although I would never run away from Severu, knowing I have the option is probably something I'll always need after what I went through with my father.

I open the book, flipping the pages in an accordion fashion. For a moment, it feels like my heart stops beating. No. This cannot be right. I cannot believe what I'm seeing. *It's empty.*

I pull out another, and another until I've checked all of the books I used to hide the money I'd saved. They are all empty.

Did Luigi find the money when he was packing the books and take it to give to Severu? But why? This is not my father's house; I am allowed to have my own money.

I vigorously shake each book again, like the money will magically fall from between the pages. Even though I've seen with my own eyes every single dollar I so carefully stashed between them is gone. A piece of paper falls out of one.

I grab it and nearly rip it unfolding it.

It's a letter in Carlotta's handwriting.

Dear Catalina,

I had to borrow your running away money. I bet you didn't think I knew you had it. You should have told me. I would never have told Papà.

Anyway, I know you'll understand that I need it. I just can't marry that man. I need to go away for a while until Papà calms down and sees sense. I'm too young to get married. Even Severu's sister got to attend four years at university. I just want to go to cooking school. The program I want is only two years long.

It's not fair that I can be married off like a piece of property. I'm not one of Papà's possessions. I am his daughter. He loves me. I know he does, but right now he's blinded by his desire to connect our family with the don's.

When I get back, I'll sell my engagement ring and pay you back. I can't right now, not until everything has settled down and both Papà and the don have realized that any marriage between me and Severu would be a disaster. He's so old and he scares me, if you want the truth.

Anyway, I love you, soru.

See you soon!

Carlotta

P.S. I'm glad you won't run before I get back. I don't want you to run at all. Once I sell the ring, we'll have enough money to get an apartment together. It's all going to be so amazing.

I read the letter over and over again, but the words do not change. My emergency stash is gone. My sister took it. And she never said a word when we were talking about her future.

I feel like I can't breathe and my chest is tight. Am I having a heart attack? I'm only twenty-five. I'm too young.

It's all gone.

"Catalina, what is wrong?" Severu kneels down beside me on the floor. "Did you fall and injure yourself?"

"She took it." I grab his arms urgently. "She took all of it."

"All of what?"

"My emergency stash. It was my safety net and it's gone. I need it," I gasp out. "It keeps me safe."

He pulls me into him. "*I* keep you safe."

"You don't understand. I need it."

He's silent for several long seconds and then he says, "I will help you get it back. What did your sister take from you?"

The pain in my chest starts to dissolve at his words.

"She took my money."

"It was in these books?" he asked, waving his hand toward the books all over the floor around me.

"Yes."

"You were hiding it. From your father?"

"From everyone, but she found it. I should have put it in the secret room, but I wanted to use the books he gave me to taunt me with my ignorance."

"You aren't ignorant."

"I'm not. I can read Latin, did you know?"

"No, but I'm not at all surprised. You are brilliant, wife. What was the money for, Catalina?"

"So, I could run away. I was going to leave after Carlotta got married, but she ran instead. And she took my money!"

"Do you still need the money? Do you want to run away from me?" His voice is carefully neutral. None of the anger I would have expected in it at that question.

I stare up at him. Of course, I don't want to run away from him. His family are so good to me. And I love him. That's got nothing to do with it. "I need it."

He nods and stands, lifting me to my feet. "Come with me."

I follow him out of the room and down the hall to his study. He stops by a painting of a man who looks a little like my husband but is wearing clothes from a different century. It must be his great-grandfather.

It's strange that we look a little like his ancestors. I'm not even related. It makes it feel like we were meant to be.

"Feel this spot here?" He takes my hand and guides my finger to a small bump hidden by the ornateness of the frame.

"Yes."

"Press it twice in quick succession."

I do what he says and the painting swings outward revealing a safe.

"It's old school, right?" he asks with a smile. "My grandfather had it installed. He wanted someplace to store my grandmother's jewels that she could get to."

Once again I'm struck by how much Severu trusts me. Even more than his grandfather or father trusted their wives. I've been in the vault.

"The combination is seven-right, thirty-two-left, eleven-right. Try it."

I just stand there.

"It's okay, *mi dolce gatto*. Open it, so you know you can." He repeats the combination.

I dial it in, going left first, then right, then left and the lock on the safe clicks.

"Now turn the handle," he instructs me.

I turn a metal wheel with spokes several rotations and the door to the safe opens. Inside, I see stacks of cash, paperwork, a gun, and on the top shelf several boxes that probably contain jewelry.

"There is about $50,000 cash in there. If you ever need it, take it. You are not trapped here. You will never be trapped again."

The full import of what he's offering hits me, and I answer the question he asked in my office. "I don't want to run away from you, but when I saw the money that I'd spent years saving was gone, I panicked."

"Does knowing you have access to this money take away that panic?" He asks me with no judgement.

I nod. "I probably need therapy."

"If you want to see a therapist, I will make it happen."

I can't hold back the words any longer. "I love you, Severu, with every-thing in me."

He stares down at me. "You love me? You're sure?"

"Oh, yes."

"How? How are you sure?"

"Because it fills my heart to bursting. The idea of a day without you hurts more than any day I spent with Francesco."

He kisses me and we end up making love on the floor of his office, the door to the safe gaping open above us.

I'm tracing lines on his chest and marveling at how much joy I have now. I have a family who loves me, staff that cares about me enough to check up on me. A husband who protects me and takes care of me and wants me to be myself and no one else.

"I'm so happy," I say.

"I am too." He sits up and pulls me onto his naked thighs. "I am not a good man, *mi dolce bellezza*. I am selfish and arrogant, but I got my comeuppance when I married you."

"What do you mean?" But I know what he's talking about. I'm not easy. He can't just pretend I don't exist and that makes me very happy.

"If you are not the center of my thoughts, you are close by. I'm jealous as hell. I need your body like air. And you are the first thing I consider when I make decisions, not *la famiglia*. You. I'm negotiating a blood alliance with the fucking Irish because it means you will be safer."

"Do you love me, Severu?" Will he admit it?

"Is love the inability to see you hurting without fixing it? Is it craving your body even when I'm so physically spent I can barely move? Is it finding time to spend with you regardless of responsibility? Is it wanting to be a better man? Is it trusting you more than any other person?"

I can't answer. My throat is too clogged with tears.

"If that is love, then yes, I love you, Catalina. But it feels like something bigger than such a small word."

I swipe at the wetness on my cheeks. "I think love is bigger than the stars in the sky."

"It's the birth of a new galaxy in my heart."

Maybe even a whole new universe. "I love you so much." I kiss him.

He says the words again when he is inside me, my legs draped over each side of his hips, our bodies one. "I love you beyond death, Catalina."

EPILOGUE

CATALINA

I breathe into the stretch as I bend forward and let my fingertips brush my yoga mat and feel no pain. It still surprises me even though I've been fully healed from my surgery for several months and had my last physical therapy session last week.

It definitely got worse before it got better though. Recovery after the surgery was hard with lots of pain. Carlotta surprised everyone when she insisted on helping me through recovery. She took time off from culinary school and was there every day, keeping me entertained and encouraging me.

She and my new family spoiled me rotten.

But Severu was my rock. He believed in me, and my full recovery. I had no choice but to believe in it myself.

They had to break my bone and insert a metal rod when they reset it because after the first break, I didn't get the follow up care I should have. There was also scar tissue that needed removing. The specialist told us it was a miracle I had not lost mobility years ago to atrophied muscles and shrunken tendons.

Severu didn't agree. "It wasn't a miracle; it was my amazing wife's strength of will. She does Yoga every single day and manages pain with a fortitude I wish every one of my men had."

His words didn't surprise me. Severu doesn't tell me he loves me very often, but he is vocal in his approval and admiration of me. For my mafia don, those words are more real than any whispered sweet nothings could be.

He was furious about me not getting the treatment I needed. If he could have dug Francesco up and killed him all over again, my husband would have. He's protective like that.

As soon as the hospital confirmed that I was not pregnant, Severu insisted I go on birth control. He wanted me to get the surgery immediately and didn't want to risk me getting pregnant and having to put it off. He also didn't want anything to complicate my recovery.

With the prospect of being almost entirely pain free in my future, I agreed. I opted for an IUD, which I had removed today when I was at the hospital for my final physical therapy session.

I didn't tell Severu, but I'm planning to.

I'm ready to have his baby.

He's going to be an incredible father. We've talked a lot about how we were both raised. He loved and respected his father, but he wants our children to learn to live with their emotions, not suppress them. Even a son that will one day take over as Don of the New York Cosa Nostra.

His belief that emotions made him weak was the reason he was prepared to marry my sister. He knows that would have been a disaster, but worse, according to him, is the thought that he never would have had me as his wife. He has nightmares about it. When he wakes, he's voracious and rough in his lovemaking, even more dominant than usual, like he needs to imprint himself on my body.

I don't mind. I adore intimacy with my husband, whatever his mood. But more and more often lately, he wants more gentle lovemaking, where he will take hours exploring my body and letting me explore his. He will stay inside me until I've climaxed at least twice before allowing himself to come. I'm not sure what drives this, but it feels a little like he's doing the same thing as when he goes all rough dominant. He's imprinting me with *us* though, not just him.

He's telling me he loves me with his body, but he's also accepting my love.

"Do you think you could keep that pose up with me inside you?"

Speak of my very own devil.

I'm in the tree position, my hands pressed together above my head, my right leg bent at the knee with my foot resting on my left inner thigh.

"If I was standing on a box, maybe, but you're too tall." Smiling, I drop my pose and turn to face my handsome husband.

He's wearing athletic shorts that reveal dusky muscular legs and a t-shirt that clings to his massive chest. "I'd say that you're too short, but that would be a lie. You are perfect as you are. My pocket Venus."

Heat climbs into my cheeks. "You're always saying things like that."

"Speak the truth and shame the devil."

"I don't think my devil feels much shame." I step up to him and press my hands against the hard plains of his chest.

"Am I your devil?"

"Mmm...hmm," I agree. "All mine."

"And you are all mine." He lifts me with an arm under my bottom and lays claim to my mouth.

I kiss him back, falling into the passion between us as naturally as breathing. I don't even realize we're moving until he lets go of my butt and I find myself standing on the weightlifting bench.

"Will this work?" His dark eyes are blazing with desire, and it takes me a second to understand what he's asking.

Then I do and I smile. I bounce a little on my toes. Very little give. "Yes."

"Then take your clothes off. It's time for naked Yoga."

I rip my sports bra over my head and toss it and then shove the matching bottoms down my legs along with my underwear before kicking them away.

Completely naked, I take a deep breath and let it out. As I do, I bring my body into the tree pose.

SEVERU

My beautiful wife lifts her foot to balance on her inner thigh and opens her sweet pink pussy for me. It's glistening with her cream already.

She is so damn perfect for me.

"Now you," she says, like she's in charge.

Since what I want requires my cock out of my shorts, I oblige her. First I toe off my workout shoes and socks, enjoying how she's already panting, her eyes fixed on my body. Yanking my shirt over my head by the collar, I'm glad I already locked the door to the gym.

Then I stand there in my shorts tented from erection.

Catalina licks her lips, her eyes going unfocused.

I shove my shorts down and then step up to her. She's right, having her stand on the weight bench has my cock lined up for entry into her slick channel. But first, I want to see how long she can hold her pose with me touching her.

Cupping her generous tits in both hands, I lean forward and take one hard nipple into my mouth and gently bite before suckling hard. She loves this, and she's moaning in only a few seconds. I finger her folds, sliding through her wet juices and spreading them around her tender flesh.

Her foot slides a little and I lift my head, staring straight into eyes hazy with pleasure. "No, *mi dolce bellezza*, if you want me to keep touching, you keep your foot right where it is."

She stares at me like I've lost my mind. "I can't."

I laugh, the sound dirty but also filled with genuine mirth. "There is nothing you can't do, wife."

Her hazel eyes light up. Her sweet beauty blooms under praise and I make sure she gets a lot of it.

When she's dripping and making desperate little sounds of need, I grip both of her hips and push my cock into her. Her greedy walls suck me in tight and it feels so fucking good.

Moving one hand around to her lower back, to keep her in place, I slide the other between us until my thumb is against her clit. Every time I thrust forward, my thumb presses and her clit pops out of its hood. She cries out as my thumb rubs her sweet little bundle of nerves.

The slow pace I have to keep so she doesn't fall is the best kind of torture, but I feel my climax coming, familiar tightness at the base of my penis.

Her pussy clenches around me and her hands come down to latch onto my shoulders. She screams as her pleasure takes her and I let myself go, ramming into her tight channel and releasing my seed into her. She shudders with aftershocks from her orgasm as I wring the last bit of pleasure from our climaxes.

Then I lift her and turn so I can sit where she was standing, her legs wrapped around me. I'm still lodged inside her, not going soft.

Fuck.

I hope she's up for another round, because I sure as hell am.

Making a decadent sound of pleasure, she rotates her hips. "Do you think we made a baby?"

My whole body goes still. The only way that would be possible is if she had her IUD removed. "Did you..."

She nods. "I want your baby, Severu."

I kiss her like my life will end if I don't. I feel like it will. This woman. So damn perfect.

She starts moving against me.

This time when we finish, we end up laying on the workout mat. Well, I'm on the mat and she's on top of me.

She lifts her head and meets my gaze. "It's alright? That I had it taken out."

"It's your body. You know I want a baby with you."

"I know you need heirs." Her expression says it's not the same thing.

"Yes, but I *want* a family with you, the wife I love."

Her smile is blinding. "I love you so much, even if you are a bossy don."

"You wouldn't want me any other way." And we both know it's true.

Still, I'm a little surprised when she says, "No, I wouldn't."

Because I am her devil, and she is my sweet beauty. Together we are perfect.

THE END

BONUS SCENE

Two Months After Naked Yoga
CATALINA

I angle the butterknife just so on the bread plate and then step back to assess the table set formally for two in the rooftop garden of our home. The hand tatted Sicilian lace runner placed over the burgundy tablecloth is the same one that was on the table the first night I met Severu.

Back then, he'd been intended for my sister and I was the spare sister. That hadn't mattered to my ovaries, which had exploded with fireworks the first time our hands touched.

His touch still has the same effect on me, only now? My lady bits don't pine. They get satisfied. Very, very satisfied.

My thighs clench in arousal and I give my vagina a stern talking to. There's no use getting worked up. Severu won't be home for another hour. And we aren't making love right away.

I have the perfect dinner and surprise planned for my husband.

The light glitters off of my engagement and wedding rings as I reach out to adjust the small rectangular giftbox beside his plate. He gave me the beautiful art deco engagement ring for our first anniversary a few months ago. The ten-carat square cut emerald with five-carat diamonds on either side is impossible to miss.

Which is my husband's intention. He's ridiculously jealous and determined that every man ever in my vicinity will know that I am taken.

Carlotta was furious when he demanded her engagement ring back, but being the intelligent man that he is, Severu didn't try giving that ring to me. It is currently sitting in the safe in his office.

He says that if Carlotta ever marries, she can have it then. If she wants it to sell, or to wear.

Once she has finished culinary school and her mandatory two years working in a restaurant kitchen owned by *la famiglia*, she won't need it to sell. She'll be allowed to inherit her portion of my father's estate left after Severu turned over the bulk of the Jilani assets to Big Sal to fund his life as consigliere.

I'm not sure yet what I'm going to do with my inheritance, but I think I will donate it to programs that serve victims of domestic violence. Severu says I can do whatever I want because as his wife, I will never need that money.

He keeps a minimum of $50,000 cash in the office safe so I know I always have a go fund.

How could I *not* love a man who is so thoughtful?

He also reminds me often that if I ever did run, he would follow. And he would find me. Of that, I have no doubt.

But I don't want to run. There is nothing in my life with Severu to escape. I love him. I love his family and now that I'm not going to every coffee klatch and fundraiser hosted by mafia wives in the city, I love my life.

SEVERU

My wife's text tells me to meet her on the rooftop.

I pat the folded papers in my suit jacket breast pocket before taking the stairs up to our home's outdoor living space two at a time. Catalina comes up here at least once a week to read in the garden.

If she's not in her office or at the piano when I come home, this is the next place I look. And I always look. We've been married over a year and my need for her has not abated even a little.

I crave her body with an addict's devotion, but even more, I crave her company.

Before marrying Catalina, I jealously guarded my time alone. Especially after the more violent duties as mafia don. Now, I would rather be with my wife. Always. She sooths the beast and entices the man.

My cock begins to harden. Sporting a semi is a regular occurrence around Catalina, so I doubt she'll be surprised.

Looking breathtakingly beautiful, my wife stands beside a table set for two. Candles burn in the silver candelabra in the center, casting a warm glow on her creamy skin.

She's got on a dress I would never allow her to wear outside our home. The same shade of green as her engagement ring, it cups her gorgeous tits lovingly, dipping low enough to expose most of her cleavage. The skirt clings to her stomach and hips, showing off the fine curve of her ass.

Is she wearing panties?

She's not wearing shoes. She likes to go barefoot at home, and I quickly discovered that I like it when she does too. Her sexy little feet make me want to strip the rest of her naked too.

"Good evening, husband. How was your day?"

I yank her into my arms. "You know it turns me the fuck on when you call me that."

"I know." The look she gives me goes straight to my cock.

Slamming my mouth down on hers, I kiss her the way I've been wanting to since leaving her delectable, naked body in bed this morning. Her lips part, like they always do and I sweep my tongue inside her mouth.

Catalina is so damn sweet.

Her hands slide up my chest and into my hair as she presses her curves against me, but then she breaks off the kiss and steps away before I realize what she's doing.

I growl and reach for her, but she dances backward.

"Save all that growly sexiness for after. It's time to eat dinner." Her smile is intoxicating.

"I would rather eat you."

She laughs. "Later. I mean it, Severu. I went to a lot of effort for tonight. Are you going to ruin it?"

I don't see how bringing her to a screaming climax, or four is ruining anything, but I sit my ass down in the chair because this romantic dinner is so obviously important to my wife.

It's then I notice the small box wrapped in shiny black paper with a gold bow beside my plate. "What's this?"

"Your present."

Two words that make even a ruthless don quake. Did I forget an important date? It's not her birthday. We just celebrated our first anniversary.

"What is the occasion?" I ask cautiously.

She grins. "Open it and find out."

It's too small to be a gun. She got me a prototype pistol not even available to the military yet for Christmas. My wife is resourceful. It's my favorite weapon now.

But this box is too small for even a Derringer. It could be a knife, I suppose. Maybe a switchblade with a titanium handle? Titanium doesn't hold an edge like steel for the knife blade, but it's an excellent material for handles.

"You're trying to figure out what it is before you open it." She laughs again, her effervescent happiness contagious. "Just open it and find out."

What could make her this happy?

And then it comes to me and my damn hands shake as I pull the bow on the present. When I open the small box, a thin white stick nestles in gold speckled tissue paper. It has two blue lines in the results window.

"Does that mean what I think it does?" I ask.

Her eyes suspiciously bright, she nods.

She's pregnant. We're going to have a baby.

Oh, fuck.

My heart feels like it's going to beat out of my chest and I jump up from the table. To hell with dinner.

I put one hand around her and press the other on her lower belly. "You are carrying my child."

She nods, too choked to speak.

This time when I kiss her, it is reverent. This beautiful creature is going to give me a child.

"When?" I ask as I lift my lips only a scant inch from hers.

"I'm due a week after our second anniversary."

That means she's a month...six weeks along? It doesn't matter. May is my lucky month.

Swinging her up into my arms, I head toward the stairs to go back inside.

"There you go, carrying me around like a caveman again."

"You should be used to it by now."

She kisses the underside of my jaw. "What about dinner?"

"Forget dinner. I need you."

"You can feed me after." Her voice has gone sultry. "I'm growing a baby, I can't be skipping meals."

That stops me in my tracks and I reverse my steps.

"What are you doing?" she demands.

Sitting down, I settle her in my lap. "Feeding our baby."

"I thought we were going to make love."

"After," I tease.

CATALINA

Severu's sex is hard under my thighs from the moment we sit down, but he makes it clear there is no way we are getting up from this table before I eat dinner.

He feeds me from his plate and shows just how adept he is at stoking the fire of my need with only one hand. My nipples are extra sensitive, which is one of the reasons I got the pregnancy test.

He slides his hand inside my dress and cups my breast, playing with my hard nipple while he feeds me small bites of Chicken Marsala. Biting my earlobe, he huffs warm air against my ear, sending shivers down my arms.

"You have to eat too," I remind him.

He takes a bite of chicken and then nuzzles the join of my neck and shoulder as he chews.

I squirm in his lap, spreading my thighs as wide as my tight skirt will allow in an invitation my diabolical husband ignores.

"Please, Severu, I need you."

"I need you too, *amore mio*."

Of all the endearments he uses with me, this my favorite. *My love*. And he knows it, knows how it turns me on. The fiend.

I turn my head and try to kiss him, but he has a piece of bread for me to bite into right there.

Sealing my lips, I shake my head. I want a kiss, not food.

"You need to eat, wife." His fingers gently twist and pull on my highly sensitive nipple.

"Kiss first."

"If I kiss you, neither of us will finish this delicious meal you prepared."

"That's not a bad thing."

"You are pregnant with my child, Catalina. I will take care of you and make sure you get what you need every single day of this pregnancy."

"How is that any different than every other day of our marriage?" I sass.

"I am glad you feel that way, now take a bite of bread."

"Fine." I take a bite and chew angrily.

My husband just smiles and swirls a bite of pasta onto his fork. When he tries to feed it to me, I grab his wrist and direct it to his mouth instead.

We finish our dinner, both making sure the other eats, but when he makes noises about dessert after our plate is clean, I'm done.

I reach up under my skirt and yank my thong down my legs and then straddle his lap and try to undo his belt. With a deep masculine laugh, he helps me and shucks his slacks and boxers down to mid-thigh without dumping me off of his lap.

His erection springs upward and I immediately press my needy center against him. I'm so wet that I slide easily along his big shaft. Every time my clitoris meets up with the bulbous head, it sends jolts of pleasure through me.

"Stop teasing me, wife."

I'd laugh at the irony of that demand if I had the breath to do so. I don't, so I just lift my hips enough that the head of his erection settles into the opening of my body.

Grabbing my hips in a bruising grip, Severu surges up and shoves his hard length into my depths.

He's so big, it's never easy to take him, but my body knows how to adjust and soon we are moving together. He spears into me over and over. I try to slam down so he'll hit my cervix, but he doesn't let me, controlling the speed and the depth of our coupling.

Sometimes, hitting against entrance to my womb is too much, but others, like now, it's what I want.

"Severu!"

"Trust me, *mi dolce belleza*."

"But I want—"

"I will give you what you need."

And he does, drawing forth one of the most powerful orgasms of my life. I shout out his name as I come, only to feel the heat of his own release deep inside me. Then he kisses me as the aftershocks shake my body.

Eventually, the kiss ends and my head rests against his chest.

Severu runs his hand up and down my back. "I too have a gift for you *amore mio*. It is not nearly as wonderful as what you have given me, but I hope it will make you happy."

Sitting up, I meet his handsome gaze. "You always make me happy."

"That is not true." He laughs.

I love his laugh and get to hear it more often now.

"Okay, maybe not always." Severu and I are both strong-willed, stubborn people.

It is inevitable that we clash sometimes.

He fishes around inside his jacket and pulls out some folded papers.

I take them and unfold them so I can read the top one. It is an acceptance of admission letter to NYU.

Excitement wars with disbelief inside me. "You applied to NYU on my behalf?"

"Yes."

"But what about security?" Will I have to take a team of four bodyguards to class with me every day?

Severu kisses me and then lifts his head, his expression sober. "You'll have to take your courses online because you can't afford to be so predictable in your schedule that you show up to the same classes every week."

I can tell he thinks I'm going to be disappointed, but I'm not. The chance to go to university is something I never thought I would have. I kiss him this time, and it's not short, soft or anywhere near chaste.

When I eventually lift my mouth from his, his eyes are gleaming with dark passion and I know we're not done making love.

I grin. "Can I attend lectures that are particularly interesting to me?"

"Yes."

"You are the best mafia husband ever." I throw my arms around his neck and hug him with all the joy coursing through me.

We are going to have a baby. I get to go to university. The De Lucas are an amazing and loving family and they are mine. Severu is mine. And I am his.

My heart is so full, I think I'm going to burst.

Severu stands and shifts my body so he's carrying me bridal style. "I've heard there are foods you aren't supposed to eat pregnant."

I laugh. What a segue, but so very typical of my husband. I've researched it. Of course, I have, but I'm also keen to hear what my OB says on the subject.

"Ask the doctor. We have an appointment the day after tomorrow." I snuggle against his chest as my powerful husband carries me down the stairs into our home.

"I will do that."

Two days later, while I sit in blushing, mortified silence, my OB tells my husband that intercourse is fine, but no, she doesn't recommend banging against my cervix.

Which explains why he's been so careful about his depth of penetration since I told him I was pregnant.

Severu doesn't stop there. He wants to know the safest positions for intercourse and if anal sex is allowed.

My OB nixes the anal sex and has a much more frank and detailed discussion with my husband about sexual positions than I am comfortable with.

"I thought you were going to ask about safe foods to eat," I mutter after she leaves the room.

"I did."

"But you had to ask about sex too?"

"It is my job to take care of you."

Apparently, that includes knowing the safest positions for sex while I am pregnant.

We leave the doctor's office with not only way more than I wanted to know about pregnancy sex, but a list of foods and beverages for me to avoid during pregnancy as well. And let's not forget the recommended Yoga poses along with those I should not try, advice to nap if I need it (and you know that means I'll be taking naps when my overprotective husband thinks I do...which could lead to afternoon sexy times, so not something to avoid), and not one, but three books on pregnancy.

It's going to be a long few months, but I'm not complaining. Severu is over-protective because he loves me. And I put up with it because I love him.

Win-win.

With more than 10 million copies of my books in print worldwide (Isn't that wild?), I'm an award winning and USA Today bestselling author with over 90 published books. My stories have been translated for sale all over the world and after a long career in traditional publishing, I've gone indie. I am loving the freedom to write the stories both me and my readers enjoy the most. My new steamy mafia romance series, Syndicate Rules features the morally gray alpha heroes and spice I love to write. I write contemporary, historical and paranormal romance. Some of my books have action adventure and intrigue. All of them are spicy and deeply emotional. I'm a voracious reader and love to talk about both my books and those I've read (or should read...good recs are always welcome) on social media. Welcome to my world where love conquers all, but not easily!

For info on my books and series extras, visit my website:
www.lucymonroe.com

Follow me on Social Media:
Facebook: LucyMonroe.Romance
Instagram: lucymonroeromance
Pinterest: lucymonroebooks
goodreads: Lucy Monroe
YouTube: @LucyMonroeBooks
TikTok: lucymonroeauthor

SYNDICATE RULES

CONVENIENT MAFIA WIFE
URGENT VOWS
DEMANDING MOB BOSS
RUTHLESS ENFORCER
BRUTAL CAPO
FORCED VOWS